What People Are Saying

Identity theft, scams, and a serial killer. *Username* is a must-read for every person who has a credit card or uses the Internet. Who's using your name? Your username? You may not know until it's too late. See yourself as a mark through the eyes of Maureen and Jennifer, master identity thieves. Their scams will shock you as you realize how vulnerable you are. Then there is the nice gentleman you could meet in a chat room, or perhaps he sends you a persuasive e-mail. He couldn't possibly be a serial killer … could he? Faulkner has penned a real who-done-it, a page turner that one could say is ripped from the headlines.

~ Lee Boyland, Award-winning author of *The Rings of Allah, Behold, an Ashen Horse, America Reborn,* and *Pirates and Cartels.*

Raw and utterly chilling, *Username* won't let you go till the very end. There is evil in these pages but one woman fights back. Courageous, strong and computer savvy, Maureen's story should be told to every woman, young and old alike. Someone's survival could depend on it.

~Carmen Stenholm, Author of *Crack Between the Worlds*

Award-winning author Joyce Faulkner debuts her newest publication in her spell-bound thriller, *Username*.

Well known for her attention to detail, Faulkner leaves nothing behind as she takes us on a chilling journey into the world of scam artists. While the internet may be a valuable resource for today's society, it is also the rich hunting grounds of scammers and stalkers. How safe are we on-line? How much information is too much?

Recommended for mature readers, this novel will leave you looking over your shoulder and turning on every light in the house long after you've read the final page…

Username is bound to find a place among the best of today's thriller titles.

~ Maria Edwards, President of American Author Society

USERNAME

JOYCE FAULKNER

ISBN Hardcover:	978-0-0934930-7-5
Paperback:	978-0-9834930-2-0
E-book:	978-0-9834930-3-7
LCCN:	2011930091

Cover Design: Joyce Faulkner

The Page Turns

Printed in the United States

To the unwary,

a warning...

Contents

Prologue—GOD BLESS THE SINNER

My mother was Southern Baptist, my father a drunk. I grew up in a violently virtuous home, but now I embrace sin. I'm a big believer in it. When I'm alone and in the dark, it's the only thing that makes me feel whole. Before I began my little projects, I was little more than a Xerox copy of a blank sheet of paper—warm nothingness. Then, sin colored me with a 48-box of Crayola Crayons and I was redeemed.

It began in May of 1958 when I was thirteen. The old man passed out on the couch while Mom pelted him with Fritos and intoned biblical warnings. I grabbed a warm Pepsi and pinched one of her Pall Malls on my way out the back door. I could still hear her squawking, "Rod? Rod!" when I turned the corner half a block from our house. I leaned against the streetlight and sucked on the cigarette. A shadow flickered across a shade in the yellow house on the corner of Elm Street. I blew smoke out my nose and stared, transfixed.

My fourth grade teacher, Mrs. Thompson, lived there. I stepped over the low picket fence and hid behind a shrub. The window wasn't quite closed. She leaned over the tub, her tits dangling, her white-streaked belly bulging. The hairy patch between her legs was Brillo-pad gray—so was her old-lady hairdo. She'd already washed her face so she didn't have any eyebrows. I unzipped my fly and stroked myself while I watched her bathe. It's my favorite memory from childhood.

By the time I was fifteen, I spent most nights roaming the neighborhood peeking at dozens of women. Soon, watching wasn't enough. I lay in bed at night and dreamed about them. Their fearful eyes aroused me and I grunted as I masturbated.

I made my first attempt at sixteen, creeping up behind a fleshy woman loading groceries into the trunk of her car. I split her scalp with a crow bar, but had to leave her when a truck turned into the parking lot. I ran like hell, terrified someone might have seen me.

I got home late, sweaty and pissed at myself. I sucked down some of the old man's scotch and felt better. I was disappointed I didn't get to rape her, but seeing the news report got me going again. I jacked off into my bloody t-shirt while my parents argued about Jesus in the living room.

Over the next several months, I made four less than satisfying attempts at rape. Each time, I lost my nerve and ran off. I lost weight. I couldn't sleep. I wanted. Oh, I wanted so much. My mother's Sunday school class prayed for me. My father gave me a beer.

I discovered 'The Scam' when my cousin Buddy got his girlfriend pregnant in the fall of 1962. He came by to borrow $200 from the old man. That was a lot of money in those days. Curiosity got the better of me and I followed him down the street, asking questions.

"Will you give it up?" He pushed me aside.

"I don't see why you won't tell me."

"I don't see why you are so curious."

"You never borrowed money before, it must be something big. You buying a car?"

"I wish," he shrugged. "I got me a little problem I gotta settle."

"You're gambling?" I imagined him meeting a bookie in a back alley, betting on the ponies or maybe greyhounds.

"I knocked Sheila up." He hitched his khakis an inch or two and rubbed his nose on the sleeve of his madras shirt.

I clapped him on the back. "You sorry sonofabitch!" Buddy was such a goodie-two-shoes that I never guessed he was doing the dirty deed with his angelic little Sheila.

"Ain't nothing wrong with my pecker." Buddy coughed and sniffed.

"A regular Don Juan." I elbowed him.

He grinned but his cheeks were red. "Now I gotta take care of it."

"How you gonna do that? Your part is over."

"For crying out loud, Rod. YOU know." He arched one eyebrow. "We got a line on a doctor who does it for $200."

"It?" I scratched my head. "Oh…It!"

Buddy stepped over my mother's over-pruned hedge to get to the sidewalk.

"How does it work?" I trailed along on my side of the shrubbery. "I thought it was illegal."

"We call a number and tell whoever answers we have the money. Then someone gives Sheila an address. Probably a rented room somewhere. She's supposed to go by herself. When she gets there, she puts on a blindfold. Someone shows up and takes the money. Then they lead her off, put her on the table, and do it. After they are gone, she takes off the blindfold and goes home."

"Just like that?"

"That's it. She never sees them."

I imagined that pretty little thing stretched out on a table with her legs wide. "Where do you get the number?"

"She got it from a girlfriend who got it from a bulletin board over at the University. She says there are numbers floating around all over the school."

"Hell of a note." Could it be that easy?

Buddy ran his fingers through his crew cut. "I gotta get going, partner. She wants to get this taken care of tonight."

"Good luck, man." I stuffed my hands in my pockets and watched him saunter off down the street towards Sheila's neighborhood. I knew where she lived. I peeked at her on Tuesdays and Fridays when her parents took square dancing lessons. She had rosy little nipples and peach fuzz between her thighs. I closed my eyes and imagined her flat stomach swelled taut like a basketball. My cock twitched and I followed him.

They were sitting in a glider on Sheila's front porch when I crept up behind them and knelt behind the railing. She nestled her head in the crook of Buddy's shoulder. I clenched my fists. It didn't seem fair. This bastard had a good-looking girl who spread her legs for him and he was an ordinary guy!

He kissed the top of her head. "You don't have to do this, baby. I'll marry you if you want."

It wasn't much of a proposal.

Sheila's stiff petticoat rustled as she stood up, smoothing her skirt.

"Where are you going?" Buddy didn't seem that upset that Sheila was passing on his offer.

"He said the Shangri-La Apartments. Number 25."

"I'll come for you if you take too long," he said as he handed her the cash.

"I'll be fine." She smoothed her long flip and threw a thin white cardigan over her shoulders, clipping it together over her bosom with a silver sweater chain.

I backed away and headed for the Shangri-la. I have long legs. I made it ten minutes before she did, tiptoeing into the unlocked apartment. The back bedroom door was closed. I tapped on it. "She's changed her mind," I called. "She couldn't get the money."

Someone inside grunted.

My loafers thumped against the hardwood floor as I walked away. In the front hall, I slipped them off and tiptoed into the kitchen to unbolt the back door. Then I ran out the front way, slamming the screen behind me. Hiding in the stairwell above Number 25, I waited.

USERNAME

A minute later, Doc Lawless slipped out of the apartment and locked it behind him. He strolled out to his black Edsel, a folding table under one arm, clutching his instrument bag. He put everything in the trunk and drove away, passing Sheila as she hurried towards the Shangri-la.

I let myself in the back way. As I unlatched the front door, I heard her start up the stairs. Backing away, I hid in the bedroom and waited until she entered the apartment.

"I'm ready," she said after a moment. It sounded like a question.

I opened the door. She fidgeted in the middle of the living room wearing a white scarf around her eyes, her thin arms crossed over her chest. I unzipped my trousers and my cock sprang free.

"I left the money on the kitchen counter." She pointed.

I came up behind her and touched her shoulders. She drew back in alarm. "There, there," I whispered as I guided her into the bedroom.

"Should I take off my clothes?" she asked.

"Yes." I watched as she unhooked her sweater guard, stepped out of her flats, and unzipped her dress. My excitement rose as she wriggled out of her petticoat and panties. I wished for the table Doc Lawless took with him as I pushed her down on the floor.

"Now what?" The scarf covered most of her face. The nylon fluttered in and out over her nose and mouth.

"Open your legs."

It was that simple.

"Oh," she squealed when I mounted her, but I put my hands around her neck and squeezed. It didn't take long. I came as she died. It was exquisite. It was better than knowing God, I WAS God. I tucked her panties and the money into my pocket before leaving. I was half way down the steps when I remembered fingerprints. I went back and wiped everything down with her panties. I couldn't resist looking in on her.

She was spread eagled, naked except for her bra and the blindfold. The little bow above her bangs was crooked. I straightened it. I pulled the bra down so I could see her nipples. They seemed bigger than I remembered. I pressed the tiny buttons inward with my index finger. They popped right back out. Ha! I yanked the scarf away from her eyes. They were bigger than I remembered too. I felt enormous affection for her, so I gave her another go. I thought of my mother as I thrust again and again into the corpse. She'd call this sin, I realized.

Then it happened.

I was awakened right there in the Shangri-la. It was sin I'd been seeking. Life without sin was dull and lonely. With sin, it was shiny and powerful. I became a disciple for sin as I ejaculated into Sheila's pretty little body.

The next day, I tacked a small sign on a bulletin board in the Student Union of a small college in the next town. "Got trouble? Ask for Rod." I put my home number.

A frightened young girl called that afternoon.

It should have lasted forever. The girls came to me like sheep, never telling a soul. Sheila was the only one I left where she lay, the others I wrapped in a rug and dumped in the woods for the critters to eat. As the years went by, I rode a bus from campus to campus, taking a room in a motel, before posting my invitation. Business was brisk. The money was good.

I told my parents that I had a job as a traveling salesman. My mother disapproved. She wrinkled her nose. "What are you selling," she asked.

I held up a brand new bible. "Enlightenment."

"Don't be disrespectful." She grabbed the book away from me and thumbed through it.

A fifty dollar bill drifted to the floor I'd hidden it in Proverbs—my version of mad money.

"What kind of filth have you been rolling in?" Her eyes glowed. "We need to cleanse you—body and soul." She pointed to the bathroom.

I was no longer a child. I drew myself up, omnipotence roaring in my ears. She startled and backed away, her fingers covering her mouth.

"I'm—I'm calling the reverend right now." She fumbled for the telephone.

"I outgrew cleansing ceremonies years ago, Mama." I liked that she was afraid of me. I turned my back on her and went into the living room where the old man toasted my success.

A few minutes later, she hurried out the back door and headed for church. Fine. Good place for her.

I dropped in from time to time to store things in the crawlspace under my room, but mostly I hunted after that.

It all came to an end in 1973. Once pregnant girls could go to a doctor, my opportunities dwindled. I wasn't the type of guy they'd go with willingly. Not like Buddy. I slunk back to my parents' house.

The day I moved back into my old room, my mother went to D.C. to protest with her church cronies. I loved her enthusiasm, fighting for my little projects that way. Ha! I hung out with the old man and had a few drinks, laughing when we saw her on TV marching in front of the Supreme Court her face contorted with righteous indignation for all those unwanted fetuses.

"At least she's bitching at someone besides me," my dad said as he tossed back a shot.

I raised my glass. "Go Mom!"

GOD BLESS THE SINNER

The woman hated sin but she didn't know a thing about it. All she knew was virtue. You never caught her sparing the rod. Oh no! I looked at the scars on my hand where she doused it in boiling water when I was four and pissed the bed. I swallowed the booze in one gulp.

Dad drifted off, snoring loudly. I switched off the TV. In my room, I took my scrapbook out of the closet. It was wrapped up inside my baby blanket. I put the soft blue fleece around my neck and rubbed it against my cheek, the book in my lap.

I didn't buy a Polaroid until I'd been at it for a year, so the first fifteen pages were just panties—mounted, neatly labeled with name and date.

I touched Sheila's panties and remembered that little pink bow above her bangs. I lifted the album to my face. Her scent was gone now. I paged through the book, fingering the underwear, enjoying the pictures. I loved my girls.

I didn't know what to do next. I was twenty-eight years old and my years of easy sin were over. I'd dropped out of high school when I found the scam. I didn't have a profession. I couldn't go back to the blankness I felt before Shangri-la. I sat on the bed, my back against the wall, my knees against my chest, sucking on my mother's Pall Mall.

I heard her come in around 2 am. "What are you doing in here? Get your butt to bed," she said to my father. He belched. I cracked my door and watched her hustle him into their room, muttering about the evils of drink. Even after a ten-hour bus drive, she bristled with virtue.

She put the old man to bed and within a few minutes, he was snoring again. Around 3, I heard the springs of their bed squeak as she climbed in beside him.

I tiptoed down the hall in my stocking feet, my loafers in one hand, and the scrapbook in the other. I stuffed newspapers under their door and wet them down with gasoline I'd siphoned from the old man's car. I lit a match and backed away as flames devoured the door.

I was half way down the block when I heard her shriek. I was sitting on a bench at the train station, when two fire engines rushed by. I hugged my scrapbook to my chest. Oh, but sin was sweet.

Chapter 1—Maureen

<u>Wednesday, October 2, 2000</u>

Jennifer's padded bra hung on the glass doorknob of Maureen's room. "Can't be leaving stuff like that in plain sight." Maureen disentangled it and threw it into the laundry basket. What if someone came to visit? What if someone broke in? She didn't want to answer any questions about Jennifer. Life was already too complicated.

She pulled a tight band over her hair. It stretched the skin of her forehead and lifted her eyebrows. A trick she learned from a cross-dresser some time ago. She applied pancake next—a shade darker than her natural skin tones, even darker base under the eyes. She took her time with her brows, thickening them with a sharpened charcoal pencil she kept in the freezer. The wig was a good one—expensive, dark brown, flecks of gray and curly.

She put on round-framed glasses and examined herself in the mirror. The wide straps of the cotton brassiere cut into her shoulders but it held the contents of the cups straight out. She bounced up and down on her toes. A slight jiggle. She twisted around to look at her rear. The special girdle rounded her butt nicely. "Not bad for an old broad," she muttered.

She pulled a pair of black pants over her substantial hips, glad for the elastic in the waist. Maureen loved pullover blouses with pictures on the front. Today's choice was black silk, embroidered with a white tiger whose eyes were turquoise blue. She slipped several bracelets over the cuff of her sleeve, enjoying the way they clattered against each other. Matching plastic earrings dangled from her lobes. Black knee-high stockings and jeweled scuff sandals with a skinny two-inch heel completed the outfit. She packed a pair of thick socks and her well-worn Nikes in her big purse, just in case.

The drive to downtown Cleveland seemed endless in rush hour traffic. She logged onto her computer at 8:10 AM. She checked her phone mail—two blocked access complaints, a manager's request to review an employee's time on the Internet and three messages from her boss, Bill Casey. Par for the course.

She reset the passwords and called the hapless early birds who'd somehow managed to type in the wrong combination of letters and numbers three times in a row. One fellow was an executive vice president. This was the second time this week he'd goofed up. An MBA from Harvard was beginning to mean less and less, she thought. People were idiots when it came to computers. She snorted. People were idiots. Period.

She called Linda to set up an appointment to answer Bill's questions in person.

"Bill says come by his office before you leave today." It was after 10 o'clock. Linda stood beside Maureen's desk with a white mug and a couple of chocolate donuts. A picture of a black dog sitting in Santa's lap adorned the cup with the name "MIDNIGHT" emblazoned below it.

"I love his sense of urgency. He fills my phone mail with messages, and then is too busy to meet with me?"

"You know how fickle he is. Is something else wrong?"

"Mr. Gorman called and wanted to know why he couldn't log onto the network." Maureen cleaned a space for donuts on her desk. "I asked him to check the connection and he said that the plug didn't fit into the cigarette lighter. I was stuck for a minute until I realized he was driving in his car."

"He was using his computer while driving?" Linda sat down in Maureen's client chair and crossed her legs.

"He said he wanted to browse the net." Maureen imagined the dorky little man careening down the highway trying to type in his password or manipulating the cursor with that little nipple of a mouse on his laptop.

"He's going to kill someone." Linda laid Maureen's donut on a napkin on the desk before biting into her own.

"Or himself." Maureen opened a note file and typed in Gorman's name with an exclamation point. She'd get back to him later. "Is that a new hairdo?"

"You like it?" Linda's hair was stiff with gel, the ends tipped with gold.

"It's dramatic."

"When you are dating a younger man, you have to make concessions."

"I see."

"Sean didn't call me again last night. He was either out or had his truck in the garage. The lights were off. I thought about dropping by and peeking in the window when I walked Midnight but I was afraid of what I might see."

"He won't like you spying on him."

"He never knows the difference. Did I tell you about the earrings I found on his dresser? I think they belonged to that doctor's wife."

"You poke around in things that aren't your business and you're going to be unhappy with what you find." Maureen lifted her glasses and rubbed the bridge of her nose. She hoped the heavy lenses wouldn't leave a permanent mark.

"Aren't you going to eat that?" Linda nodded towards the remaining donut.

"I'm on a diet." Maureen patted her well-padded thigh.

"You are always on a diet." Linda picked up the pastry between her thumb and forefinger and took a bite.

"It's a constant battle after you get to be a certain age."

"What would YOU do, Maureen?"

"I'd find someone else."

Linda swallowed. "That's what I should do, but it's not so easy for a divorced woman to find a decent date. The younger ones like Sean think they're doing you a favor. The older ones are either married or divorced. Married men bad mouth their wives but won't leave them." She picked crumbs off her blouse with shiny blue fingernails. "On the other hand, the divorced ones are so bitter. They bad-mouth their ex's, but they aren't interested in long-term relationships with anyone else. All any man wants is sex anyway. I want that too, but then once they get it, they get nervous and leave me with the bill."

"What bill?" Maureen was thinking about Gorman. This wasn't the first crazy phone call she'd gotten from him. Was this an opportunity?

"For dinner. For drinks. Whatever. I end up paying."

"Don't."

"Oh sure." Linda stretched. "Sometimes they won't meet you if you don't pay. They say they can't afford to go out." She stood up. Break was over. "Want to do lunch today?"

Maureen had several cases coming to a conclusion in the next few months. She SHOULD tend to them, but keeping an eye on Linda was more fun. "I have errands to run, but I can do them tomorrow. How about the Galleria?"

"Oh goodie! I love the black bean soup at the Café Sausalito." Linda headed back toward the corner office, wobbling in her over-high heels.

MAUREEN

"Crazy woman," Maureen murmured as she logged onto PeopleSoft. Gorman. There he was. Sales Manager for the northeastern district. Social security number, marital status, home address, salary, last review. She sighed. These dopes always made more money than they deserved. She copied the information over to an Access database she kept on a CD.

Maureen and Linda sat in an indoor courtyard decorated with potted palms. A brawny waiter brought their diet colas and Linda's black bean soup.

"What's wrong with Mark?" Maureen gestured towards the young man with her eyes after he walked away.

"I tried already. He's gay." Linda stirred sour cream into her soup.

"How do you know?"

"He told me. He's HIV positive."

Maureen made a mental note to check Mark out. He didn't look sick. It might work out if no one else knew about his status. She eyed him as he served a couple at the next table. He was bulked up with a thick neck, broad shoulders, and muscular arms while his waist and hips were narrow. Too bad the best looking ones were on the other team.

"Did I tell you the dating service came through? I have a date with a fellow named Bard Bailey." Linda dumped the silver-serving dish of ranch dressing on her salad and dug in. "Can you imagine a name like that? Makes you wonder what his mama saw, doesn't it?"

"Is this the first one?" Maureen cut her lettuce into bite-sized pieces and pushed them around on her plate.

"They sent a couple characters my way a few months ago. I chatted with one fellow on the phone for a month before deciding to meet him. He worked for the water utility. We set it up to meet in the parking lot of Danny's bar. I figured I could drive off if I didn't like what I saw."

"And that's what you did?"

"Not at first. He parked beside me so that the windows on the driver's side of our trucks faced each other. He was no Tom Cruise but he was nice looking. A little older than I expected and maybe a bit worse for wear, but basically okay. Then I realized he had a glass eye."

"Lots of people have glass eyes, Linda."

"Well, I never knew one before. He lost it in Viet Nam. Some sort of thorn put it out." She shuddered—sticking out her tongue and rolling her eyes, her hands limp at the end of her wrists. The elderly couple at the next table startled, the woman twisting her head to stare at Linda in alarm. Mark hurried towards them but Maureen held up her hand and shook her head. Linda had a way of setting off chain reactions.

"If everything else about him was fine, what's the big deal?" Maureen didn't see Linda ever finding the right person. She had too many requirements—not too old, not too fat, no obvious flaws.

"I know, but he should have told me about it. I feel bad, of course, but I got to thinking about what my ex would say if I took up with a one-eyed man. Charlie is physically perfect, you know. He was a football player in high school—all state. My girlfriends thought he was gorgeous. We were the perfect couple what with me being a cheerleader and all."

Maureen had heard all that before. "So what happened with the fellow with the glass eye?"

"Walter." Linda sighed. "His name was Walter. He wanted to take me for a drink. Now that I think about it, he probably would have paid, but I couldn't do it. What would people say? I'd rather be alone than have people think the only man I could get was damaged goods."

Middle-age spread and divorce had robbed Linda of her self-esteem. Sometimes her unselfconscious prattle made Maureen feel bad for her. "What makes you think this Bard Bailey is going to be any different?"

"I gave the dating service what for after my experience with Walter. They have it in my file now—no one with any physical problems. It's more than just appearances. I want someone who can take care of me for the long run. Wouldn't do to find someone and have him croak on me."

"Surely you want more than that?"

"Well, I want someone who's fun to be around, of course. Someone who looks like Mel Gibson would be nice. I don't think it's unreasonable to want someone who is attentive, do you? And, I never thought I'd say this, but I want someone who doesn't care how long his cock is."

"WHAT?" Maureen sucked diet cola up her nose and choked.

"Oh shush! Don't look at me that way. I've been out there dating for a long time. They are all so worried about their equipment. They either want you to comment on its magnificence or they apologize about its insignificance. I mean, who even notices?"

Maureen looked around the restaurant, hoping that Linda's voice didn't carry. "Well, yes, I see what you mean." She shook her head, searching for a new topic of conversation, trying not to laugh. "So when are you going to see him?"

"See who?"

"Bard Bailey, silly."

"Oh, yeah. Bard." Linda's laugh was the lighthearted giggle of a thirteen-year-old. "This Friday."

"Where are you meeting him?"

16

"At Danny's, of course. In the parking lot."

"You nut." Maureen shook her head. Mark brought their entrees. "Are you married, Mark?" Maureen glanced up at him, poking at her omelet with her fork.

"No ma'am. Going to school."

Mark's eyes reminded her of the antelope at the Cleveland zoo. Wary but sweet. "What are you studying?"

"Biochemistry."

"Case Western?"

"Yep." Mark ground black pepper onto Linda's pasta.

"Grad student?"

"Of course."

"Good luck." Maureen cut her omelet into small pieces.

"Thanks, ma'am." Mark gathered up their salad plates and hurried off to the kitchen.

"What was that all about?" Linda whispered, her eyes twinkling. "You made old Mark nervous as hell."

"Just getting to know the man."

"Hmmmm. I think you like him. Too bad he's not available as they say."

"That kind of availability isn't required." Maureen did find Mark interesting. Very interesting, indeed.

"I was wondering if you'd mind dog-sitting Midnight in a couple of weeks. Sean and I are going to drive over to Pittsburgh to watch the Browns play the Steelers and Charlie's going to be out of town too," Linda said as they shared an umbrella walking up East Ninth.

"Sure."

"I don't mean just feed him. Like let him come to your apartment? He gets hyper when I'm not there. The doggie shrink says he's not over the divorce yet."

"The doggie shrink?"

"Don't laugh. He was one depressed puppy until we figured out what was wrong."

Maureen shook her head. "Well, we wouldn't want Midnight to get depressed again. There is a problem though. They don't allow dogs in my apartment complex. If he was a little guy, I'd try to sneak him in, but Midnight's a handful. Someone's bound to hear him galloping around."

"Why don't you spend the night at my place? The leaves are changing. You and Midnight can go for walks. He loves chasing the ducks. I'll even give you a hot pink key."

"A what?"

"I color code my keys. House keys are hot pink, cottage keys are blue, and storage is silver." Linda laughed. "Charlie got me doing that the first year we were married. He caught me standing in the rain sorting through my keys."

Maureen thought about it. Jennifer was supposed to run down to Columbus and check on a case. However, plans could be changed. This was a wonderful opportunity. Two days to explore the Hinckley property. "I think I can manage. I might have to run out a couple of times. You think Midnight would be okay if it wasn't more than an hour or so?"

"If it's during the day, he'll be fine. Just put him in the pen in the woods to the left of the house. It's another story if it's at night though. He gets paranoid and barks his fool head off if you leave him out there after dark."

It began raining and they scurried the last few yards to the East Ohio building. "I can take him with me. It's not a big thing." Maureen was in a hurry to get back to her desk and make a note about Mark. Her toes were cold even inside her Nikes. She stamped her feet, eager to strip off the damp socks and change back into her jeweled sandals.

Linda seemed oblivious to the cold. The fluorescent lighting in the foyer wasn't kind to her. The too-young hairdo, didn't flatter either. Yet, at forty-seven, she was a sparkly pixie. Everyone liked Linda, even Maureen.

"I'll bring you the extra key. Sean and I are going to leave out right after work that Friday. I'll make my mother's special recipe chili for you before I leave."

"That won't be necessary." Maureen mentally rearranged her schedule. A weekend in the country would do her a world of good. "I'll talk to you about it when it gets closer."

"I appreciate it, girlfriend." Linda hugged Maureen.

Maureen tensed. She wasn't prepared for hugs. What looked natural didn't necessarily feel natural, but Linda didn't seem to notice anything unusual. The woman was both naive and kindhearted. The very qualities that would keep her in trouble, Maureen thought.

Maureen cleared the minutia of her job by mid-afternoon. Time to check on those most likely to get in trouble. She pulled up the software that allowed her to see if employees were talking by instant message to anyone outside the network.

There were two ongoing conversations. A woman in Human Resources was discussing medical benefits with an employee who was home after a hysterectomy. The employee was milking it, although Maureen couldn't blame her. A month just wasn't long enough. The other conversation was between the Director of Finance and a housewife in Fresno. She peeked in long enough to understand that this was a long and involved erotic seduction. The company didn't mind the tone of the exchange so much as the four-hour length of it. She logged the IM session and forwarded it to the man's manager. The VP of Finance would embarrass the man this time. If there was a next time ... well, there better not be a next time. The company sent out memo after memo warning people that their use of corporate phones, computers, and faxes were not private. It was sheer stupidity when they abused the system anyway.

She turned to the request for the log of a certain employee's browsing trail. That meant the manager had noticed a decline in the man's performance. She retrieved the logs for the last three months and printed them out. Lots of time on ESPN.com and WSJ.com. There had been some discussion about whether they were appropriate sites during work hours. The decision from above was to buy a corporate license for WSJ.com and as long as the bulk of ESPN.com was before work, during lunch, or after work, she was to turn a blind eye to the browsing. Maureen had snickered when she got the memo. Men ran the company and they needed their sports fix.

This fellow, an accountant, must have been betting though. He spent almost all day every day browsing the various sports sites. She retrieved his phone logs on a hunch—hundreds of calls to the same long distance number over a three-month period. Area code 702. She looked it up. Las Vegas.

She wasn't supposed to check his employee file, but she peeked anyway. "Why was this guy still working for the company?" She said to herself.

Suspended twice before—once fifteen years ago for cornering a secretary and feeling her breasts, once for performance. This joker was due for a comeuppance. "Idiot," Maureen grumbled as she prepared the package that would seal his fate.

Finished for the day a good two hours before quitting time, she pulled up her notes. "MARK! From the Café Sausalito. Student at Case Western. HIV +? Get license plate number?" She thought for a moment and typed, "Biochemistry. Grad school. Masters? Doctorate?"

She'd have Jennifer follow him and pick up some additional information that way. Somehow, Mark didn't strike her as gay. Maybe he told Linda that to fend off a pass or something. She'd have Jennifer check that out as well.

Maureen returned to Gorman. Cyrus B. Fifty-two years old. Divorced. He'd had a serious accident before he hired on with the company. There must have been a court case about it, because his medical files had been subpoenaed and they were now part of the public record. When he agreed to a physical upon being hired, he signed a form allowing the company access to his records. They were all there. She scanned them.

They were routine. The man claimed he didn't smoke. Other than high cholesterol, everything seemed normal. Then she saw it—a visit to St. Luke's Emergency Room for a broken arm caused by a car accident. Why did he go all the way over to St. Luke's for treatment when he lived in Parma? He must have either been in the area or he was trying to hide something, but from who? She checked the date. Two years before his divorce. Aha! She checked the day of the week. Wednesday.

Mr. Gorman was on the wrong side of town at 2 o'clock in the morning—seeing a woman who wasn't his wife, she guessed. She bet he'd been drinking as well. That's why he was sued. Someone else was hurt, probably a lot worse than Mr. Gorman.

From his goofy calls for help with his laptop, she figured he still drank. Maybe not a lot, but she bet he drove his car when he drank. A trip to the courthouse was in order. She was convinced she'd find at least one DUI since the car accident.

She checked company records. He had two insurance policies—one term at $10,000, the other whole life at $50,000. Both listed Miriam Gorman as the beneficiary. His daughter? His ex-wife? She looked further. Perfect. She pulled up her note file. Miriam Gorman. Mother. Miriam lived in Parma too. Maureen decided to send Jennifer over to take a look—maybe steal Mrs. Gorman's mail if the opportunity presented itself.

"You wanted to see me, Bill?" Maureen stood at the door of Bill Casey's enormous corner office. Everything gleamed. No loose papers or stray paper clips. Linda kept things in pristine order.

"Have a seat!" He waved her in, the phone pressed against his ear. "I'm on hold."

Maureen set her briefcase on the small round conference table and sat down in the plush client's chair.

"Would you take a look at this?" He tossed a medium sized post-it note across the desk.

Maureen scanned it. In a large looping script, Linda had written: *Call your wife. She has a wild hare!* She looked up at Bill in surprise.

He shrugged. "Imagine having a mind like that?"

"What does she mean? A rabbit?"

"I talked to Morgana. She told Linda she had an idea and that I better call her before she spent a lot of money."

"Oh, I see. Did you catch her in time?" Maureen laughed.

"Nope. Seems we are booked on a cruise up the inside passage next summer."

"Congratulations."

"I only hope the new system is installed and working by then." He slammed down the phone. "My damned earlobe is numb. If they want to talk to me so bad, they can call me back later."

Maureen raised one eyebrow. "Didn't like the music?"

"Rap."

"I prefer show tunes, myself."

"I'd have waited ten more minutes if they'd been playing country." He sat Marine Corps stiff in his chair, a left over trait from when he was a Master Sergeant. His short brush cut was left over too. She wasn't sure where he got his penchant for decorative plaques though. The walls were full of them—awards for performance, inspirational quotes—even his granddaughter's bronzed baby shoes. He folded his hands on the desk. "So, what can I do for you, Maureen."

"I don't know. You called me."

"I did?"

"You left three phone messages and an email."

"I'm like that. I want to make sure you know I'm trying to get in touch with you."

"I did. That's why I'm here." She loved repartee with Bill Casey but it was getting late and she wished he'd get to the point.

"Jack called again. He doesn't like changing his password every month. He likes PREZ. He can remember it."

"Everyone can remember it. It's on his vanity plates and his Cross Pen. He wears a tie that says PREZ over and over again. It's probably the PIN for his bank accounts, for God's sake. Anyone with half a brain can get into any of his files, and when someone does, he'll be all over us. Rules are rules, Bill. If I let him break them just because he's the President, I'll have to let everyone break them."

"You are tough."

"Only because it's necessary."

"There's no other alternative?"

"You mean like taking his fingerprint or scanning his retina?"

Bill folded his hands and twiddled his thumbs. "He's not ready to pay for that kind of technology."

Maureen raised her eyebrows.

"Yossarian would appreciate this situation." Bill Casey was a Catch-22 aficionado. He quoted it at every management meeting.

She folded her arms across her chest.

"Not responding to pressure?" Bill's eyes twinkled.

"You either trust my judgment or you don't."

"I trust you, but it puts me between a rock and a hard place. Jack's a stubborn man. He doesn't like change."

"Are you going to back me up?"

"Hell yes, I just hoped I could get you to back down so I wouldn't have to go toe to toe with the big guy."

She stood up. "Anything else, boss man?"

"Have Linda bring in a first aid kit. Someone's going to have to patch up my scratches after I emerge from the lion's den tomorrow."

"She went home already."

It was after dark when Maureen got home. She locked the door behind her and stripped off her clothes. She hung the silk blouse in the closet, but everything else went into the laundry basket. Putting the wig on a Styrofoam head, she creamed her face to get rid of the heavy pancake make-up.

After a long hot shower, she rubbed her body with a rough towel and coated herself with jelled baby oil. The loose cotton pajamas felt wonderful after a long day wearing that huge brassiere. Padding barefoot into the kitchen, she made herself a bowl of cereal and sat down at the counter to eat it, reading her mail.

She sorted it into several piles. There were two birth certificates, a passport, and several credit cards under a variety of names. It was becoming a full time job just keeping up with the records for her projects. She was glad to see that two banks had sent the all-important PINs for Mastercards she'd already received. Now she could retrieve cash from them. She got nervous when her checking account dropped down below $10,000 and she refused, as a matter of principle, to dig into any of the various savings accounts, Certificates of Deposit, or brokerage accounts she maintained. Of course, she never touched the money she kept in Switzerland. That was for a rainy day or for when she decided to retire.

She emptied her bowl and rinsed it while her computer booted. Her equipment was top of the line. She didn't believe in running things on a shoestring. You have to have the right tools if you want the best results.

She relaxed in her ergonomic chair. Logging onto AOL, she checked her email under all seven usernames. Mostly spam, but a few notes from potential targets. She answered them all, careful to respond in the manner each expected. A housewife in Detroit had included her address and telephone number in her signature file. She saved the information to her database, shaking her head. It was amazing how much intimate information people gave out to their online 'friends.' Then she went to Yahoo. Then she went to Hotmail. Her correspondence took the better part of two hours.

Next, she turned to financial matters. Her last deposit had been credited to her Morgan Stanley 401K. The market was up and she was pleased with the overall progress of the account. While she was at it, she checked Jennifer's affairs as well. Everything seemed in order although the check for Jennifer's new Saturn hadn't cleared yet. She'd have to call the dealership and make sure they deposited it. These little details could screw up the works if you didn't keep at them.

It was getting late when she slipped in the CD she'd made at work and loaded today's information into her main database. She added the credit cards and birth certificate data before settling down to research Mr. Gorman. She hacked into the Motor Vehicle Registration database and found that he drove a twelve-year-old green Volvo. Plate Number: SALTY. She sighed. Get real. Who'd he think he was? Jimmy Buffet? It was disappointing. She'd hoped he drove a Hyundai or an old Pinto. She checked newspaper archives. No sign of a macho middle-aged hobby like a motor scooter or skydiving—just a picture of him at his daughter's wedding with a garter stretched over his head. She tapped the monitor with her nail. That old demon rum. She grinned.

Chapter 2 – The Strangler
<u>Thursday, October 10, 2000</u>

Dick Longren maneuvered the Sunset Limited down the narrow dirt road. The recreational vehicle smelled new. Everything was wrapped in heavy plastic including the chairs. This was the best gig he'd had in years—delivering RV's from manufacturers and/or dealers in one part of the country to customers and/or dealers in another part. Every trip was a different route with a new vehicle. He slapped the steering wheel with the heel of his hand, chortling to himself. The police would never figure it out.

He pulled up to the KOA office. A round man with a baldhead and white chin whiskers sat behind the counter reading Popular Mechanics. Dick pulled his fishing hat low over his sunglasses and raised his voice to a nasal tenor. "Got room for a Limited, forty-foot? Internet connection?"

"Howdy, stranger. How long you want to stay?"

"One night."

"Got a space over by that Chinook. It's real quiet. Those folks are visiting relatives for the next couple weeks." The man gestured with his head and Dick turned to look. The space backed up against the woods. It would be a bit of a maneuver, but it was possible. It suited his purposes too. If you didn't count the empty RV, the next nearest neighbor was over a block away.

"Any decent places to eat?" Dick never cooked in the RVs he delivered. People paying upwards of $200,000 wanted their vehicles in pristine condition. A trace of grease on the stove or breadcrumbs in the microwave was a big no-no. It's not that he gave a damn one way or another, but his affairs were delicate. He didn't want to draw attention to himself even though a complaint about a dirty kitchen would not alert anyone to his real mission.

The Strangler

"There's a *Denny's* over near the interstate." The old man took Dick's American Express card and swiped it through the reader on the register. He turned it over to examine the signature before handing it back to Dick.

Although he was holding his breath, Dick knew it was okay. He didn't plan on using this particular name much longer anyway. It wasn't hot, but you didn't get to be fifty-seven years old in this business if you weren't careful. He signed the receipt with a big 'D' followed by a thick horizontal line with a slight squiggle towards the end for the 'g.' He loved messing with handwriting experts—like they could tell anything about anyone based on how you do your ABCs.

The Sunset Limited was a monster and it took a while to get it in its proper place. He was sweating by the time everything was set up for the evening—and hungry. He retrieved a small scooter mounted above the bumper and set it up on the kickstand. The helmet was in one of the storage bins under the RV. He put on his thick leather jacket. This was his last run of the year with the Honda. It would be too cold before long, at least in the northern states.

He kick started the scooter and cruised through the camp. There were RVs of all sizes and shapes. The women were intriguing. A gray-haired femme fatale smiled through the back window of a Winnebago. He nodded and lifted a hand in greeting. Just around a shallow curve, a big-butted red-head came out of the laundry area. He touched his helmet with two fingers, almost as a salute.

These camps were crowded with tin cans full of honey. He looked forward to a quick review of the area once it was dark. It was a risk because men usually accompanied these ladies.

He wasn't worried. He began peeking when he was thirteen years old. In all that time, there was only one close call. A naked girl caught the glint of his glasses through her bedroom window, but by the time she raised the alarm and her father came barging out into the yard with a baseball bat, Dick was long gone.

USERNAME

He was a lot younger then, of course, but he could still sprint. He jogged two miles every day during hunting season just to be sure. The day he could no longer run like hell was the day he'd retire. He learned his lesson though. He no longer wore glasses. He was one of the first in the United States to have Radial Keratotomy surgery on his eyes. He could see better than a teenager now.

He turned onto the main road and headed toward the interstate, accelerating once he was past the outer bounds of the RV camp. The waitress at *Denny's* was a cute little thing. She reminded him of his cousin Buddy's girlfriend Sheila.

This girl wore a nametag identifying herself as 'Susanna,' a silver ring in her eyebrow and pink glitter fingernail polish. He flirted with her and she got so flustered she had to come back to ask him whether he wanted pancakes or toast with his Slim Slam.

He closed his eyes and imagined his hands around her throat, the look of surprise and then horror, the tightening of her muscles and then the slow relaxation. His erection pressed against his fly. HE didn't need any Viagra. He knew a secret other men his age didn't, the eroticism of power. Knowing you have the ability to take a life whenever you want—that was the best aphrodisiac of all.

He gave Susanna a big tip and winked at her. The teenager blushed. He bet she hadn't yet been introduced to the joys of sex with a man older than her grandpa. He toyed with the idea of raping her, but decided to pass for now. He had other fish to fry, so to speak. Maybe he'd catch her another day. The sheer arbitrariness of his decision made him feel potent and strong. Life or death—it was up to him.

It was dusk when he parked the Honda near the Sunset Limited and secured it to the RV with a chain. As eager as he was to explore the camp, it was still early. He went inside and set up his laptop on the kitchen table.

The Strangler

Rummaging through the slim leather carrying case, he found his mouse, a wireless card, and the power converter. While everything was booting, he collected his digital camera from the cupboard over the refrigerator, a portable printer specially made for photographs, and his beloved scrapbook.

He uploaded the photos from the night before. There were ten of them. The first was at the mall in Indianapolis as Iliana drove up and parked beside the RV. The second was after she was inside. She brought along a bottle of Bailey's Irish Crème as a gift. He told her it was his favorite drink, but of course, he wouldn't touch the stuff.

The bitch was nervous about getting into the vehicle. She didn't tell anyone she was meeting him, she said. Good, that's the idea. She wanted to light up a cigarette as he pulled out of the mall and headed towards Columbus, but put it back into her purse when he scowled at her. It wouldn't do to have the Sunset Limited smelling like stale smoke. The next pictures were after she was dead. He licked his lips. They were his favorites.

He opened them in Photoshop and touched them up a bit—cropping some of them, sharpening the focus on others. When they were perfect, he printed them. He bought the best paper. It made a difference. He opened his scrapbook and paged through it, enjoying the pictures and sniffing the panties. The scent had gone out of the older ones but he sniffed them anyway.

Certain photos excited him more than others and he paused to appreciate them, his hand inside his pants. One of the pictures from last night was going to be in that category—the one with Iliana lying naked on the plastic-covered bed in the rear of the RV, a long pink scarf knotted around her neck, the bottle of Bailey's Irish Crème stuck in her vagina.

He held it up to the light. She had a grotesque bunion on her left foot. He'd not noticed it before. It reminded him of his Grandmother and that excited him even more.

30

He played with himself until it was pitch black outside. It was time to get rid of Iliana. He put on latex gloves. He was glad it was October. Folks would head for home in the next week or two or they'd go south. He turned out the lights before slipping out the door. He listened. Distant voices towards the bathrooms and laundry.

He was confident no one could see him from there. Unlatching the aft storage bin under the Limited, he took out an orange hand truck. It took a minute to assemble it, locking the joints with metal pins. Then he pulled out the large package.

He was glad she was a small woman. It was more complicated with the heavier ones. He'd wrapped her in several layers of plastic and then a final covering of brown butcher paper secured with heavy twine. She was stiff. He stood her up against the footrest of the hand truck and tied her to the back railing.

He looked around once again before pushing the body off into the woods behind the RV. He trudged along for almost an hour, enjoying the cool darkness. It was his last time to be alone with Iliana and he treasured the moments.

Deep in the glade, he found the perfect spot at the base of a tree. He laid her in a small depression and spent time covering her with brush, dried saplings, and lots of crackling leaves. He was in no hurry. It would be a long time before anyone found her. He took an extra moment to masturbate over her grave, a special tribute. He'd been talking with her online for over two years and she never guessed what he was. What a dumb bitch!

It was midnight by the time he found his way back to the camp. He made the rounds, peering into the windows—pausing to

The Strangler

appreciate an elderly woman folding clothes in an Airstream near the gate. The only other view was of a middle-aged couple getting it on in a tiny trailer near the office. He watched for a while but he couldn't see much more than the man's scrawny arse moving up and down. He glimpsed the woman's legs wrapped around the man's waist, but it was too dark to tell if she was wearing polish on her toes. He got bored after a few minutes and went back to the Sunset Limited.

He undressed and sat in front of the computer in his underwear. He logged onto the Internet and checked his mail. There was a note from Marianne22 in Zanesville, Ohio.

"I'm looking forward to meeting you, Raymond. I do hope you won't mind that I'm not as young and beautiful as you might have wished for. I do love you and I'll do everything I can to make you happy."

I'm sure you will, he thought before sending her a quick email. "Can hardly wait to meet you, love. I'll reach the Colony Square Mall shopping center tomorrow around 10 pm. You can't miss me. I'll park outside Sears. My RV looks like a blue, white, and green bus. Pull up in front of me and flash your lights. Until then, hugs and kisses from your limey lover." He chuckled as he typed it. He'd never pretended to be a Brit before.

He changed usernames and checked for email from his other loves. He had discovered long ago that it paid to keep several possibilities in the queue. Some were easier than others. A woman in Saint Louis came to visit him forty-five minutes after he first messaged her. Others took years to develop. You couldn't predict what a woman might do.

After answering his mail, he decided to mine some new targets. After all, he'd be down two after this trip. He clicked on Member Directory and pulled up the search form. He thought for a moment. He hadn't taken anyone in Cleveland in twenty years.

USERNAME

The last time was when he was Lance, a flight attendant for Continental Airlines. He followed a woman out of long-term parking at Hopkins International. That was when he still broke into houses. He was a nervy little twit back then.

He typed in "Cleveland" in the location box and checked "Female." He thought about what else he might want. Ultimately, those two qualities were sufficient. He didn't ask for much, he chuckled to himself.

Several hundred hits. No way he'd go through all of them. He scrolled through the profiles. Some put their ages, the younger ones, and the ones pretending to be young. He decided to pass on married women this time. They were missed too quickly. The one's that proclaimed themselves single were okay, but he zeroed in on the divorcees.

It amused him that they saw themselves that way. They wanted you to know someone had wanted them once upon a time. He looked for women in their late forties and early fifties. They were more willing to believe the scenario he created for them. He wasn't sure why.

In the end, he found ten. Pulling up "The Letter," he modified it for each one and emailed it off. "The Letter" was one of the best scams he'd come up with since he pretended to be an abortionist back in the 1960s. If he worked it right, it had the same advantage. They came to him at a time and place of his choosing. He closed down around 1:30 am.

Packing everything away, he stretched and yawned. It had been a long and satisfying day. He checked his supplies—plenty of rope, big heavy plastic bags, rolls of brown paper, two balls of twine. He ran his fingers through the long yellow scarf hanging on a hook in the closet—pink for Iliana, yellow for Marianne. He kept a knife in his duffel. He hadn't even needed it with Iliana. She'd been putty in his hands.

The Strangler

He retrieved his sleeping bag and unrolled it on the big queen sized bed at the rear of the RV. He stretched out and relaxed.

Life as The Lone Wolf had been good. Forty years this spring. He couldn't think of anyone else who'd been as successful. They caught that stupid-assed Ted Bundy right away. Jeffrey Dahmer didn't last long either. Here he was after all this time, still active. He'd shown them all.

Chapter 3 – Jennifer

Tuesday, October 15, 2000

Jennifer brushed her light brown hair into a high ponytail. She rummaged around Maureen's dresser for an elastic band to hold it. There was nothing that would pass. Not even a rubber band. She stamped her foot in frustration. She WASN'T going to spend three hours teaching aerobics with her hair hanging down like a damp mop. She found the scissors in the kitchen, stuck blades down into a small vase. Holding the ponytail even higher, she cut it off and laid it on the sink. She hated the damned thing anyway.

She went back to the mirror in the bathroom and snipped at the remaining hair until it was less than an inch long all over her head. There. That was more practical. Cooler. It made her more noticeable, but even so, she'd never stand out in a crowd. Her afternoon at the mall proved that.

A wide assortment of clothes lay across Maureen's bed, most with the price tags attached. There were several pairs of expensive silk slacks in size sixteen for Maureen—navy, brown, black and gray. Jennifer had stuffed them down the front of her own pants and pulled the big loose blouse over them. Everyone thought she was pregnant. She was so swift not even the cameras caught her.

At Lane Bryant, she bought an eighty-dollar blazer and then tucked three knit shells in the same bag. She even stole a couple of those funky brassieres that Maureen wore. Jennifer held one of them up to her chest, trying not to giggle.

For herself, she found a cute leopard print leotard along with sheer black tights and black aerobic shoes at Kaufman's. She didn't need them but they were too easy to pass up. She dropped them in her big black bag and wandered back out into the mall.

She was spectacularly successful in the food court. She focused on women with small children. One left her belongings lying unattended on a bench while she chased her two year old around the center fountain. Unnoticed, Jennifer slipped her hand into the diaper bag and retrieved the woman's change purse. Piece of cake!

Not too much later, she bumped into an old gentleman standing in line at Sbarra and picked his pocket. Loaded down with loot, she worked her way out of the mall, stopping to lift a pair of sunglasses in a velveteen bag from the Sunglass Hut. She sometimes wondered if people were blind or if she was invisible.

Sitting on Maureen's bed, Jennifer sorted through the old man's wallet. There was a thick assortment of credit cards and a driver's license. Morton Minor, born 1935. He was bald with a big nose. In the paper money section, she found a small sheet of white paper folded in thirds. A thick headline read, "Have you seen this woman?" A photo of a thin-faced woman with big hair and lots of make-up was labeled 'Iliana Minor Johnson.'

Iliana was a real Schnauzer. She had a snout as big as the old man's. Born in 1959, Iliana must be his daughter. Poor old Morty looking for his child who'd gone missing. Oh well, maybe Maureen could do something with it.

Then she hit pay dirt. There was four twenties, a ten and two fives in the main folder, three hundred dollar bills hidden in the secret compartment. These old codgers must not believe in banks. She took the money and left everything else for Maureen.

She didn't expect much from the young mother's purse, but it was her lucky day. Aside from a Kaufman's credit card and a driver's license, there was a brand new Social Security Card in the name of Donald O. Tamarind. Initials DOT. She giggled. Now why would a parent do that to a kid? Jennifer put it aside. Maureen could use this one for any number of things. The number would be pristine. All in all, it was a good haul.

She glanced at the clock beside the bed. Time to get ready. She stripped to her bra and butt-thong. The new tights had a silky feel to them as she pulled them up over her thighs. The leopard spotted leotard showed a little more cleavage than she liked, but there was this young guy in the class who would appreciate it. Okay, so that wasn't in the plan, but she was no nun.

She put on her trench coat and tied it around the waist. Her new aerobics shoes went in her bag along with a towel and a change of clothes. Anything else? She looked around her.

Maureen could put all this stuff away when she returned. Who would have thought these projects would be so much work? It was worth it though. A few more months and she'd be fixed for life. She could be herself then. What a relief that would be!

Jennifer had parked the Saturn under a tree not far from Maureen's Acura. A yellow Post-it note stuck to the steering wheel said, "Danny's Bar. Tonight. Eleven-thirty. Watch Linda." Maureen was always leaving little notes around. Remember to do this, remember to do that. After two hours of aerobics, it was going to be a long night. Jennifer sighed as she pulled onto Pearl Road and headed towards Strongsville.

The parking lot at the gym was full. She nosed the little car into a narrow spot next to Kyle's sleek Beemer. He was sleek too. She'd had her eye on him for months now. She tossed her bag over one shoulder and locked the Saturn. She longed for things to be normal again, to go out, and have dinner with a boyfriend rather than running around all over the place supporting the projects. When things settled down a bit, maybe she'd call old Kyle.

Jennifer

The first hour was step aerobics. Twelve yawning people leaned against the mirrored walls in thick-soled cross-trainers and work-out clothes. She stood on tiptoe to reach the benches stowed on the top shelf of the equipment closet.

"Can I help you with those?" His voice oozed like spilt honey. Men on the make were so obvious.

"If you can hand them down to me that would be great." She put a little flirtation into her smile.

"That's okay. I'll set them up."

The smell of his aftershave was intoxicating. She busied herself with the music selection, while he spaced the benches six feet apart in two rows. The class required an upbeat tempo—a bit of Selena, some rock, a little disco. She tried a medium paced mambo, leaning over the CD player and rocking her hips.

She was aware of Kyle's eyes on her buttocks. She hoped it made him nuts.

"Okay, wake up!" She clapped her hands and everyone took their places behind their step benches. This was a class of professional people—women in their early thirties and men in their early forties. "Let's start with a short warm-up and then some stretches." Her voice was almost a baritone. She made an effort to raise it a half-tone to add excitement to the class. These people were fat and sassy. She intended to work their butts off.

The music swelled. Jennifer led them through a series of movements designed to prepare their muscles for stretching. Taking a deep breath, she bent her knees before reaching for the ceiling with both hands, lengthening her torso. Putting the back of one heel on the bench, she enjoyed the tension up the back of her leg and into her trim buttock. It was important to keep her body working well. You never know when one might have to run away, she thought as she eyed Kyle's thick biceps.

The music changed tempo and she moved in time to the beat, watching Kyle's reflection in the mirror. He matched her pace.

The rest of the class moved faster too, although a tall, chubby woman in the back row missed her step and twisted her ankle. Jennifer pretended not to notice and the woman continued her movements with her teeth clenched. What an ass! Jennifer had no patience for show-offs who didn't know when to quit.

The next number increased the pace again. A balding fellow with a round belly began breathing through his mouth, a wet huffing sound. The chubby woman broke off and sat down to rub her swelling ankle. Jennifer smirked to herself.

Kyle hadn't broken a sweat yet. Their eyes met in the mirror and he nodded. Fueled by the electric current between them, Jennifer increased the complexity of the steps. She swung her arms higher and lifted her thighs, building the intensity of the work-out. Another woman dropped out.

"Damn, girl!" A lean black woman called out and the group laughed, causing one of the men to lose the beat.

Jennifer glanced around the room. The duds were sitting on the floor—their backs pressed up against the back wall, their legs splayed outwards. Everyone else was having fun. Kyle's thin sleeveless t-shirt was damp now. His eyes focused inward. His lips moved as he counted to himself.

"DOUBLE TIME! YEAH!" Jennifer pumped the air with her left fist and sped up again. The class followed her movements and the room filled with various hoots, whistles, and grunts.

Jennifer kept her breathing even and deep. She couldn't do anything about the flush on her face or the beads of sweat forming on her upper lip. She held the pace throughout two songs, her heart pumping. Pushing the students and herself, she enjoyed the sheer physicality of the class.

"Cool down," she said as the next song slowed. Whimpers of relief met her announcement as everyone began the process of coming down off the exercise-induced high. She glanced at Kyle.

Jennifer

He was no longer staring at her. Jennifer didn't blame him. She didn't care anymore either.

As their heart rates dropped to normal, she took them through another intense stretching routine. The camaraderie evident during the height of the class gave way to silent introspection as they sat in the straddle position and leaned down over their legs. Jennifer put her nose on her knee and exhaled. Leaning forward, legs wide, elbows on the floor, she whispered, "See you next week."

She didn't wait to see them collect their gear and file towards the showers. Slipping out the back door, she headed towards the smaller workout room where the next class awaited her.

A huge change of pace, this was a class for those over sixty-five or for folks with physical ailments that prevented them from standing for any length of time. The whole routine was performed sitting in straight back chairs. Even so, this group required more of her than the other.

The old ladies wanted to chat. They brought her small gifts and recipes. The old men winked and tried to pat her bottom. Each member required attention. No matter how well they knew the routines, no one was interested in doing anything in unison. They weren't here for the physical experience but because they enjoyed each other's company.

The hour seemed like three. Afterwards she herded them like so many clamoring geese towards the locker rooms. Mr. Graber was a garrulous fellow with thick glasses and arthritic knees. He used two canes to find his way out the door to his big ten-year-old Cadillac. Jennifer couldn't believe the old man was still driving. He was at least eighty-five. Nearly running over Mrs. Reese who was hobbling across the parking lot towards a dented Ford Escort, he skidded to a sudden stop and laughed as she scolded him. Tipping his hat, he pulled out onto Pearl Road. Horns blared, tires squealed. How did he last this long? Jennifer wrote his license plate down on the palm of her hand with a Magic Marker. She also wrote down Mrs. Reese's number before waving good-bye.

Back in the locker room, she copied the numbers to a notebook she kept in her bag. Peeling off her leotard, she stepped into the shower and soaped herself with a natural sponge. Her hair was short enough now to dry with a towel. She didn't bother with make-up. Eschewing underwear, she put on a pair of light cotton trousers with a tie waist and a thin over blouse. She paused in front of the mirror. With a colored scarf over her head and wrapped in her trench coat, she didn't recognize herself.

Her eyes drooped. She couldn't wait to get back to her apartment and go to bed. She slid behind the wheel of the Saturn and yawned.

Damn! Maureen's note was still there. Damn!

There was no way she was going to last until 11:30 without something to eat. She headed towards the nearest McDonald's and ordered a Quarter Pounder with Cheese, large fries and a Diet Coke. She had to laugh at herself about the Coke. Who was she fooling?

She drove over to Danny's Bar and parked under a dark tree at the corner of the small lot. It was only 10 o'clock, but Linda's old van was already there. Jennifer tore into the sandwich. Sipping her coke, she settled in for a long evening praying Linda would get tired and go home to bed. She wouldn't count on it though. The goofy woman was obsessed with finding a man.

Linda came out of the bar and looked around. Her van sat under the streetlight at the edge of Danny's lot. Jennifer was pretty sure she wouldn't notice her crouched down in the Saturn with her half-eaten sandwich. Linda glanced at her watch and climbed into the van. A distinctive thump echoed through the night as Linda locked all four doors. Just in case, Jennifer guessed.

Linda had piled her hair on top of her head with one long tendril curling down her back. Her fringed western shirt hid her wide hips while her high-heeled boots made her appear taller. She probably smells to high heaven too, Jennifer thought. Linda tapped out some inner rhythm on the steering wheel while she waited.

Jennifer sighed and bit into a salty French fry.

Within a few minutes, a gleaming new Isuzu Trooper pulled into the parking space next to Linda. It was a Limited Edition—black with a light-colored metallic paint around the wheel wells and along the bottom of the doors. Bard Bailey wasn't as new or fancy as his SUV. Sporting a two-day-old beard, he looked like a middle-aged version of a blue jean commercial. He got out of the truck and leaned against the fender. Linda must have liked his looks because she rolled down her window and called to him, "Hey, good looking!"

Bard tossed his cigarette and ground the butt under his heel. He strode across the gravel parking lot with a pretentious John Wayne swagger. "How are you, darlin?" He bent over to peer in Linda's window.

Linda's voice was softer, but Jennifer could hear her plainly. "That's a nice looking truck you have there."

Bard stepped back, folding his arms across his chest. "I thought you might like that. I brought it along special for you to see." His tone had changed.

Jennifer sat up straighter. "Something's not right," she muttered.

"Oh?" Linda seemed puzzled.

"It's a hell of ride, let me tell you. Luxury and practicality all rolled into one. Even so, only a certain kind of person drives a Trooper—someone who likes to challenge both herself and her vehicle. Someone who needs four-wheel drive for off-roading, but prefers an automatic when dealing with the Interstate. Someone who no longer needs what I call the 'Mommy Van.' Someone just like you." He thumped the roof of Linda's van.

Jennifer couldn't make out Linda's face through the dark windshield, but she imagined her eyes were wide with surprise.

"It's a nice car." Linda sounded doubtful.

"You want to give it a spin?" Bard Bailey gestured towards the Trooper.

Linda shook her head. "I didn't come here to buy a car."

"No? What DID you come here for, little lady?"

Linda didn't answer and the silence swelled between them.

"Come on, give it a try." Bard dangled the keys just beyond Linda's reach. "You'll love it. It's perfect for you. Come on, we'll have fun."

Linda pushed the door of her van into Bard. He backed away, holding his elbow. She was more than a head shorter than Bard and fifty pounds heavier. She yanked the keys out of his hand and ran around to the driver's side of the Trooper.

"Get in."

Bard ducked his head and automatically obeyed the command in Linda's voice.

The engine came alive. Bard had barely closed the passenger door when Linda hit the gas. Gravel flew and the rear end fishtailed as they passed Jennifer. Country music blasted the neighborhood as Linda made the first turn on two wheels.

Jennifer started the Saturn and made a U-turn. The lights of the Trooper were disappearing over a small rise by the time she pulled out onto Route 303. She accelerated. Just beyond the corner of Center and West 130th, the SUV lay on its side in a shallow ditch. Heart pounding, Jennifer skidded to a stop a few feet away and wound down her window.

The passenger door popped-open and Bard emerged, frowning. "You stupid bitch!" He yelled back into the overturned vehicle.

"Oh please." Linda stuck her head out the opened door. Her hair had come undone and was hanging around her face.

Bard put his arms around her waist and pulled. "Do you know how much that's going to cost me?"

"How the hell would I know, asshole?" Linda pressed her boots against the dash, her arm around Bard's neck, struggling to get out of the Trooper. Her cheeks were red. Jennifer wasn't sure if she was hurt or embarrassed.

"I'll sue you. I'll take every penny you have." Bard swung Linda around and set her on the road. One of her boot heels flew off into the darkness.

"Then you'll be an asshole with a buck ninety-eight." She put her hand on her cheekbone, wincing.

Bard clenched his fist and took a step towards Linda. "Don't mess with me, bitch."

Jennifer beeped her horn. They both jumped as if they had been so caught up in their confrontation they had been unaware of the Saturn's headlights illuminating them. "Can I help you?"

Linda shielded her eyes with her forearm and squinted. "Will you take me to Danny's bar?"

"Sure. What about him?" Jennifer gestured towards Bard who was pacing back and forth on the berm of the road, a cell phone at his ear.

"He can take care of himself." Linda crossed in front of the Saturn.

"HEY! You forgot this!" Bard pulled Linda's purse out of the Trooper.

She hobbled across the road.

He held it over his head. "What do you want me to tell the police when they get here?"

Showing remarkable balance in her broken-heeled boot, Linda kicked his shin and grabbed her purse when he crumpled in pain. "You slid off the road." She headed back towards the passenger side of Jennifer's car.

"They didn't tell me at the agency you were fat." He spat, rubbing his leg.

"They didn't tell me you were ugly." Linda got into the Saturn and slammed the car door behind her.

"Lover's quarrel?" Jennifer asked as she drove off leaving Bard standing in the middle of the road shouting obscenities after them.

"Blind date." Linda rubbed at her eye with the heel of her hand

"Didn't work out?"

"He didn't like the looks of me so he tried to sell me a car."

"Looks like you got even."

"Not yet." Linda stared out the window.

Jennifer pulled into Danny's parking lot.

"Thanks." Linda slammed the door and disappeared back inside the bar.

Jennifer parked under the tree. Getting out of the Saturn, she crept across the parking lot and peered into Linda's van. A soft bell dinged when she opened the door. Reaching across the steering wheel, she retrieved the keys dangling from the ignition. The hot pink one was easy to find.

Chapter 4 – The Hunt

<u>Wednesday, October 16, 2000</u>

Dick got into Orlando around six. He stopped at a do-it-yourself carwash and rinsed the road dust off the Sunset Limited. Using a sock stuck on his hand, he wiped down the inside with lemon-scented oil. No more fingerprints. Not his, not Iliana's, not Marianne's. Not even little Susanna's from *Denny's*.

He smiled to himself. Going back to pick up that little piece was like putting a cherry on top of a deluxe hot fudge sundae. Not only did she have a ring in her eyebrow, she'd pierced her left nipple and her right labia. It made for great pictures.

He checked in all the closets and storage bins. It wouldn't do to leave some little something in a corner somewhere. When he was satisfied, he stored his sleeping bag and scooter in a rented garage. Then he delivered the RV, collected his money, and took a taxi to the Crowne Plaza on International Drive.

He loved staying in nice hotels. The idea that there were hundreds of hoity-toity people in the surrounding rooms excited him. He imagined them watching porn movies, calling room service, sleeping—not one of them knowing what lurked in their midst. He sat on the bed and turned on the TV.

John Walsh was blasting some scumbag murderer. Dick leaned back on his elbow, his mouth open. He couldn't help but love that guy. If his father had more balls or his mother had less, Dick might have been some hotshot TV host too. He liked the way they reenacted crimes while Walsh did a steamy talk-over. He sometimes lay in bed remembering his own adventures and imagining John Walsh's voice describing the action.

46

He was tickled when Walsh did several episodes about his career. The producers didn't realize they were talking about the same guy, of course, and he found that amusing. The cops never put together his abortionist scheme in the 1960's. For one thing, he never stayed in one area very long. In those days, there was no good way for the different jurisdictions to share information even if they wanted to. For another, Dick left his girls deep in the woods. After a few weeks, they were nothing but scattered bones.

The shame associated with unwanted pregnancies helped. Everyone knew chubby young girls often disappeared only to return home a few months later having lost their baby fat. They told few people they were pregnant—even fewer that they were going to get rid of it. By the time anyone got worried or suspicious, Dick had moved on to other states and other girls.

The cops weren't looking for Rod Hanley either. There were three bodies in that house when it burned down and the incident was labeled a murder/suicide. That was because in those days, you could be elected coroner if you were twenty-one, registered to vote, and a high school graduate. One of those bodies had been there since Buddy disappeared a few months after Sheila died, but the idiot coroner didn't notice. The detectives presumed the incinerated young man with the bashed in skull was Rod. He chuckled every time he thought about it!

However, in 1975, the Feds did figure out that string of murders along I-40 through Oklahoma, Texas and New Mexico were the work of one fellow. That was back when he was hauling logs. That had been a great gig.

The truck had a comfortable sleeping compartment where he kept his girls while he drove the highways listening to loud rock music and smoking thick cigars. Sometimes he'd crawl in the back with them and paint their toenails with bright red polish. Sometimes he held them in his arms, brushing their hair and applying lipstick. It

47

The Hunt

was the only time in his life he could keep them with him in air-conditioned bliss for a day or so after they died.

A few years later, he did several girls in Canton, Ohio while he was working for the gas company. That was a stupid move. A hick trooper somehow put two and two together. Dick busted his butt getting out of town and he stayed clear of Stark County even now.

Walsh ran a program about the killer who got into a women's dorm at the University of Arkansas back in the early 70s. Even though the TV people got the facts wrong, he was much happier with that report. Fifteen in one night was a world record and he was proud of it. Not even Richard Speck was THAT successful.

It had been easy too. He followed one of the coeds into the building and hid in the bathroom off the front foyer until after curfew. The headmistress had a small stone elephant decorated with glass beads standing just inside the door to her apartment. He used the beads to strangle her.

She was a tough old broad. He enjoyed the way she tried to buck him off just before she died. The old woman had a closet full of old fashioned shoes. She must have been hot back in the thirties. He spent a few minutes struggling to get a pair of thick heeled, open-toed sandals on her deformed feet, fumbling with the delicate ankle straps. He lost interest after a while and wandered out into the dark lobby.

Moonlight glowed through huge glass windows. He swallowed the urge to howl. Nine floors of sleeping beauties awaited him. He was God—choosing this one, passing over that one, spending time with one girl, simply bashing in another's head and moving on.

John Walsh's voice quivered with outrage as he told the story. Dick relived the thrill every time he watched that piece, and they played it almost as much as they did the one about John List. Of course, there was a big difference. They caught John List.

Oh, how he loved sin.

USERNAME

The show ended and he switched off the TV using the remote. Logging onto his computer, he attended to his correspondence. He was eager to see if the ladies of Cleveland had responded to 'the letter.' Four women had yet to answer. If they hadn't answered by now, they wouldn't ever so he wrote them off. A couple responded with "No thanks." One woman got all bent out of shape and said, "Don't send any more emails!" Another sent him a note that said, "Nice Try!"

An email from LindaLu48 had some potential. "Dear Lone Wolf," it began.

"I read your letter with great interest. I have been lonely since my husband left me. I never realized how much I depended on Charlie. The bathroom wallpaper is peeling and the toilet sticks. I find myself waiting for him to fix them even though he doesn't live here anymore. I go to the grocery store and fill the cart with his favorite foods. I drive past his house just to torture myself. I can't get it into my head that he doesn't want me anymore. I never suspected he didn't love me.

"It's been almost five years, but I don't know how to date anymore. When I was a young girl, I had lots of boyfriends, but I seem to have lost the knack for flirting. A couple months ago, I tried the singles group at church but it was embarrassing, everyone eyeing each other. We all knew what we were there for. We were all the same—losers. I'd rather be alone than go through that again.

"I bought this computer for work. My boss likes being able to leave me dozens of emails every night—you know, 'type this tomorrow,' 'call so and so at three,' that kind of thing. I have to admit I never thought of using it to find a friend until now. I'm a dignified person, you understand, but your letter spoke to me. I hope you'll write again.

Sincerely,

The Hunt

Linda"

Dick grinned. Bingo. He stretched and popped his knuckles. "Dearest Linda," he typed with his index fingers.

🦁

Thursday, October 17, 2000

The next evening Dick took a shuttle to the airport. The Orlando terminal was crowded with stores offering an abundance of Mickeys, Donalds and Goofys—everything from fluffy house shoes to framed drawings to ashtrays and statuettes. He dodged a young couple pushing a big black pram filled with stuffed animals. No baby in sight.

Sticky-fingered kids with red foil balloons tied to their wrists wandered around the terminal eating ice cream on a stick. He tried not to look at them.

He got on the neon-trimmed tram and found an empty corner. A toddler clung to his mother's leg and tried to play peek-a-boo with Dick. He hugged his laptop to his chest and stared at himself in the shiny windows of the train as they sped toward their gates.

The planes from Orlando to Pittsburgh were always packed in economy. He upgraded to first class using his Amex card. Boarding first, he settled into the wide leather seat and accepted a glass of Chablis from a middle-aged flight attendant.

"Don't I know you?" Her eyes crinkled at the corners when she smiled.

"I take this flight a lot." He squirmed in his seat. He knew who she was at once. She hadn't aged as well as he would have thought. She was a young recruit back when he was known as Big Lance, the homosexual stud of the Chicago to Cleveland route. Her name was Candy then, now the pin on her left breast said 'Candace.'

"I never forget a face, just have a hard time with names. I can't place yours." She leaned over to pick up a magazine lying on the seat next to him. Her thick perfume made his eyes water. "Don't you worry, I'll figure it out." She moved on to the old couple in the seats behind him.

He wore a rug and a fake moustache. He had darkened his graying eyebrows and perched fake trifocals on his nose. He doubted she would make the connection, but he buried his face in a glossy magazine anyway. A photo layout of a beautiful beach proclaimed the wisdom of retiring to Costa Rica.

He peeked over the top of the page to appreciate Candace's round buttocks when she bent over to serve the man across the aisle and then again when he noticed she was wearing provocative open toed shoes instead of her uniform pumps.

Once they were airborne, she brought him a can of tomato juice. She started to open it but he held up his wine. "Can I save it for later?" He stretched his mouth wide in what he hoped was a winning smile.

"Are you sure?" She tossed her hair.

"Just leave it with me, I'll open it when I'm ready." He winked and stuck the tomato juice into the slash pocket of his jacket. Her long neck had turned scrawny somewhere in her forties. She wore a cheap locket on an expensive chain. He wasn't sure but he thought the baby peering out of the gold tone heart was a boy. She was a bit long in the tooth for a kid. A grandchild, maybe?

He tried to ignore her, but the demon was aroused now. Shivering with anticipation, he imagined knotting a scarf around her throat, her eyes wide with recognition and horror as she slipped away. "You wouldn't be interested in having dinner with an old man would you?"

The Hunt

She hesitated. He guessed it had been a while since a gentleman offered to buy her a meal. "We won't land until after nine and I have a midnight flight to Detroit. That's not much of a layover."

"I'll have you back long before then." He licked his lips.

"How about a restaurant in the airport? There are several TGI Fridays in the terminal." Her faded eyes sparkled. Unlike Linda, Candace still knew how to flirt.

"That's perfect." His dreams of renting a car and driving her out into the woods crumbled.

"I'll meet you at the main restaurant a half hour after we land." She flashed him a quick smile and returned to her duties.

"Terrific." He sank back into his seat and stared into the darkness outside his window. It would be harder to manage inside the terminal but he'd figure out a way.

Dick waited until the plane emptied before collecting his backpack from the bin over his head. The area cleared quickly.

He stood on the moving sidewalk, trying to appear inconspicuous. A man in a rumpled suit coughed and Dick moved to allow him to pass. The bookstore was closed. So was the post office. A few yards away, Concourse B converged on a food court and shopping mall.

Dick stepped off the moving sidewalk and sipped from a water fountain mounted on the wall. A pilot in his fancy-assed uniform hurried past. Dick stood up and headed toward the food court.

A loud beep. A woman in an electric cart full of tired-looking young men in golf clothes swerved around him. Startled, he jumped aside. The majority of the people from Dick's flight were on the escalator heading down toward the trams that would take them to retrieve their baggage. Dick slowed his pace, looking around for an opportunity.

Mid-day, this area was packed with travelers rushing to catch their flights, but it was nearly nine-thirty and the gates nearest the food court were empty. He found a mop and pail and a small orange sandwich board sign that said, "Closed for Cleaning" in front of one of the johns. He stuck his head around the corner and peered into the bathroom.

A chubby man in a green jumpsuit was loading paper towels into the dispenser. Block letters on the front of his baseball cap identified him as 'Grady.' A yellow plastic radio hooked to his belt snaked wire up his back and across his head into tiny earphones plugged into his ears. Bouncing to some private rhythm, Grady was so absorbed in what he was doing that he didn't see or hear Dick slip into one of the stalls behind him.

Dick took off his small knapsack and hung it on a hook on the door. He wanted to make sure nothing happened to his laptop. He found a black nylon sock in one of the side pockets and slipped the can of tomato juice into the toe. He held it up and it swung in a slow arc. Perfect. He opened the door of the stall enough to peek out. The janitor rummaged through a cart filled with cleaning products, rocking his head from side to side.

Dick's plan was simple. He'd jump out, conk this bozo on the head, and steal his jumpsuit and cleaning cart. He'd lose the rug and glasses, but keep the moustache. Then he'd wait near the ladies room by TGI Fridays across from McDonald's.

When Candace went inside to powder her nose, as he knew she would, he'd put the sign outside to keep others out. Once he was sure Candace was in there alone, he'd slip inside, dispose of her, and leave her in a stall. It was risky, but he was experienced—and oh so hungry. Besides, killing someone in an airport would pop John Walsh's eyes out. No one had ever been so bold.

When he was done, he'd mop his way out the door and wander away, leaving the sandwich board in the hall to keep folks out of the restroom until he was long gone. He'd find a men's john in another part of the terminal, get rid of the green zippered work clothes, and saunter down to baggage claim. End of problem. End of Candace, he chuckled to himself. He tingled with excitement. The hunt was on.

Grady shook his watermelon-sized buttocks to music only he could hear. He was shorter than Dick and a lot younger. Moon walking backwards, he picked up a big bottle of liquid detergent for the soap dispensary. Singing in a hoarse, off-key whisper into the end of his mop handle, Grady closed his eyes, the hand clutching the bottle extended as the final notes echoed in the empty bathroom.

Dick charged, but the stall door opened inward rather than outward and it slowed his momentum. The janitor finished his performance and opened his eyes at just that moment. His face registered surprise and then alarm as Dick rushed forward intent on tackling him. Grady stepped back, squeezing the soap bottle convulsively. A stream of viscous pink liquid shot across the few feet that separated the two men and coated Dick Longren's glasses. The world went pink a moment before Dick slammed his head into the younger man's doughy belly.

The bottle of soap dropped to the tiled floor and they both fell on it. Its contents gushed out in a wide puddle. Straddling Grady's slippery, squirming body, Dick swung the sock in a wide arc, aiming to crush his skull. The janitor jerked his head to one side and the tomato juice can hit the floor next to his ear with a dull thud.

Eyes bulging, Grady turned into a whirlwind of pummeling fists, kicking feet, and snapping jaws. Cursing in Spanish, he grabbed for the sock as Dick swung it again. A sharp elbow caught Dick across the bridge of his nose. His glasses skittered across the floor under one of the stall doors and landed behind the commode.

Grady's meaty fist connected with Dick's mouth and blood spurted. Finding his footing, he backed away, holding his mouth.

The bastard was trying to hurt him! He struggled to get his balance, but his feet slid on the soapy tile.

"You peesasheet!" The panting janitor lay on his back. His arms and legs churned as he rolled over and rose to his hands and knees. "Whasyerproblem, asshole? I'm gonna kill chou, chou sonofabeetch." Grabbing the cleaning cart with one hand, Grady struggled to pull himself to standing position but his feet slipped out from under him and the cart tipped over, spilling a pail of water and splashing Dick's pants.

Dick decided it was time to run away. However, Grady Ramirez, the spreading pool of water and pink soap, the upset cart and several mops lay between him and the door. The can of tomato juice inside the sock dangled beside his thigh. His heart pounded in terror.

He tried to squeeze between Grady and the toilet stalls but a sneakered foot smashed against his ankle. Jesus! Dick swung the sock and caught the man under the chin with the tomato juice can. Grady's baseball cap flew off. Eyes rolling back into his head, he dropped backwards like a felled tree, stunned.

Dick glared at the body, his hands on his hips. This jerk tried to kill him. The very idea! With a force born of fear and outrage, he swung the tomato juice once again, but it hit the edge of the sink counter rather than his intended target prostrate on the floor. The can split open and splattered juice all over the bathroom, the man on the floor and Dick.

How did he get himself into such a predicament? He'd never been so rash before. He prided himself on his caution. Someone could walk in any minute. This vicious thug on the floor could come to his senses and attack him again. He tried to kick the thick body before him but his supporting foot slipped and he fell against one of the stall doors.

The Hunt

Shocked by his own inability to destroy his enemy while he was down, Dick turned and ran. Sliding around the corner into a tiled foyer leading to the carpeted hallway, Dick froze. It was never a good idea to run away from the scene of a crime. He leaned against the edge of the door, trying to catch his breath.

A teenager in oversized shorts, high topped Nikes and an enormous t-shirt trotted toward the bathroom.

"This john is closed." Dick pointed to the orange sign.

The boy's eyes seemed to linger on Dick's mouth which was still bleeding.

Dick wiped away sweat and tomato juice with the back of his hand. "Rough landing. Bit my lip."

"Shit happens, dude." The boy hefted the duffel he was carrying to the opposite shoulder and headed down the concourse toward the far gates.

Dick watched the kid, trying to decide what to do. Something dripped down the side of his face. He touched his cheek. His fingers came away red. Tomato juice. No problem. He had a handkerchief in his knapsack.

It was then he realized he'd left it in the bathroom stall. Shit! His airline tickets were in the chest pocket in his jacket. He patted the back of his slacks. His personal information was safe in his wallet. FINGERPRINTS! The fake glasses. His computer!

He glanced both ways. No one was coming, so he went back inside the bathroom.

The janitor lay on the floor with his eyes closed. Dick went to the stall and retrieved his knapsack. Where were the damned glasses? THERE. Two down. He squeezed into the stall and fumbled behind the toilet. Twice his fingertips nudged the slippery specs and they slid beyond his reach. Grunting, he wormed around the commode until he retrieved the glasses and tucked them into his breast pocket. Relieved, he slipped the backpack over his shoulder and started for the door, side stepping the soapy puddle.

The janitor's hand shot out and grabbed him by the ankle.

Dick screamed.

Who WAS this idiot? He tried to run but Grady held on tight. Dick turned and pummeled Grady's head with his fists. He took a step and the heavy body slid on the floor along with him. He clutched the post of one of the stalls to steady himself and kicked at the man's chest and shoulders. Winded, his energy waned. No matter how hard he tried, he couldn't dislodge the thick fingers around his right leg.

"Get away from me, get away!" Dick fought but the monster at his feet was heavier and stronger. The janitor pulled himself up Dick's body, hand over hand, until he was standing.

"What's chour problem, man?" Grady backed Dick up against the far wall and pushed his face to within an inch of Dick's nose. A dark bruise was forming under his chin.

The knapsack pressed into Dick's shoulder blades. He felt small and helpless before Grady's fury. "Get away from me or I'll call the cops." His voice quivered.

Grady sneered and slammed him against the wall. Dick imagined the small computer screen cracking. In desperation, he grabbed the man's thick, black moustache with both hands.

"OW!" The janitor howled and jerked his head back, freezing when Dick's grasp threatened to pull the thick mustache out by the roots. Eyes watering, the chubby man whimpered in pain and rage.

Dick felt Grady weakening. He gritted his teeth and pulled harder. "You asshole. It didn't have to come to this."

The Hunt

Nose running, Grady grabbed Dick's moustache with both hands as well. "Let go, man. Let go or I'll pull chour freegin' leep off."

The two of them clung to each other's moustaches for several seconds, the whites of their eyes showing. The corners of Dick's mouth turned downwards and he stamped on the man's foot, grinding his heel into the tongue of Grady's tennis shoe.

Something in the janitor's eyes changed and he jerked. As Grady's nails tore into Dick's upper lip, the fake moustache came off in his hand.

"Holy sheet, man!" Grady's eyes widened in horror as he stared at the bit of hair in his hand. It was then that he noticed the tomato juice drying on his fingers. He let go of Dick and backed away. "BLOOD! Someone's bleeding, man!" Drops of sweat appeared on his forehead. He swayed, grabbing for the counter.

"You did it. I'm bleeding!" Dick spit a bloody wad of saliva onto Grady's white sneaker and hissed through his red-stained teeth.

The janitor blanched and fainted dead away, still clutching the fake moustache. His head thumped against the wet floor.

Dick ran.

He ran out the door, down the long concourse, past TGI Friday's where Candace stood waiting for him, down the escalator, squeezing past an old lady with a straw purse filled with Florida keepsakes.

Fear buzzed in his ears. Neither tram was there. They ran a few minutes apart. It couldn't be too long.

He needed to pee. He danced from foot to foot, resisting the urge to cross his legs. He glanced behind him, half expecting to see Grady lumbering after him. An electronic sign above his head flashed. The train pulled into the loading area. He looked over his shoulder once more. A uniformed guard was coming down the escalator.

"Jesus!" He whimpered.

His bladder was bursting. The glass doors on the other side of the train opened. Two people on the tram exited and headed toward the escalators. The guard reached the train lobby. Oh God! Dick turned his back and gritted his teeth.

The sliding doors on his side opened and he hurried into the first car. The guard stepped into the last one. Dick couldn't tell if the man was looking for him or not. He gripped the chrome pole as the tram whisked him back to the main terminal.

The train stopped just behind security where several people in uniforms gathered to peer into a nun's valise. Dick was the first one off the tram. He hurried down the next set of escalators heading towards Baggage Claim and the taxi stands outside the glass doors.

The row of shuttles, cars, and vans seemed endless. He hurried to the stand where several people were in front of him. He forced himself to be calm, but he was relieved when it was his turn. He crawled into a shiny new Avalon painted taxicab yellow. "Where to?" A skinny black man glanced over the back seat at him.

He drew back into the darkness. "Number One Oak Tree Spur in Sewickley, just off of Winding Road."

"You're on."

Normally, Dick would have enjoyed the fact that the cabbie was impressed with his upscale address. Not tonight. In the privacy of the cab, Dick squeezed his legs together, praying he wouldn't leak. He touched his tongue to the cut on his lip. Spitting onto his handkerchief, he scrubbed tomato juice off his hands and face. He glared at the driver who was watching him in the rearview mirror. The driver returned his eyes to the road as they pulled out of the airport and headed towards Sewickley.

The Hunt

Dick saw his own reflection in the window. Unlike the strong, invincible man he'd seen in Orlando that morning, the face he saw was tired, old, and weak. Stupid! Carried away with his own good fortune, he went too far. Since when did he have to involve a third party to take a woman? Since when did he try to take on someone as brawny as Grady the Janitor?

The taxi turned off Beaver onto Winding Road. The trees were losing their leaves. Hunting season was over. Dick's anxiety turned into deep sadness. At the top of the hill, he paid the driver and headed across the grass to the tiny rock house. His shoes still squished. He took them off and set them on the front porch. He didn't want to track anything into his living room.

His clothes were filthy—covered with slimy soap, tomato juice, and sweat. He took off his trousers. There was a large bruise on his left thigh and his ankle was swollen. Scratches crossed his forehead. The bastard left marks on him!

In all the years he'd been at this, he was wounded only a couple of times. He once got a black eye when a dying girl pulled a shelf down on him. Then a few years ago, he racked up his knee by running into the sharp corner of a nightstand. Grady the Janitor had messed him up pretty good in comparison.

He stood in front of the toilet, moaning in relief as he emptied his bladder. He stepped out of his damp underwear. "Please, oh please," he said to himself. Squatting, he poked at the BVDs before picking them up to sniff. Thank God. Only soap. No trace of urine.

After a hot shower, he wrapped himself in a warm robe. The bald spot near the crown of his head was getting bigger. His skin seemed looser. Damn, he never noticed that before. Was this the day when he crossed the line into old age? He touched his cock. It seemed smaller, softer.

Maybe it was time to call it quits and go to Costa Rica. He was going to be fifty-eight in a month. It had been a close call. He could have been hurt or caught. He thought about how John Walsh leered every time they nabbed someone big. Maybe he didn't rate as a scumbag anymore. After all, Candace was winging her way to Detroit unmolested. He couldn't meet his own eyes in the mirror.

He crawled into bed and pulled the covers up to his chin. The remnants of his baby blanket were pinned to his pillow. Not much more than a few shreds of the soft material remained. He rubbed it against his cheek, his forefinger flicking his eyelashes. What would he do without his scams? Was this how it happened? One day you find you can't hack it anymore? He rolled over onto his stomach and buried his face in his pillow.

Chapter 5 – Projects
<u>Friday, October 18, 2000</u>

The light on Maureen's phone was flashing when she arrived. She hung up her jacket and sat down to listen to her phone mail, pencil in hand. Eighteen messages, ten of them from Bill Casey starting around 4 AM.

"Sheesh, Bill. Don't you ever sleep?" Maureen scribbled on her yellow phone pad. Three messages were the same question asked in different ways. He must have been having security nightmares. She pressed a key to move to the next message. The hairs on the back of her neck prickled and she spun around.

"Didn't mean to scare you." Bill stood at the door of her cubicle. "I've been waiting for you to get in."

"Is something wrong?"

"All these news reports about viruses are getting to me. Diane Sawyer did an exposé on TV last night. I'm an old mainframe man. Security used to be simple. You buy RACF and assign someone to handle permissions. Only people you had to watch out for were employees. No one else gave a damn." He sat down in her client chair and crossed his ankle over his knee.

"Employees are still your main worry."

"Yeah. Practically all of them now. Used to be it was only the IT people. Now every pimple-faced runt out of high school can take us down."

Maureen sipped her cooling coffee and set the mug on its coaster. "Who's been asking questions?"

"CEO."

USERNAME

"Let me guess. His thirteen year old grandson hacked the public library."

"Twelve year old niece—and it was the Girl Scout site."

"She get a badge?"

"Smart-aleck."

"Me or her?"

Bill Casey was the most attractive ugly man Maureen had ever met. He made her think he liked her and that was utterly charming. He fidgeted in the chair and it squeaked. "I need to know if we are protected."

"We are as safe as the company is willing to pay for, Bill. I've told you this before. There's no such thing as a risk-free system. We can tighten things up more but there's a price tag."

"What should we do?"

She thought for a minute. "Increase my budget."

"This may be our best opportunity. They are listening for the first time in a long time. Write up a proposal."

"It'll be on your desk in the morning."

He stood up. "Things have changed too fast for an old fart like me. I'm trusting you to keep us safe, Maureen."

#

The elevator doors opened on the 18th floor. The lobby smelled of oiled wood. Inlaid in golden oak and dark mahogany, the *First Life* logo gleamed underfoot. Maureen held her security badge against the reader and the glass doors swung open.

She preferred the bathrooms on the Executive Office floor when she needed a good cry. Instead of beige metal stalls, each toilet was in a tiny private room with its own bowl of potpourri.

Projects

The heavy oak door hung on brass hinges. Even the doorknobs were fancy—glass cut to look like lead crystal. She squinted. Maybe they *were* lead crystal. Closing the lid, she sat on the commode. She hated when people were nice to her—when they trusted her. Her breathing quickened and her eyes welled with tears.

It would help if Bill Casey was a jerk. The idea of letting this nice man down was hard to bear. She could only hope she'd covered her trail well enough that the company wouldn't find her little maneuverings until she'd been gone a long time. She ticked through all the places she'd touched the system, hoping that she'd covered everything. She hiccupped. First rule of security—no one thought of everything.

She unrolled the soft premium toilet paper and blew her nose. It was time to move on. She was losing her nerve and anxious people make mistakes. If things had been different last Friday, she might have scored big and be gone by now. All the premiums were up to date. Everything was set and ready to go. Linda could have died in the accident or Bard could have done her in. Hell, Linda might have done herself in. The fact was, it didn't happen.

Maureen reviewed the odds. Linda was a goof. She did stupid things. She had accidents all the time. She went off with strange men. Linda was a reasonable bet. One of these days that bet was going to pay off. So why she so relieved that Linda was okay? Maureen didn't understand herself. Business was business. Wasn't it?

The sinks were marble. Laying her glasses beside the crystal faucet handles, she splashed water onto her face. The lights above the mirror looked like tulips made out of shells. She rubbed her swollen eyes. The heavy liner smeared. Damn.

She blew her nose again and began the arduous task of reapplying makeup. Maybe it was time she changed her tactics. Waiting for something to happen could take a long time. Maybe she should give things a little push.

Back at her desk, her phone was still flashing. She turned on her computer. An icon flickered at the bottom of her screen. "You have 97 messages." Ignoring it, she logged into her brokerage account.

Almost! The Swiss accounts were close too. She COULD go tomorrow if necessary.

With a few keystrokes, she brought up Travelocity. Prices were a bit high. She shook off her impatience. She could afford to go, but she couldn't bring herself to do it yet. It wasn't quite enough. One more project—just one more.

She scrolled through her private database. Cy Gorman was coming along. She had opened a Platinum MasterCard and an American Express card in his name with the address of her own post office box. The MasterCard had a $12,000 limit and a cash advance potential for the same amount. She was waiting for a $6,000 Visa too. American Express expected payment in full each month which limited its usefulness for her purposes. She'd save it for an emergency. The cards themselves were stored in her safety deposit box and the numbers were in the database. Unsure how to invest these funds, she was tempted to feed the Swiss account—or maybe the Caribbean one.

She'd acquired Miriam Gorman's social security number, birth certificate, and health records. Miriam fell twice in the last year. The first time she broke her arm, the second was much more serious. Even though the old lady recovered from those accidents, she was ninety-four. How long could she last? Maureen made a note to apply for a passport in Miriam's name since the old woman never had one.

Maureen took out a small insurance policy on Miriam by accessing the *First Life* database and making the necessary entries. She tinkered with the program so the computer thought it had received a monthly payment from Miriam for years while protecting against discrepancies in premiums paid and money deposited in the company bank accounts.

It would take a good auditor a year to figure things out even if they were suspicious. Maureen would be basking in the sun on some luxurious island by then. Miriam's mail was being forwarded to one of Maureen's post office boxes. When Miriam died, Maureen would submit a claim in Cy's name. The check would come to Cy's address of record in the database, which was one of Maureen's post office boxes as well. It was a simple thing to deposit the check into the account Maureen set up in Cy's name. It was even simpler to write a check on that account made out to cash. Bingo.

She also set up a much larger policy on Cy Gorman himself with Miriam as beneficiary. She figured Cy for a good bet. Jennifer discovered he was a member in good standing with Alcoholics Anonymous although, judging from his enormous liquor bills, he had been off the wagon for months. He traveled long distances by car for *First Life*. Jennifer followed him south to Clarksburg where he checked into the local Holiday Inn with three or four bottles of Crown Royal and didn't come out for two days.

Maureen wondered how much work he did for the company. Checking his log, she saw he'd read his email when he first arrived but didn't touch his accounts the three days he was in West Virginia. At this rate, *First Life* would sack him before Maureen could collect. That meant a ton of work for no good reason.

It was easier to touch up his accounts. Not too much. His performance had never been very good, just enough so he'd still be with the company when the inevitable happened. The hourglass on her computer flashed and the deal was done.

She checked the status of the projects Jennifer started at the mall last week. Mort Minor gave up accounts at most of the department stores, two Visas, three MasterCards and a Diner's

Club Card. He had written his address on the card the makers of his wallet provided.

She forwarded his mail to her post office box and awaited a chance to review his bank statement. If Morty's account was sufficiently robust, she'd order checks. She didn't dare use his existing credit cards for revenue since he might have reported them as stolen. She just opened new ones that Morty would never know about.

She hadn't decided what to do about Iliana. It could be an opportunity if the woman was truly missing and stayed that way. She had the woman's birth date and her father's name. Maybe she could get a birth certificate and a passport. She might be able to work backwards and get a social security number. She'd have to think her options through.

She ordered credit cards for Donald O. Tamarind. She'd milk those accounts for money until someone noticed. On impulse, she opened a small life insurance policy on him with his mother's name as the beneficiary. You never knew. She once collected a tidy sum when a homeless man froze to death. It was a fluke that she acquired his personal information. Some street kid mugged him, took whatever money there was and threw the ragged old wallet away. Jennifer found it in a bus stop on East Ninth.

Albert Graber, Jennifer's septuagenarian student, was a major disappointment. He'd gone bankrupt twice. His bank account was overdrawn and no one would give him credit. Leona Reese wasn't much better. She lived on social security. No assets. No savings. She stored their names away, but she didn't expect they'd ever be useful.

That brought her to Mark Stevenson, the buff waiter from the Galleria. Jennifer followed him to his car one night—a Jaguar with a vanity plate, BRBSBOY. A bit playful for a fellow studying at Case Western. Maybe Linda was right about Mark's sexual status.

Projects

She made a note to have Jennifer find out who BRB was. Some rich old man with AIDS?

Jennifer would keep after Mark. He had to go home sometime. Once she had his address, Maureen would have the post office forward his mail to one of her boxes. All it took was filling out a form. All kinds of interesting things came by mail—checks, bills, catalogs, legal documents, even his grades. Companies printed account numbers on people's bills.

At the very least, armed with names, addresses and account numbers, she could hack into a utility's customer database to find out his social security number. With that, everything else about him was hers—even his medical records.

Maureen stood naked in front of the fogged up mirror in her bathroom, her body damp from her shower. The baby in the next apartment cried. She cocked her head, listening. Heavy footsteps. A soft voice cooing. The baby quieted. She ran the tips of her fingers over the long scar starting at her navel and disappearing into her pubic hair. She sighed. It wasn't what she wanted anyway.

She wiped the steamy mirror with a towel. A fuzzy image of a strange face appeared in the damp glass. She sighed. The accident had broken her nose and she never liked the new one. Popping the contact lenses out of her eyes, she put them in their case. They floated in the solution like soft brown raindrops. She smoothed heavy cream over her forehead, removing the dark eyebrow makeup. Her wet hair clung to her skull.

The projects had taken their toll. She was bone tired. The stress of posing as someone else was getting to her. Hell, she hadn't used her own name in years. Her eyes burned. "What have I become?" She peered into her own eyes.

USERNAME

The original Maureen Tippleton was her roommate in college—a pretty young woman who'd just graduated with honors in computer science when she died in an airplane crash near Dallas.

It was the first time someone she knew died. Stunned, she packed the dead girl's things to send back to Owensboro—clothes, books, pictures, a box of personal papers. As she worked, she found an official copy of Maureen's birth certificate with a seal from the state of Kentucky. Attached to it with a pink paper clip was her social security card. This was Maureen Tippleton's legal identity, she realized. It was the only way to prove that she ever existed.

That was the moment the projects began, although she hadn't used Maureen's identity until she came to Cleveland and applied for work at *First Life*. For a moment, she thought she might cry again. Then she put on her pajamas and went back to her computer.

Chapter 6 – Conscience

Monday, October 22, 2000

Jennifer braked as she approached the first drive-way on Linda's property. It curled around the pond and approached an A-frame cottage where Linda's boyfriend Sean lived. Fifty yards later, the second driveway was a straight shot to the garage under the main house. A thick grove of pine trees led to a clearing a half mile down the road. She turned off the headlights and pulled in.

Her hands shook as she gathered her burglary tools. Lights flickered through the trees. She checked her watch. Eleven-thirty. Linda was up late, but it was a work night. Bill Casey was having a staff meeting in the morning. She'd have to go to bed soon.

The reality of what she was contemplating hit her. Closing her eyes, she bumped her head lightly against the steering wheel. This was nuts. Linda was a sweet, wacky woman. Jennifer imagined Linda's flashy lopsided grin and fluttering hands forever stilled. Her stomach rolled and she hiccupped. No! Starting the engine, she backed out of the clearing bouncing over the shallow ditch onto River Road.

She slammed on the brakes and put the car in park. It was going to happen anyway, of course. Sooner or later, Linda was going to bumble into trouble. More trouble than she could handle. That's what drew Maureen's attention to her in the first place.

She was a terrible driver. She'd been in two fender benders in the last year. Once when Jennifer was following her, Linda jumped out of her van in the middle of Pearl Road and banged on the trunk of the car ahead of her, screaming and cursing.

On top of that, she had terrible taste in men. She was so desperate for attention that she went home with strangers she met at bars. She was overweight and from the flush on her cheeks, Jennifer bet

Linda's blood pressure was sky high. It was only a matter of time, but Jennifer needed the money now.

She pulled back into the clearing, easing forward until the Saturn was hidden from the road. The lights still glittered through the leaves. Was something wrong? Her heart pounded in alarm. She got out and crept through the woods. She knew her way. She'd spied on Linda many times before tonight.

She knelt behind a tree at the edge of the drive-way. The side of the main house was to her right. The kitchen door opened out onto a large covered porch facing the woods. It was dark.

Voices in the distance. She moved so she could see around the corner of the main house. Across the duck pond in the front yard, the A frame blazed with light. On the deck, a sullen young man reclined in a lounge chair with his arms folded over his chest. Linda paced in front of him, pausing to shake her finger in his face from time to time.

Jennifer relaxed. Another fight with Sean. That seemed to be their post coital routine. She couldn't understand what Linda saw in Sean, nor could she see why Sean spent time with Linda. Talk about a mismatch.

She was too far away to hear what they were saying which meant they were too far away to hear her if she bumped into something in the main house. This was her chance. She crept up the back steps. At least she didn't have to break in anymore, she thought as she inserted the hot pink key into the lock.

It was surreal standing in Linda's dark kitchen, looking for a way to cause an accident. She never had to before. If you were patient, things happened naturally. People who engaged in risky behavior died early. It was a basic principle of the insurance industry. You could bet on it, but it was hard to figure the timing.

She concentrated on the problem at hand. Gas made sense in terms of getting in and out. She could pull the stove away from the wall, disconnect the hose, and then push the stove back in place. It would take a while for the concentration of gas in the air to reach explosive levels. By then, Jennifer would be back in Strongsville.

She turned towards the stove. Switching on a tiny penlight, she froze. A box of homemade cookies sat on top the oven, wrapped in colored cellophane. A card on top said, "Happy Birthday, Maureen."

Her fingers trembled as she reached out to touch the card. "Dammit, Linda." She must have checked out Maureen's personnel file. That's probably what the damned staff meeting in the morning was all about.

A whimper and scratching sounds made her jump.

"Midnight! It's me, boy." The dog knocked her to the floor. She fell on her stomach with Midnight's paws on her shoulders, nibbling at her right ear. The penlight rolled across the linoleum. "Aw, come on, boy. Get off me."

She turned over on her back and the big dog licked her face. He was invisible in the dark kitchen but he could see her fine. He was wide-awake and ready to play. She could feel his tail whipping back and forth in joyous recognition of an old playmate.

"Can't we do this another time?" She tried to push him away but he rushed her again, hitting her in the chest with his nose. She fell backwards, her head thumping against the floor. The tip of her left pinkie stung. She tried pushing herself to a sitting position by placing her palms on the linoleum, but the floor was wet and she slid back down. Something cut deep into the soft tissue between her thumb and forefinger.

"Stop it, Midnight." The dog was much stronger than she was. "STOP IT!" Her hand hurt. Midnight tried to lick it. That's when she realized she was bleeding. The penlight lay against the baseboard. Its dim illumination cast long shadows and made the small pool of blood seem glossy black. She fumbled for it and stuck it in a pocket near her knee. She grabbed the corner of the cabinets with her right hand, holding her left to her chest, and hoisted herself to her feet.

Jennifer couldn't figure out how she'd cut herself. She didn't want to drip blood onto the living room carpet, but she wasn't sure if she could still hear Linda and Sean arguing. She stood in the archway trying to decide what to do. Midnight slipped on the bloody floor and fell, his nails making scraping sounds. It was too risky to stay any longer.

She took a clean dishtowel out of the third drawer from the top near the sink and wrapped it around her hand. So much for murder, Jennifer thought as she found her way to the back door, making a wide berth around the spots of blood she'd left on the kitchen floor. Midnight tried to squeeze out behind her, but she pushed him back in. His whining yips followed her down the steps.

Reaching the gravel drive, she peered around the corner of the house. Sean leaned against the railing, holding Linda in his arms. Her shoulders shook. Jennifer couldn't tell if she was laughing or crying. Either way, the fight must be over.

Jennifer turned and ran into the woods. Her hand throbbed. She stopped to rest at the foot of an oak two hundred yards from the house. The pinkie finger was stiff. She could feel something hard in the cut in the fleshy part of her hand. Not daring to pull out her penlight that close to the house, she rewrapped the towel and headed towards the point on River Road where she parked the Saturn.

Her legs were quivering when she found it twenty minutes later. She unlocked the door and climbed in, laying her head on the steering wheel. "Oh, God." The hiccups began again. "Not Linda."

Conscience

This had to end. It was a downward spiral. First shoplifting, then fraud. Fear of being stranded without enough money had driven her to the brink of murder. Enough, she thought. Enough.

Besides, the longer it went on, the more likely someone would get wise. She'd worked Cleveland years before and walked away with forty-eight thousand dollars. At the time, she thought that was a pretty good haul. Of course, that was the problem. She didn't really know how much money it would take to make her feel safe. She only knew that she didn't have enough yet.

First Life had been an opportunity she couldn't resist—the ultimate payoff. Even so, what a fool she'd been to come back to Ohio. She didn't dare go downtown. Someone might recognize her. Limiting her activities to night time in the suburbs was minimal protection. Strongsville was a bedroom community after all. She was careful with her appearance, but who knew who she might run into at the *Giant Eagle*? This time when she left, she was never coming back.

⁂

The key to Maureen's apartment stuck. Jennifer wiggled it and bumped the door with her hip. Hurrying into the kitchen, she flipped on the lights with her elbow. She was a mess. Her blouse and pants were stained with ugly splotches of dark brown. The bleeding had stopped, but her hand hurt like the devil. She unwrapped the stiffened towel and took a look.

A long cut traversed the finger from the pad of the pinkie down past the first knuckle. It was more of a deep scratch. The cut in the web between her finger and thumb was more serious. She could see a small bit of white glass imbedded in the wound. After several unsuccessful tries to remove it with the fingers of her right hand, she collected Maureen's eyebrow tweezers from the medicine cabinet and pulled out a half-inch piece of glass. "Dammit, Linda. Why don't you sweep up when you break something," she muttered.

Wincing, she poured peroxide on the wound and wrapped her hand in gauze. A band-aid around the pinkie was all that was necessary. She helped herself to some of Maureen's scotch and plopped down on the couch.

What a night, she thought. In the first place, there was Midnight. He was a lovable creature, bounding around the pasture behind the A-Frame, barking for the joy of hearing his own voice. In the second place, as goofy as Linda was, Jennifer liked her. It was fun hearing about her crazy adventures, fun watching her get stuck in a newspaper dispenser over at Perkins that time, fun watching her almost catch the attention of the local hunks at Danny's bar.

It was incredible the amount of bad luck that girl had and it was equally incredible to see the good-humored twist she put on all these stories. Linda would make a great stand-up comedienne, the only woman in Cuyahoga County who couldn't get laid. Jennifer was relieved that the house on River Road wasn't filling up with gas. It was one thing to rip off insurance companies, it was quite another to kill someone—especially when that someone was a friend.

She took a sip of her drink. Was that true? Was Linda a friend? The scotch burned its way down her gullet and her eyes watered. Maureen had set up several checking accounts in Linda's name and secured the usual array of credit cards. There was a passport and an Ohio driver's license with doctored photos. Even after all that work, the idea of collecting the money stuck in Jennifer's craw. Going after the insurance money was no longer an option either. She sighed. Yeah, maybe Linda was a friend.

It didn't start out that way. Maureen met Linda her first day at *First Life*. As Bill Casey's secretary, Linda helped Maureen get settled—bringing her pens and pencils, scissors, a stapler, a calendar and a desk mat.

Conscience

"You're going to need this. Trust me," she'd said as she handed Maureen a brick of Post-It Notes. "Bill has insomnia. He spends half the night leaving everyone phone mail messages, and then he comes in early and leaves everyone a ton of emails."

Maureen accepted the note paper. "What are the messages about?"

Linda set a *First Life* mug on Maureen's desk. "Anything that's on his mind. Usually work."

Maureen was eager to log on to her new computer. "I appreciate all of your help."

"That's okay. I just thought I'd break the ice. Are you from around here?" Linda plopped down in Maureen's client chair and crossed her legs.

"No, I grew up in Kentucky. Who is the database administrator?" Maureen turned on her computer.

"Charlie and I got our dog Midnight from a breeder down there." Linda unsnapped a charm she wore around her wrist to show Maureen a picture of a good looking man playing with a black Labrador retriever. "Charlie's long gone but I still have Midnight." The smile was bright, but the eyes were sad.

Maureen's computer beeped as it went through the log-on process. "The database administrator?"

"Bick Taylor. He's a friend of my ex's. They grew up together in Medina. A nervous little guy. Reminds me of a jittery hamster with his nose twitching and his heart going pitty-pat." Linda closed the locket and leaned back in her chair.

"What's his background?" Maureen watched the various programs loading on her system out of the corner of her eye.

"Accountant. What else?" Linda slapped the arm of her chair and laughed. "Complete with a pocket protector and bifocals."

Maureen looked around, uncomfortable with all the eyes and ears Linda was drawing to their conversation. She lowered her voice, trying to appear casually interested. "Much experience with computers?"

"Bick? Are you kidding? You'd have thought Bill had asked him to jump off Terminal Tower when they moved those records to the computer. IBM scares him to death. He's worried he might make a mistake, God forbid—and if he does make one he scurries around looking guilty." Linda screwed up her face to demonstrate.

Maureen smiled into her computer monitor and typed the start-up password. "What about the auditor?"

"We don't have one." Linda hid her yawn behind her blue acrylic fingernails.

Maureen sat up straighter. "Oh?"

"Well, not one that works for us all the time. Bill hires a friend of his wife's—a little red headed bulimic who comes in here every three or four years and turns the waste paper baskets upside down."

"She into computers?"

"How the hell would I know?" Linda stood up, tugging on her sweater to get it down over her hips. "If you want to know who keeps condoms in their paper clip cup, I'm your girl, but the technical credentials of a consultant we use once in a blue moon is beyond me." She marched down the hall with her long earrings swinging back and forth.

"Bitch," Maureen murmured as she reset her password.

Jennifer finished the scotch and rinsed out the glass. It wasn't until Maureen completed research on *First Life* employees that Linda surfaced as a possible mark. Divorced with no children, she lived

Conscience

alone on an isolated twenty-acre piece of property in Hinckley that was worth a fortune.

That's when Maureen got to know Linda. That's when Jennifer started following her. It seemed like the perfect gig, but now it was so much wasted effort. It wasn't like she was an amateur either. Jennifer had worked projects since her early twenties. She knew the score. You don't get friendly with marks. Ignore that rule and pay the price. She was going to lose a lot of money over some goofy woman who didn't even know she existed. It was nuts.

Jennifer didn't feel like driving back over to that tiny storage room of an apartment in Parma. Her hand ached. She peered through the blinds. The Saturn was parked in the far corner of the lot. It probably didn't matter. Only the old busybody in the upstairs apartment ever paid any attention.

This two apartment deal seemed like a good idea in the beginning, but it was getting to be a pain. Paranoia was giving way to the frustration of everyday inconveniences. There were only so many hours in a day and she was starting to take short cuts. She needed a place where not so many eyes watched.

"What the hell," she said out loud. It was one more problem and she was tired of problems.

She switched out the living room lights and went into Maureen's bedroom. Stretching out on Maureen's bed, she fell asleep cradling her injured hand.

Chapter 7—Changes

<u>Monday, October 22, 2000</u>

Dick lay in his recliner and pointed the remote at his TV. He was sure there was a special on the Discovery Channel about Jack the Ripper. At first, he was disappointed. A fellow named Steve tackled a crocodile while his good-looking wife watched. Dick imagined what it would be like to rape that little nugget. She wore khaki shorts and a shirt with lots of pockets, feminine macho. She wrestled with prehistoric animals too. There was a scab on her left knee and dust on the seat of her pants. Very exciting.

He took a sip of *IC Light* and slipped one hand down inside his pajamas. It would be tough getting her away from old Steve though. His penis drooped. Damn. He decided he didn't like Steve, but after the commercial, the crazy bastard poked at a deadly puff-adder with a stick. Dick laughed with delight. The little guy was entertaining, he'd give him that much.

A branch scratched against his window. He jumped and hid behind the chair. Holding his breath, he waited for the Feds to kick in the door. Would John Walsh be with them when they came for him? He imagined the clip of him shuffling out of the house in chains while the announcer assured the audience there would be details at eleven. After it was all over, John Walsh would go on Larry King Live and the two of them would snicker about how they caught him.

The wind rattled the branch against the window again. No one was coming in, he realized. When he stood up, his knee cracked and he rubbed it. Not even a month ago, he was knocking off women left and right, three in his last trip alone. He'd been bold and he'd been bad. Then he ran into that son of a bitch Grady. One stupid move and here he was cowering behind a recliner.

Changes

Growling, he kicked the recliner. Damnit! A sharp pain shot through his ankle.

He limped into the kitchen for another beer. The refrigerator was empty except for a jar of dill pickles and a squeeze bottle of Hellman's mayonnaise. He'd been too nervous to visit the *Giant Eagle* since the close call at the Pittsburgh Airport, living off of stale bread and strawberry jam for almost a week. Even that was gone now.

He slammed the door and went into the bedroom to get dressed. Stripping off his pajama bottoms, he caressed the yellowing bruises on his ankle. He couldn't get over it. Grady wanted to hurt him—*did* hurt him. What was this world coming to?

He had to deal with this funk, he realized. It was just a birthday. It didn't mean anything. Okay, this was a tough business and maybe it WAS time to retire, but he still had to live. He put on a golf shirt and dark trousers. He rubbed his cheeks, bristling white. He needed to do something about that. Well, maybe not. Who'd guess an old codger like him was a wanted man? John Walsh didn't even have an old photograph of him like he did of John List.

Dick stood behind the front door. Should he go out in the yard? Anything could be waiting for him. He opened it a crack and pressed his face against the jamb. There was no one hiding in the burning bushes. He stepped onto the porch, half expecting to hear a guttural voice screaming at him to freeze.

A moment passed. No bullets slammed into the front of his house, no SWAT team rushed forward with automatic weapons. His breath fogged in front of his mouth and lips. The trees were losing their leaves. He could see all the way to the river. There was no one there. Grady the janitor had spooked him. That's all.

It was dark when he crawled into the Jeep and headed down the hill into Sewickley. The Giant Eagle was a bit of a drive, but it was worth it. It was a huge store with a cornucopia of options—dry cleaners, pharmacy, bank and video as well as normal grocery store products.

He took a cart and started through the produce department. He picked up a firm tomato and held it to his face. It smelled of summer when his mother peeled and stewed bushels of them. She'd make macaroni and cheese, which he loved, and then spoon stewed tomatoes on it, which he hated. Then she made him pray before she made him eat it. His stomach lurched.

He looked around.

No one was watching.

He poked a hole in the tomato's skin, spit into it, and put it back. He glanced over his shoulder. In the next aisle, an old woman frowned as she picked potatoes out of a large bin. Her dress rode up, revealing her blue streaked calves. He licked his lips and grinned. He could take her in a heartbeat if he wanted.

Whistling to himself, he continued shopping.

The cart was half full when he came to the meat counter. He stared at a thick piece of lean beef. It was blood red. Suddenly, he saw the reflection of a face in the saran wrap—a familiar face. He glanced up. Buddy stood behind the glass case. He wore a white hat over his fuzzy blonde hair and clear plastic gloves. A stained white apron covered his Izod shirt and preppy chinos. Dick backed away. The boy watched him with his mouth open. His front tooth was chipped.

Dick wheeled the cart around and headed down the candy aisle. He was imagining things. Buddy was dead. It had been an accident—not like his projects, not like his mother and father. Everyone liked Buddy—even Dick. It was a shame what happened to him.

Dick never knew for sure why Buddy started following him. Perhaps Dick's mother put him up to it. All Dick knew was that

Changes

he came back from meeting one of his girls in Tulsa to find Buddy waiting for him at the bus station.

"Where ya been?" Buddy leaned against a lamppost, his jaw twitching as he chewed his Juicy Fruit. "We've been worried about you, Rod."

The hairs on the back of Dick's arms rose in alarm. It wasn't that he minded being caught so much as he minded being stopped. He loved meeting his girls.

"Business. My business." Refusing to look at Buddy, Dick retrieved his fat suitcase from the belly of the bus.

"You aren't in any trouble, are you?" Buddy grabbed Dick's elbow. "Cause you know that would break Aunt Myra's heart if you were. You're all she has, Rod. Her baby boy."

Dick jerked his arm away. "What kind of trouble would I be in? I'm not the one who knocked up some slut." It was a low blow and Dick relished delivering it.

Buddy recoiled as if slapped.

Dick glared for a moment. Then he grabbed the handle of his suitcase in both hands and waddled down the sidewalk, the muscles in his arms quivering with the weight.

Buddy followed along beside him. "This has nothing to do with that, but believe me, I've been through hell. I'd hate to see anything like that happen to you. I don't know what you are up to, but you've changed. When you're home, you spend hours in your room all by yourself. Then you disappear for weeks. And the money! You never had two dimes to rub together. Now you're loaded. What's going on, man?"

"I got a job." Dick paused at the corner waiting for the light to change.

"A job? What kind of a job?" Buddy folded his arms over his chest and raised one eyebrow.

"What do you care? Maybe I'm selling bibles. Wouldn't that make Mama happy? Maybe I'm selling booze? There's one for Dad. Either way, it's none of your business." The light changed and Dick dragged the suitcase across the street.

Buddy slipped his hand around the handle of the big Samsonite case as if to take it away from Dick. "What do you have in that suitcase, Rod? It weighs a ton, you can barely lift it."

"Leave me the hell alone, Buddy." He yanked the suitcase away and hurried down the sidewalk, leaving Buddy standing in the middle of Sherman Street, his hands in his pockets, his head cocked sideways.

Dick knew there would be trouble with Buddy. He'd not been the same since Sheila died. At first, he retreated to his room, lying on his bed, staring at the ceiling. Then, after he'd answered all kinds of questions from the police for months, he got angry. Then he got nosey. It's not that he suspected Dick. Why would he? He was curious about Dick's comings and goings. Too curious.

A block from his house, Dick's arms hurt. He sat on the suitcase and lit a Pall Mall. The leaves in Mr. Olney's orchard rustled. Dick squinted. He could just make out Buddy hiding behind one of the apple trees. Shit! He tossed the half smoked butt onto the pavement and ground it out with his heel.

The last few feet before he reached his yard were excruciating. There were blisters on the palms of his hands and the muscles in his shoulders ached. He backed up the three steps to the door, bumping the suitcase as he went.

His mother was at a revival in Cincinnati. His father was snoring on the couch. Programming for the day was over and the TV blared white noise. Dick got himself an *IC Light* out of the fridge and sat down on the chrome and plastic dinette chair.

He stared at the suitcase and sipped the beer. He'd never brought one of them home before. Unsure as to what to do with her now that he had her here, he relaxed and let his mind wander. In the living room, his father stretched and farted. Dick held his breath. Smacking his lips, the old man rolled onto his belly and began snoring again. Two sheets to the wind, Dick thought.

It was close to mid-night. The dog next door yapped. Something knocked over a garbage can across the street. A hoot owl wailed. Dick figured Buddy was peering in the kitchen window right now.

He grinned to himself. Dumb shit! Draining the beer can, Dick crushed it against his forehead and tossed it into the sink. Leaving the suitcase setting in the middle of the kitchen floor, he padded to his room and stripped down to his underwear.

Buddy was kneeling on the floor in front of the big case, fiddling with the lock when Dick returned. "You're a nosey son of a bitch, Buddy."

Buddy barely turned his head. "I want to see what you got in here." He pulled a screwdriver out of his back pocket. It was Dick's old man's screwdriver. Buddy must have got it off the table in the tool shed.

"Well, don't mess up the lock. Use these." Dick tossed Buddy the key. He opened the fridge and took out another *IC Light.*

"You better watch that stuff. You're going to be as bad off as Uncle Al." Buddy muttered as he inserted the thin piece of metal into the cheap lock. Flipping up the catches, he opened the suitcase. "Jeez, Rod. What the hell is this?" The suitcase was filled with small packages wrapped in white butcher's paper and marked with a black pen.

"What does it look like?" Dick opened the chest freezer and rearranged the boxes of frozen potpies and TV Dinners.

"You brought a side of beef from Tulsa?" Buddy picked up one of the soft packages marked 'chuck' and turned it in his hands. "It'll be spoiled." He held it under his nose before handing it to Dick.

Dick took it and placed it in the freezer. "You crazy son of a bitch. How the hell would I fit a side of beef in this little case?"

Buddy picked up another one—smaller, softer. It wasn't marked. Dick opened a drawer near the stove, keeping his eyes on Buddy. "Well, it's obviously meat of some kind."

Dick grinned. "Go ahead. Open it."

"You're stealing meat? Is that what this is all about?"

"See for yourself." Dick fingered his mother's marble rolling pin inside the drawer.

Buddy peeled back the brown tape and pulled the thick white paper away. Inside, tightly wrapped in Saran Wrap, was a small piece of pale flesh topped with a tiny pink nipple. He looked up into Dick's eyes, his mouth open. "God, Rod."

Dick hit him in the face with the rolling pin, breaking his nose. Buddy dropped to the floor, unconscious. The second blow fractured his skull. Dick continued hitting him until he couldn't swing the rolling pin any more. He stood over the body, covered with blood. As his breathing slowed, he heard something else—his father's loud snores from the living room.

"Jesus, Buddy. You dumb shit. Look what you made me do!" Stepping over Buddy's body, he repacked the packages into the suitcase. The blue Samsonite luggage was splattered with blood.

Time was running out, little Suzie was going to start stinking soon. He wet a cloth and wiped down the suitcase. Grunting, he carried it out to the carport and put it in the trunk of his father's Plymouth. He'd take her to the woods later.

Back inside, he wrapped a sheet and several towels around Buddy's head. Struggling to pull him down the hall to his bedroom, he stepped on a broken tooth with his barefoot. "Goddamn you, Buddy!" He kicked the dead body.

Changes

At the front of the grocery store, Dick looked over his shoulder. The young man in the meat department was watching him. Dick gave the cart a shove. It rolled into a rack of magazines near one of the check-out counters where a half dozen people stood in line. He left it where it landed and hurried through the video store and out the door. Finding the Jeep parked near a cart return, he put both hands on the front fender. "No, no, no!" he muttered to himself.

A young man in a Porsche parked beside him. "Sir? Are you all right?" Dick backed away, his eyes bulging. It was another Buddy.

He got in the Jeep and left the clean-cut young fellow standing by the cart return. As he pulled onto Steubenville Pike, he saw John Walsh drive by in a red Toyota. He accelerated until he came to an abandoned drive-in theater a mile or so down the road. No one was coming the other way. No one was behind him. He parked near the ticket stand and turned off the engine.

He was sweating again—and thirsty. Maybe he needed to see a doctor. He pressed two fingers to the base of his throat. His pulse was too fast to count. He peered into the rear view mirror and stuck out his tongue. He wasn't sure what he was looking for on his tongue. Moss? His stomach growled.

He turned around and headed back toward the *Giant Eagle*, slowing as he neared *McDonald's*. Fast food seemed safest. He wouldn't have to be around anyone. No. He wasn't going to do that. There was a *Denny's* a few feet further down the road. He pulled into a parking space in front of a stand of newspaper machines.

He forced himself to go in. It was late. A middle-aged couple sat in a corner booth. In the smoking section, two elderly lesbians ate burgers and ignored him. The hostess put him in a small booth near the kitchen. He ordered tuna salad.

While he was waiting, he downed a coke and ordered a second one. He couldn't imagine himself as a sick old man. On the other hand, his libido had slowed. In recent years, he'd only hunted three or four times a year. However, up until now, he'd felt good, looked good. He held up a thick hand in front of him—steady as a rock.

The left pinkie jerked. He blanched and stuck his hand in his pocket.

The waitress brought him his tuna fish. He dug in, ravenous. Winter was coming soon. Maybe he'd take a break. Slow down. Watch TV. Play on the Internet. Maybe he'd write his memoirs.

He wondered if people like him did things like that. It would be great if he was the first. He'd hide it, of course. The mysterious envelope sent to some famous lawyer on the event of his death. Then after he was gone, they'd all talk about him with wonder and awe. John Walsh would do a special. Maybe they'd feature him on The FBI Files.

Another Buddy walked into the restaurant. The hostess showed him to a booth behind Dick.

I'm not afraid of you, Dick thought. He glanced over his shoulder. Buddy peered around the big laminated menu and grinned. His broken teeth glinted in the harsh light.

Dick faced forward. "I killed you once," he muttered. "Don't get in my way or I'll kill you again."

He gritted his teeth and pushed his half-eaten lunch away. Damned spook. He wasn't going to let a ghost push him around. He clinched his fists and stood up. Pausing a heartbeat, he turned to face Buddy.

A husky man and two kids stared back at him, French fries in hand. At first, Dick thought it was Grady the Janitor, then he realized this man didn't have a mustache.

Changes

The little girl hid her face in her father's leather Steeler Jacket. Her brother extended his middle finger and grinned. There were holes where his eyes were supposed to be.

"Stop that, Rod." The father scolded.

"Cute kid," Dick told the man. "Reminds me of me." He picked up the check from their table and walked away.

"Thank you," the kids called after him in unison.

Stupid little bastards.

Upfront, the cashier had two big moles on her left eyelid. "Was everything good?" She smiled.

He stared at her moles as he paid the two checks with a twenty and a ten. They were like flesh-colored peas stuck between her lashes. He thought about how they would look in his scrapbook and licked his lips.

Her eyes changed and he realized he'd scared her. Good. His cock stirred and power rushed back into his body.

He stuffed his wallet into his inside breast pocket. He was going to go back to the *Giant Eagle* and buy groceries. No one was going to stop him. The flame inside him might have flickered but it was still burning.

He didn't see any more Buddies or John Walshes as he drove home. He locked the Jeep in the garage and carried in his groceries. He ate a small dish of strawberry ice cream. It was the first time in a week he wasn't hungry. He felt even better after a long, hot shower. Putting on his favorite pajamas, he sat down at the computer.

He checked out the ten most wanted. Satisfied that none of his names were listed there, he went to the next website on his bookmark list, Court TV. He liked that dark haired woman lawyer named Vickie something, but there wasn't much about her on the web page, and nothing about him. Then on to John Walsh's page. He was relieved although it was no surprise. No one had found him because no one was looking for him.

He opened his email and scanned the messages. There was an email from LindaLu48.

"Dear Lone Wolf,

I hope this finds you well. I loved your last note. I know what you mean. I used to think anything was possible—that I'd grow up, marry a prince and live happily ever after. I guess I did marry a prince, but he cheated on me and left me. I have a girlfriend who thinks I was crazy to throw away a good marriage because of that, but I think HE was the one that threw away everything when he chose to sleep with that woman. The thing of it is, I don't like who I've become. I'm pushy and controlling. I find something wrong with everyone I meet. No one seems safe enough. I hit them before they can hit me.

Last night, I broke up with a young man I've been seeing. He was living in a cottage on my property. I got so mad when I found out he was STILL seeing other women that I kicked him out. I feel bad about that today, but I'm sticking to my guns. At least, so far.

I was obsessing about him, I guess. I listened to his phone mail, went through his snail mail, read his email. I followed him all over Cleveland and got upset when I saw him with all those other women. Every time I confronted him, I walked away trying to believe in him. Each time, I thought this is it. He won't cheat anymore. How silly of me! HE never made that promise.

I'm turning over a new leaf. I'm going to live my life differently. I'm not going to put unrealistic expectations on my relationships. I'm not going to force things. I'm a beautiful woman. I don't need to do that. (I wish I really believed that.)

I'm looking forward to hearing from you.

Sincerely,

Changes

Linda"

Dick read the note twice. Turning over a new leaf? Was it that easy? Just decide not to do something you've always done? He doubted it. He closed the email message and went on to the others.

There were 129 emails. He scrolled down through his message list, deleting junk mail and porno. That left 40 letters from his marks. Some of those women he'd been working on for years. A couple of them were close to the big meeting.

On impulse, he deleted them. He went to the address book and deleted their addresses, too. It was a gesture. He had saved them to a cd just in case his computer crashed. He could get them back at any time. Even so, he felt empty without them. They were his future girls. How could he live without something to look forward to?

It's not that easy for people to change, he thought as he pulled up a blank email form.

"Dear Linda,

You do sound like a beautiful woman. Do you have a photo you can send me? I like to visualize the people I'm corresponding with.

I understand your feelings about wanting to change. I think we are all programmed to do the things we do. I've often longed for a different life than the one I have, but I was destined to be who I am. I was put on this earth to clean up the garbage, to thin the herds. It's not something I asked for or even wanted in the beginning. Although I must say, I'm good at what I do and I like it very much now.

I have special talents. To give them up would sacrilegious. I will never be finished. When I die, someone else will take my place. My spirit is infinite even if my body is not.

USERNAME

You are the same. You have a destiny. You have a program and a purpose. Stay the course.

Your friend,

The Lone Wolf"

Dick sent the email and logged off. He went outside and sat on the front porch. The moon lit the waves of trees spreading out before him. Frost was forming in the yard. He rubbed the goose bumps off his forearms. He took the pack of Pall Mall's he'd bought at the *Giant Eagle* out of the breast pocket of his pajamas and lit one with his gold Zippo. It had been years since he'd smoked a cigarette. The smoke filled his lungs. It was like going home.

Chapter 8 – The Truck
<u>Wednesday, October 23, 2000</u>

Maureen was the first in. She tossed her coat over the back of her chair, picked up the receiver and retrieved her phone mail. Linda's voice sounded frantic.

"Maureen, there's something wrong with Midnight. I came home to find him covered with blood. Only thing I can figure is he found a piece of a cup I broke last week. I'm taking him to the vet as we speak. Funny thing though is that he seems fine. I don't see any cuts on him. I'll let you know what the doctor says."

The second message was calmer. "Maureen, the Doc can't find a thing wrong with Midnight. I guess he caught a mouse or something, but if he did, he sure didn't leave anything but the blood. Charlie came over to check on him after we got back from the vet and he chewed me out good for being so careless. I deserve it, I guess. It was quite a scare. Anyway, it's ...uh, oh my God, four-thirty and I haven't been to bed yet. I'm taking tomorrow off. Bill will have a fit, but he'll get over it. I'll catch you later."

The rest of Maureen's phone mail messages were from Bill Casey. In the last one, he postponed the staff meeting until the next day. So much for a birthday surprise, she thought. Of course it wasn't really her birthday, but she felt cheated anyway.

The office came alive around her as people booted up their computers. She spun her chair around so that her back was to the door of her cubicle. With trembling fingers, she logged on. Her email icon blinked. Bill Casey had questions. Good. She didn't want to think about Midnight or Linda or Mark Stevenson or Cy Gorman or Miriam or any of the others. She didn't mean anyone any harm. She just wanted the money.

USERNAME

Friday, October 25

Two days later, Maureen pulled into the long driveway off River Road. Midnight yipped and bounded across the yard to meet her. She parked in a gravel turnaround a few yards from the garage. A gleaming black and silver Trooper, so new that it still had dealer's plates, sat near the back door, loaded with blankets, hibachis, and several coolers.

The dog danced around the Acura until Maureen turned off the ignition and opened the door. "Hey Boy!" Sixty pounds of wiggling energy, Midnight jumped up into her lap, squeezing in behind the steering wheel. She moved the seat back to give them more room and wrinkled her nose. "What have you been eating? Skunk innards?" The big dog licked her face and jumped down into the yard, rolling onto his back with all four feet in the air. She got out and knelt on one knee to scratch his belly.

"You spoil him." Linda leaned against the front fender of the Trooper, her arms folded over her chest.

"You should talk. I'm not the one that took him Christmas shopping or had his picture taken with Santa." Maureen gave Midnight a snack from a box she kept in the Acura. He snapped it up and chewed it with his back teeth.

"What do you think? Sexy, eh?" Linda pointed to the new Trooper with a beer can in her hand.

"Why a truck?" Maureen asked as she struggled to her feet, shading her eyes against the setting sun. No longer the center of attention, Midnight raced off into the woods, leaves crunching under his paws.

"I like sitting up high where you can see. It's got four-wheel drive, a great stereo, lots of cargo space. It's perfect for a woman with a dog. Besides, I've been kind of itchy lately. Maybe it's approaching menopause, maybe it's dry skin. Either way,

Midnight and I might take it across the Kalahari Desert some day."

"The Kalahari?"

"You know, that big empty space in the middle of Africa? Besides, I like to take away something from each of my relationships. This was Bard Bailey's contribution."

"I thought you didn't like Mr. Bailey."

Linda rubbed an imaginary fingerprint off the hood with the sleeve of her orange Cleveland Brown's sweatshirt. "I don't. I like the Trooper. I had to drive all the way to Rocky River to get this. Want a beer?"

"I'd rather have wine."

"I have wine coolers in the fridge."

"That'll do."

"Beer's quicker." She pointed to the Styrofoam coolers in the back of the truck.

"I thought that was liquor." Maureen laughed. She liked who she was when she was around Linda. "What did you take away from Charlie?"

"This estate." Linda gestured at the rolling land around her. The house was a simple cracker box with a large back yard edged up against the woods. The front lawn swooped down forty yards to a small duck pond which separated the main house from the A frame cottage where Sean lived. "It belonged to Charlie's aunt and uncle. They willed it to him when they died in an airplane crash back in the 80s. I would never have asked for it, but Charlie knew how much I love it here. He signed it over to me during the divorce settlement."

"That was generous of him."

"Charlie's a generous guy, but he did it because I didn't ask for alimony," Linda said as they climbed the porch steps. "I think he wanted to be sure I was okay."

"Charlie's family is loaded. You are a secretary. I'm not sure that was fair."

"I don't know. It was over. Besides, I have enough to get by, especially if there's no house payment. The kind of taking care of that I need has nothing to do with money." Linda opened the screen door, draining her beer can before following Maureen inside.

Linda's divorce arrangement puzzled Maureen. She would have wanted the property and alimony. She took great satisfaction in owning things. You couldn't count on people the same way you could cash. Besides, how else could you keep score?

Midnight raced out of the woods and up on the porch, nipping at the seat of Linda's jeans just before the screen door slammed shut. "Lord, he's in a mood tonight. He knows I'm going somewhere and he's reminding me he wants to go too." She danced around the kitchen trying to avoid the dog's playful snapping.

After a few minutes, he turned his attention to Maureen while Linda leaned against the counter panting. "We'll go for long walks, won't we, boy?" Maureen pulled the dog's floppy ears. Midnight wiggled away, hit the screen with his nose, and was off for the woods again.

"Look at him." Linda chuckled. "He's so wild he flunked out of puppy school. He was distracting the other mutts and they made us leave."

"We'll have fun, don't worry."

Linda poked through the refrigerator and retrieved a small bottle. She twisted the lid but it refused to open. "I was going to make chili on my day off, but I got all involved in buying the Trooper and never got around to it. So don't expect chili."

"That's okay. I can whip something up."

Linda found a pair of pliers in the drawer next to the sink. She fitted them around the stubborn cap and grunted when it refused to move. "Oh no, I had to cook stuff to take with us anyway. Football food. I made enough sauerkraut and kielbasa to feed an army. Barbeque Ribs. I even made my mom's special spaghetti sauce. I left you a quart in the fridge. There are all kinds of noodles in the canisters by the sink. Take your pick. I was going to leave you steaks to grill out on the porch, but I wasn't sure you could handle Midnight. He has a bad habit of stealing stuff off the grill."

"That rascal!" Maureen took the bottle away from Linda. The lid came off with a single twist. She grinned and tossed the cap to Linda who shrugged and caught it. "When did he get to be such a thief?"

"He was born that way. He'll steal anything—hotdogs, steaks, ham, bread. Bread is his favorite. When he was still a little guy, a friend invited us in to her house for tea. She had just come back from the market and wasn't finished putting things away. There was a loaf of Roman Meal on the kitchen table. We'd no sooner come in the back door than Midnight broke loose, grabbed the bread and ran around the house knocking things over."

Maureen laughed and scratched Midnight's ears.

"I don't know why we chased him," Linda continued. "No one wanted the damned bread after he'd salivated all over it anyway. I had to buy the lady a new loaf of bread and pay for broken bric-a-brac. She hasn't invited us over since."

Linda led Maureen through the house. It was an explosion of personality. Colored magnets covered the refrigerator. Linda's collection of antique cookie jars filled a hutch—and a shelf over the cabinets and a glass case in the dining room. Maureen cringed at the thought of what Midnight could do to all those ceramic figurines and prayed it wouldn't happen on her watch.

Framed pictures of Linda's parents, of Charlie and of Midnight covered the living room walls. Maureen sat down in an old oak rocking chair in front of the picture window and sipped her wine cooler. A thick afghan made out of variegated crocheted squares was draped over the back of a white brocaded couch. An upright piano sat in one corner with an assortment of unburned candles on top. The legs of the piano bench bore deep gnaw marks, as did the back lower corner of an upholstered chair. A well-chewed squeak toy lay in the corner.

"Did you ever live here with Charlie?" Maureen's eyes lingered over a photo of Charlie with his aunt and uncle posing by the marble fireplace.

"Oh no. We used to come out here to picnic, of course. Heck, I lost my virginity in the eleventh grade in the A-frame over there." She pointed. Maureen turned to gaze out the picture window. The cabin was perched on a small rise in full view of the main house. "There are tons of hiking trails on the property. Aunt Helen used to keep horses here too. I'd come out and go riding with her right after Charlie and I first got married. There's great cross-country skiing in the woods behind the cottage, too. We each had an ATV for the rest of the year. We had lots of fun out here."

"It sounds like it. Do you miss Charlie?"

Linda took a quick sip of her beer, avoiding Maureen's eyes. "Don't be silly. I miss Charlie like I miss the measles. He was a part of my childhood and now I'm grown."

Realizing that she must have hit a nerve, Maureen let her gaze drift out the window again, sipping the too sweet wine. Canada Geese and mallards floated in the pond.

A muscular young man in jeans and a brown football jersey stepped out on the deck of the A-frame just across the water. He

The Truck

locked the front door before slipping a backpack over his shoulder and starting down the steps. At the foot of the stairs, he picked up a piece of gravel and skipped it across the surface of the water. The birds rose lazily, squawking.

"Is this Sean coming now?" Maureen asked although she knew it was.

"Look at him. You'd think he was eighteen." Linda waved at Sean through the picture window. He ignored her as he clambered over a row of bushes, jumped over the small creek that fed the pond and cut across the lawn where more ducks and geese roosted. After a couple of strides, he stopped, lifted his foot, and stared at the bottom of his shoe. Then he wiped the sole on the grass, took a couple more steps, and wiped it again.

Linda sighed.

Maureen wrinkled her nose. "What do you see in him?"

"I can't imagine at the moment. He looks better with his clothes off?"

Sean finished cleaning his shoes and started up a grassy slope towards Linda's house. "I don't know, I think you can do better."

"I'm not sure I can anymore, girlfriend."

The women got up and went out on the porch, watching as Sean opened the two doors to the storage compartment of the Trooper and tossed his backpack in.

"Yo, Linda! You ready to roll?" Sean acknowledged Linda's presence without looking at her. Midnight ran out of the woods and jumped on his back. They scampered around the back yard like big puppies as Maureen and Linda came down the backstairs.

"Sean, this is my friend Maureen."

"Yo, Maureen!" Sean tossed an orange across the yard and Midnight chased it. Rather than fetching it, the dog bumped it with his head like a soccer player as it arced down towards the ground. It went forward a few feet more and then he bumped it again. Only when the orange had lost all of its forward momentum did Midnight pick it up and carry it back to Sean.

"Nice to meet you, Sean." Maureen extended a hand.

"Yeah." Sean slapped the palm of her hand lightly before turning to Linda. "You ready?"

"I'm ready, I'm ready." Midnight trotted back with the orange in his mouth and dropped it at Linda's feet. Linda squatted and rubbed his ears before hooking a leash onto one of the links of Midnight's choker collar. "He's going to be upset when I leave. How about taking him for a walk?" She handed Maureen the leash.

Maureen smiled. "Have fun."

"Yo!" Sean pulled his baseball cap over his eyes and crawled into the passenger door.

Linda hugged her. "You too."

Maureen tugged on the leash. Midnight resisted until Linda threw the orange down the hill toward the pond. The dog took off, jerking Maureen's arm and forcing her to follow. She turned to wave as she hurried off.

"Maureen?"

"Yeah?"

"Here." Linda tossed her the house keys and hurried around the Trooper, her ponytail swinging with each stride. They were halfway down the hill when Linda started the truck. Loud rock music boomed across the property.

Midnight whirled at the sound of the stereo and charged back towards the driveway, barking. Maureen ran behind him, pulling on his leash and ordering him to stop. Linda gunned the engine.

The Truck

Sean thumped the outside of the door as Linda turned onto River Road.

By the time Midnight and Maureen got to the end of the driveway, the Trooper was on Center Road headed toward Hinckley. The dog stared down River Road, his tail stiff out behind him, whimpering. Maureen knelt beside him, stroking his back. "You can't count on people, buddy. That's the way it always is. Sooner or later, they leave you behind."

Midnight crashed into Sean's computer desk. A tiny video cam fell off the top of the flat screen monitor and rolled across the floor. He raced to retrieve it.

"Sssssh." Maureen held her gloved finger in front of her lips. Midnight cocked his head, his eyes glowing yellow in the half-light. "Can't you look around without making noise? What kind of a burglar are you?"

Midnight sank to the floor and covered his nose with his paws as if embarrassed by his faux pas. Maureen didn't think she needed to worry about anyone seeing them. The A-frame was only visible from the main house, but it never hurt to be careful. She enjoyed going through people's houses when they weren't there. It gave her a sense of power. She knew everything about them, but they didn't know she existed.

For all his boorish appearance, Sean kept the cabin spotless. There was a place for everything. His counters were wiped down, his floors mopped. There was no garbage in his garbage pail, no dust on the furniture. His bills and legal papers were filed in manila folders and stored in an unlocked lock box under his bed—which was made.

She pocketed a book of his checks and a credit card she found in the top drawer of the dresser. His clothes hung in a pine wardrobe. The shirts appeared to be ironed and the trousers were folded over the bottom rung of wooden hangers. Yo, Sean, Maureen thought. I gotta get you to come clean *my* apartment.

She sat down at his desk in the loft over the great room. He has a nice system, Maureen thought as she booted the computer. You could tell a lot about someone by how he organized his electronic files. She pulled up the file manager—lots and lots of folders filled with jpgs. He had the normal software packages loaded and a few of the not so normal.

Maureen was sure he'd been indulging in some 'explorations.' It looked like he'd broken into the public library a time or two—maybe a few other places, but nothing too ambitious. The kid was no amateur, though he was a bit naïve about security on his own system. Nothing was passworded except his email account and it didn't take a rocket scientist to figure that one out. She typed in "BROWNS" and she was in.

He had a nice collection of pornography, pretty much what Maureen would have expected. She wondered if he sold it. There was no trace of drugs in the house and she had looked everywhere. It was strange since he had an extensive set of contacts for a young man. She copied his address book to a disk. She scanned his calendar. "Old Sean is popular," she said to Midnight.

He had a date for every night of the week. He'd also been out every night the week before. Jennifer had followed him. Lenore was the doctor's wife. Peggy was a housewife over in Medina. Cindy worked at Wal-Mart. They were all considerably older than Sean. Maureen didn't get it. She wasn't attracted to kids. She liked rich older men with solid portfolios.

Coming down the metal spiral staircase, she realized there wasn't much here. Sean was exactly like he seemed, a bored young man in a boring job taking advantage of the sexual frustrations of lonely women. He wasn't the first. She would use his ID from time to time but he wasn't going to be the one to make her rich.

She loved the cottage though. Made of logs and glass, it consisted of a two-story great room, a bedroom, a kitchen and a loft. A garage and large storage room filled the ground floor. A small deck off the loft held a couple of redwood lawn chairs, a much larger deck off the great room held a picnic table, a glider and a gas grill. The windows were tall and unfettered by curtains or shades. Braided rugs covered the polished pine floors. The furniture was new and comfortable—nothing too frou-frou, but not plain either. It was perfect.

She locked the door behind her and followed Midnight down the wooden steps. It was a bright night. Even so, it was hard to see the black dog once he was more than a few yards away. She hurried to keep up. With a loud bark, Midnight scattered the sleeping geese. They honked and flapped their wings. Maureen laughed. The cool night air caressed her face and she enjoyed the smells of mossy water, birds, grass and dog. No question about it. This was the place.

After every argument, Linda claimed to kick Sean out. Yet, the days and weeks ticked by and he was still living there. Maureen needed to figure out a way to encourage Sean to leave.

Sunday, October 27

Maureen planned on asking Linda about renting the cottage as soon as Sean left seconds after they returned from Pittsburgh.

"Yo, Maureen." He petted Midnight, never meeting Maureen's eyes.

"Sean." Maureen nodded.

He tossed his backpack over one shoulder and disappeared around the corner of the house, not even offering to help unload the Trooper. Maureen knew he was in a hurry. He had a date with Lenore in forty-five minutes.

"Did you have fun?" Maureen turned her attention to Linda who had unlocked the hatch on the Trooper and was tossing field chairs, cushions, and boxes full of trash into a big heap near the back bumper.

"Not really." Strands of hair had slipped from her ponytail and hung down at the nape of her neck and around her ears. Streaks of red darted through the whites of her eyes.

"Do you want to talk about it?" Maureen picked up one of the Styrofoam coolers and carried it up the steps to the back porch.

"I don't think so. Not yet, anyway."

Midnight jumped up into the truck, wagging his tail and nuzzling Linda's cheek. She put her arms around his neck before pulling the dog down from the truck and closing the hatch.

Maureen met them on the top step. "I think I'll get my butt on home. Work day tomorrow." She hoped Linda and Sean had had an argument. It would make things so much easier. She decided to put off discussing the cabin with Linda until later.

"Thanks for taking care of my baby." Linda held Midnight by his collar. He whined and lunged, trying to get away from her and follow Maureen down the steps to her car.

"It was no problem. We got along great." Maureen put the key in the ignition of the Acura. The bell toned repeatedly. Midnight yelped. "I'll take him any time you need a dog sitter."

"He likes you. Look at him!"

"Is there anything I can do?" The bell was annoying. Maureen started the engine, lowered the window, and stuck out her head.

"No, nothing." Linda pulled Midnight back into the house and closed the kitchen door.

The Truck

Maureen headed for the nearest *Dairy Queen*. Ordering a small M&M Blizzard, she leaned back in her seat and sucked the cold sweetness through a straw. She'd get the lowdown from Linda tomorrow. Then she'd have a better idea of how to proceed. If she was lucky, Linda would be sick of the libidinous Sean Harper and would be in the right mood to kick him out. If she wasn't lucky, she'd have to figure out how to encourage Sean to leave on his own.

Chapter 9 – The Following
<u>Friday, October 25, 2000</u>

Brown wrapping paper lay on the floor around the base of Bill Casey's desk. A cardboard box full of packing foam sat in his lap. "Isn't it great?" He held up the heavy wooden plaque.

Linda cocked her head. "What is it?"

"It's an award for speaking at a small business organization's dinner last month in Shaker Heights." He rubbed the brass plating with his cuff.

"Yeah, but what IS it, Bill?" Maureen stepped back and squinted.

"It's a thing-a-ma-jig, you know."

Linda laughed. "A what?"

"It's art. It doesn't have to be anything but a design." He propped it up on his credenza, rolling backwards in his chair to admire his prize. "Sometimes you just have to let nothing be nothing."

"I don't know, it looks like a goose or duck or something with a long neck to me." Maureen sat in Bill's client chair, a tablet in her hand, ready to note down whatever issue Bill had on his mind when he called her to this meeting.

Linda stepped forward and frowned. "That's not a long neck, Maureen. That's a big penis."

"Oh, Man!" Bill grimaced. "Why would you say a thing like that?"

"Well, *look* at it."

Both Bill and Maureen leaned forward, contemplating the shape of the brass and wood engravings.

The Following

"It's like those IQ tests where you can see two different pictures in the same design—you know, like if you look at it one way you see a clown and if you look at it another way, you see Jesus?"

"Oh God, I see it!" Maureen clapped a hand over her mouth, smothering a giggle.

"I see the goose now." Bill twisted his head sideways.

"So imagine the goose is the background." Linda pointed.

"Aw, Man!" Bill leaned back slapping his own forehead with the heel of his hand.

"Now who would send someone an award like that?" Linda gave Bill's chair a little kick, making a face at Maureen.

Bill took another peek. "Oh, Man!"

"It's no big deal, Bill." Maureen wiped her eyes with a knuckle.

"What do you mean no big deal? I don't want a big dick hanging on my wall." He picked up the plaque and put it back in the box.

Maureen and Linda both burst out laughing.

"It's not funny."

Maureen found Bill's embarrassment charming.

"What if Jack came down here?" He glanced at the door. "What if Morgana came to visit?"

"Oh Bill, don't be so glum. I'm sure no one else would notice it." Linda gathered up the brown paper, smoothing it out on Bill's desk and folding it.

"I can't even see the goose now," he said as he folded the box lid.

"He doesn't want to be with me. That's the bottom line." Linda's eyes were red and swollen although they were dry at the moment. "We hardly said a word to each other at the game. The sex was good, but then he fell asleep and I was all by myself again." She leaned forward in Maureen's client chair and covered her face with her hands.

"Maybe there's not much to talk about." Maureen handed her a box of Kleenex, glancing over her shoulder to reassure herself that the man in the next cubicle was on his smoke break.

"It's just that I want someone who acts like it's a nice thing to go to bed with me." Linda's voice squeaked with the effort to push wind through her tight vocal chords. "He didn't even say good-bye last night. Just rushed off like he had something better to do."

Maureen choked on her secret knowledge of where Sean was going. "So why do you want to be with him? He's not someone you can have fun with. Find another guy. Someone who recognizes your value."

"I'm beginning to think men are incapable of being faithful. They are driven by their gonads and nothing else matters but their next score." Linda scraped her fingernail back and forth over a rough spot on Maureen's desk.

"I'm sorry, Linda." Maureen didn't know what else to say.

"Sean has a saying. When you put your penis in a woman, she goes crazy. I almost think he's right. Once I have sex with a man, I feel the need to check up on him. I want to know everything about him—where he goes, who he sees, what he's doing. I'm afraid he'll cheat on me, I guess."

Maureen understood getting even. She understood the need to follow people in order to collect information about them. However, what Linda described seemed so undignified and pointless. "You know, when you look for trouble, it's easy to find," she struggled to find the right words.

The Following

"I keep thinking that if I had been more alert, Charlie wouldn't have strayed." Linda's face twisted in anguish as though Charlie's betrayal was only yesterday.

"I know this is a radical thought, but why did it matter so much that he had sex with someone else?"

Linda pulled several tissues from the Kleenex box and blew her nose. "I couldn't live with someone I couldn't trust."

"Was he good to you?"

"Extremely."

"Was he home every night?"

"Always."

"Did he hit you?"

"Charlie? Are you kidding?" Linda crumpled the tissues and threw them in Maureen's waste paper basket.

"Was there anything else wrong with him?"

"Well, he wasn't much of a kisser." A weak smile.

"You gave up all of that because of a one night stand?"

"A promise is a promise, Maureen."

"It's a question of perspective. If I had a man who adored me, who gave me anything I wanted, who was fun to be around and who was around whenever I needed him—well, I guess the everyday means more than a quick fumbling in the back of a cop car."

Linda folded her arms over her chest. "He LIED to me. I hate being lied to."

Maureen looked down into Linda's eyes. They were welling with tears. "Did you ever lie to him?"

"No! Of course not!" A small pause. "Not about anything important."

Maureen nudged Linda's knee. "We all lie about something. It's human nature."

"Oh? What do *you* lie about, Maureen?"

She patted her own buttocks and grinned. "My weight."

Linda stared at her for a moment. Then the corner of her mouth twitched. "Oh you!" She giggled, covering her lips with her fingertips.

"Actually, I'm a size six. I just want you to believe I'm a sixteen." Maureen's eyes twinkled behind the big round lenses, relieved that Linda's gloomy mood had broken.

"You're too funny." Linda laughed, then her expression darkened and she bit her lip. "The question is, would you lie to your husband about seeing someone else?"

"In a heartbeat. Are you kidding?"

"Okay, okay. So I don't weight 120 pounds anymore." Linda threw up her hands in mock capitulation. "And I really wear a size 9 shoe instead of a size 8."

Maureen held up her cup and clicked it against Linda's Midnight mug. "I rest my case. You are as big a liar as I am."

"It's a sad testimony to our degenerate society, isn't it?"

Maureen drank her water. "Well, from one lying stalker to another, let's get back to work and continue this conversation at lunch. Okay?"

"*The Galleria?*"

"You're on." Maureen returned to her databases with a sigh.

"I met a new man," Linda said as they rode the elevator up to the second floor of the *Galleria*.

The Following

"Yeah? Does this mean that you have decided to dump old Sean?"

"After the way he acted this weekend, I think I might."

"He's no good for you. Besides, if you want to chase him out of your cottage, I'll rent it from you. You won't even be out one month's rent." It was easier to bring it up as a half-joke.

"You mean it? You'd want to live in Hinckley?"

"I love Hinckley, besides I'm getting tired of living in an apartment building. I'd like to be more out in the country. Maybe we could drive into work together, save on gas and parking."

"That would be great." Linda tried to hug Maureen.

Maureen stiffened and stepped back. "That means you'd *have* to get rid of Sean." She held Linda at arm's length, but patted her on the shoulder hoping that would satisfy Linda's need for affection.

"I've kicked him out twice in the last month. This way I have a reason to make it stick." Linda's eyes turned inward and her voice drifted off as though she was talking to herself.

Maureen lapsed into silence as they stood in line at the *Café Sausalito* waiting to be seated.

"Hey, Ben. Where's Mark?" Maureen asked as the host led them to a table in the atrium.

"Didn't you hear? He was hurt over the weekend. Someone tried to carjack that Jag of his. He wouldn't give it up and some little bastard pistol-whipped him. Left him for dead in the middle of Ontario Street." The maitre d' helped Linda push in her chair.

"Oh God! That's awful. How is he?" Linda put her hand on the man's forearm, her face filled with concern.

"It doesn't look too good. They don't think he's going to make it." The man's big eyes were gloomy. "You never know which day will be your last one, do you?"

Mute, Linda and Maureen accepted their menus.

110

"Rachel will be over to take your orders." Ben backed away.

The edgy humor from Bill's office seemed long over. Maureen stared at the list of entrees, mentally reviewing the details of the life insurance policy she had purchased on Mark Stevenson. If he died, it would be double indemnity. She added that figure to the total in the bank in Switzerland. She clenched her fist. Maybe this was it.

"I can't believe how dangerous this town is sometimes." Linda closed her menu. "I'm afraid to walk down the street at night."

"It's dangerous everywhere." Maureen wondered if Mark would hang on for a long time or if he'd give up the ghost quickly.

"You remember when that woman was beaten and raped in our parking garage? She rolled her window half-way down to talk with someone who approached her car and he reached in and pulled her right out." Linda shivered. "It was months before I'd bring my car downtown after that."

Linda's comment brought Maureen back to the present. "When was that?"

"A few years ago. Now that I think of it, it was before you came to *First Life*. The lady was a friend of Bill's. She went to school with Morgana."

"Did she die?"

Linda glanced up at Maureen. "No, but of course, she's never been the same. There's better security in the garage now. It's safe enough. Don't worry."

"Right behind our building?" The familiar seemed safe sometimes just because it was familiar. Maureen made a note to research the rate of crime in Cleveland garages. Maybe parking downtown was risky enough to bet on.

The Following

"It's hard to believe, isn't it?" Linda unfolded her napkin and laid it in her lap. "There was a young girl who was a clerk at a convenience store over in Lakewood. A robber stabbed her. They said it was a non-fatal wound, but she died anyway."

Who parked downtown, Maureen wondered. Managers? Maybe they got monthly passes as a perk or something. She realized that Linda had stopped speaking and was waiting for her to comment. "Infection?"

"The thought that anyone would want to hurt her was so traumatic that she chose not to live." Linda glowed with the romance of the whole thing.

"That sounds like urban legend to me." Maureen rearranged the sweeteners. "You know, like the story about the woman who died because a black widow spider made a nest in her beehive hairdo? All those baby spiders chewed on her scalp I guess."

Linda obviously hadn't heard the spider story. "Yeccch!"

"Or the story about the couple out on a lover's lane who nearly got murdered by a fellow with a hook for a hand?"

"You are nuts, girlfriend."

"You gotta know whether or not you are being kidded. Every other fellow is out to con you." Maureen felt a sudden urge to lecture Linda for her naiveté.

"I'm careful." Linda reached across the table to pat Maureen's hand. "You are as big a worrywart as Charlie."

"It's worse online, you know. People are out to take advantage of the gullible—or at least shake them up." Maureen wagged a finger at Linda, serious words spilling out even as she tried to be playful.

A waitress came to the table. "I'll have the black bean soup and diet coke." Linda smiled up at her before turning back to Maureen. "I think I could recognize a scam when I see one. I'm a grown person after all."

"I'll have the Caesar salad and iced tea," Maureen said to the waitress who nodded and wrote down their orders on a small pad. "You might or you might not. A lot of smart people have been caught up in some of these things. My uncle used to go down to the local Wal-Mart to meet his 'buds.' They'd bullshit and smoke and complain about politicians. Then one day, a friend of the family, an officer of the Savings & Loan where they kept their money, called his wife. He'd taken three thousand dollars out of their savings account to help one of these guys. Of course it was too late. The *Wal-Mart* gang had moved on by the time the police got there. My uncle was crushed. He hung out with these characters for months and thought he knew them."

"Oh, the poor fella. I bet he was so embarrassed." Linda shook her head.

"These people are good at finding soft spots and the Internet has extended their reach right into your home."

"Most folks know when someone's trying to con them," Linda insisted. "It's only the very old or the very young that are vulnerable."

"You think?" Maureen accepted her tea from the waitress. "Bick Taylor called me all upset because someone sent him an email with a link to a Web page. Seems someone was claiming to be in the business of taking new-born kittens and molding them into different shapes, like cubes and tubes. There were even photos on the site of these fuzzy little characters inside bottles and a price list. He was outraged and wanted to set up a mass mailing to all employees to report it to the Humane Society."

"Well, I don't blame him." The corners of Linda's mouth turned down in disapproval. "That sounds horrible."

"Except that it was a joke. Someone with a twisted sense of humor put together the Website, computer generated pictures and all. If

The Following

he'd read the whole thing, he would have realized it, but he got so upset that he didn't get to the punch line."

Linda stripped the paper off of her straw and dropped it into her diet coke. "People are sick."

"Then there are chain letters. They are worse than just a waste of time."

"What's wrong with chain letters? I forward them on to my friends all the time."

"They take up computer resources for one thing. If they get loose in a corporate system, they can fill up an email server and take it down in a few hours. If I send out a message to ten people and they each send out messages to ten people and those people do too, you can have millions of messages clogging the system before you know it."

"Oh Maureen, you are such an IT person." Linda sipped her cola. "It's always about the equipment with you."

Maureen sighed. "No, not just that. People are doing a lot of dangerous things over the Internet. You can get into trouble without realizing it."

The waitress brought their food.

Linda stirred sour cream into her soup. "I love the Internet. It makes me feel better when I'm alone at night knowing that there's always someone out there to talk to."

"I know but remember that you don't know anything about these guys. They could be out to rob you or rape you."

"Not my friends. I've talked with them for ages. I may not have met them in person, but I know them. I know their hearts."

Maureen thought about their earlier conversation. "What if they are lying?"

Linda put down her spoon and raised her eyes to Maureen's. "They could be, but how do you know if anyone is lying?"

114

"That's my point. You knew Charlie better than you know these guys."

Linda took a deep breath. "It's changed out there. I've changed. Men don't come on to me like they did when I was young and pretty. Maybe I do get my heart broken from time to time, but taking a chance is better than being alone forever."

Maureen swallowed back her irritation. How did people get to be so stubborn?

Chapter 10—John Walsh
<u>Sunday, November 10</u>

"Dick. Oh, Di-ck!" The old woman's Eleanor Roosevelt soprano quivered.

Lord, how he hated Sundays. He glanced in the rearview mirror.

Oona Barrett filled the backseat. She pointed to the window separating them, her eyes wide.

He pressed a button and the glass slid open.

Her breath was raspy. "Did you see that guy?"

He scowled. "Where?"

"Back there," she panted. "The one with the black stocking cap?"

He glanced behind him. A group of young men were playing football in the park. It was cold. Half of them wore black knit Pittsburgh Steeler caps. "Which one?"

"The ugly one."

He turned right and started up the hill. "Okay."

"I think he's wanted by the FBI."

He was sure that none of the young men was Buddy. "Oh?"

"It's what's his name. I saw him on CNN. He's a rape murderer. I'm sure of it." She rummaged in her purse until she found her inhaler. Her lips were turning blue. Whoosh. She sprayed medication into her lungs. Her long, slow exhalation was ragged.

He glanced over his shoulder as he eased around a tight curve. "Are you okay?" The damned woman was going to die before he got a chance to kill her.

She waved her hand, her lips moving but no sound coming out.

116

"Should I stop?"

"Fine." She forced the word out. "I'm fine."

It was a bitch working for a four hundred pound asthmatic like Oona Barrett. Every time she got excited, he ended up rushing her to the clinic. "Are you sure?"

"Take me home, Dick." She coughed into a handkerchief, her eyes watering.

At the top of the hill, he drove up the cobblestone drive and parked in front of the mansion. Getting out of the car, he hurried around to open the back door. "Take deep breaths." He offered her his arm.

The wheezing continued. "I have to call the hotline."

The tips of his ears burned. "I don't think they have a hotline on Sundays."

"Don't be silly. You can always call a hotline." She lunged forward, her fingers digging into his flesh. The car groaned. He locked his knees and pulled. It took two tries to get her out of the Lincoln. The sour odor of disease overwhelmed him and he took a step back.

"What are you going to tell them? You saw a kid that looked like someone they had on the show, but you don't know who?" He rummaged in the back seat for her cane.

She tugged her black silk dress down over her belly and straightened her coat. "What *is* his name? I saw it just the other night. He kills them with a pickaxe."

"It would be pretty hard to sneak up on someone with a pickaxe, Miz Barrett." He handed her the cane.

"Maybe if I tell them what he looks like they can help me guess." She hobbled up the gentle slope on swollen legs.

He shuffled along beside her. "It's the FBI. They have hundreds, maybe thousands of guys they are looking for. Most of them are ugly dudes with black hats. They don't have time to deal with you unless you can say which criminal you saw."

She stopped to catch her breath. "They have all these pretty blonde-haired girls answering the phones and looking at computers." She poked him with her cane.

He gritted his teeth and helped her up the porch stairs. "I think you are confusing TV with the FBI."

"Maybe it wasn't a pickaxe, now that I think of it. What was it? A sword?" She paused as she reached the top step.

"I don't know. I didn't see the show."

She shook a finger at him. "You saw the guy, didn't you? Maybe you should call them."

"No ma'am. I didn't see a thing." He opened the door.

"It was a shotgun. He kills them with a shotgun."

"Everyone uses a shotgun. What's that going to tell them?" He tried to guide her through the door, but she snarled and batted him away with the cane. "Get back! I can do this myself."

The maid hurried to help the old woman into the house and he backed away, glad to be rid of her for the day. The trip to church wore her out and made her meaner than usual. She'd sleep now, her snores drifting out her bedroom window all the way down to the old stone house where he lived.

He prayed that she'd forget all about the FBI by the time she woke up. This was a good job and he wasn't ready to leave yet. The apartment was nice and the estate was secluded. Who would think to look for him here? He drove the Lincoln down to the garage.

He didn't have to do much—just keep all of Oona Barrett's cars clean and drive her around once in a while. He got out and pushed open the rickety old garage door.

In fact aside from church, she didn't go out much anymore. The servants took care of her and her rich, dead Daddy's fine house. She lounged around eating massive amounts of food and watching three televisions at once. He parked the Lincoln between an antique Mercedes and a spotless Jeep Wrangler.

He didn't mind her lifestyle. It gave him plenty of time for his scams. She let him have his pick of the vehicles to run his personal errands. It wasn't long before he began to think of her Daddy's fleet of expensive automobiles as his own.

Other than whining about little things, she pretty much left him alone. She was half blind and half deaf. It made her the perfect boss.

Dick sat in front of the TV, his feet propped up on the ottoman. John Walsh was on Larry King.

"It's nice to see you again, John." Larry reached across the desk to shake his hand. "I understand you spent the last couple of days with the Hancocks."

"It's good to be back." John Walsh was wearing a dark suit instead of his trademark leather jacket.

Fascinated, Dick learned forward as if to touch the screen. John Walsh's eyes crackled with passion and he still had a boyish face. It wasn't fair. Even though they were the same age, Dick looked and felt ten years older.

"How's the Hancock family holding up, John?"

Dick startled out of his reverie at Larry's question. What family? He turned up the volume.

John Walsh

John Walsh narrowed his eyes. "There's nothing to prepare you for what some animal has done to your child."

"I can't imagine it," Larry King sure didn't look his age either. Maybe it was makeup? Dick decided to do a little experimenting, maybe add a few tricks to enhance his disguises.

"They are devastated, Larry. We featured their daughter twice on America's Most Wanted, so I got to know Otto and Alma Hancock. They knew she'd never run away. As time went by, we had to fight to keep their spirits up. Now their worst fears have been realized."

"Are there any clues as to who might have killed Miss Hancock?" Dick decided to buy himself some suspenders just like Larry's—and maybe a striped shirt with a white collar.

"You know we can't go public with details, Larry. That would compromise the investigation."

"Let me ask it this way, John. Do you think whoever did this will ever be caught?"

"Like most of these creeps, he made some major mistakes. Those mistakes will be his undoing. I think he'll be caught soon."

Dick laughed and shook his fist. Go, John. Go! He loved it when John Walsh got revved-up.

"Let me take a break here," Larry said. "When we come back we'll talk about what the FBI found last week in that pond in Indiana."

As they went to commercial, a video shot from a helicopter hovering over a round barn south of Indianapolis flickered onto the screen. Four firemen in thick blue nylon jackets carried a litter up the slope of a muddy water hole twenty yards from the corral.

Dick's gut twisted. Shit! They found Susanna, the little waitress from *Denny's*. His mind raced. Did he leave anything for them to find? He left her clothes at a Salvation Army collection bin in Mississippi. He doubted anyone would recognize them that many states away. The body was in the water for weeks. They weren't going to find any DNA.

Larry King was back.

"Let's take a call from Oona in Sewickley, Pennsylvania. Are you there, ma'am?"

"Mr. Walsh. I think you are wonderful, tracking down these criminals like you do." A breathy voice wheezed over the line.

John Walsh smiled. "Thank you, ma'am."

Dick looked through the window at the mansion on the hill. "Bitch!"

"Do you have a question?" Larry liked to move things along.

"Yes. I think I saw some one that was on your show, but I can't remember who. What should I do?"

Dick ground his teeth. The woman was an idiot!

"You mean you don't know the name of the person you saw?" John Walsh looked puzzled.

"It was that fellow that killed people with a gun."

Larry King looked at John Walsh and shrugged.

John Walsh took charge. "Ma'am, I suggest you go to our website. You'll find pictures there. If you recognize anyone, then you can call."

The web address flashed on the screen.

"HA!" Dick leaned back on the sofa and put his feet on the ottoman.

"Back to the Susanna Hancock story." Larry King took back the lead. "What kind of a person does something like this?"

"It's most likely Susanna was taken by a sexual psychopath. Some weirdo who had done this before."

John Walsh

Dick loved when John Walsh used those big words.

"It's heartbreaking, John." Larry looked sad.

"I have a personal message for this scumbag." John Walsh turned to face the camera, the muscles in his jaw twitching. "Don't think you can get away. We'll find you sooner or later. I'll find you. If you try it again, I'll find you faster."

John Walsh's eyes burned into him, just like Buddy's did. A bead of sweat trickled down his ribcage.

Dick turned off the TV. He wasn't going to panic. Yes, he'd been down in the dumps since that deal with Grady the janitor. Yes, the depression was worse this year than last, but he was coming down from the highest of highs. Hunting had gone well even if Candace did get away.

He tossed the remote onto the couch and went into the kitchen. The refrigerator was empty again. He sighed. Sunday night. The only place open now was *Denny's*. He'd pass. There was a bottle of Johnny Walker Black in the cabinet above the sink. He took a quick swig and shuddered.

His laptop sat on the table. Why not? He logged onto the Internet. There were two emails from Amber44D who was seventeen and naughty. He clicked on the link in the body of her message and looked at the pictures. She was scrawny but her rubbery breasts were enormous. She held them up and smiled as though she was very proud.

He scanned through the photos hoping to find one that showed her feet. Ooooo. She wore a little toe ring. His breath caught in his throat. He tried to construct a fantasy, but Amber44D was too perfect and the excitement drifted away after a few minutes.

He yawned and returned to his email. There it was. Lindalu48. He opened it.

"Sweetheart,

It's happening! Sean will be moving out the end of this month. A friend of mine from work will be moving in two days later, so there's no going back this time.

Maureen is a little hard to get to know, but she's a sweetie underneath it all. Midnight loves her and dogs can tell about people, you know. It'll be fun to have her living in the A-Frame. I'll look after her and she'll look after me.

I know you want to come see me, but I beg you to be patient. Things are a little crazy now. Once Maureen gets moved in, I can leave Midnight with her and come see you. How about that?

By the way, I've attached a new photo. Midnight and I came back from a long walk the other day and found Charlie waiting in the driveway for us. He had a new digital camera he wanted to try out. It's a nice picture of the property. That's me and Midnight collecting the mail. In the background you can see my house and the A-Frame. Isn't it pretty?

Don't be angry with me, baby. Our time will come.

Love and Kisses

Linda"

Damn her black little soul to hell! He knocked the mouse off the table where it dangled, flashing red lights. Linda was the perfect off-season tryst. Divorced. Lonely. Desperate for reassurance.

Hinckley was only three hours away. He could be there and back in one evening. She was like a silver koi in a barrel. He was ready to reel her in and now out of the blue, she put him off?

He stood up to retrieve the mouse and kicked over his chair. Damn! He hated Sundays. Wasn't spending the morning with Oona Barrett bad enough? It took a half hour to clean her stink out of the Lincoln. Then John Walsh practically dared him to kill again.

He popped his knuckles and sat back down at the computer. There was still the jpeg attached to Linda's email. He downloaded it. Bright autumn colors filled his screen as the photo appeared. Linda had gotten all gussied up to go for a walk? Her dark auburn hair was a mass of elaborate curls. She knelt in front of a mailbox, hugging a big black dog. Except for that dazzling ear to ear smile, she looked like anyone else in the world.

He used his mouse to zoom into a small portion of the photo right over Linda's head. Ah. The last piece of the puzzle. He smiled and zoomed in even closer. "Try and stop me, John Walsh," he muttered.

He changed usernames and tapped at the keyboard. Maybe Sundays aren't so bad after all.

Chapter 11 – Linda Lu
Tuesday, November 13, 2000

Maureen sipped her coffee and thumbed through *The Plain Dealer*. A small headline on the second page caught her attention. West Sider Dies after Carjacking!

"Someone you know?" The waitress stood over her with the coffee pot.

"He worked at one of the restaurants down in the *Galleria*. A nice young man. He never regained consciousness, it says." Maureen's eyes flew down the article. If she got the request for death certificate submitted this week, she should get a check by the end of January. The timing was perfect.

The woman refreshed Maureen's cup. "Makes you wonder what this world is coming to."

Maureen emptied two small packages of sugar into her cup. "I hope they caught the son of a bitch that did this to him."

There were several credit cards in Mark's name stored in her safety deposit box. She took the cash advances out of two of them a few weeks back. Collecting the maximum out of the other two was a priority.

She didn't expect the executor would check Mark's credit report for quite a while if at all. Unpaid bills in Mark's name were piling up in a post office box in Parma. Creditors trying to get in touch with him about these unpaid debts were calling the cell phone that she'd set up in his name—including the cell phone company. The phone itself was in a landfill, the battery long run down.

Even if they did manage to track down Mark Stevenson, he was dead. She was one of thousands of people that he might have bumped into during his life.

"His poor mother." The waitress left a bill on the table. Maureen didn't know if Mark had a mother or not. She didn't know anything about him except that he'd paid off.

Maureen called *Acme Furniture Rental* and arranged for her couch, desk, dinette set, bed, nightstand, dresser, and TV to be picked up the day of the move. Linda's cottage was furnished and the rent was less too. She was saving a ton of money on this deal.

She sat back in her chair. Oh Lord, she thought. I *am* a creature of habit. I don't have to economize anymore. I'm loaded. I'm beyond loaded. She drummed her fingers on her desk, enjoying the moment. It should be enough, she thought, but it wasn't. Just a little more, one more big score and then she'd quit.

She scrolled through the choices available to her on the *U-Haul* Webpage. All she had was computer equipment and clothes. Maybe a pickup truck would be the best option.

"What the hell are you doing?" Linda stood in the door of her cube. Maureen checked the time at the bottom left of her monitor. Ten-fifteen. It was routine now, she guessed.

"I'm making arrangements to rent a truck, what does it look like? I don't want to spread this move over more than one weekend."

"Now why would you do a stupid thing like that when I have a brand new Trooper that you can use? It wouldn't hold a refrigerator or anything like that, but you should be able to move the stuff you have in a couple of trips." Linda set her mug on the desk and stretched.

"That's nice of you but I can't take your new truck. What if something happened to it?"

"Don't be silly. It's insured. Take it, take it."

"Thank you." Maureen spun her chair around to look at Linda. "I pray this doesn't spoil our friendship. You know, too much of a good thing."

Linda looked different. Softer. Her face was scrubbed so that her skin glowed. The dark liner was gone as well as the thick layers of mascara. Her hair was brushed and shiny—no rats or hairspray. She set a greeting card on Maureen's desk. "How can there be too much friendship? It'll be great, like one great big pajama party. We'll have fun."

The card had a picture of a big dog. Maureen assumed it was Midnight. All black animals look the same in Polaroids. It was a 'Welcome to Your New Home' card. Inside was a big, smudged paw print. "I take it this is from Midnight?" She picked it up and ran her finger over the photo. She never had a pet when she was a kid. Living in apartments, moving from town to town, she'd never had time for one as an adult either. Someday.

"Well, I may be a bitch, but my prints don't look like that." Linda raised the mug and laughed.

Something in her tone made Maureen look up again. "You're in a good mood. What's going on?"

"One of my best friends is moving in."

"Uh huh."

"I got Sean out of my system once and for all." Jennifer spent four hours the night before following Linda who was following Sean. She didn't give up the chase until Sean settled in with a blonde at a bar in the Flats. Linda was crying when she drove past Jennifer headed towards I-71.

Maureen raised an eyebrow.

Linda Lu

Linda shrugged. "Okay, so I'm *trying* to get Sean out of my system."

"It's something more than that."

"I've found a new guy." Linda lowered her voice as though confiding a secret. "An older man."

"I thought you didn't care for the older ones."

"I didn't think I did, but Peter's different. He's a gentleman."

"What does he look like?"

Linda put her fingers over her mouth and giggled. "I don't know."

"Oh?"

"I met him on the Internet. We've not actually seen each other yet. Although I sent him a few pictures of me."

"Oh, Linda." Maureen's mouth went dry. "What do you know about him? Where does he live? What does he do for a living? Is he married?"

"He's not married. He's never been married."

"Don't you think that's odd? An older man who's never been married? I mean, does he still live with his mommy? Is he gay? Ugly? Stupid?"

"Maureen!" Linda sat down in Maureen's client chair. She was wearing soft silk slacks and her thighs whispered against each other as she crossed her legs. "He's none of those things. He was so busy with his business that he never got around to getting married. His mother's been dead for years. Stupid is not how I'd describe him. And he's definitely not ugly!"

"If you've never seen him, how do you know he's not ugly?"

"He doesn't write like an ugly man—or a gay one." Linda said as though the issue was closed. "He's very intense. Sexy."

"How can you tell?"

"I just can. People are more intimate on the Internet. They do and say things they'd never do if you knew them in person."

"How did you meet him? A chat room?"

"Oh no. He sent me a letter. It was a wonderful letter—so wonderful I had to answer him. Then he answered me. Then I answered him back. It's been going on for a month now. We had our anniversary last night."

"Anniversary? No, don't answer that. Tell me about the letter."

"It came out of the blue. He introduced himself as Peter Good, a businessman who sometimes comes through Cleveland. We've spent all kinds of time together since then—talking, talking, talking. I've never been with a man who liked to talk like Peter does. He said he was tired of searching for relationships in singles bars and church socials. He had bad luck with dating services—just like me. Friends and relatives set him up with a series of unmarried ladies who all dreamed of being married ladies. None of that was what he wanted."

Maureen swallowed and bit her lip to keep from smirking. "What's the story with his name? It might as well be the name of a porn star—and, after all is said and done, what does he want?"

"A friend. Imagine that? He wants a date when he comes through Cleveland. Someone to hang out with. Someone to have dinner with." Linda clasped her hands over her chest.

"You aren't going to burst into song, are you? I think old Peter just wants someone to have sex with. Once."

"Well, yeah, he wants that too." Linda's cheeks reddened. "More than once though. He wants an affair. He said so right up front. He wants someone to spend quality time with when he's in town."

"That doesn't sound like something you'd go for. What's up?"

Linda Lu

"He's rich."

"Rich?"

"Millions."

"He told you that on the Internet? He probably lives in a cardboard box under a bridge."

Linda folded her arms over her chest. "No he doesn't. He's got a mansion and a condo and all kinds of land. An RV too. And a houseboat."

"Wait till he takes you home. You'll have to sleep in his box because the mansion is being used by gypsies and the condo is being refurbished."

"There's still the RV and the boat." Linda laughed.

"The boat's in dry dock and he forgot where he parked the RV."

"That's why God gives you expensive hotel rooms."

"With champagne and caviar." Maureen added to the image.

"And roast pheasant under glass."

Maureen leaned back in her chair and shook her pencil at Linda. "I'll make you a bet. He wants someone to visit in Cleveland so he doesn't have to get a hotel room while he's here. He'll decide he loves your cooking and the two of you will watch TV while your famous chili bubbles on the stove. He'll mooch a night's stay, dinner, and a little nookie. Won't cost him a red cent."

"I'll take that bet. He's already offered to take me with him the next time he comes through in his RV. What do you think about that, girlfriend?"

"I think you're nuts. You've been down this road before. Remember the guy who offered to take you to the Ritz for dinner? You drove across town to meet him the first night he IM'd you. What if he'd been the boogie man instead of a pimply faced teenage boy who couldn't afford an ice cream cone?"

"I'm smarter than that now."

"Uh huh."

"I am. I know Peter. We've become very close. He sent me flowers the other day. I don't know how he knew my real name and my address, but they were gorgeous. Expensive roses."

Maureen startled. "Doesn't it bother you that a total stranger could figure out who you are and where you live?"

"I was flattered that he went to the trouble to find out."

"Oh Linda," Maureen sighed.

Saturday, November 17

Maureen parked beside the A-frame. Linda called to her from the main house across the pond. "Hey, girlfriend!" She hurried across the frosty grass, her hands in the pockets of her parka. Midnight romped ahead of her, yipping in welcome.

"Empty yet?" Maureen waved in greeting. Midnight put his nose to her crotch. "How ya doing, boy?" She pushed him away and gave him a squeaky toy she'd ordered from *PetSmart* online using Morton Minor's new credit card. Waggling his tail, he carried it up the wooden stairs to the deck and plopped down in front of the door to gnaw on it.

"He certainly loves you," Linda said as she gave Maureen a welcoming hug. "And yeah, Sean vacated the premises this morning. I don't know how clean he left it though. You know how guys are."

"I brought some stuff, just in case." Maureen popped the trunk of the Acura and retrieved a cardboard box filled with detergents, furniture wax, mop heads, sponges, and other cleaning supplies. She didn't think there would be much she'd have to do. Old Sean was a pretty clean fellow. She took great pleasure in ordering the products from Quixtar using his credit card though. It seemed right to her after the cavalier way he had treated Linda.

"I've got a big fire going in the cabin. I figured it would warm things up for you." Gesturing towards the smoke coming out of the rock chimney with her head, Linda took the box from Maureen's hands and headed up the steps.

"That was nice of you." Maureen took another box out of the trunk and closed it with her elbow. She noticed that Sean left the garage door open. "After all of these years of living in apartments, I'm excited to have a garage and all this extra storage. I thought about backing the Acura in and unloading all this stuff in there just for the novelty of it, but I was afraid I'd scratch up the car."

"It's not the biggest garage in the world." Linda held the door open for her. "Sean kept it neat because he couldn't get his pickup in there otherwise."

"Well, I'll practice getting in and out of there some other day. By the way, I brought lunch. I thought you might like some of Slyman's corned beef." Midnight picked up his toy and rushed inside just in front of Maureen, almost tripping her in the process.

"I thought I smelled something wonderful. I can't believe you drove all the way down to St. Clair Avenue on your day off just because you knew how much I love it. You are going to have to be careful of Midnight though. He loves Rye Bread and will go after corned beef like a cat after a mouse."

"Not to worry. I thought of that and brought him a sandwich too." Maureen set the box down on the kitchen table. Midnight laid his snout on the table and begged with his eyes.

"Would you look at this place?" Linda spun around in a small circle as she inspected the A-frame. The cottage was spotless. Sean had even mopped the floors before he left. "He wasn't much of a boyfriend, but he'll make someone a wonderful wife."

"Doesn't look like he left us much to do." Maureen opened the kitchen cabinets. They had been wiped down. Not a crumb remained. No little circles where jars of honey or marmalade once sat. No leftover grains of salt or sugar. "What about the bathrooms?"

Linda opened the door to the washroom just off the kitchen. "Gleaming."

"Good. Let's eat." Maureen took the sandwiches out of the box and laid them on the table along with big cups of root beer. "This is enough to give us heartburn for days."

"Chocolate Pie?" Linda picked up a box from out of the carton.

"And Key Lime. I wasn't sure which one you liked."

"Baker's Square? Damn! You know how to throw a picnic." Linda put the two pies in the sparkling clean refrigerator right next to an open box of Arm and Hammer. What twenty-something male living alone kept a house this clean? What was Sean up to? Wiping away fingerprints? Getting rid of evidence? What had she missed about him? Maybe she ought to keep an eye on him after all.

"I imagined we'd be working off the calories but it looks like we'll have to store them in our fat cells."

"Oh good, I hate exercise." Linda opened a sandwich and put it on the floor for Midnight who jumped on it.

"I didn't get him any root beer. I presumed he would prefer water." Maureen carried the other sandwiches to the great room and spread out a picnic on the floor in front of the fire.

"I wouldn't count on that. He likes just about anything wet or sweet." Linda followed her with the drinks in hand.

A weak beam of sunlight broke through the clouds and lit the great room through the huge front windows. "It's beautiful here,

Linda. It reminds me of the house a schoolmate of mine had when I was in college. It was on a lake and you could sit and look out the window at people paddling canoes, kids doing cannonballs off of a little dock, fishermen with strings of tiny bream. They all looked like they were having such fun."

"Didn't you have fun?" Linda bit into her corned beef sandwich.

"I would have, I guess. I didn't like that girl though. She was quite a snob. Acted like she was doing me a big favor to invite me. Her name was Maureen, would you believe."

"NO! Maybe she was uncomfortable having another Maureen around. Sometimes kids don't' like to share things they consider their own. There was another Linda on the cheerleading squad and we hated each other's guts. She could do the splits better than anyone else on the team, but I looked better so I got to be the Homecoming Queen. There I was all dressed up with a rhinestone tiara and a big ribbon pinned to my formal. I looked right at her and waved. Oooh, that got to her. She was so jealous."

Maureen broke off half of her sandwich for Midnight who had eaten his and was begging for more. "Linda was a popular name in the forties and fifties. Lots of Lindas and Marys and Karens. There were two or three of each in my class."

"Names do seem to go in cycles don't they? The people in our parent's generation had Shirleys and Maudes and Deloreses. My mother's name was Pauline," Linda said with her mouth full.

"And in the sixties it was Cynthia and Amanda. A few Sunshines and Rainbows thrown in for good measure during the summer of love." Maureen was only a kid that summer but she thought it was ridiculous. Everyone throwing away their possessions to find themselves.

"Then we got into Kristins and Samanthas. You had to call them that, too. No Krissies or Sammies." Linda made a face. "I had a cousin who insisted we call her child Anastasia even though the kid told everyone her name was Stacey."

Midnight lay down next to Maureen and laid his head in her lap. She stroked his head. "Then it got fancy. Kaitlyn and Brianna. Everyone went Irish there in the eighties."

"Maybe only the Irish were having babies during that decade. Didja ever think of that?" Linda giggled.

"Maybe so," Maureen said, enjoying the warm glow of the fire. "You ready for pie?"

"I'm always ready for pie."

Maureen pushed Midnight off her lap and got to her feet. "A piece of both?"

"Hell, yes. Bring me it on." Linda sat in front of the fire like a cat, flexing and pointing her stockinged feet. "I've often thought that you are trapped by your name. I mean, would I be the same person if my mom had called me Heloise?"

Maureen froze for a moment, staring at the pie in her hand. "Probably not. You'd have a newspaper column about wiping down your front door with vinegar or some such."

"YIKES! Not my thing. Of course, I could see Sean doing that column. What if your mom had named you Susan or Sharon? Don't you think that would have changed your outlook on life?"

Maureen cut them each a tiny piece of the chocolate pie. She once used the name Sharon. In fact, she had used lots of names in the past few years. It didn't change who she was although it sometimes changed how people treated her. The best names for women her age were Sheila and Joanna. They had an upper class ring to them—like Jennifer and Patricia did for women a few years younger. "I don't know. I think a person's experiences might change who they are, but not their names." She carried the dessert plates into the great room.

Linda reached for the pie. "I always wanted to be known as Josephine. When I was a kid, I had a little playmate named

Josephine. I thought it was so much more exotic and romantic than plain old Linda." She stuck her finger into the whipped cream on top the chocolate pie. Midnight sat up on his haunches and whimpered.

"So change it to Josephine. What's the big deal?" Maureen sat down cross-legged in front of the fire.

"See what I mean? That would be hard for a Linda to do. I'm steeped in ordinary. I live two miles from where I was raised. I'm a Clevelander through and through. More important, I'm a west-sider. I live in the same suburb where I went to school. Everyone would think I was crazy if I changed my name to Josephine. I'm stuck in Linda-dom. You are different. You've traveled all your life. You can be any body you want and people will just accept it."

Maureen stared at the fire. She had reinvented herself many times. When it was all over, would she be able to stay one person? Or would she feel compelled to keep changing? Was she doomed to spend the rest of her life moving to new towns, making friends who never really knew her? It was a gloomy thought. "How are things going with you and Peter?" She didn't like talking about herself.

"He sent me a CD today. Some blind Italian tenor. Wasn't that sweet? Every day or so he sends me a present."

"You mean Andrea Bocelli? Do you like him?" Maureen rattled the ice in her root beer and Midnight moaned, begging for a drink.

"It sounds nice. I don't understand a word. Peter says it's very romantic, but how would I know? At least with Sean, the rapsters were speaking English of a sort."

"The bloom is off the rose?"

"Oh no. I like Peter. He has the sweetest voice. Very deep and sexy."

"You gave him your phone number?"

"No, he just called me one day. We've had some long, wonderful conversations. Some nights, I drift off to sleep with his voice in my ear. I feel like I've known him forever. He understands me like no man ever has. Lots better than Charlie ever did. You see, he was betrayed too. His mama was a real bitch. She ran off with a preacher and left him and his daddy to fend for themselves. He's angry, even now. So he knows how it feels to be cheated of something that was supposed to be yours."

Maureen frowned. She couldn't figure out what Peter Good's game was, but she didn't believe he was the god of understanding Linda described. Linda was her friend now. She didn't want some other con sticking his wick in her business. "You be careful. I'd hate to see you get hurt again."

"This is different, Maureen. Peter loves me. He's willing to take care of me. He's even willing to marry me."

"You haven't met him yet. How can you be discussing marriage when you don't have a clue what he looks like?"

"Oh, Maureen. You're acting like Charlie again. Peter's a sweet, innocent soul without a vicious bone in his body. You have to trust my judgment on this one."

Chapter 12—Sean

<u>Friday, November 22</u>

Sean knocked on the window. Jennifer jumped and checked her watch. Eleven o'clock. She'd been sitting outside Danny's Bar for two hours.

"You're in my way." He pointed to his pickup truck. It was covered with a fine layer of snow. "Get outta my way." Jennifer rubbed her eyes.

She must have drifted off. It was getting harder and harder to keep up this schedule.

Sean beat on the hood of the Saturn with his fist. "Come on, Sweetheart! I gotta get home." He swayed back and forth, his breath making fog in front of his face.

Jennifer rolled down the window. "Keep your shirt on. I heard you the first time." She turned the key in the ignition. The Saturn whined, but didn't start.

"Get that thing outta here," Sean growled. He kicked at her bumper, missed, and staggered backwards. "I got a date."

"Lay off, Asshole." She showed him her middle finger. "You touch this car one more time and you'll be on your ass." She tried the Saturn again. It caught. She turned on her windshield wipers to knock off the snow. The defroster blasted cold air on her face.

"It's about time." Sean lurched over to the truck, covering his eyes with his hand to protect them from the glare of Jennifer's headlights.

Jennifer backed out of the lot. She didn't care where the little prick went anymore. She was tired and grouchy. She headed back toward Strongsville.

Her fingers were cold inside her mittens. I could have gotten frostbite, she thought as she wiggled her toes. What did she hope to achieve with Sean? He was out of Linda's life and out of the A-frame. Perhaps it was a case of the devil you know? This Peter sounded worse than Sean to Jennifer.

Lights reflected off the rearview mirror into her eyes. Someone was following too close to her back bumper. The two-lane road glistened with late night frost. She accelerated. The vehicle behind her sped up as well. A loud horn beeped. "You crazy bastard," she muttered to herself. Her wheels slid in the new snow and she hit her brakes. The lights behind her moved to her right towards the ditch, then the driver overcompensated and veered to the left. Sean's pickup truck sped past her before losing traction again and sliding sideways.

Jennifer came to a full stop, watching as the truck spun around two full times before it wrapped around a tree on the left side of the road. The tree broke off and fell against the electrical wires, knocking them to the ground. They writhed and sparked. She could hear the crackling from inside the Saturn twenty yards back from the accident. "Stay inside the truck, Sean. Stay inside," she whispered as she watched the driver's side door opening. She flashed her lights and beeped her horn. Frantically, she rolled down the window. "STAY INSIDE THE TRUCK. THE WIRES ARE DOWN."

Sean squinted into the bright lights. His head was bleeding. He staggered toward the lights, stepping directly on the live wire. Jennifer covered her eyes, screaming inside her head.

Chapter 13—Hinckley
Wednesday, November 27

"This is Linda. I can't come to the phone right now, but your call is important to me. At the beep, please leave a message with your name and number and I'll get back to you when I can."

Dick slammed the receiver onto the base. He'd been leaving messages since Sunday and no answer. Where the hell was that bitch?

First, she put off their meeting. Now she's not answering the phone or his emails. Was she playing with him? He bent down a metal blind and peered out the window.

Oona Barrett's mansion sat on top of the hill like an extravagant version of the Psycho house. He could see the cook through the kitchen window. Her head bobbed. Maybe she was whipping potatoes or something.

Breathing heavily as his excitement grew, he pulled on his jacket and zipped it up. Clenching and unclenching his fists, he thought about creeping up behind the cook, hooking his forearm under her chin and lifting her up off her feet. Oh yeah. Sin. His breath fogged when he opened the door. The chill stopped him.

He couldn't take the cook just because she was there. What the hell was he thinking? He was getting impulsive and that would come back to bite him in the butt, if he didn't watch out. Glancing at the mansion one last time, he turned toward the garage instead.

Most crimes aren't solved. He was living proof of that. Getting caught used to be the last thing on his mind, but things changed in recent years. Now the police collected all kinds of crazy stuff off bodies. Saliva and semen and hair and bite marks. Who knew what part of him lay in some evidence locker somewhere? These days, he made an effort to make sure his girls disappeared forever.

He discovered the Internet in the early-1990s when he bought a computer. The services were expensive then. Almost three dollars a minute. He haunted a chat room called 'Over Forty' where he watched aging divorcees flirt with strangers night after night. Ever so often, the chatters planned a party where they made real passes at each other. That's when he began developing 'the letter.'

The Internet was perfect for his purposes. There was a universe of women out there willing to accept the stories he told them at face value. He pretended to be whatever and whoever they wanted him to be until he got them alone. He chose the time and place. He chose the technique.

As long as he followed the script, the rendezvous went like clockwork. He was never good at adlibbing, not even when he was a young man. Whenever he tried it, there was trouble. Taking Susanna on impulse was a big mistake. He could see that now. He got greedy and careless.

It could have been a catastrophe. The 'letter' was working fine. Why take chances? That meant staying clear of people you knew like Oona Barrett's cook. Nothing drew the police quicker than a murder in your own back yard.

In the garage, he tossed a flashlight, a roll of duct tape and a shovel into the back of the Wrangler. He preferred when they came to him, but he'd already invested time and money in Linda

Knight. No way was she weaseling out now. He rummaged on the workbench for a knife.

In the trunk of the Lincoln, he lifted the carpeting and took out a couple thin pieces of metal. Ohio required a license plate on both the front and rear of the car. He squatted down in front of the Wrangler.

It was mid-afternoon when he pulled onto Route 60 and headed toward the Turnpike. He had a map to Linda's property in Hinckley thanks to Mapquest. She should be alone. Sean moved out of the cottage over the weekend and Maureen wasn't supposed to move in for another two days. He'd cut that black lab's throat if it got in his way. He imagined the fear in Linda's eyes when she woke up to find him looming over her. He'd teach her what it meant to dump him.

Chapter 14 – Moving In

<u>Wednesday, November 27</u>

Jennifer wiped her nose with last year's Kleenex dug out of the pocket of Maureen's heavy winter parka. She packed several boxes of books into the trunk of Maureen's car. It was time to get out of the sour smelling apartment and get some fresh air. No one could sleep all day and all night too.

Sean was dead and there was nothing anyone could do about it. Moving would keep her busy at least. Maureen could bring the bigger stuff using Linda's Trooper this weekend.

The old woman on the fifth floor peeked out her window, watching Jennifer scrape the frost and snow off of the Acura's front window. The nosey old bat probably thought she and Maureen were lesbians. All the more reason for moving out to Hinckley. Going from two apartments to one made sense. It would be cheaper. Easier, too—less running back and forth.

She drove through Hinckley. Turning into the drive headed towards the A-frame, she saw something move in the darkness just beyond the deck. A deer?

Linda's house was dark as expected. When Maureen finally got through to her, Linda said she was going to take the dog over to Charlie's and go visit Sean's mother and father. They were east-siders, so Jennifer didn't expect Linda to be back for several hours.

Her headlights illuminated the cottage at the end of the lane. It still seemed like Sean's home. Wind swept snow across the driveway. The digital thermometer in the console of the Acura informed her that the temperature dropped five degrees since she left Maureen's apartment in Strongsville.

143

Moving In

No way was she going to stand out in the weather unloading the car when she didn't have to. Using the remote, she eased into the garage closing the door behind her. The Acura filled the tiny space. She opened the door gingerly and squeezed out.

Her back to the wall, she side-stepped around the left back fender. Her fingers found a knob. The door opened inward. The storage room echoed back her breathing. The light from the garage pierced a few feet into the darkness. A bicycle hung on one wall and a snow blower sat back in the gloom. She didn't have anything to put in there. She backed out.

Popping the trunk with her key fob, she lifted a box to her shoulder, circled the car and climbed up the wooden stairs to the kitchen on the second floor. She set the carton on the table and flipped on the lights. The cleaning supplies set in the corner where Maureen left them, but a mop had fallen over. She picked up the mop and leaned it against the wall.

She unzipped the over-sized parka from the bottom and took off her gloves. The cottage was beautiful. Nicer than anyplace she had ever lived before. The pine woodwork gleamed. She walked into the great room. Sean's ghost filled the space.

A cool breeze chilled her cheek. Standing in the middle of the braided rug, she looked around—listening. The fire was long dead, but the flue was closed tight. She stuffed her hands into her pockets. The light from the kitchen cast long shadows.

Then she saw it. The door to the deck was ajar. She was sure Maureen locked it the last time she was here. She turned out the kitchen lights and peered through the front window. It was impossible to see if anyone was out there. She stepped onto the deck, looking toward Linda's house. Something flickered deep in the darkness beyond the pond. Then there was nothing. She rubbed her eyes. Maybe the wind blew the door open?

She went back inside the darkened cottage, closing and locking the front door behind her. "Is there anyone here?" There was a tickle in the back of her throat. "I'm going crazy," she said to herself and shrugged.

The house was cold. Squatting in front of the fireplace, she opened the flue, took an artificial log from the stack next to the hearth and lit it with a long match. It caught and a long bluish puff of smoke rose into the chimney. She stared into the flames, fascinated.

In front of her, on the pinewood floor she noticed spots of dirty water reflecting in the dim light. Her own footprints? She rubbed her hands together then held them to the flame. The fine hairs on the back of her neck prickled. She came in through the garage, her feet never got wet!

Someone grabbed the bottom of her parka and pulled it up over her face. Her upper arms were pinned next to her ears with the jacket inside out from her armpits up. "HEY!" she yelled and flailed, trying to pull it off.

Strong hands wrapped around her from behind. "Don't scream and I won't hurt you." A deep voice rasped in her ear.

Terror overwhelmed her and she screamed.

"Shut up, you little bitch!" He hissed. "I'll break your neck and think nothing of it!"

Somehow, she brought herself under control. Fighting back panic, she mumbled through the jacket quilting, "Who are you?"

"Your worst nightmare, little girl." He jerked her backwards, his big arms crushing her chest, the parka bunched up under her chin, her arms high in the air.

The small metal strip between the wooden floor of the great room and the tile of the kitchen raked under her heels. The windows. He didn't want anyone outside the cottage to see what he was going to do to her. That meant he was going to hurt her. Panic took over again.

Moving In

There were windows in the kitchen as well. Even before she heard the door open, she knew he was taking her down to the first level. The garage might be full of car, but the storage room was the perfect place for a rape. Murder too.

She forced herself to think. The man behind her was tall. She could feel his belt buckle pressing between her shoulder blades. She could smell his sweat. She pressed her sneakers against the floor to slow their progress. The rubber soles squeaked against the kitchen tile as the man struggled to get her through the doorway.

"No! NO!" She kicked at his shins with her heels.

"Umph!" He loosened his grip. Taking her chance, she grabbed the doorjamb with both hands through the sleeves of the parka.

He wrapped his arms around her chest and jerked as he went through the door, pulling the jacket down to her waist. The sleeves pulled down below her wrists. She grabbed the doorframe again as soon as her hands were free. She kicked behind her, catching him on the side of the ankle.

He bellowed and hit her in the small of the back with his fist.

The blow shocked and infuriated her. The man pulled on her waist, "Let go or I'll kill you right here. All I have to do is snap your neck."

He was lying or she'd already be dead. She clung to the doorframe, kicking and screaming. The cut between her left thumb and forefinger throbbed. Her pinkie was still sore and she felt it beginning to slip loose. He hit her again, crushing her fingers beneath his fist. She felt the pinkie break. She let go and they both fell down the wooden steps backwards.

She heard a double thud and realized the man's head had hit the front bumper of the Acura, which was less than a yard from the bottom of the stairs, and then the cement floor. She fell on top of him, sinking into his belly. He expelled air from his mouth like the shush of a leaking balloon.

Pulling the parka the rest of the way off her head, she struggled to get up off of him. The pain in her finger was intense. Glad that Maureen's jacket was several sizes too big, Jennifer dropped it beside the wooden staircase.

The garage light had timed out and it was even darker than the kitchen. She pulled herself to her feet, disoriented, and unsure which direction to turn. Feeling for the rough concrete block wall with her hand, she stepped over the man's body and headed toward the garage door.

Damn! She couldn't get out that way. She didn't know where the controls were mounted. She couldn't go back towards the stairs. Her attacker lay there moaning. The thought of another encounter with him made her shrink against the wall. The only way to get away was to drive out.

The remote was inside the car. There was less than two feet between the wall and the Acura. Running her fingers over the front fender, she sidestepped towards the driver's door. Still blind, she found the door handle. It was a tight squeeze. She sucked in her stomach and slid in one leg at a time, pulling the door closed behind her.

She patted the pockets of her jeans looking for the car keys. Nothing. She closed her eyes, imagining them in the right hand pocket of the jacket, which was turned inside out and lying in a dark corner of the garage.

She was going to have to run for it. She fumbled in the console between the front seats trying to find the remote. The man made scratching noises as he regained his senses and tried to get up in the cramped space. The front of the Acura shuddered as he pulled himself to his feet.

"God! Oh God!" Her fingers found a hairbrush, then Maureen's cell phone, then a digital pedometer. "Where is it? Where *is* it?"

Moving In

Cough drops fell on the floor. The man leaned against the front of the car and then started up the stairs to the kitchen.

Using her damaged left hand, she felt the inside door panel until she found the lock. She tried to wait, counting his footsteps as he mounted the stairs. A loud crash. He must have missed a step. "GODDAMNED BITCH!"

She waited, fingers trembling, eager to lock the doors but afraid to alert him to her presence. He stopped moving. She fancied he was listening. She was sure he could hear her respirations. Moments passed.

If he didn't find her on the second floor, maybe he'd leave. Where was he? In the kitchen? Still on the stairs? The silence frightened her. She pulled down on the switch. All four doors locked with a loud thump. Stupid, Jennifer told herself. She held her breath.

The man clambered down the steps and squeezed around the car, pressing his face against the glass trying to see her. "I know you are in there," he said, kicking the side of the car. She wasn't sure he *did* know that, so she remained motionless. He leaned against the wall and put his feet on the side of Maureen's Acura, rocking it. She could just see him when he moved. She cowered in the seat, still feeling around the passenger seat for the remote.

"Open the door."

She refused to answer.

"I know you are in there. You can't get away."

She bit her lip.

"I said get out of there." He kicked the door panel repeatedly. "GET OUT! GET OUT!" The car shuddered.

He stopped. She could feel him outside her window. What was he doing? Thinking? He needed a tool to break into the car, she realized. There was nothing in the garage. No crowbars, no hammers, no screwdrivers—but he didn't know that. The darkness hid everything from him.

Her fingers wrapped around the remote. Relief rushed over her, then anxiety. If she opened the garage, the lights would come on. Easier for her to see him, easier for him to see her. She dry swallowed, unsure what to do.

He was moving. Sliding against the wall, feeling for a light switch, she guessed. He found the open door of the storage room. She heard him inside fumbling for the light.

Were there tools in there? She couldn't remember. It was now or never. She eased herself over to the passenger side of the car and unlocked the door. She paused, listening. He was still in the storage room. She pressed the button.

The overhead light came on and the garage door ground open.

She squeezed out of the car.

"DON'T THINK YOU CAN GET AWAY!" He crashed into something inside the storage room.

Jennifer caught a glimpse of the man — thick sweater, dark down vest, corduroy slacks, knit cap pulled low over the forehead, as he emerged from the storage room.

She ran for the open garage door on one side of the car as he ran for it on the other. The gravel crunched under her feet as she headed towards River Road. The man was close behind her, but she was lighter and faster. She felt him falling behind.

As Jennifer reached a line of trees, she glanced over her shoulder. He was a dark hulk lumbering across the yard. Panic took over and she sprinted through the blackness. She didn't even feel the rock roll under her foot. The fall took her breath away. He was on her before she could move. Two swift blows to the side of her head and she went limp.

Moving In

She lay on her back on the concrete floor of the storage room. Her head ached when she opened her eyes. The man was out of breath. She could hear him wheezing, see the tortured rise and fall of his chest—but she couldn't make out his features. The light from the garage was behind him. He'd removed her shoes.

"Sleeping beauty awakes." He panted as he stripped her left sock off. "This will keep you out of the snow."

Her right heel caught him in the lower belly, her left hit his thigh. He gasped and staggered backwards. She kicked twice more and he fell against the bicycle hanging on the wall. He slid to the floor and the bike fell on top of him. Jennifer jumped to her feet. He lunged for her and she kicked him in the face.

"Argh!" Blood streamed from his nose. She raced out the door, running with one bare foot into the night, heading towards the duck pond. Pain shot through her toes. It was several seconds before she realized that they were just cold. She hid behind a bush, waiting for him to emerge from the A-Frame.

A few seconds later, he rushed past her, muttering to himself. Terror melted into anger. Fury flushed her cheeks and made her forget her aching feet. She wanted to kill him! She stood up, her fists clenched.

He disappeared into the trees beyond Linda's house. She knew where he was going—the small turnaround off River Road several hundred yards from Linda's drive behind the woods. She hobbled back to the cottage, crying out as the icy gravel cut into her sole.

Entering through the garage, she closed the door to the storage room after retrieving her shoes and sock. The keys were in the pocket of Maureen's parka. She disentangled it and put it on. Her one sock was wet. She stripped it off, fuming as she got into the Acura barefooted.

Huge dents and scratches covered the slick silver finish of Maureen's car. The heating system blew cold air at first, then warmer. The garage door was closing behind her as she drove down the lane toward River Road.

There in the distance, she saw a dark-colored Jeep back out of the turnaround a half-mile away. She was almost on him, when the Jeep accelerated. The Acura was a powerful car. She pulled to within a few feet of his back bumper. Ohio plates. She memorized them. He ran a stop sign as River Road dead ended into Center. Turning left, he headed towards the Hinckley Reservation.

"You don't know your way around, do you?" Jennifer murmured. She saw him glance into the rearview mirror as she made the same turn, her headlights reflected off his mirrors.

The Jeep turned left off the side of the road, bouncing over a shallow ditch. It was pitch black out. He disappeared into a frozen cornfield. She slammed on her brakes and backed up. The Jeep lights flickered from time to time in the distance. Every once in a while, she imagined they rose into the air, then sank into the muck.

She lowered her window and screamed into the night, "I hope you break your neck!"

There wasn't much she could do at this point. She was barefoot and her toes were half-frozen. The right side of her face ached from where he'd hit her. Her left hand throbbed.

She was under no illusions that the license plates would be valid. An orange light shaped like a gasoline pump flashed on. The Acura needed fuel. She'd not planned on following anyone tonight, never expected to run into some loony son of a bitch intent on raping her.

She made a u-turn and headed toward Strongsville. She passed Linda on Pearl Avenue coming back from the funeral in Shaker Heights. The Trooper zoomed past. Linda must not have seen the Acura.

Moving In

Should she warn her? She kicked herself. Why did she care about this silly woman? The man was gone now, but still she worried.

Jennifer's anger changed back to fear. Who was he? What did he want? No way was she going back to Hinckley until daylight. Besides, how would she explain being there in the first place? She took out Maureen's cell phone and tapped in Linda's number. No answer. Since Sean's death, Linda hadn't wanted to talk to anyone. Phone mail was full.

"You're on your own, Linda." Jennifer pulled into Maureen's apartment complex and parked under a streetlight. Her sock was still damp. She slipped it on and put on her left shoe. "Yuk!" She wiggled her toes. The right sock and shoe was warm from sitting in front of the car's heater.

Was he a burglar? Was he after Linda? Someone who knew Sean? Thoughts flipped through her mind. What should she do? What could she do? Linda didn't know she existed. All contact had been through Maureen except when she rescued Linda from Bard Bailey. She had to protect the projects.

Looking around her, she got out of the car. The front door was dented. She squatted down, running her fingers along a deep scratch. The bastard! She loved that car. Her left pinkie ached. It had swollen to the size of a frankfurter. The cut below her thumb had reopened during the attack and the bandage was stained. She sighed and went into the building, looking over her shoulder every few steps.

Chapter 15 – Peter Good

Switching to four-wheel drive on the fly, Dick Longren glanced into his rear view mirror as he bounced through the frozen cornfield. The Jeep bucked as he hit some invisible rock. The wheel jerked to the left, wrenching his wrist.

The bluish headlights disappeared in the darkness behind him. Afraid to relax, he kept his foot on the accelerator and the Jeep leapt over a ditch, slamming the crown of his head on the overhead bar, knocking his false teeth loose. He hit the road and skidded sideways.

Who the hell was that wildcat? It wasn't Linda. He had a picture of Linda. She was fleshy and pliable. This woman was all bones and prickles. He touched his upper lip and sniffed. His nose was no longer bleeding but it hurt like hell. He rubbed his scalp. He had a goose egg up there.

Up ahead was a main road. He turned toward Medina. He glanced at the rearview mirror. No blue headlights. He veered right onto Medina Road. No one followed. After several blocks, he pulled over to the berm.

He fished a handkerchief out of his back pocket and blew his nose. Switching on the dome light, he examined himself in the rearview mirror. His nostrils were red-rimmed and bruised, but nothing seemed to be broken. He pushed his teeth back into place and clamped them together with a loud snap. His bladder was full. He held his knees close together.

The girl was downright vicious. Not even Grady the Janitor was so heartless. In all his years in this business, he'd never run into someone like that. He remembered the way Sheila struggled weakly before giving in to him, soft and submissive. Now *that* was a woman!

The pressure was intense. He put the Jeep in gear. Not too much further, near the crossroads of Ohio 18 and 42, he found a coffee shop. Two identical Harley Davidson motorcycles gleamed under the neon lights out front. He parked beside them. Stepping inside the shop, warmth encased him like a hug. However, his nose was crusty and he couldn't enjoy the comforting smell of brewed coffee.

He nodded to the clerk. "Do you have a public john?"

The young man wore his hair straight up like Bart Simpson. Popping his gum, he pointed to the right. "You are going to have a cup, aren't you?"

"I promise." Dick headed toward the bathroom.

"Really, man. You can't just come in here to take a leak." The boy put his hands on his hips.

"I'll drink a whole damn pot, okay?"

"I'm putting a menu on that table for you."

"Fine." Annoyed, Dick pushed open the swinging door. A muscular man in a tight t-shirt and black leather pants stood in front of the urinal. His balding head shone pink under the yellow lights. He glanced over his shoulder at Dick who hurried to a second urinal to relieve his aching bladder.

"Looks like you're going to have a couple of shiners there, buddy." The man zipped his leather pants.

"It hurts." Dick tried to keep the whine out of his voice as he shook himself dry and tucked his penis back inside his shorts.

"A woman?" The man's immense biceps rippled as he washed his hands in the sink next to Dick. He turned to the blower and pressed the start button with his elbow.

"It's always a woman." Dick splashed cold water on his burning nose.

"They never know what they want. They give you the come on, then when you get going, they put up a stop sign." The man rubbed his hands together under the noisy blower. He had a slight lisp so that 'stop sign' came out 'thop thign.'

"Things have changed over the years. Not for the better if you ask me." Dick looked around, his hands in the air, water streaming down his cheeks.

"Having a problem?" The man slipped on a thick leather jacket, which had been thrown over the top of the stall doors.

"No towels!" He had no intention of bending down and putting his head under the blowers. "Can you believe this place? They expect you to buy something, but they don't even provide you with a damn towel." It had been a long frustrating day and Dick had a three-hour drive in front of him.

"Hold on, buddy. I'll get you some napkins." The burly man sauntered out the door, the chains on his jacket clinking.

Dick looked at himself in the mirror, pressing his upper and lower dentures together. He pulled his lips back to check the seal. It was one hell of an evening. He'd tried and missed before—that was part of the game. When he was hunting in the early years, he missed as many as he caught. However, he'd never had one try to hurt him before.

"Here ya go." The man brought him a sheaf of napkins. "At least they buy good quality, thick ones."

Dick was taken aback by the fierce-looking fellow's friendliness. "Thank you." He patted his bruised face with the napkins and wiped his hands dry.

"My name's Bo Janus." The biker offered his hand. His smile was glittery with a shiny gold cap on his right front incisor. "Would you like to join me and my brother for an espresso?" It came out 'ethpretho.' This was the kind of fellow Dick expected to run into in a noisy bar, not the men's room of a coffee shop.

Dick squared his shoulders, trying to appear taller. "I'm Peter Good." He shook Bo's hand. The grip was soft and amiable. Something wasn't quite right about Bo's eyes. Dick stared until he realized he was being rude. "I can't stay too long, but I'd love a cup of coffee and a quick sandwich." Bo was not the kind of man Dick wanted to offend.

"Come on, then. My brother's waiting." Bo slapped Dick on the back. Dick smiled without showing his teeth, wondering why Bo was being so nice to him.

The heels on Bo's black boots scuffed against the linoleum as he strutted into the coffee shop. A skinny gray braid dangled over his collar. Dick thought maybe he'd grow one too. Maybe he'd buy a hog. He never tried a biker identity before.

Another man in leathers sat at a corner table facing away from them. Two identical black helmets sat on the floor beside him. A long silver ponytail hung down his back and he was balding in the exact same place as his brother, Dick noticed.

"Derek, this is Peter Good. I invited him to sit with us."

"Fantastic." Derek turned around with a wide grin on his face.

"Wow." Dick's jaw dropped and his eyes widened.

"Don't stand there and gawk, have a seat." Derek pulled out a wrought iron chair and patted the seat. He had a gold cap on his left front incisor.

"Everyone's surprised when they first see us." Bo laughed.

"I'm sorry. I didn't expect it." Dick's upper plate wiggled when he spoke. He felt the server's anxious eyes on his back and sat down.

"I'm the evil twin." Derek twirled his long white moustache, his eyes twinkling. "Old Bo was Mama's favorite."

"How did she ever know which one of you was Bo?"

"He's left and I'm right." Bo turned his chair around and straddled it, his chin on the back.

"What?"

"We're mirror images of each other." Derek pointed to his left eye. It was green. Bo's right eye was green.

So that's what was different about Bo, Dick thought. He'd once tried to kill a girl with eyes like that—one blue, one green. He looked from one brother to the other. Their gold teeth glowed in the fluorescent lighting of the shop. "Bo and Derek aren't really your names, are they?"

"Hell no, man. Our mom named us Simon and Noah when we were born, but we dropped the biblical when we bought our first Harleys. Who ever heard of bikers with names like that?" Bo gestured to Bart Simpson to bring them menus. A blue snake tattoo wound around his right forearm. Dick glanced at Derek. Sure enough, the same serpent curled the opposite way up his left.

"I guess so." Dick accepted the menu printed out on red construction paper. "But what did your mom think?"

Derek tapped a long nail on the chicken sandwich. Bart Simpson nodded and wrote it down. His hair didn't even bounce. "Stella? She thought it was a hoot. She likes that skinny little actress. She still calls us Simon and Noah though." Derek's lisp wasn't as pronounced as Bo's but he still had trouble with his esses.

"Mothers are like that," Dick said. "I'll have the tuna please and the Spiced Mocha."

"Tomato Bisque and Coconut Mocha." Bo patted his lean belly. "Have to watch my girlish figure."

The server frowned. Not expensive enough, Dick guessed. "What about you? Anything to drink?"

157

Peter Good

"How about some iced chai?"

"Tough guys." The boy muttered under his breath as he headed back for the counter.

Bo and Derek slapped their palms together in a noisy high-five. "Why do you suppose he thinks tough guys don't drink chai?" Derek's good humor was infectious, but Dick was still cautious. Strangers didn't invite you to have dinner with them for no reason.

"People are never what they appear to be," Dick said rubbing his left wrist. Driving the Jeep cross-country aggravated his arthritis. Not that he had a choice this time.

"No, they never are. You for example appear to be a wealthy man—dressed well, clever, middle classed—but something tells me that's not all you are."

Dick squirmed in his seat. His eyes darted around the small coffee shop looking for John Walsh or the Feds. "I'm nothing, nobody."

"So tell me, Mr. Nobody. What the hell happened to your face?" Derek leaned back in his chair, his thick forearms crossed over his chest, his white eyebrows making a sharp V over his nose.

"The love of a good woman, bro," Bo said.

"What did she do? Hit you between the eyes with a frying pan?" Derek inspected Dick's wounds, cocking his head first one way and then the other.

"Something like that." Dick wished Bart Simpson would bring the food.

"We've had our share of women problems. Isn't that so, Bo?"

Bo took a breath as if the story he was about to tell was painful. "My ex-wife used to beat the shit out of me every Saturday night and twice on Sunday. Itty-bitty gal, too. Had some temper, that one."

"Did you hit her back?"

"Stella would never stand for us beating up on women." Derek rolled his eyes.

Dick enjoyed the way his cock throbbed when he hit a woman, his fist sinking into soft flesh. "What happened to her?"

"She ran off with the milkman. Probably beating up on him as we speak." Bo rubbed his palms together as Bart Simpson served them their drinks. "It does set you back on your tail though. Took me a long time to get back into the game again."

"Really?" Dick sat up straight in his chair, interested. "How long before you felt better?"

"Couple months before I tried again. Couple years before it worked again." Dick imagined Bo's poor little incapacitated wienie. Two years was a long time to do without.

"Old Bo was in love with that little firecracker. I told him right from the beginning that she was no good for him, but he couldn't see it." Derek sipped his chai.

"That's right. I should have listened, but I had my heart set on her. I'd think I was ready to let go and turn over a new leaf, then I'd get to thinking about her—get to wanting her, before you know it I was on my way back home. Fact is, I never did leave her. She left me."

Dick nodded. "I keep thinking I'm going to turn over a new leaf, but it never works out. I get itchy and that makes me do stupid things. Today was stupid. I flat out jumped the gun. I knew I should have waited."

"Shot your wad, did you?" A small dimple appeared near the corner of Derek's mouth when he smirked.

"What? No, nothing like that." Dick couldn't stop looking at the twins. He sniffed. Burnt chocolate. Who were these guys? Demons? He shuddered. Was he losing his grip again?

Derek laid his arm on the back of Dick's chair and leaned over to whisper in his ear. "They don't like that, Big Pete. You go off ahead of them, it pisses them off."

"Your sandwiches." Bart Simpson set the plates down in front of them. "Your soup." The bisque sloshed over the edge of the bowl onto Bo's placemat. "Anything else?"

"Check with us later, boy." Bo growled and Bart backed away. "Kids today." He dipped his spoon into the soup, holding his pinkie in the air.

"Course, I didn't do much better." Derek patted his chest with the tips of his fingers. "I got in with a married woman. She said she was going to leave her man and come with me. I had visions of her riding behind me on the Harley, heading into the sunset, like that Meatloaf video. Then one day, she turns up pregnant and won't even come play anymore. Everything's for that kid now. Broke my heart."

Derek's sordid confession amused Dick. "It's best not to go in half-cocked. If you got a plan, stick to it," Dick lectured them, shaking his finger. "You give into those feelings and anything can happen. You get careless and you end up like this." He pointed to his own misshapen nose.

"I don't know that I ever planned to fall in love." Bo slurped his soup. "I just see someone and know I have to have her. It's too late to plan anything then."

Dick bit into his tuna sandwich and chewed. "There's such a thing as getting greedy."

"Greedy? Wanting more than your share?" Derek slapped the table with the palm of his hand, sloshing Bo's soup again. "Are you one of those perverts who takes two or three at a time?"

Dick thought about the dorm in Fayetteville, his mouth full. He'd done twelve that night. Or was it eight? He couldn't remember for sure.

Bo thumped him on the bicep with his fist. "Is that right, Pete? You one of those perverts?"

He swallowed his tuna, grateful it gave him time to think of a worthy come back. "Only if I'm lucky, Bo. Only if I'm lucky."

They all laughed. "It's hard enough for me to catch one, let alone multiples," Derek said. "But if it ever came my way, I'd sure as hell not turn it down."

"Me neither, bro."

"You fellows done here?" Bart Simpson hovered around them, picking up Dick's plate the moment he ate the last potato chip.

"I dunno. I think maybe I might go for one of your great big banana splits." Bo winked at Dick. "Soup for the abs, ice cream for the soul."

"I'll have strawberry cheesecake and more chai." Derek gave Dick's shoulder an intimate little squeeze.

"How about you? Dessert?" Bart Simpson turned to Dick, his pencil posed over the pad.

Dick wanted to go home and fall asleep. "None for me. I've got to get on the road. Just bring me my check."

"No, no. You don't have to do that, buddy. Bo and I'll take care of the check." Derek shook the chair again. Dick's teeth rattled inside his mouth.

"I can't ask that of you." Dick reached for his wallet.

"I said, we'll take care of it." Derek's blue eye froze Dick in his tracks.

Dick burped. "Uh, thank you. I appreciate it." He got to his feet wondering if they were going to rough him up for the chance to buy his dinner.

"No problem, Peter. We enjoyed jawing with you." The twins pushed back their chairs. Derek stepped forward to pump his hand, then Bo.

Dick zipped up his down vest and pulled the knit cap over his ears. "Hope to see you all soon," he said as he hurried out of the shop. They waved to him, their gold incisors glowing. Bart Simpson wiped down the counter, scowling.

Dick unlocked the Wrangler and crawled in. Who picks up someone in the men's room and buys him dinner? Maybe when there have always been two of you, you never feel vulnerable. You always have your brother to back your play. He'd never had anyone except Buddy and that wasn't the same thing.

He turned on the light and studied the map. He could see the twins through the front window of the coffee shop, eating their ice cream. They were downright spooky. He wanted to get away from them. Starting the Jeep, he drove south on 42 heading toward Massillon where he hoped to find the Ohio Turnpike.

It was late—already eleven o'clock. His body ached. The abortive attempt to find Linda was stupid. The frantic search of the main house had turned up no clue as to what happened to her. He'd wandered down to the A-Frame only because there was a light in the loft. He'd thought maybe Linda was cleaning for her new tenant.

When she stopped answering his emails, he'd spent the better part of a week dreaming about her. She was like fudge—soft and gooey and made just for him. Masturbation didn't satisfy the deeper hunger. He needed to take her out before she got away from him.

When he found the cottage was empty as well, the disappointment was bitter. He turned out the light in the loft and sat down on the top step of the spiral staircase. Should he go on back to Pittsburgh? Should he find someone else? Maybe he should just sit and wait until Linda came home.

It was all taken out of his hands when he saw blue headlights drive up the lane. It was a gift, a freebie, he thought as he watched the tiny woman go out onto the deck, squinting into the darkness.

People are never what they appear to be. The skinny witch nearly killed him.

He put on a CD. Andrea Bocelli's voice filled the Jeep. He fantasized as he drove east toward Pittsburgh. He dreamed he'd done the skinny one and laid her out on the bed in the A-frame and then waited until Linda came home. Ah!

Two men on big motorcycles blew past him on the Turnpike. The noise made him jump and he twisted the steering wheel sharply to the right. His wheels hit the grooves dug into the berm. He felt the vibrations deep in his testicles. He corrected and pulled back into the right lane. Were the Biker Twins following him? Were they waiting up ahead? Did John Walsh send them?

An hour later, he came to the toll turnstiles near the state line. They were brand new. A couple years back, they had been rammed by a semi that burst into flames. He braked as he approached. Pulling into the one on the far right, he handed the woman his ticket.

"Four-fifty," she said, yawning. It was approaching two am.

He braced his feet and lifted up his buttocks to get to the wallet in his back pocket. The pocket was empty. He patted the seat under him. Nothing. He felt queasy. He tried the breast pockets inside his vest. What could he have done with it? The woman in the tollbooth tapped her purple fingernail on the cash register. "I'm looking for my wallet," he told her. She pointed to a parking area just the other side of the booth and closed the sliding window. He pulled around under a streetlight.

He found his flashlight and got out of the car. He checked under the front seats. He couldn't imagine the wallet in the backseat, but he checked there as well. He patted his buttocks once again and his chest. Then it dawned on him.

The evil biker twins from hell! That's why they bought him dinner. They picked his pocket. They probably paid for it with HIS money. "Son of a Bitch!" He kicked the front tire. The bastards sweet talked him and stole his money. He paced back and forth, furious at his own gullibility. It was fundamental—people aren't nice. He'd learned that when he was five. STUPID!

"Do you have the toll or not?" A trooper pulled up beside him in his cruiser.

"Someone stole my wallet."

"I heard that one before."

"A set of biker twins."

"Right."

"Forget it."

"Got the toll or not?" The man put the car in park and switched off the engine, frowning.

"I got the damned toll. That's not the point." Dick was furious. There was close to four hundred dollars in that wallet. It was a long day and his teeth were loose. He got his ass kicked by a broad and now two middle-aged goons in leather robbed him. All he wanted now was to go home.

"Pardon my saying this, but show me the money." The trooper held out his palm.

"Very funny." Dick opened the glove compartment where he kept a twenty-dollar bill, just in case.

"You want change?" The trooper was young.

"Hell, yes. I want change." He still had to pay tolls in Pennsylvania.

"Stay right here then." The cop turned on his heel and strode over to the first booth, chatting with the woman inside.

Dick slammed the glove compartment, trying to remember what all was in that wallet besides money. No credit cards this trip, thank goodness. Which ID was he carrying? He couldn't remember. He'd told the twins his name was Peter Good. That should confuse things enough to keep them off his back. None of his IDs led back to his real address. He sighed. Not too much harm done. Let the Bobbsey Twins have the damned money.

The trooper returned with his change. "Drive carefully, sir, and don't try that wallet shit again. Just pay the toll."

"Right."

Dick got back into the Jeep and headed toward the next row of tollbooths where he picked up a new ticket. Fog clouded the road in front of him. He slowed, keeping a close eye out for deer. "Shit!" He thumped the steering wheel. What if the biker twins hadn't stolen his wallet? What if he'd lost it at Linda's house? What if that bitch who attacked him had it? He pulled to the side of the road, sweating.

It didn't matter. It was the same whether it was the psycho biker twins or a psycho bitch. It was just money. No one could trace the ID. Two deer trotted across the highway in front of him.

He grinned. His good luck was returning. If he'd been driving normal speed, he would have hit them. It's okay, he told himself as he pulled back onto the turnpike and accelerated.

"Shit!" He slammed on the brakes again. It *did* matter. Fingerprints. He wore gloves when he was inside those houses, but the wallet had been handled barehanded for months. What should he do? Go back? No, that would be even more stupid than the rest of this endless day. He thought for a long time. There was nothing he could do but pray that the twins were busy counting his money—and if it was in one of Linda's houses? He prayed it wasn't. He pulled back onto the highway. A huge eighteen-wheeler hurtled by, shaking the Jeep and startling him. He was sure Buddy was driving it. He snapped his jaws and growled.

Chapter 16 – Starting Over
<u>Monday, December 2</u>

Maureen pulled into the parking lot of the post office on Pearl Road next to a black Beemer. Taking out a large ring with dozens of tiny keys, she flipped through them until she found one marked '3342." Iliana Minor Johnson's passport was in P.O. Box 3342. She slit the envelope with her fingernail and opened the small blue leatherette book. She smiled at her own photo. She looked fresh and pretty. The red wig and green contacts flattered her pale features. It was almost time to become Iliana. Jennifer's experience at the cottage the other night was proof of that. Maureen was more than ready to move on.

She tucked the envelope into her bag and squatted. Her bulk made it difficult to check the mailboxes on the lower level. P.O. Box 2800 was empty. She sighed. Mark Stevenson's so-called sister was still waiting for *First Life* to pay off. Maureen didn't want to leave Cleveland until that money was deposited in her Swiss Bank account. Off balance, she struggled to stand.

"Here ya go." A tall man held out his hand to help her.

Maureen startled with recognition. It was Kyle, the hunk who attended Jennifer's aerobics class every week. "Thanks," she said, lowering the timber of her voice as she put her hand into his.

"You look familiar. Have we met?" He asked as he pulled her upright. His eyes drifted downwards to her enormous bosom, a flirty grin on his lips.

Maureen straightened her clothes, shuttering her eyes behind the thick glasses. "I don't think so." Jennifer had thought Kyle was sexy, that he was attracted to her. What a laugh! He's a pig like the rest of them, Maureen thought. She lifted her bag over her shoulder and started for the door.

Kyle put his hand on her elbow as they went out the glass doors. "You live in Strongsville? We must have run into each other before somewhere."

"No, we haven't." She jerked her arm away and headed toward the Acura. He was a pushy pig too!

She felt him close behind her, too close. "Don't get bent of out shape, ma'am. I didn't mean to upset you. I love older women!"

Stung, she spun around, her fists clenched. "Look. I don't know you. I don't WANT to know you, okay?" She unlocked the Acura using her key fob.

He stepped back, his hands open in a mocking peace gesture, smiling the smile of a man who knew he was attractive. "What the hell happened to your door?" He appraised the damage. "Looks like someone kicked the hell out of it."

His deep raspy voice chilled her. Was he the one? She got into the car and locked the doors. Kyle tapped on the window. "Look, I have a good man who can fix that for you." He held a business card against the window. It said, "Kyle Parker, 440-729-STUD."

Maureen put the car in reverse and backed out of the space. Kyle stood in the parking lot, laughing as she drove off.

Carrying a large pepperoni pizza, Maureen climbed the back stairs and knocked on the kitchen door.

"What the hell did you do to your hand?" Linda wore jeans and a ratty sweatshirt. There were circles under her eyes.

"Closed it in the car door!" Maureen set the food on the counter and took off her parka. She wrinkled her nose. Dishes were stacked in a sink of souring water. The garbage can was overflowing. Without thinking, Maureen tossed wadded up sandwich wrappers and greasy napkins into a red and white chicken box.

"Just leave it." Linda wore huge fluffy house shoes shaped like gorilla faces. "Charlie still has Midnight." She scuffed into the living room. The drapes were open and the cottage was framed by the picture window.

Maureen followed her, picking up a half-empty soda can off the floor beside the rocker and collecting old newspapers off the coffee table. "Don't you want something to eat?"

"Eventually." A pillow lay against the arm of the couch. Linda sat cross-legged on the middle cushion, covering her legs with a blanket.

Maureen couldn't put it off any longer. "I'm sorry about Sean, Linda. I'm sorry I've waited this long to come see you too."

"That's okay. I wasn't here anyway." She picked at her chipped fingernail polish. "He wasn't my boyfriend, you know. It's funny. I don't know what we were. Once in a while sex partners? Friends? Landlord-tenant?"

"He was a nice boy." Maureen stood by the couch. Linda stared out the window without speaking. A single tear trickled down her cheek. Maureen looked away. When she stole a peek a few minutes later, Linda was still crying. Turning back to the kitchen, Maureen found a plastic bag under the sink and focused on cleaning up the trash.

Linda was lying on the couch when Maureen finished. "That was nice of you."

"No problem. I like to keep busy."

"No. I mean about Sean being a nice boy."

Maureen sat in the rocker. It squeaked when she leaned back. "His folks okay?"

Starting Over

"I don't think so, but I don't know them very well."

"When are you coming back to work?"

"Tomorrow. That's all the vacation time I have. Besides, it's all over now."

"That's good."

Linda turned her head on the pillow and stared out the window. It was snowing again. "You may have guessed this, but Sean reminded me of Charlie when we were young. It was like going back in time—at least sexually. Charlie was so into being a cop. That's why I spent my nights alone back then. Sean, well Sean didn't see any reason to spend time with me at all unless he found himself without a date."

"I'm sure Sean thought you were great."

Linda's laugh was a short bark. "You think?"

"He was young and insensitive."

"I used him. I think that's what makes me feel so bad. When the sex was over, I bitched at him for not coming over more often. I bitched about his other women. The truth be known, there was nothing to talk about once we put our clothes on. Bitching filled in the long silences. He absorbed my anger at Charlie until he had enough. Then he'd leave. I never once thanked him for giving me a small piece of himself once in awhile."

"There's nothing you can do about that now." Maureen rocked back and forth in the chair. She did understand. Kind of.

"That's just it, Maureen. I'm sorry Sean is dead and I'm sorry I wasn't nicer to him when he was alive, but not *that* sorry. I've been laying here thinking about that. I'm just upset that I won't have someone to bitch at because I'm lonely or horny or sad. I hate what I've become."

Maureen turned to look out the window too. "Everyone is sad and lonely and horny. You don't own that monopoly."

"Not you. You seem to have it all together. You have goals. You take care of yourself. I noticed that the first time we met. You know who you are. Me, I haven't felt like myself since Charlie left. I never wanted to have a career. I was the kind of girl who wanted to grow up and have a husband and babies. Charlie and I had fun when we were first married. The babies never came along though. Maybe they would have, but you have to have sex to get pregnant. I was mad at Charlie and I held out on him. I held out for years. I thought that we would have babies when I got through punishing him. It floored me when he told me he was leaving. I had been a good girl. I wasn't the one who sinned. He should be making it up to me. I remember standing at the door watching him pack his clothes in his car. I couldn't believe it."

"So what are you going to do now?" Maureen squirmed in her seat. The snow would make it difficult getting back to Strongsville. She wondered how she was going to extricate herself from this conversation and get out of there.

Linda pulled sheet after sheet of tissues from a Kleenex box sitting on the coffee table. "I'm going to change. I decided that just before you got here. I'm going to work on myself—maybe take some classes, maybe take up a hobby. I'm going to focus on being interesting." She blew her nose, tossed the used tissue into a waste paper can near the couch, and sat up. "I'm not going to be so needy that I torment the people I'm with and I'm going to be more selective."

"Good for you." Maureen stood up. "You will be happier."

"It's going to be hard for me. My mother used to read me fairy tales about a charming prince who rescued you from bad guys and made you happy forever after." She pulled more tissues out of the box.

"It never happens that way. That's why they are fairy tales." Maureen laughed and headed for the kitchen to fetch her parka.

171

Starting Over

"So I see. It's beginning to piss me off." Linda stuffed her tissues into the front pocket of her jeans.

"Is it still okay that I borrow your truck this weekend? I've only got a few big things left to move and I banged up my car the other day."

"Can you do me a couple of favors at the same time?" Linda scuffed to the kitchen. Maureen had put all the dishes in the dishwasher and wiped down the sink with something piney. Linda filled a glass with tap water, drank it down and refilled it. "Damn, crying makes me thirsty." She gulped down the rest of the water.

"Sure, what do you want me to do?"

"First off, I'm meeting my friend Peter Good this weekend. If you would give me a lift to the mall, I'd appreciate it."

"He's meeting you at the mall?" Maureen raised one eyebrow.

"He's coming through town with an RV. It's easier to park them in big parking lots."

"Are you sure about this guy?" Maureen wondered just how different the changed Linda was from the old one.

"Oh Maureen, he's wonderful. He listens to me and understands. He was worried because I wasn't online or answering the phone the last few days. I told him about losing Sean and he was so kind. He's coming to see me to take my mind off this tragedy."

"Oh, he is?" The idea both alarmed and annoyed Maureen. "What do you know about him? Did you check him out? Is he who he says he is?"

Linda's nose was as red as her eyes. "It's about time I learned to trust again, don't you think?"

"Oh Linda!"

Linda put her arms around Maureen and kissed her cheek. "You are a grand friend. Thanks for caring about me. I'm a grown woman, it's about time I act like one."

"Okay, okay." Maureen patted Linda's back. "I'll shut up about the gentlemanly Peter Good. What else did you want me to do?"

"I'll be gone all weekend. Don't give me that look." Linda shook her finger at Maureen. "If you would go get Midnight from Charlie's house and bring him home after you are through moving, I'd appreciate it. He's been over there since the morning I found out about Sean. I don't want him getting too used to staying with Charlie."

"You got it. What time do you want me to come pick you up?"

"How about around six on Friday evening?"

"Sounds good. I'm going to leave another couple boxes of things at the cottage. Is there anything I can do tonight before I go?"

Linda caught Maureen's hand and pointed to the swollen pinkie. "One thing. Will you get this finger set?"

"It's not that bad." Maureen winced and held the hand against her chest.

"It's going to heal crooked if you don't do something now. Go down to the clinic on Pearl. They are open all night. Won't take long."

It had been a long time since anyone cared about her. "Yes, Mother." Maureen laughed. "I'll go take care of it after I leave off this load."

"This is going to be fun," Linda said as she walked Maureen to the door.

"What?"

"Being neighbors."

Starting Over

Maureen drove out Linda's driveway, turned right on River Road and then turned right onto the lane leading to the A-frame. She opened the garage door and drove in, looking around, her stomach tight. She checked the storage room, before she lowered the garage door. She put the remote in one pocket of her parka, the car keys in the other. It fit her much better than it did Jennifer.

She wandered through the second level, flipping on lights in the kitchen and in the great room. She examined the locks on the front door. The deck was snowy. No recent footprints. Her heart thudded as she climbed the spiral staircase. The closets were empty. No one in the loft. She turned sideways to get down the stairs, her wide hips throwing her balance off.

Two small lamps on either side of the bed provided dim light in the bedroom. She checked the wardrobe and the bathroom. A box of new bathroom accessories sat beside the commode. Brand new towels and sheets filled the linen closet. That was thoughtful of Linda given everything else she had on her mind. Some of Maureen's clothes hung in the walk-in closet between the bathroom and the bedroom. Jennifer's were there too—and their shoes.

Maureen wandered back into the great room. She had already unloaded the books. They sat on the pine bookcases either side of the stone fireplace. She sank into the large sofa across from the mantel, her legs stretched out in front of her. Closing her eyes, she breathed in the smell of wood and tile and cleaning products.

Funny. It comforted her knowing that Linda was nearby. She hadn't used any of the credit cards she'd taken out in Linda's name. She wasn't sure why. It just didn't feel right.

She opened her eyes. It was the first time she had a place to display her books in years. "My word," she muttered to herself as she got up. "I haven't seen that in a while." She crossed the room and stood on tiptoe, hooking the bottom of its binding with her fingernail to pull it out.

It was her eighth grade yearbook. She sat back down on the couch, holding it in her lap. It opened naturally to the page with her photo. She was such an ugly little thing—frizzy hair, blue plastic framed glasses, braces. Of course, there were thirty-three other pictures of funny looking children. The eye was drawn to any one of them, but not her. She was invisible even then.

She paged through. There she was in math class, an intense little girl focused on her geometry teacher. A photo in the back showed her onstage, singing. She had been so excited about the chance to sing a solo. Her mother paid for a singing coach to prepare her. It didn't matter that her voice was thin and shrill. They both had visions of her ending up on stage at the Metropolitan. She even made her own costume—something faintly Germanic. That was before the boys started giving her the business. Opera was not popular among middle class kids in the early 1960s.

She ran her fingers over the picture. Nothing had turned out like she thought it would. There was Jennifer on her horse. The little bitch never did let her ride it. Maureen was there too, already beautiful. They had never been friends no matter how hard she'd tried. Her lips twitched.

The cabin creaked. She tensed, listening. Was he coming back? Who could he be? Maybe it was one of the men at work? She took a big breath and pushed those thoughts from her mind. It was time to get back to the old apartment. She closed the book and replaced it on the shelf.

Friday, December 6

Friday was a beautiful day, but it was already dark by the time she got out to Hinckley. She stuck her sunglasses in the holder over the windshield and parked the Acura in the garage at the A-frame. The frozen grass crackled under her sneakers as she trekked across the land between the two houses.

Linda came out on the porch and tossed Maureen the keys to the Trooper. "I'll be there in a minute." She wore her hair down, soft around her face. The make-up had been toned down—light lipstick, a touch of mascara. Her long skirt, belted knit over-blouse and boots were simple and elegant. This must be the look required by the mysterious Peter Good. She went back inside the house, the storm door slamming behind her.

Maureen unlocked the Trooper as she walked toward it. It was a strange looking beast—square, boxy and tall. She opened the smaller door on the hatch and set her bag in the rear compartment. Several boxes of Linda's things sat in a far corner.

She climbed in behind the wheel and felt around for the seat adjustment, raising and lowering it to find the right position. She was playing with the mirrors when Linda came out wearing a long down-filled coat.

"I thought you'd have the truck all warmed up by now." Linda teased as she crawled into the passenger seat. She was a bit taller than Maureen, but she had trouble getting into the tall vehicle too.

"It took me this long to find the radio." Maureen laughed as she stuck the key in the ignition.

"You know, you can start the truck using the remote if you want."

The engine roared to life. Maureen put the car in reverse and backed into the turnaround. "Other than the fact that it's cool, why would you want to start this thing remotely?" Changing to drive, she pushed down on the accelerator and threw gravel, jerking Linda's head back.

"Sheesh! You're going to break my neck before I get a chance to meet my Prince Charming." Linda gripped the handle mounted on the side of the car above the door window. "You might want to turn it on in the mornings while you are drinking your coffee.

That way all the windows are defrosted and the seats are warm when you get in."

"Sounds like a good way to get it stolen if you ask me." Maureen scanned the dashboard, over-steering so that the truck veered first too far to the right, then too far to the left.

"My God, girlfriend. Relax, it's not that hard to drive."

"It feels strange." Maureen hit the brakes too hard. "Where are the lights?"

"There." Linda pointed.

"Great." Maureen flipped them on and spun out as she turned onto River Road. "I'm so high up I feel like I'm going to tip forward when we go downhill."

"Being up high is the point. You can see everything. Besides, no one's going to mess with you in a truck like this. People will cut you off in a smaller vehicle. They don't dare when they see you coming in something this macho." Linda patted the dash.

They headed toward Hinckley. Maureen wasn't sure she was going to get used to the different feel of the Trooper compared to her Acura. "Where is he going to meet you?" Maureen felt the vibrations from the road through the steering wheel.

"Food Court."

"How will you know him?"

"I won't. He'll know me."

"My God, Linda. What if he's not what you think? What will you do? Have you thought of that?"

"I'll call you to come get me. I have my cell phone." Linda patted the pocket of her coat.

"Do you have your mad money?"

"Twenty bucks tucked into my bra."

Starting Over

"You know how to get away from him if he tries to jump you?"

"Kick him in the balls."

"You have some pepper spray?"

"Good heavens, Maureen. I'm going to meet a sweet old man, not Jack the Ripper. Don't worry."

Maureen drove into the entrance road and circled the mall. Finding the right entrance, she pulled up to the curb. "You will be careful?"

Linda squeezed Maureen's hand. "Not to worry. I'll be fine."

"Have fun." It was hard for Maureen to be sincere about that.

"A simple weekend of drugs, sex, and rock and roll."

"Take pictures."

Linda waved as Maureen drove off in the Trooper.

Maureen wasn't sure she knew which house belonged to Charlie. He sometimes slept in an apartment in Strongsville with his woman friend and her children, but he stayed home when he was dog sitting. The new girlfriend didn't like Midnight.

Maureen pulled into the paved driveway of a huge house. The yard was small but well groomed. Unlike the cracker box styles of the houses around it, the house looked like maybe Charlie had designed it himself. She remembered that Linda told her Charlie loved building things. He and his uncle had built the A-frame when he was a teenager.

She left the truck running, got out and approached the door. It was oak and stained glass, oddly feminine for a man living alone. Midnight barked when she rang the doorbell. A handsome man opened the door. The foyer was large—a big chandelier, hardwood floors, curving stairway to the top floors. Midnight rushed out, knocking her backwards in his enthusiasm.

178

"You must be Maureen." Charlie held the door open for her to enter.

"Thanks, but I can't stay. The truck's running."

"Well, hold on then. Let me gather up Midnight's toys."

Maureen hooked the fingers of her right hand under the dog's chain collar. "Come on, boy. Let's get you in the truck." She herded him toward the passenger side of the Trooper.

"He loves going for a ride." Charlie carried a big box of doggie goodies to the back of the truck. "He'll want some of these. I took him shopping the other day and bought him new things. This will protect your shoes and nylons." Charlie's eyes sparkled with life and energy. He was one of those rare folks that Maureen liked on sight.

"We'll have a good time," she said.

"I'm sure you will."

Maureen didn't know what else to say. Charlie's good looks made her nervous. She got back into the truck. "I'll take good care of him."

"I don't doubt that for a minute." He stuck his hands in the pockets of his trousers. He seemed to be studying her. She lowered her eyes. He looked like a bulldog. If he got interested in something, she was sure he'd never let go. Good quality for a detective but it was disconcerting.

"Good bye!" She wiggled her fingers at him and backed out of his driveway.

Midnight barked. Charlie watched as she drove off. It wasn't until she got to Hinckley that she realized he hadn't asked her about Linda.

Chapter 17 -- The Jeep
<u>Saturday, December 7</u>

Dick was flying. The small aches and pains he had endured over the last few weeks quieted. He spun the steering wheel full to the left, then to the right. The wheels skimmed over the ruts and leapt over potholes filled with crusty water. The sun glittered through the bare trees as he raced through the forest toward the summit.

He wound around the mountain. Up and up and up. Near the top, a small parking lot preceded a picnic area crowded with tables and grills. Huge pine trees stretched towards the sky and shaded the graveled area. No one came up here this time of year. It was his special place and it was good to be back.

He pressed the accelerator to the floor. Bouncing over a rotted log, he raced through the trees dodging tables, broken saplings, and large rocks. The lookout appeared in his windshield. He pushed a moment longer before braking. The Jeep skidded to within inches of the small wooden barrier.

He sat for a moment, panting. The land spread out below him and he was the master of it all. He left the door open. The music swelled, the meaning of the Italian words didn't matter. That's why he liked it so much. It could mean anything he wanted it to mean.

Balancing on the barrier just above the cliff, he turned his face toward the sky -- stretching his arms over his head palms up.

"AAAAAAAAAAAAAAAAAAAAAAAAAAAAAHHHHHHHHHH HHHHHHHHHHHHHOOOOOOOOOOOOOOOOOOOOOOOO!!!!!!! !!!!!" A wordless howl of joy. Feral. He was back—strong and virile. Endorphins raced through his body. "FUCK YOU, JOHN WALSH!"

Sunday, December 8

He reached home before dark. The massive six-car garage on the estate used to be a stable. It was warm inside. He parked over the drain. Getting out of the car, he put his palms on the front fender and leaned forward in a modified push up. He'd been driving for hours. Soreness was setting in. He stretched and then moaned, clutching his back. JESUS! He ripped off his down vest and threw it in a corner.

Mud covered the Jeep. Gravel stuck in the treads of the tires. Yawning, he found the utility vac and plugged it in. Pulling back the ragtop, he vacuumed the front seats keeping an eye out for hair and other debris.

The panties were on the floor on the passenger side. He rubbed them against his cheek before sticking them in the pocket of his trousers. The backseat and the carpets were stored. He had no need for them in his line of work. Bits of plastic lay scattered near the hatch. A dirty shovel was propped upside down behind the driver's seat.

He collected the knife and stowed it behind a loose stone near the sink. Dots of blood or mud covered the first garbage bag on the roll. He shredded the bag with his teeth and nails and stuffed it in the garbage can near the workbench.

He unplugged the vac and put it away. The hose was stored on a reel. Tugging on it, he rolled the cart closer to the car and turned on the water. Mud and grit dissolved and swirled into the drain. Grunting, he pulled the plugs in the floor and sprayed the inside of the car. Tiny bits of dirt and hair washed out of the cracks. He squirted lemon scented dishwashing detergent into the floorboards. Soapy water drained out of the open holes onto the stable floor. The final rinse was steaming hot. The Jeep sparkled.

The Jeep

It was 10:30 before he finished. Standing in the doorway of the garage, he reflected on his weekend. He left the woman's clothes in a dumpster behind a strip mall in Brecksville. Her purse went in a garbage can near a paved trail in the Metroparks. He dropped her wallet, minus money, ID, and credit cards, in a library near Twinsburg.

She'd been a heavy woman. It was a struggle getting her in and out of the back of the Jeep. Even so, she was delightful. It had been a long time coming.

Leaving his muddy shoes on the back porch, he carried the digital camera and the roll of plastic bags into the house and set them on the counter. His fingers were stiff. He pressed against each knuckle, enjoying the loud satisfying pop. She'd pulled on his sleeve when she was losing consciousness and tore it under the arm. He cut it into strips with a pair of long skinny-bladed scissors. The pieces went into a plastic garbage bag he kept in the cabinet under the kitchen sink.

The high-powered showerhead shot hot water onto his skin. He opened his mouth and stuck out his tongue. He soaped under his testicles, shampooed his thinning hair, and rinsed grit from the lines in his neck. Something dark was stuck under all ten fingernails. He scrubbed them with a stiff bristled brush. The water turned brownish below his feet before swirling down the drain.

He stood in the steamy bathroom rubbing his skin with a rough towel. He swabbed his ears with a Q-Tip and trimmed the hair in his nostrils with the same scissors that he'd used to cut up his shirt.

Removing his teeth, he set them to soak. It was then that he saw the redness on his cheek. He leaned forward to peer into the magnified mirror. Three parallel scratches, fairly deep. It was nothing. He pretended to shoot at himself in the temple with a finger gun, farting loudly. His toothless grin stretched across his face like a bloodless wound.

USERNAME

Falling backwards on his bed, he stared at the ceiling. The plaster pattern formed a picture of John Walsh's face.

"You aren't going to catch me," he said out loud. Rolling over onto his side, he pulled the covers up over his shoulders. He felt safe and secure for the first time in weeks. Sleep took him softly.

Chapter 18—Missing

<u>Sunday, December 8</u>

"What the hell does she see in this truck?" Maureen said to Midnight as they started down a steep hill. He wagged his tail. A sharp curve appeared. She pumped the brakes, throwing them both forward then pressing them back in their seats. She was too far to the right and the front tire caught the edge of pavement. Midnight slid off the passenger seat into the foot well, whimpering.

She twisted to look behind her on the winding two-lane highway, easing forward on the berm. A car swept over the rise less than one hundred yards behind her. "Damnit!" She slammed on the brakes again. The wind from the passing vehicle rattled her windows. Midnight looked up at her with enormous pleading eyes. "I'm trying, boy! It's like driving a refrigerator box."

She pulled back onto the road. The SUV was heavier, slower to accelerate. She missed the surge of power she got from the Acura. A delivery van came over the rise. The driver beeped his horn and swerved into the left lane, ducking back in behind the Trooper when a Toyota full of habited nuns appeared in the opposite direction.

"Sunday drivers!" Maureen pressed the pedal to the floor. Midnight yelped and cringed under the dash. The tires squealed and left black marks on the pavement.

The van nosed up close to her back bumper, whipping out onto the passing lane as soon as the way was clear.

She slowed as the irate driver mouthed profanities at her. "What's a big truck like that doing on a back road like this anyway?" She shouted out the window.

Trembling she turned onto River Road. "That's IT!" She told Midnight who had scrambled back up onto the seat. "We're putting this thing away as soon as we unload it."

Just before the driveway to the big house, they turned into the tree-lined lane leading to the A-frame. Backing up to the deck stairs, Maureen leaned over and opened the passenger side door. Midnight jumped out of the Trooper and dashed toward the ducks that were clustered together towards the far bank of the half frozen pond. Barking, he bounded down to the water's edge, stopping short of getting his feet wet.

Maureen slid down out of the high truck seat, keeping an amused eye on the playful dog. She tramped around to the back of the truck and pulled open the two doors. "What are you doing? It's not like this is the first time you ever saw ducks!"

Midnight ran around the pond and disappeared behind the cabin. She took a box full of peripherals out of the Trooper. The dog came full circle behind her and nipped at her thighs as she climbed the stairs to the deck. She danced away from him, giggling. She was afraid he was going to get a tooth caught in the thick padding of her girdle, but he did make her laugh.

Aside from Midnight being good company, Maureen felt safer with the big dog on the property. He wouldn't harm a fly, but he barked at anything that moved in the dark. No one would be able to sneak up on her with him around.

It took less than an hour to unload the last of her computer equipment. She came out onto the deck. Midnight snored beside the front door. She tromped down the steps and got into the Trooper. There was one last carton in the back of the truck filled with some of Linda's things.

Maureen shook her head. That kind of thing invited thieves. Someone needed to scare her, she thought. Explain the ways of the world. She'd have another little talk with Linda when she got home—tell her about what had happened to Jennifer right here in the A-frame. She wasn't sure how she was going to explain Jennifer to Linda, but after all, they were neighbors now, living on the same property. An eye to security would keep them both safer.

Before she could start the engine, Midnight woke with a start and begged to go with her. "I'm not going that far."

He jumped up and put his front paws on the door. "Oh for God's sake, crawl in." She sighed and opened the back door. He crept over the front console to take his place beside her, his tongue dangling out the side of his mouth. She scratched his ears before turning the key.

She drove around to Linda's driveway and pulled the truck into the garage under the big house. It was dusty and half filled with boxes. She went into the house. Midnight rushed past her and disappeared into Linda's bedroom.

"Come on, boy. Let's go." She slapped her thigh and made kissing sounds. When the dog didn't come right away, Maureen went searching for him. He had found a rawhide bone and was lying at the foot of Linda's unmade bed gnawing on it. A large bouquet of dead flowers sat on the nightstand. A small card said, 'Your secret admirer, Peter.'

Maureen picked up the vase, intent on throwing the flowers away. Linda would never understand. She wasn't sure she understood herself. Men came and went in Linda's life. This one raised Maureen's hackles. He frightened her too. Perhaps because she couldn't figure out his angle and she was sure he had one.

Jennifer followed the others to find out their habits. Maureen reviewed their personal records. She knew everything about them. Peter Good was anonymous, out of reach. That implied he had something to hide.

She picked up the card and turned it over. Nothing on the back. She re-positioned it where Linda left it. "You don't know who you are dealing with, Mr. Good," she muttered to herself.

Midnight lifted his head at her words. "Bring it with you. We got to get out of here. She'll be home soon and it would piss her off if she found us here." She picked up the bone and shook it. He grabbed it and they engaged in a brief game of 'tug of war.'

"Think you can outdo me, do ya?" She wrestled the bone away from him and took it into the kitchen.

Midnight growled and scampered about, squeezing past her as she held the backdoor for him. Yipping, he crouched on his front legs, his rear end wagging back and forth with his tail. She tossed the bone out into the brown winter grass. He chased down the steps and into the backyard. She walked across the drive headed for the pond. Midnight caught up to her, carrying the toy in his mouth.

"Let's go get dinner," she said.

Monday, December 9

Maureen leaned back in her chair. Small envelopes flickered across the screen of her monitor. The computer growled. The compact disc recorder hummed. She was stealing records from a credit agency. It looked like it would be a gold mine of personal information. No longer would she have to send out fake surveys to email lists gleaned from Internet profiles.

She eyed the clock in the lower right hand corner of her monitor. It was after eleven and Linda hadn't come to see her. She'd worked at *First Life* for two years. Almost every day, Linda showed up at ten-fifteen to fill her ear with new problems and adventures.

Missing

Maureen was disappointed and hurt, almost like a spurned lover. She thought Linda would want to talk about her date. Had this asshole been so wonderful that Linda forgot her friends? She stared at the screen waiting for the phone to ring.

Maybe they had an accident or something delayed them. Maureen chewed on a hangnail and checked the clock again. She picked up the phone and called Linda. Last Friday's message. She tried the house in Hinckley. The machine picked up. Linda's husky voice urged the caller to leave a name and number.

Maureen went back to work. Even though she planned to pull up stakes and move on to a new life very soon, the database might come in handy as a backup. You never knew when circumstances would change. She selected more records. The CD whirled in its case.

How well did she know Linda, she wondered. Would she stay away without telling anyone? It was strange, but was it that strange? Linda was hungry for love of any kind. Sex was a tonic to her. What if Peter Good was her Prince Charming? Would she find the courage to break away and come home? Would she even want to?

Then again, what if Peter Good was the devil? Her throat went dry. She swallowed twice. What if Linda wasn't coming back? She squeezed her eyes shut, imagining Linda being scared or hurt. She leaned forward, pressing her forehead against the edge of her desk and dabbing at her upper lip with a Kleenex.

The huge brassiere cut into her ribs. Her glasses irritated the bridge of her nose and left little red marks. She took them off. I don't care, she said to herself. I don't care, I don't care, I don't care. It was a mantra.

The computer finished its sequence and the mechanical sounds ceased. Maureen sat up. What if Peter Good wasn't what he appeared to be? Could he be the one at the cottage? If so, what was he looking for?

Maybe he was using Linda to get to her. Was he one of her projects? If so, how did he find out about the scams? She was positive no one could trace anything back to her. Or could he? She shivered at the thought.

She slammed her fist down on her mouse pad. "Ouch!" Pain shot through the bandaged finger. She'd still not found her way to the Doc in the Box. Her finger would be crooked just like Linda said.

Such thoughts made her crazy. It was lunchtime. She put on her parka and mittens. The new knit pants Jennifer stole at the mall bunched around her thighs. Her legs whispered against each other as she walked. She was half-way to the Terminal Tower when she stopped in the middle of the sidewalk. "The cops!"

People swirled around her, their noses red and running in the freezing air. No one seemed to notice her standing there. She was as invisible as a pigeon pecking at garbage on the sidewalk. Pedestrians stepped to one side and continued on their way, lost inside their own lives.

"The cops," she said again. Snowflakes floated down, lightly touching the statues near Public Square. Deep in thought, she crossed against traffic, horns blaring around her.

What if Linda never came back? After a few days, Bill Casey would call her family. After enough time passed, her parents would call the cops — and then, they would come out to the place in Hinckley. When that happened, her life was going to change.

Christmas decorations filled the store windows inside Tower City. She stopped to stare at the faceless mannequins in a shop window. They'd go through Linda's house first. Her fingerprints were on the vase in the bedroom. What an idiot she was!

The Trooper was parked in Linda's garage! Charlie had seen her driving the truck on Friday. Sooner or later, they would talk to him. How much had Linda told him about her? Someone goes missing. About the same time, he sees someone else driving her car. That would make anyone suspicious.

She rode the escalator to the food court. It was a noisy blur. Business people did business on their lunch hours, women with children shopped, high school kids played hooky. A couple of uniformed cops sat at a table by the windows overlooking the Cuyahoga, munching on gyros. She turned her back to them, hoping they hadn't seen her.

Would the Hinckley authorities handle the case? Or would they call in Cleveland detectives? Didn't matter, someone was going to be all over Linda's activities. Anything unusual was going to draw a lot of attention. She was going to have to dismantle her operation as it pertained to Linda.

It would be easy enough to cancel credit cards and close bank accounts. She could shred the passport and other documents, cut up the cards and the half dozen driver's licenses for different states. The public records had to be changed before the authorities got suspicious. That made her nervous. It meant hacking into the Motor Vehicles Database again. Not a trace could remain. Her fist curled inside the mitten, the pinkie aching. The bastard, she'd get him for this.

The movie theater beckoned—cool anonymous darkness. She bought a ticket for *The Lord of the Rings*. It was vaguely familiar. Back in college, the original Maureen wore a button that said, 'Frodo lives!' She was intrigued, but she never got around to reading the book. The auditorium was empty except for a middle-aged couple making out in the back row.

She found a seat, took off her parka and covered herself with it. When she picked up Midnight on Friday evening, Charlie never asked any questions. He just helped her get the dog into the SUV.

The cops would find that damned black and silver truck with the vanity plates, 'MIDNITE' in Linda's garage. Then they'd talk to Charlie and then they'd come to her. It went through her mind again and again, an endless circle. There didn't seem to be anything she could do about it.

She should leave. Dump Jennifer and leave, but she couldn't do that. There were too many outstanding issues with the targets. There were over a dozen post office boxes awaiting checks, birth certificates, credit cards, death certificates and passports. It would take awhile to make other arrangements. One never left money on the table. She needed time.

It came to her as the main feature began. She'd hide the truck! Yeah, that would work. She'd hide the truck and tell them that Linda drove off to meet someone on Saturday instead of Friday night. If no one found the Trooper, then why wouldn't they believe her?

There were some new rental garages over on St. Clair. She'd drive the damn thing into Cleveland, hide it in a leased storage unit and then take a bus out to Strongsville. The bus stopped not far from Jennifer's apartment. She'd pick up the Saturn and drive it out to Hinckley.

Mid way through the movie, she got up. She couldn't wait until Bill Casey got worried about Linda not showing up for work. She needed to get rid of the Trooper right away. How would she explain being gone? In the lobby, she took out her cell phone and tapped in Bill's telephone number, ready to plead a migraine. His phone mail picked up. She ended the call without leaving a message.

She hurried out into a snowstorm. Traffic slowed to a crawl. Buses circled the square. City workers had already salted the sidewalk. The Acura sat in a lot not far from Jacobs Field. She stamped her feet and rubbed her hands together while the attendant labored to free it from the enormous maze of snow-covered cars. The dented door brought back the rage. She'd get whoever did that too, she thought as she got in.

Missing

It was around 2:00 PM when she eased onto East Ninth Street. Hoping Linda had come home, she dialed the Hinckley house again. She hadn't. Maureen's nose burned like she was going to cry. 'I don't care, I don't care, I don't care," she chanted through clenched jaws. I-71 South was icy. Snowplows were doing their best, but it took two hours to get to Hinckley.

She parked in the garage under the A-frame and hurried up the steps to fetch the Trooper's keys, which were hanging on a hook in the kitchen. She thumbed through the file of credit cards and IDs, selecting one and pocketing it.

Midnight was glad to see her, jumping up to put his paws on her shoulders. "I guess you would like to go for a quick walk, wouldn't you?"

The snow was ankle deep in the yards connecting the two houses. Midnight ran towards the woods the other side of Linda's driveway, lifting his leg against a tree before disappearing into the thicket of trees.

Maureen unlocked the backdoor and stepped into the kitchen, leaving wet footprints on the linoleum. She sighed and slipped off her shoes. Hurrying to Linda's bedroom, she collected the flowers and the card. What to do with them? She couldn't just throw them in the trash.

In the kitchen, she drained a cup of brownish water from the bottom of the vase into the sink. She set everything down on the table and retrieved a towel from a drawer under the counter. It was hard for Maureen to squat so she got down on all fours to wipe up the water she'd tracked into the house. This excess bulk had to go. No matter what she was doing, it got in the way.

She slipped the card into her parka pocket, picked up her shoes and the vase of dried out flowers. She turned on the lights in the garage without opening the door. Using the remote on the key fob, she started the Trooper. "Cool," she said out loud. She made a note to get a remote ignition on the next car she bought.

The truck's engine roared in the small confined space. She set the vase in the luggage compartment behind the backseat. The vibrations from the motor caused it to fall over on its side. The dry flowers crumbled and left tiny flecks in the carpeting.

She pulled the carton of Linda's stuff closer to her and moved things around, making room for the vase. There in the bottom of the box was Linda's laptop computer. "My God, Linda! You are nuts!" Maureen couldn't imagine anyone being so careless with a computer. Pulling it out of the box along with a power supply and a box of disks, she set the vase against the inside corner of the box and propped a big flashlight against it.

She got into the truck and opened the garage door using the remote. Backing out into the snow, she felt around on the console looking for the windshield wipers and the defroster. It was already getting dark. She pressed a button and the passenger side window whined open. "MIDNIGHT! Come on, Boy! Let's go home!"

A distant bark answered deep in the woods. She opened the door. He rushed up to the truck, ears flopping, and crawled in, soaking wet. Once inside, he shook himself from head to toe, splattering Maureen and the inside of the truck with icy water.

"Hey!" She held her arms over her face. "Cut it out, boy."

The dog curled up on the seat and looked up at her.

What would happen to Midnight if Linda never came back, she wondered? Linda loved this big goofy character. Maureen teared up. "Looks like it might be just you and me now. Would you like that?" She put her arm around Midnight. He was wet, but she didn't care.

She closed the garage door and backed into the turnaround. The drive was treacherous. Centering the truck between the two rows of trees that lined the narrow lane, she headed for River Road.

Missing

Back at the A-frame, she had to pull Midnight out of the truck. The Trooper was warm and he was reluctant to jump down into the cold snow. She picked up Linda's computer and grabbed Midnight's collar. He resisted and she had to drag him up the steps and into the great room.

Once inside the house, Midnight headed for his doggie bed and curled up, eager to finish his nap. Maureen filled his food dish and refreshed his water. With weather like this, she had no idea how long it would take her to get downtown and back. She didn't want to leave the laptop where someone could find it. In the bedroom, she slid it under her mattress.

Wednesday, December 11

"Three days. Not a phone call or email. It's not like her." Bill Casey scratched his blonde buzz.

"I thought she'd be back by now." Maureen sat in his client chair, a notepad in her lap. Bill's office was noticeably messier.

"You don't think something happened to her, do you?"

"She's an adult, Bill. She has a right to go out on a date."

"Did you meet this Mr. Right of hers?"

She shook her head.

"No, I thought not. She never even mentioned him to me and you know how Linda is, she tells everyone when she gets a pimple. Nothing is private as far as she's concerned."

"It is strange. She left Midnight with me. You know how she loves that dog. You'd think she'd be back for him."

"Maybe her mother knows where she is." Bill thumbed through a brass Rolodex, the cards flipping through his thick fingers.

"Maybe." Maureen had grown increasingly depressed by Linda's absence. Bill's concern made her feel guilty but she wasn't sure why. She folded her hands in her lap, wincing.

Saturday, December 14

"Do you remember me? I'm Linda's ex-husband." Charlie's eyes were electric. He stood at the door, bundled up in a double-breasted navy P-coat. His jeans were wet to the knee from his hike across the lawn from the main house.

Midnight barked and jumped into Charlie's arms, licking his face. "Hello, Boy! How are you, buddy?" He staggered under the weight of the wiggling animal.

"Hello, it's good to see you." Maureen covered her nervousness with a wide smile. "Come on in, I have a fresh pot of coffee and some Krispy Kremes I picked up this morning."

"Thank you, ma'am. Let me get these boots off before I go tracking gunk through your nice clean house." Charlie set the dog down inside the door. Peeling off his boots, he set them on a rack outside the door on the deck.

She never realized what the rack was for. Totally familiar and comfortable with his surroundings, Charlie stepped into the great room in his stocking feet. The cottage was his more than hers, Maureen realized as she took his P-coat, scarf and cap.

"You look half-frozen. Why don't you have a seat in front of the fire and warm yourself?"

"Looks wonderful!" Charlie squatted in front of the hearth. He removed the screen and jostled the logs with a poker. "Feels great, too." He added another piece of wood and sat cross-legged on the rug in front of the fireplace. Midnight lay down beside him, his chin on Charlie's knee.

Missing

Maureen frowned as she watched them together. She'd come to think of Midnight as her dog over the last week. It hadn't occurred to her that Charlie might claim him. She hung Charlie's damp things in the kitchen. She set mugs on the table, sugar cubes and a carton of Hazelnut creamer. "Please, let's have some coffee." There was a tickle in the back of her throat. She thought sure she might have a coughing fit if he didn't say something to her soon.

"It's been a long morning. That coffee smells like heaven." Charlie got up and wandered into the kitchen.

"The cold weather makes me want to stay inside all day, curled up in front of the fire with a good book." Maureen poured coffee into Charlie's mug. "I don't have any regular cream, but this stuff is great. Makes plain old coffee taste exotic." I'm blabbering, she thought. Don't act nervous or he'll be suspicious.

"Terrific, I'll try some." Charlie scratched Midnight's ears with his toe.

"I'm afraid I don't have much of a selection. The Krispy Kremes all have maple icing. That's my favorite. My dad used to buy them for me." She opened the box and held it out to him.

He picked out two and laid them on the plate in front of him. "I'm guessing you know why I'm here." He had a way of searching a person's eyes.

"Linda?"

"Have you seen her?" He bit into the donut.

"Not since last weekend. Is there something wrong?"

"Her parents are worried. They haven't heard from her in two weeks. They live in Florida, you know. They called me to come check."

"That's nice of you."

"We may be divorced but she still means a lot to me." His voice was low and sincere. Maureen was surprised. She'd been under

196

the impression that Charlie and Linda were no longer close, their conversations restricted to matters concerning the property and Midnight.

"She lent me her truck so I could move. I picked up Midnight last Friday, as you know." Why did she say that? It sounded so practiced. "Anyway, she wanted it back because she had a date on Saturday."

"She didn't say where she was going?"

"No, I'm afraid not. I just know her from work. We thought we'd get to know each other better once I got moved in, you know."

"You should have called."

She was startled. "Why?"

"I would have come for Midnight. I'm sure he's been a handful."

"Oh, no. It's okay. We've had fun. I didn't have your telephone number. I wouldn't have called in any case though. I keep thinking she'll be home soon."

"You were worried about her?" He narrowed his eyes. She squirmed in her seat.

"Not worried so much. I didn't know if she goes off like this once in a while or what. She's a grownup, after all. I just wondered where she was."

"Linda is as naïve as a child. She thinks everyone is as harmless as she is. I worry about her sometimes. Her parents do too, especially her dad. He was my mentor when I was a rookie. We are still good friends."

"I didn't know that." There were a lot of things she didn't know about Linda, it seemed.

"What about your friend? Does she know Linda?"

Maureen startled. "My friend?"

"That pretty young thing I saw shoveling your lane this morning?"

"Oh, you mean Jennifer."

"Does Jennifer know Linda?"

"I don't think so."

"Does Jennifer live here too?"

Maureen didn't know what to say. There was only one person on the lease. Would Charlie know that? Did he have access to the lease? She better not lie, she decided. "Uh, Jennifer is a friend of mine. She came out to have dinner with me last night and it was so bad she decided to spend the night." She felt like she was talking too fast, stumbling over her words.

"Where is she now?"

"She was chilled through. She said she was going to take a shower to warm up."

"Funny, I don't hear the shower. The pipes rattle, you know. I haven't gotten around to fixing them."

Maureen laughed. "Yes, they do rattle. She must have finished showering by now. She's taking her time getting dressed."

Charlie finished his coffee. "Tell you what. I'm going to go check out the property. Make sure everything is okay. I bet old Midnight would like a good run, wouldn't you, boy?" Midnight's tail thumped against the floor. "Anyway, I'll come back in a few minutes and maybe I can catch Jennifer then."

"Okay. I'll tell her." Maureen collected Charlie's things and gave them to him.

"It was nice getting to know you a little, Maureen. Linda spoke so highly of you."

"She did?" Maureen wrung her hands, thinking about her original plans for Linda.

"Oh yes, she said you were her best friend." Charlie put on his jacket.

"That was nice of her."

"That's Linda. She's a real nice girl."

She stood at the window watching Charlie and Midnight tromp through the snow. What was she going to do? She didn't doubt that he'd hang around until he got a chance to talk with Jennifer.

She went back to the bedroom. She'd have to do the only thing she could do. Give him Jennifer. The dark brown wig went on the head form sitting on her dresser. She took off her glasses, rubbing her nose. Popping the dark brown contacts out of her eyes and putting them in the solution, she used cold cream to remove the heavy makeup.

The big over blouse came off next and the knit pants. She stood in front of the mirror in her underwear. Peeling off the padded girdle, which gave her Maureen's heavy buttocks and thick thighs, she began to feel more like herself. She removed the huge brassiere and the enormous prosthetic breasts. The soft plastic adhered to her skin when she sweated and it was always a relief when she took them off.

No time for a shower, she dusted her flesh with talcum and put on Jennifer's jog bra, jeans and sweater. Without the extra padding and Maureen's dark eyebrows, she looked like a different person. She found the blue contact lenses for Jennifer's persona. The light brown hair cut short, easy on the makeup. She sat on the bed and pulled on Jennifer's heavy socks and snow boots.

Charlie and Midnight were hiking through the woods, just visible through the trees. She slipped on her jacket, hat and mittens. The mittens were important. Charlie had seen Maureen's hands. It would never do for him to realize both of them had a broken pinkie finger. "Good morning, Charlie." The voice was too similar to Maureen's. She tried again, higher. "Good morning, Charlie." It was the best she could do. A risk she'd never take if she had a choice.

She tromped through the snow, following their footsteps. Midnight raced out to meet her. She never could fool Midnight. "Don't mess this up for me," she said under her breath. Charlie saw her and waved. She waved back as she approached him. "Good morning, Charlie," she said.

Chapter 19 – The Letter

Saturday, January 4, 2001

Maureen missed Linda. She missed Midnight even more. She sat cross-legged on the couch with Linda's computer in her lap. Her head dropped forward to rest on her chin and she snored, the warmth of the fireplace enveloping her.

She was exhausted. In the weeks since Linda disappeared, she'd made arrangements for her exit from Cleveland. Given the circumstances, she decided to leave the Maureen identity behind.

She had several new backup identities to choose from — Miriam Gorman, Iliana Johnson, Mark Stevenson. Disguises wouldn't be as necessary where she was going. She'd never been there before. No one would recognize her.

After the initial kick she got out of turning the socially snobbish, very slim, very pretty Maureen Tippleton into an obese middle aged woman, the outfit was hot, bulky and uncomfortable. She was eager to get rid of it. The real Maureen was dead after all. It didn't matter anymore.

Jennifer Bright, on the other hand, still had some life in her credit history. She was a very fashion conscious woman even now. In the time that Maureen used Jennifer's IDs, her disguise was minimal—just enough to protect herself if she ran into someone from Cleveland who remembered her first visit.

After thumbing through a few magazines, she went shopping for her next look. A bright red acrylic wig. Black-framed square-lensed glasses like the real Jennifer wore. She bought emerald green contacts and high fashion makeup. It was nice to wear designer clothes after so many months of plus sized fashions.

Money was not a problem, but she couldn't bring herself to waste it. She didn't want to quit her job until the very last minute. She made a good salary and had amassed a month's worth of vacation. Jennifer's earnings weren't as significant. She needed her time for other things so she submitted Jennifer's resignation at the dance school the week after Linda went missing.

The IM bell rang. "Hey Doll, what's up?" HotToddy asked.

Maureen jerked awake. This was the first evening she had time to check out Linda's Internet account. She went through her financial spreadsheets, her small collection of photos and her various folders, but there were still hundreds of new and old emails to go through. She'd drifted off after the first few, which were mostly spam.

HotToddy wasn't on Linda's Buddy List. Maureen checked HotToddy's profile. A bisexual actress in Chicago with a husband and three children. Loves sewing.

"Have we met?" Maureen typed into the answer box of the IM and hit SEND.

"Not yet. I saw your profile and thought maybe we'd hit it off," HotToddy answered.

"Not interested," Maureen typed.

HotToddy was insulted. "Fine."

Maureen yawned and scrolled through the latest emails. It was going to take forever to get through them all. There were fifty-six offers for products to make Linda's penis longer. Out of curiosity, Maureen clicked on the link. They were selling penile weights. She giggled at the image of a naked man walking around the house with weights tied to his genitals.

There were dozens of queries about home businesses. Most were variations on multi-level marketing. Deleting those items plus the pornography ads, Maureen cleared out the mailbox well enough to see what remained.

Linda belonged to several groups having to do with romance. Could one of the people participating in these groups be Peter

Good? Maureen read some of the emails. Filled with loneliness and hunger, none of the comments were from Linda. She was a lurker. She signed up for a user group, received the emails, probably read them all, but never commented or provided others with information about her life and interests.

Given Linda's eagerness to talk, Maureen was surprised. She would have thought Linda would be sharing her life with everyone in the group. It was, of course, dangerous to do such a thing. Maureen lurked several groups herself searching for wealthy older people. Folks provided scam artists with an abundance of material without realizing it.

She created a database file and added a record for each person who participated in the groups and for anyone who sent Linda an email in the weeks before her disappearance. She created a field to differentiate these people from the ones Linda seemed to know in some capacity.

She decided to sort first by username and then by date going from earliest communications to latest. There were about twenty different names — people who populated Linda's online life.

Linda communicated with her father in Florida almost every day until the Friday she disappeared. Maureen read their emails with a sense of sadness. Her own father and mother died when she was in high school. She remembered them with fondness, but it was hard for her to imagine what it would be like to know them as an adult. Linda's dad gave her advice about the plumbing, talked about his Aunt Mim who was in a nursing home, congratulated her on the purchase of the Trooper.

Linda also exchanged emails with several men including Charlie and Sean. She loaded them into her database, adding a field to identify email communicators. She'd check them all out starting with their emails to Linda and their profiles. People leave all kinds of clues as to their real identities. Sometimes they even provide

The Letter

you with specific information like where they lived or their telephone numbers.

It didn't appear that Linda logged her Instant Message conversations. That was too bad. You could pick up a lot there because people got involved in conversation and let down their guards.

She could do a cross-reference of the forty or so names Linda kept on her Buddy List. She created a field in her database that said "Buddy List (Y/N)." There were only a few who had not communicated with Linda via email. Maureen added those names to the database.

Then she went to Linda's address book. This provided her with a lot more information on some of the names. JohnnyT449 was also John Tompkins. His telephone number was 614-449-5538. There was no street address, but Maureen recognized the 614 area code as Columbus, Ohio.

She added fields for real name, address, city, state and telephone number to the database. After thinking about it for a minute, she added a memo field, then a field identifying gender and another for family members.

The IM box lit up again. MurrayBigCock asked her if she wanted to see teenagers having sex with farm animals. She closed the message without answering.

It took a couple of hours to fill the database from all those sources. She ended up with ninety-three records. She had full information on six of them—Charlie, Linda's parents, Bill Casey and two women. None of these people were high on Maureen's list of suspects. However, there were forty-two records with telephone numbers. Some would be cell phones, but she should be able to get addresses from the rest. If nothing else, she could identify the city and state from the area codes.

Maureen was concentrating on collecting data when she heard the distinctive sound of a door opening. That was the signal that someone on your Buddy List had logged on. It slammed shut before she had a chance to see who it was. She checked Linda's Buddy List. The box had one entry: (The Lone Wolf). The parentheses meant someone with the username of The Lone Wolf had logged on and off. People did that all the time, it didn't mean anything. She went back to work.

It was after midnight when she made her first query—those records that were male, not family, was on the Buddy List and had sent Linda email. Ten names appeared. The Lone Wolf was one of them. "Hmmmm," she said to herself. "It's a place to start."

She went back to the emails and found the ones sent by The Lone Wolf. She sorted them in order they were sent and opened the first one.

"Dear Linda,

First off, I am not writing you because I think you might be interested in the kind of relationship I am seeking. I am writing you because ... well, I don't know how I am going to explain why I sent you this email.

I guess the reason is that you have a profile in the member directory, which indicates that you live in the Cleveland area, and also lists your marital status as 'Married.' As such, you are probably open to communicating via email and from your age may have been married for quite a while, like me. Of all the profiles I've seen, yours was one of the few that caught my eye. You see, I am looking for a love affair ... a very real passion-filled can't-wait-to-see-her-again kind of love affair.

I relocated to the Washington DC metro area for a new position that requires a lot of travel, and with a firm that will be catering to several clients in the Cleveland area. As I will be the point man for these projects, I will be spending time in your area. In the interest of being open and up-front I feel that I should mention that my wife did not relocate with me to the DC area for reasons that I won't go into here, and that I will be living and traveling alone for a number of years.

The Letter

Yes, I hear the sound of you hitting the delete button. Please, please, hear me out. I married very young and went straight from a promising high school student to brand new husband to very attentive young father. While I don't regret any of this, I hope you can understand my desire to be just a little 'bad' — but still be bad safely. Now may be my best opportunity to have that 'fantasy love affair' all men wonder about, and under circumstances in which I would also be able to give my lover the time and attention she would deserve.

I am a white male, tall (six foot plus), large frame, brown hair, blue eyes, clean-shaven, and 53 years old. I have some of the traditional middle-age spread but carry it well. In addition to being a non-smoker and non-drinker, I am drug-free and disease-free. I tend to be on the quiet side until you get to know me and I am guilty of having a quirky sense of humor.

A college educated professional, I work hard but also enjoy getting away for the weekend or even just an evening. Conservative in action, liberal in thought, mature in nature and values, I have found it most comfortable to be 'proper in public' and 'passionate in private' when it comes to interpersonal relationships. While I enjoy the company of a woman, I can be trusted to be discreet … and I am looking for just ONE lover.

My interests are varied. I enjoy everything from museums to amusement parks, from the outdoors to bookstores. My friends describe me as both a 'gentleman' and a 'gentle man' but chalk both up to an old fashion sense of common civility … plus excellent luck in my choice of parents.

I have no reason to think you might know of anyone who would be interested in the kind of relationship I described, but maybe you do. I am seeking a very unique woman. She has to be interested in an exciting yet sensitive love affair, interested in being a best friend, interested in a passion-filled yet rational romance, and all that on an occasional basis.

If you happen to know someone whose life can be enhanced by a lover, who is in need of some passion and perhaps doesn't even realize it yet … please tell her about me. I would like to find her. I would like both of us to find each other.

Warmest Regards, Peter"

Maureen laughed out loud. What a jerk! I'm sending you this letter to see if you want to have an affair because you have the qualities I've been looking for—you are married and you live in Cleveland. If you aren't interested, do you know someone who is? Was *this* the famous Peter Good?

Of course, Linda was divorced. She must not have changed her profile when Charlie left. Embarrassed? Forgetful? Didn't Linda tell her that Peter Good had never been married? When had they confessed these little lies to each other?

It was late and Maureen had to go to work in the morning. She decided to print out all of Peter's letters to Linda and all of Linda's answers, put them in order and read them that way. It would make more sense. She copied everything to a floppy disk—the database, all of Peter's emails and all of Linda's. Maureen could print it all at work tomorrow. Maybe she could find out more about the amazing Mr. Good.

She yawned and logged off. She wrapped the phone cord into a tight roll and unplugged the power supply. Everything went back to the bedroom with her. The still warm laptop went under her mattress, the wires in her nightstand drawers. No sense leaving stuff out to lure the curious.

Charlie Knight didn't say so when he came to visit, but she was willing to bet he still had a key to the cottage too. Besides, the longer Linda was gone, the more upset her folks got. They might show up at her door any day now. She couldn't blame them. She didn't mean to miss Linda, but she did.

Chapter 20 – The Lone Wolf

Dick Longren logged off and pushed the chair back from the table where his laptop sat, his palms in the air and his mouth open. LindaLu48 was online! It was impossible. There were no computers where he left her. Trembling, he went to the refrigerator and took out a Budweiser. Twisting off the cap, he downed half the bottle and wiped his upper lip with his sleeve.

What should he do? He paced back and forth in the narrow kitchen. Glancing at his watch, he drank the rest of his beer and opened a second. Damnit! He had to know. He dropped the bottle into the sink. It fell over, foaming into the drain.

The keys lay on the counter. He scooped them into his pocket and grabbed his down vest. His frozen boots sat on the front porch like impertinent gargoyles, leather tongues hanging out of the untied uppers. He stood on the cold cement in his stocking feet, struggling to slip on one stiff boot then the other.

His eyes adjusted to the dark as he hobbled across the gravel drive to the old stable. Fortunately, the old woman seldom used the Jeep and it had a full tank of gasoline. Not bothering to change the license plates this time, he tossed the big flashlight and a shovel into the back. The garage door stuck on a rock. He kicked the stone away with his heel and threw his weight against the stubborn swollen wood.

He reached the Pennsylvania Turnpike by 1am and turned west. She was his special girl, the one who rescued him from old age. Maybe it was a sign. Maybe she wanted to see him again. It had been a month but it had been cold. She would still be there. The thought excited him and he pressed down on the accelerator.

Sunday, January 5

It was almost morning and he was exhausted when he got home. Nothing like this had ever happened before. He'd gone back to visit his girls many times. Not once had he ever forgotten where one of them lay. How could he have lost this one?

Standing two feet deep in some parts of the forest, deeper in others, the snow was an icy barrier keeping them apart. The bare trees all looked alike in the dark. He had tramped through the woods for hours never seeing anything that was familiar.

He parked the Jeep in the stable, dripping with water, tires muddy. Turning out the lights, he limped toward the house. Maybe she WAS gone. As impossible as that seemed, he had seen her online with his own eyes.

Of course, it could be a ruse. He didn't put it past John Walsh to do something that low down and dirty. The man was obsessed, so much so that he would cheat and lie. Dick leaned his head against the doorframe as he took off his boots. Walsh had done it before. When they did the episode on the dorm in Arkansas, he had deliberately misstated the facts. Dick had left twenty corpses, not the five reported by John Walsh. What was this world coming to when you couldn't even believe a TV show?

He stripped off his clothes and stuffed them in the laundry bag. He was stiff and cold. The shower warmed but didn't soothe him. Not bothering to wash himself, he stared into space with his mouth open. It was his imagination. She was out there, sleeping under the snow. Somewhere.

He crawled into bed—wriggling and turning, yanking on the sheets, tucking the comforter around him. The remains of his baby blanket were pinned to his pillow. He caressed it and stroked his eyelashes until he drifted off to sleep.

The Lone Wolf

He woke at noon, his mouth dry and sour. His back popped as he stretched. When he sat up in bed, the muscle in his right calf contracted and he screamed, "Damn. Damn. Damn." He rubbed the leg with both hands, whimpering.

Since he turned fifty, it had always been something. Warts. Muscle cramps. A painful ingrown nail that turned the side of his big toe black. Indigestion. Just looking at a fresh tomato caused acid to rise in his throat and then scorch its way back down.

The knotted muscle continued to plague him. He got up and tried to put his heel down on the cold floor. Jesus! He pulled on a new pair of crew socks, wiggling his toes. His joints ached as much as his head.

A hot lunch at the *Cracker Barrel* in Robinson Town Center was in order. White gravy over country fried steak, white gravy over mashed potatoes, white gravy over biscuits. Enough cholesterol to kill him instantly. His boots were limp and soggy from last night's excursion. Nikes were fine, he decided as he went back inside to fetch them.

A note was stuck in his mailbox at the end of his sidewalk. "If you don't keep that Jeep clean, you won't be allowed to use it. This will be your only warning. Oona Barrett."

He crumpled the note in his fist. "Bitch," he muttered. He'd never put up with her if the address wasn't so prestigious and the rent so cheap. It wasn't a lie. He did live here. He just never told his girls about the caretaker's shack which had been converted into a tiny apartment at the back of the estate.

He spent hours in the stable grooming the Barrett fleet, but when the old cow finally hobbled down to look, the Jeep was in bad condition. Salt coated the sides and the windscreen. Mud caked the wheel wells, flaps and tires. Bad luck.

He got out the hose to wash it down. He narrowed his eyes. What the hell was the old woman doing in the garage anyway? She could barely walk. His stomach growled, but he pulled out the hose to clean up first.

Did she send the cook to spy on him? There were all kinds of things in the garage he didn't want her seeing—like the stack of stolen license plates under the tool bench. He gritted his teeth until the plate popped loose again.

🦁

<u>Friday, January 10</u>

The Instant Message appeared as soon as he logged on.

Wide8nch: "Hi there, I am Steve in Ft Lauderdale Florida. I am 33, divorced, and traveling to Pittsburgh on Business. I will be there next Tuesday. I am an executive, 6 ft 2, 190 lbs., blue eyes, brown hair and I work out often. I have a nice build with a hairy chest. I am very well endowed. (8 thick inches...NO LIE). I am honest, nice and disease free. IM me and lets talk."

These guys were perverted. They'd drive you crazy if you let them. Dick answered back, "I'm short, fat, dumpy with hair on my back, black moles and stinky feet. I have blue hair and brown eyes and I lay on the couch all day. I have a skinny one-inch cock...NO LIE. I'm on welfare and I lie like a whore. Still wanna chat?"

"Very funny," Wide8nch responded. "Want to give me the truth now?"

Dick paused. He wasn't quite sure what the truth was anymore. Whatever it was, he wasn't about to share it with some homo. "I'm into women."

"Me too," Wide8nch said.

"Then go find one."

"Don't have to get huffy." The man logged off.

"I might as well be walking the streets down on Liberty Avenue." Dick remembered an earlier Pittsburgh when the buildings weren't so tall or so new and when business was conducted leaning against a wall with a whore on her knees in front of you. He found it all degrading and uninspiring. He much preferred his girls. He may not have been their first but he was their last. He chuckled with satisfaction at that thought.

He started through his emails. He'd been neglecting them. There was a note from the RV distributor in Indianapolis. The first delivery of the year was a *Grand Escape*. An old couple in South Carolina wanted one. They requested delivery by the first of April. He checked his calendar. That would work out fine. Might still be a bit dicey when it came to weather but he'd been doing the job for four years now. He could handle it.

He pulled up Mapquest and plotted the trip. It would take him through Clarksburg, West Virginia. He pulled up the Member Directory and typed Clarksburg in the Location box. Under the advanced options, he selected female. Under marital status, he typed in Divorced. Thirty-four names came up. It was a small town. Scrolling through, he read the profiles. One in particular caught his eye. JenniferB29. Her hobbies and interests included aerobics, jogging and martial arts. In the Quote box, she'd put: "Moving to new city, looking for a special friend."

He hit the "WRITE" icon and opened up an email form. Finding the Word file named 'The Letter', he cut and pasted it into the form. He wasn't much of a typist. It took him a half hour to modify it to fit Jennifer's profile. He was sending it off when the Buddy List door opened.

It was LindaLu48. He sat still—his index fingers posed over the keyboard, trying to decide what to do. If it was the real Linda, would she say hello to him? No doubt, she would be upset. Would she respond if he said hello to her?

He brought up the Instant Message form. Maybe if he tried to explain — no, how does one explain the excitement of strangulation to the person being strangled? He deleted the form.

If it was Linda and she was alive, she would have had to walk all that way to find help. She was a chubby woman. That could not have set well with her. If there was one truth he learned from his employer, it was that chubby women don't like to walk.

If it was Linda and she was dead, her ghost would be pissed off, especially if she didn't quite make it into heaven. He figured that's what happened with Buddy since none of his girls ever bothered him before now.

Then there were the other possibilities. If it wasn't Linda, then who was it? Her ex-husband? Something prickled between his shoulder blades and he spun around to see what was behind him. Nothing. Well, at least not Linda's husband.

Maybe it was that skinny bitch he'd grabbed in the cottage near Linda's house. He rubbed his nose remembering how she kicked him there. He couldn't imagine she would be online pretending to be Linda though. She wasn't the computer type. She was the kick-you-in-the-balls type.

He remembered the hard muscles in her arms where he'd pinned them over her head. Her legs were like pistons and she had a voice like a screech owl. She must be the new tenant Linda told him about. He caressed his crotch imagining himself pressing those thick thighs open.

The worst scenario was the most likely he had to admit. He popped his knuckles. His eyes flitted around the room. The corners were dark. Did the curtain move? Unable to withstand the tension a moment longer, he got up and checked the door. Locked. He ran his fingers over the latches to be sure the windows were secure.

Sitting back down, he opened the IM and typed in: "Is that you?" He paused, unsure whether to hit the SEND key. Facing another day without knowing was more than he could bear. He moved the curser to the SEND button and pressed the left button.

"Who else would it be?" LindaLu48 answered.

"Where are you?"

"Exactly where you left me."

Dick gasped. Urine trickled down his leg and pooled under his foot.

Chapter 21 -- The Seduction

Friday, January 10

The IM door slammed shut.

"Well, la-di-dah!" Maureen sat on the couch with her heels on the coffee table, Linda's laptop propped on her knees. A metal baseball bat leaned against the arm of the couch. "Talk about sensitive." She frowned and fondled the bat, reassuring herself it was in reach.

The A-frame glowed with lights in every room. Maureen grew more nervous each day that passed without word from Linda. When Charlie took Midnight, she felt alone and frightened for the first time. She stopped at a hardware store on the way home from work and bought new locks for the front door, the door between the kitchen and the garage and for the storage room.

The plastic bag sat on the floor beside the baseball bat. Scanning the instructions, she realized she didn't have the right tools. Thank God tomorrow was Saturday and she didn't have to work. She'd mosey over to Linda's house and rummage through the tools in her garage.

An IM appeared from Wide8nch. "Hi there, I am Steve in Ft Lauderdale Florida. I am 33, divorced, and traveling to Cleveland on Business. I will be there next Thursday. I am an executive, 6 ft 2, 190 lbs., blue eyes, brown hair and I work out often. I have a nice build with a hairy chest. I am well endowed. (8 thick inches…NO LIE). I am honest, nice and disease free. IM me and lets talk."

Wide8nch wasn't on Linda's Buddy List nor was he in her address book. Maureen paged through the emails. There were none from him over the last few months. He must have picked Linda's

215

username at random. She ignored the IM and continued clearing out the new emails that had accumulated on Linda's account since the last time she checked.

"Cat got your tongue?" Wide8nch persisted.

She closed his IM box.

A log cracked and fell onto the grate in the fireplace. Maureen jumped. Were there footsteps in the kitchen? She twisted her head to check behind her.

"Slut! Fat Sow!" Wide8nch offered for her consideration.

She clicked on SETUP on the Buddy List Box.

"You fool everyone. You don't fool me." Wide8nch continued.

She selected Preferences and Privacy. Her heart skipped a beat. Linda had a list of people she had blocked — twelve usernames. Why hadn't she checked this before?

"You are so ugly no one can stand looking at you."

Maureen typed "Wide8nch" into a box above the original block list and hit the ADD button. Wide8nch's tirade ended. She closed his window. Then she pulled up her database and added the twelve screen names Linda had blocked.

Three of them were already in the file — xxxJwalshxxx, BuddyBoy5 and BigRedRod. Spats between friends? Did Linda tire of these three guys? Had they done something to annoy her? Frighten her? There were emails from all three of them. She copied them to disk so she could print them.

There was a telephone number for BuddyBoy5—412-988-4200. A Pittsburgh exchange. There was a note in the memo field for xxxJwalshxxx. "Crazy as shit!" Linda had written.

Maureen logged off the laptop and picked up the printouts documenting The Lone Wolf's relationship with Linda. As the fireplace warmed the roof, a large chunk of icy snow slid off the eve and crashed to the ground outside the great room.

Dropping the papers on the floor in front of the hearth, she jumped up and grabbed the bat. No way was anyone going to sneak up on her from behind again. She checked all the places where an attacker could hide—up in the loft, in the closets, in the garage, in the storage room.

Enough! She forced herself to relax and went back to the great room. Gathering up the printouts, she sat on the rug and leaned back against the sofa.

"Dear Linda,

I'm sitting here staring at your lovely face and dreaming about what it would be like to touch you. Thank you so much for the picture. I don't have a video cam or a scanner so I can't return the favor.

I'm glad to hear that your divorce is final. That kind of thing can be so hurtful. I have a little confession to make. I hope you won't hold one small white lie against me. When I wrote you that first letter, I didn't know you. I didn't know how I would feel. You see, I am not married. I've never been married. You must understand that a man in my position must be careful. There are too many women out there who would try to take advantage of my wealth. I've had some very unfortunate experiences. As I said earlier, I'm both shy and passionate. I need an equally passionate woman in my life.

I hope this doesn't make any difference to you. I close this letter with some anxiety and wait for your answer.

Warmest regards

Peter"

The Seduction

Oh sure, I'm really not married and I have a lot of money. Do you forgive me? Maureen turned the letter upside down and smacked it on the sofa cushion beside her. What the hell happened to the high falutin language of the first note?

Picking up the next email sent, she began reading again.

"Dearest Linda,

I was so relieved to get your email. I was scared you would dislike me for my little deception. To know that it makes no difference to you was a thrill. I would like to talk with you further in an environment that is more spontaneous. Would it be possible to meet you online tonight around 10:15? I'll put you on my Buddy List and eagerly await your arrival.

Your friend,

Peter"

He was a strange combination of Peter Lorre and Peter Pan, Maureen thought. She yawned. Two letters and he was putting her to sleep with his banality. She put this one aside as well.

"My darling,

Our conversation last night thrilled me. I have been thinking of you all day today. I can't believe how close we have become in such a short time. There are so many things I want to share with you. I'm making a list.

See you tonight online.

Love

Peter"

One IM conversation and they are Romeo and Juliet, Maureen thought. It was disgusting to watch other people flirt. In normal life, men hit on women. Their proposals were accepted or rejected. Then, everyone moved on. The Internet introduced virtual wooing. It seemed more ethereal but in reality, the seduction was preserved with more permanence than most marriages. His copy, her copy, the server's copy, hard copies—the words lived on forever.

"My love,

Email is no longer enough for my hungry heart. Dare I suggest that you let me call you? I spent the night wondering what your voice might be like … a soft tenor? Mellow? Alto?

Meet me on line tonight and we can discuss this next step. I promise not to call you unless you say it's okay. I promise to follow any rules you might make. Just let me have your number.

Your loving suitor,

Peter"

Gag me with a spoon! Maureen mimed sticking a finger down her throat. The original Jennifer used to say that all the time when they were in the seventh grade.

Disgusting as it was, this letter was troubling too. If Linda gave him her home telephone number, he could have gotten her home address from a reverse directory.

Peter could come visiting anytime he wanted. Maybe he already had! She thought of the intruder who'd attacked her in this very room and shuddered.

Maureen had no doubts that Peter was conning Linda, but what did he want? Money? That's what most cons were after, but this guy gave her the willies. She had a horrible thought. Maybe he just wanted Linda. To rape her? To hurt her?

"Darling,

The Seduction

To hear you makes me want to touch you. I know you told me you need time to deal with this new kind of love — but make no mistake, love it is. Please let me call again tonight. It doesn't matter what time. I don't care if it's only for a few minutes. Please my love!

Loving You,

Peter"

Maureen shuffled through the printouts. The rest of the emails were the same goo. Each one asked for more intimacy and more information. However, information flowed one way. Peter asked and Linda answered. Of course, that was Linda's pattern. She loved talking about herself.

Nowhere did Maureen find Peter's telephone number or address. Maybe he gave them to Linda by IM or phone. She checked Linda's address book. Nothing but Peter's name, email address and a dollar sign in the memo field.

She stopped. Listening.

God! She laid everything down and stood up. The couch sat in front of the fireplace, its back to the kitchen, the spiral staircase and the front door. A twenty-foot cable connected the laptop to a phone jack beside a bookcase, which sat against the wall between the kitchen and the great room. A hutch with pewter plates sat in a dark corner.

Feeling foolish, Maureen unhooked the phone line and tried to shove the hutch across the pinewood flooring. It moved an inch. She pressed her hip against the side of the cabinet and pushed harder, grunting.

It took her almost an hour to rearrange the furniture so that the back of the couch pressed against the wall. It wasn't as cozy, but no one could sneak up behind her.

She took the disk out of the laptop and climbed the spiral staircase, dragging the baseball bat behind her. Her computer system was set up in the same spot as Sean's had been. The electrical outlets were there. She slipped the disk into the drive and opened the first file. It was from BuddyBoy5.

"That was a cute trick with the IMs, Linda. Don't think you can hide from me. I know who you are. I know where you are. I even have your telephone number at home and at work. I can find you any time. When you stop at a red light in that black and white truck of yours, look in the rear view mirror. It could be me."

What was the story here? Was BuddyBoy5 bluffing? The hairs on Maureen's neck bristled. Were there any other kinds of threats, she wondered as she scanned through the emails.

"I saw you last night. Your house set at the end of a long drive. There were woods behind it, a duck pond and a funny looking log house in front of it. I climbed a tree and watched you bathe. Your belly bulges and your tits droop. Just as I like them. I will find you some day. Count on it.

Buddy"

He had been here—somewhere on this property, watching Linda. Was BuddyBoy5 the one that attacked Jennifer? She touched her broken pinkie, remembering the sudden darkness, his breath in her ear, the terror.

A monster had Linda and it was her fault. She knew something was wrong, but she was so wrapped up in her projects that she never said a word about it. She visualized Linda's face as she got out of the Trooper, rushing to her date with Peter. Maureen's breathing increased until she was gasping.

In the loft, Maureen's back was to the stairwell. The hairs rose on her arms. She turned her head, listening. Nothing. She turned back to the computer. Somewhere in the darkness below, the A-frame creaked.

She sighed and turned off the computer. Using extension cords, she turned the desk and system around so that her back was to the corner. The stairway was visible beyond her monitor. She could see out the window by turning her head to the left. "Okay." She felt better.

Wiping the sweat from her brow, she flipped on the computer again and logged onto the Internet. It was eleven p.m. She yawned. There were still things she had to do. She couldn't rest yet. She started through her screen names, checking the emails. Maureen1128 had few messages that weren't spam or notes from Bill Casey.

MiriamGorman had nothing but porn and offerings for products to insure her financial security. Maureen got a good laugh over that one. She'd used Miriam's new credit card once to pay for the garage where the Trooper was stored.

Maureen went to Google and typed in "Pepper Spray." Eighty-one thousands hits. She went to the first Website on the list.

Personal Security Devices, Inc. One vial of pepper spray doubled as a fountain pen. Another attached to your key fob. A third hung from your belt. She selected the biggest one.

They had stun guns too. A great variety. Some looked like what they were, others masqueraded as cell phones or flashlights. In all the years she worked her marks, she never needed a weapon. She picked one that claimed to put an attacker down for fifteen minutes. Using Miriam's card and a P.O. Box address in Strongsville, she checked out. She might never need any of this stuff but she was prepared, just in case.

She glanced through MortyM788's credit report, happy with what she saw. She'd used his new MasterCard to purchase a solitaire game, several pieces of security software, a cell phone and the new disguise.

JenniferB29 was her newest ID, created the week before. To throw potential investigators off her track, Maureen set up a profile that indicated JenniferB29 lived in Clarksburg, West Virginia. She'd spent many days there following Cy Gorman. It was a small town and she knew her way around. Perhaps she'd pick up a mark or two from the area.

To Maureen's surprise, there were fifteen emails in Jennifer's mailbox. Fourteen were ads. The fifteenth was from BuddyBoy5. She stared at it for a moment before rummaging through the printouts. Thumbing through them, she found the email. It was the same name. How did BuddyBoy5 find JenniferB29? She opened the letter.

"Dear Jennifer,

First off, I am not writing you because I think you might be interested in the kind of relationship I am seeking. I am writing you because ... well, I don't know just how I am going to explain why I sent you this email.

I guess the reason is that you have a profile in the member directory, which indicates that you live in the Clarksburg area, and also lists your marital status as 'Married.' As such, you are probably open to communicating via email and from your age may have been married for quite a while, like me. Of all the profiles, yours was one that caught my eye. You see, I am looking for a love affair ... a very real passion-filled can't-wait-to-see-her-again kind of love affair."

"God!" Maureen printed out the email while she found the letter Peter Good sent to Linda. She laid them on the desk, side by side. "God!" She ran her finger down the letter, line by line.

"I am a white male, tall (six foot plus), large frame, brown hair, blue eyes, clean-shaven, and 53 years old. I have some of the traditional middle-age spread but carry it well."

The Seduction

The same goofy language, the same twisted thinking. Maureen scanned down further.

"My friends describe me as both a 'gentleman' and a 'gentle man' but chalk both up to an old fashion sense of common civility ... plus excellent luck in my choice of parents."

No! It was Maureen's worst nightmare come true. She scanned down to the ending.

"I have no reason to think you might know of anyone who would be interested in the kind of relationship I described, but maybe you do. I am seeking a very unique woman ... she has to be interested in an exciting yet sensitive love affair, interested in being a best friend, interested in a passion-filled yet rational romance, and all that on an occasional basis.

If you happen to know someone whose life can be enhanced by a lover, who is in need of some passion and perhaps doesn't even realize it yet ... please tell her about me. I would like to find her. I would like both of us to find each other.

Warmest Regards,

Willie"

Maureen sat back in her chair "You son of a bitch!" She crumpled the emails and threw the wadded up paper over the railing into the Great Room below. "You lying, cheating, bastard."

Her mind buzzed. If Buddyboy5 and The Lone Wolf were the same person and that person abducted Linda and that person was hunting again, that could only mean one thing.

She put her hands over her face. She knew it was possible—had even guessed it might be true, but she somehow kept it at arm's distance.

"Murderer!" She dropped her head onto the desk and sobbed. "Why did you have to kill her? Just because you could?" The grief choked her like the parka the bastard threw up over her face. She cried until her head ached and no more tears would come, then she lay there a bit longer, thinking.

Then, anger and grief overcame fear. Sitting up, she blew her nose and typed:

"Dear Willie,

I was thrilled to get your email. I have to tell you up front that to my sorrow, my marriage has dissolved. That's why I moved to this God forsaken little town. My new job is interesting, but I don't know anyone and I'm so lonely. I'm used to having a man in my life.

I hope this change in my circumstances doesn't eliminate me from your consideration. Jennifer"

"Here, kitty, kitty, kitty!" She murmured as she hit the SEND button.

It was after midnight and she was exhausted. She inched down the stairs and hurried into her bedroom. Brushing her teeth, she thought she heard something out on the deck. She turned off the faucet and stuck her head out of the doorway.

This is ridiculous. She spit into the sink and rinsed her mouth. I'm not going to let him get to me. I'm going to get him! She put on a tent-like flannel gown and crawled into bed.

The door to her bedroom was open. She could see the great room from where she lay. Yawning, she pulled the covers up over her shoulder and rolled onto her side. Her eyes drooped and she snored. What was that? She sat up. There was no one at the door, no one in her closet, no one in the bathroom.

The Seduction

The pillows were too soft. She took three of them and rolled them up together, propping her head against the bedstead so she could watch the door. "I'm going to get you, BuddyPeterWillie," she said out loud. "I'm going to make you pay." She drifted off to sleep, her chin on her chest.

Chapter 22 -- Swordsmen
<u>Saturday, January 11</u>

The bathroom mirror was steamy. Dick Longren's crotch was raw and inflamed. Wrapping himself in his terry cloth robe, he limped into the living room. The apartment smelled of cleanser and Pine Sol. The washing machine hummed. He took the laptop off the kitchen table and set it on the top shelf of the linen closet. He backed up, squinting. The computer had eyes and they scorched him. He wrapped it in several bath towels, put it back on the shelf and closed the levered doors.

His stomach growled. It had been hours since he'd eaten. Now that he was clean, he felt calmer. He opened the refrigerator and stared at the food inside. Nothing looked good. A frozen dinner seemed the best choice. He removed the box and put it into the microwave. He poured himself a glass of milk and laid silverware on the counter.

The bell rang and he retrieved his food. As he closed the door to the microwave, he saw Buddy's reflection in the oven window. He fumbled the steaming dish of macaroni and cheese. "Leave me alone, Buddy. We're even now. I'm all clean." He set his dinner on the counter. Peeling back the clear plastic film over the food, his eyes lingered on the microwave. "That wasn't my fault, you know. You are the one that started it."

Buddy continued staring at him. Dick poked the macaroni with his fork. "You know how Mama was. It didn't matter that we were only kids."

Buddy could never let things go. "Is it that Sunday School thing again? I can't believe you are still holding it against me. Besides, you got off scot-free even though you were the big boy. I was the one she punished."

The half-pint class had gone on and on and little Roddie had to pee. The teacher was a sleepy-eyed woman with gray hair, gray eyes and gray skin. Roddie didn't like her. She smelled like a dead fish. "Only a few more minutes and then you can go." She pursed her lips and continued on with the lesson. It had something to do with someone burning a bush.

Roddie was fascinated with fire. He loved ripping strips off his father's newspaper, piling them up on the floor and lighting them with his mother's Zippo. Twice his mother caught him and doused the flames with water. Twice she paddled him with a wide piece of balsa wood that used to have a spongy orange ball attached to it with a rubber band.

The thought of water made the urge to urinate even more intense. Roddie danced from foot to foot, holding himself and whining. "Please, Miz Rather. I gotta go." He looked up at her with pleading eyes.

"You are too little to go by yourself and I have all these other kids to watch after. You are going to have to hold it, young man."

Roddie puckered up his face and sniveled. "I gotta pee, Miz Rather. I can't wait."

"Hush! You're disrupting my class."

He bawled louder, snot running down his top lip.

"I mean it, shut up!" Miss Rather closed her Bible with a snap and swung it at Roddie, smacking him across the buttocks and knocking him to his knees.

"I'll take him, Miz Rather." Buddy was a year older than Rod.

"Go on, get out of here." Miss Rather rolled her eyes and shook her head. "I'd love to just once be able to do our lesson without that little beast throwing a tantrum." She shook the Bible at him. "I'm going to tell your mother, Rod. She'll take care of you."

Buddy held out his hand and helped Roddie to his feet. One shoestring dangled and he tripped on it. "Let me tie it for you." Roddie held out his foot. He liked his cousin. He had toddled along behind him since they were babies. Buddy made a large, loopy bow across the top of Roddie's shoe.

Miss Rather opened the book and returned to her story. The other children kept their eyes on the two boys. Miss Rather clapped her hands. "Pay attention!" They startled and turned their attention to the Bible lesson.

"Come on, Roddie. Let's go." Buddy led Roddie out the door and down the hallway to the men's room in the annex of the old church. The bathroom had two stalls, a urinal and two sinks.

Neither boy was tall enough to use the urinal. Buddy opened the door of the stall nearest the door and the two of them lowered their trousers. Roddie released a long golden stream into the toilet. Buddy did too, holding his penis in one hand.

The two streams crossed before splatting into the toilet water. Roddie shook himself and his urine hit Buddy's stream. "HA! HA!" He giggled. "It's like sword fighting."

Buddy responded by pushing his hips forward. "Mine's bigger than yours."

"HA!" Roddie turned toward Buddy, missing the toilet and hitting Buddy's shoes.

"Like Robin Hood." Buddy squealed and backed away, tripping over his lowered pants. Roddie attacked, swinging his penis and the battle was on.

Lost in their game, the boys yelled and laughed. They didn't even notice when Reverend Falt came in. He grabbed them by their collars and pulled them apart. Roddie's final squirt splashed the big man's left pant leg. "Uh oh," he looked up with frightened eyes.

Swordsmen

The reverend stepped over puddles of urine and pulled the boys over to the sink. "Clean yourselves up." He turned on the faucets and handed them paper towels, which they stuck under the water.

"It's your fault," Buddy muttered as he wiped his penis and thighs.

"No, yours!" Roddie scowled.

"What possessed the two of you to make this mess?" Reverend Falt asked as they pulled up their drawers and zipped their trousers.

Buddy hung his head. "I dunno."

"Me either." Roddie hung his head too.

"Where's your mother, Buddy?"

"She didn't come today."

"How about yours, Rod?"

Roddie couldn't bring himself to answer so he pointed.

"She's in Sunday School Class," Buddy said.

"Let's go get her." The reverend opened the door of the bathroom and waited for the boys to troop past him. They walked down the hallway, their damp shoes squishing with each step. At the last door, the man stopped and knocked on the door. "Stay here," he commanded. Buddy and Roddie cowered against the wall.

Roddie's mother appeared at the door. She cocked her head to one side, her eyebrows raised and her mouth open. Reverend Falt whispered in her ear. Her look of curiosity changed into a scowl.

"They were just being boys. They need to understand that kind of thing can't be tolerated, but don't get too upset over it."

"Upset? You tell me my five-year-old son is a pervert and then say don't get upset?"

"Boys will be boys, Mrs. Hanley."

"Not my boy."

She stormed out into the hallway, grabbed Roddie by the wrist and marched out of the church. Roddie squealed and fought. Buddy followed along behind them.

"Let go, let me go. Stop it." Roddie kicked at her ankles and she slapped him.

"How dare you embarrass me in front of the congregation? I won't have you behaving this way." She swung at him again.

He ducked and pulled his wrist out of her grasp. "I hate you," he screamed and ran off down the street.

"You're filthy!" She shrieked after him.

He stopped at the corner and spun around, his hands on his hips. "We were just playing!"

"You don't play in the church." Mother and son faced each other across several yards, both red-faced. Cars sped past making it hard for them to hear each other.

"We're sorry. We won't do it again, Aunt Myra." Buddy tugged at Myra's elbow, his lower lip quivering.

"Go home, Buddy. I'll call your mother when I get home. She'll take care of you."

Tears welled up in Buddy's eyes.

It upset Roddie to see Buddy cry. "You *won't*. You won't call her!" Roddie stamped his feet, yelling over the noise of the street. She started towards him, her fists clenched.

Buddy threw himself between his aunt and his cousin. Myra pushed him out of the way and he fell off the curb into the path of a car.

"BUDDY!" Roddie covered his face with his hands.

Swordsmen

Myra grabbed Buddy's arm and pulled him out of the way, banging his face on the curb as she did. "Are you crazy? Are you?" She shook the sobbing little boy. Then she hugged him. He put his arms around her neck. "I'm sorry, Buddy. You could have been killed. I'm so sorry."

He cried on her shoulder, a scrape reddening his cheek, a bruise forming on his forehead. Roddie stood rooted to the spot, his mouth open, his nose stopped up. Myra took a shuddering breath. "Go home now, Buddy. I'll call your mother later." She patted the frightened child on the back.

"We didn't mean to do anything wrong, Aunt Myra."

"Go home." She stood up.

Buddy cut across the neighbor's yard and disappeared into his house down the street. Myra looked down at Roddie. "What am I going to do with you? It's bad enough that you wet the bed. Now they tell me you peed all over the men's room."

"We were playing." He didn't know how else to explain himself.

"Is there something wrong with your pee-pee?"

He stuck out his lower lip. "No."

"You haven't been playing with it, have you?"

"No."

"Cause you know what happens to boys who play with their pee-pee."

"What?" Roddie looked up at her, his eyes wide.

Myra paused for a moment. Roddie waited, anxious to know what was going to happen to his pee-pee. "The boogey man will come and cut it off." She sliced through the air with the side of her hand.

Roddie put his hands over his crotch and stepped back in horror.

"But you don't play with your pee-pee, right?"

232

Roddie shook his head.

"Okay, then. Let's go home and get you cleaned up. You stink."

They crossed the street and headed towards the house. The screen door slammed behind them. His dad snored on the couch, unhearing. "Go run a tub of hot water, Rod." Myra pointed to the bathroom.

He trudged into the bathroom and undressed.

"Wake up and listen to what your son did." He heard his mother say to his father. He peeked around the corner. She stood over the couch, nudging the sleeping man.

"What?"

"He peed all over the church bathroom. He and Buddy were sword-fighting with their urine streams."

"Good for them." He belched and rolled over.

"I've never been so embarrassed."

"Boys will be boys."

"What is it with you men that you think this kind of thing is cute?"

She paced back and forth, smoking a Pall Mall. Roddie's dad waved her away and pulled a blanket over his head. Roddie closed the door to the bathroom and turned on the water. He tried to be very quiet, hoping she would get over it.

He was in the tub when she came into the bathroom carrying a basket full of cleaning products. "I don't want you to be like other men, Roddie. I want you to be a good boy and keep yourself clean, do you understand?"

He didn't understand but he nodded.

"From now on, anytime you wet the bed, anytime you miss the toilet, anytime I hear of you 'playing' like you did today, I'm going to clean you up good." She took a can of Ajax Cleanser out of the basket.

Roddie didn't want her giving him a bath. He was old enough to do it himself. His flesh squeaked against the bottom of the bathtub as he backed away. She dumped the white powder on a sponge and came after him.

"NOOOOOO!" Dick screamed.

Buddy's reflection was gone. It had been many years since Dick peed his pants. The shame was intense. He hated LindaLu48. She did this to him on purpose. His thighs felt clammy.

He didn't want macaroni and cheese anyway. Leaving the food on the counter, he went back into the bathroom. The robe dropped to the floor at his feet. The skin around his cock and balls burned. The redness stretched down his thigh. He touched himself. Not clean enough. He found the can of Ajax and dumped it onto his washcloth.

Chapter 23 – Dangling
<u>Monday, January 13</u>

"ARGH!" The pain was intense. Dick sat up in bed, spreading his fingers and then clenching his fists. The joints were sore and swollen. Swinging his legs over the side of the bed, he stared at the wall. Should he get up?

It was winter. There wasn't much to do in winter. Just wait. Smacking his lips, he stretched and belched. The floor was cold. He hobbled to the bathroom to relieve his bladder. Wincing, he shook the last drops off his penis. It stung. Red welts covered the flesh around his privates. He hated the cleansing ceremonies.

He stared at himself in the mirror, sucking in his belly and flexing his pectorals. The hair on his chest was white. When did that happen? His dentures were soaking in a class on the sink. He sucked in his cheeks so that he looked like a gasping fish. Little Roddie used to do that. He expelled the air out of his lungs in a long wheeze. It was no good.

Splashing cold water on his face didn't help either. He staggered into the kitchen and opened a cold beer. He might be losing his physical prowess, but experience counted for something. Didn't it? He downed the Budweiser and opened another one, holding the frosty bottle against his burning balls.

He hadn't been out and about during the day in months. At first, he had been afraid he'd run into Grady the Janitor. Then he realized no one cared if two guys had a fight in the bathroom of Concourse B at Pittsburgh International.

The run-in with that wildcat in Hinckley was worse. He'd made a career of knowing which ones to take and which one to pass up. It was unlikely she could identify him, but leaving one alive like that was a mistake.

He spent the winter cowering in his apartment expecting the cops or John Walsh or the Biker Twins to show up at any time. Then when it looked like he was regaining his grip, he lost one of his girls.

That was the worst blow of all. She was his and he lost her. These blunders were amateurish. It was embarrassing. He set the warming beer on the counter and went to the bedroom to dress.

His normal clothes hurt too much. Even his underwear hurt. He slipped on soft gray fleece pants and a thick sweatshirt. Wool socks and expensive walking shoes, the blue down vest, the knit hat—his winter stalking clothes. It was fitting.

He stood on his porch and stretched. The river glittered through the trees. He glanced at the big house. The old buffalo was asleep. She never got up before noon. He wouldn't be needing her money now.

He hiked across the drive to the stable. He unlocked the Jeep and drove it into the courtyard. Getting out, he threw his weight against the garage door to close it. He always intended to fix it. Maybe get one of those fancy-dancy electronic openers. Oona Barrett had more money than God. She could afford it. He never got around to it. Never would now.

The gravel crunched under his tires as he started down the hill. He accelerated, skidding around the tight curves. No reason to be careful now.

Sewickley was a charming village—quaint on purpose. He nosed the Jeep into a slant-parking space in front of his favorite Chinese restaurant. Might as well get something he enjoyed.

An irritable Asian waiter in a black waistcoat took his order. "Wonton Soup and Cashew Chicken. Green Tea." He sat near the front window so he could keep an eye out for John Walsh.

He laughed at himself. John Walsh would never find him now. He got up and moved to another table in the corner. The waiter scowled at him. "Give me Diet Coke instead of Green Tea." Why worry about his health now?

The waiter scratched out something on his pad and wrote in something else. "Diet Coke."

"No. Change that. Make it regular Coke."

"The man rolled his eyes.

"I don't care. I want what I want."

"Fine. Coke." The waiter turned to leave.

"One more thing!" Dick held up the chopsticks encased in paper.

The waiter raised one eyebrow.

"Bring me a fork."

The little man in the waistcoat sighed.

Oakland teamed with young women. It was one of his favorite places. Parking the Jeep in the parking lot adjacent to the Carnegie Museum and Library, he crossed the street. Which was better? The dinosaurs or books? He went around to the Forbes Avenue Entrance.

The diplodocus stretched from the front of the room to the back, a monstrous skeleton. They'd built a little glass wall around the tail. He used to be able to reach down and stroke those giant bones. He loved the gritty, waxy feel of them, but they wouldn't let you to touch them anymore.

He looked around for the guards. They were busy with a lost little boy. He took off his gloves and laid them on top of a nearby glass case. Bending down, he stroked one of the tail joints. The guard glanced his way. Dick stood up and put his hands in the pockets of his vest. Avoiding the man's eyes, he wandered into the next room.

He squatted in front of a tiny horse no bigger than a poodle. It sat a few feet away from the great saber toothed tiger. It was obvious that the tiger was meant to eat that pretty little horse. Comforted, he took one last look at the wooly mammoth exhibit and he was ready for the library.

There was a door between the museum and the library but they wouldn't let him use it. He had to walk all the way around the building. Damned inexplicable rules.

Nodding to the guards at the desk, he climbed the stoop to the first level. His footsteps echoed in the marble hallway. He avoided the main room where they kept the computers. He felt their electronic eyes on him all the way to the first landing. On the second floor, he found his favorite book toward the back of a bank of bookshelves. The reading table was in the corner.

He thumbed through until he found the pictures. They always excited him. It was a romantic option he kept in mind since he first read that many killers ultimately kill themselves.

His favorite photograph showed a man who committed suicide by cutting himself in two with a band saw. He turned the book sideways. How did one manage such a feat? The victim's lower body perched on a platform behind the blade, the upper part of the severed torso lay on the floor.

The logistics of such an act were mind-boggling. There was the question of pain. How long did one have to lie there while the saw worked its way through your flesh? The destruction of a body gave him pleasure, but he couldn't imagine doing that kind of damage to his OWN body.

Who would be around to appreciate his work? Of course, Oona Barrett would call in the cops and they might take pictures, which would end up in books like this one. He rubbed his penis through his fleece sweatpants and flinched. He was still sore and still soft. This was not the method for him.

Then there were people who strangled themselves. Two of these pictures were of guys dressed in women's clothes. Hanging from their necks with their toes centimeters from being able to touch the floor, their penises dangled obscenely out of their lace panties.

Fascinated, he ran his finger over the photos. It was an interesting option, but he wasn't a transvestite. That was too bad. It wouldn't be as much fun in his own clothes. What would he wear? His Fruit of the Looms? Crew socks? An Izod shirt? He imagined the old woman breaking into the apartment when the stench got too bad. No, auto asphyxia was too embarrassing.

There was a photo of a young girl who laid her neck across a railroad track before an approaching train. The results stirred him.

He once had an apartment in The Pennsylvanian, which also housed the train station. At the end of Grant Street in downtown Pittsburgh, it was a beautiful building. He thought of the horror-stricken passengers running along the platforms—police and paramedic sirens screaming as they rushed to the scene, the shrieks of the children when they saw his severed head. It had possibilities. If it hurt, it didn't hurt long.

However, it had the same drawbacks as the band saw approach. You had to contort yourself like Gumby and hope you got it right the first time.

Shooting yourself seemed to be a popular approach, but he wanted something with a bit more creativity. Any Tom, Dick and Harry could shoot themselves. However, he did enjoy the story of a fellow who shot himself in the head twice with a shotgun. Now THAT was a screw-up.

There was suicide by cop. Going out in a blaze of glory would make for a great news day on CNN. He imagined himself—defiant to the end, shaking his fist and spitting curses out of the window of a burning building. John Walsh would show the clips over and over.

Of course, part of the allure of suicide is being able to control your own death. What if the cops chose NOT to gun him down like a dog? More and more they were using non-lethal ways of capturing their prey. What if they squirted that foamy crap all over him? How humiliating was that? He imagined the Biker Twins from Hell sitting in their den, watching TV, eating popcorn and laughing as he writhed inside that gelatinous goo.

Jumping seemed the most romantic option. He imagined himself executing a perfect swan dive, splatting on the pavement below in front of an enormous crowd of horrified women.

Pittsburgh had some attractive high spots too. The Cathedral of Learning was in walking distance of the Library. He wouldn't even have to move the Jeep to a new parking lot. The USX Building rose out of the downtown area but off the top of his head, he couldn't remember if there was an outdoor deck.

Most local jumpers seemed to prefer one of the high yellow bridges strung over either the Allegheny or the Monongahela Rivers. Dick closed his eyes and imagined the Golden Triangle. He had it! It was perfect. He slipped the book up under his sweatshirt and crept out of the library.

As usual, there were orange barrels directing him from one detour to another. Thirty minutes later, he found himself on West Carson Street headed west. Just beyond Station Square, a small turn-off led him down by the Allegheny to a dirt parking lot. He locked the Jeep—leaving a clear handprint on the shiny hood, the suicide book on the front seat and his scrapbook of panties and photos in the back. After all, what he was about to do required an informed audience.

It was cold that close to the river. He pulled his knit hat lower over his ears and lifted the collar of his vest. He patted his pockets. Damn! He left his gloves at the museum. They were his good leather ones too! Irritated, he stuffed his hands in the slash pockets of his vest.

A wooden staircase led to a bridge over Carson Street and then to the Duquesne Incline Station. The building reflected another era when people rode down Mount Washington to work in the Steel Mills. He bought a one-way ticket and stared through the window of an antique door as the train eased into the dock.

A bell rang and the doors to the passenger compartment slid open. A sour-faced woman and two little boys got out. The kids bounded into the station like overactive puppies. The woman yelled at them to settle down and they ignored her.

Dick pushed open the door and entered the inclined train. The lone passenger, he sat on the bench seat at the end of the car so he could watch the city recede below him. The bell rang and the doors slammed. As he rose above the station, the Allegheny and Monongahela rivers merged to form the Ohio right in front of him.

Three Rivers Stadium sat across the Allegheny from the Triangle. They were supposed to tear it down soon. The city wouldn't be the same without it. The fountain on the tip of Point State Park lay dormant for the winter. He missed it. He loved the way the water spurted hundreds of feet in the air before falling back into the pool. Nothing was like it used to be. Nothing but the Incline itself.

Pittsburgh glittered in the sunshine. This was definitely the way to go. KDKA would be on site in minutes, beating even the police. Should he jump as soon as he got to the observation deck? No, he'd wait until the News choppers arrived. He wanted the video cameras focused right on him when he jumped.

Dangling

The car going up passed the car going down near the mid-point of the ride. A tiny boy waved at him from the other train. Dick gasped and stood up, pressing his face against the glass. Little Roddie disappeared down the mountain. Dick sat back down, this time facing forward.

At the top station, Dick stepped into a museum of sorts. A tiny woman with bright orange hair molded around her face like a bubble sat in the ticket booth.

"Good afternoon, young man." Her voice was as shrill as a cricket's chirp. "Not too many people out in this cold."

He nodded.

"You from Pittsburgh? The view is tremendous, isn't it? This Incline has been here a long, long time. I've got souvenirs — photos, drawings and paintings. You interested?" Her lipstick bled into the tiny lines around her mouth. She smiled and batted her fake eyelashes.

"No, thank you. I didn't come for that."

"That's too bad. I've got some nice stuff."

"Maybe another time." Of course, he knew there wouldn't be another time. It was almost over.

A short hallway lined with old photographs of the city led him to the observation deck. Cold wind whistled around his ears. He was alone. It occurred to him that the plump little lady selling tickets and souvenirs was the last person to speak to him. She'd remember it later when that pretty blonde woman from KDKA interviewed her.

At the far corner, he crawled up onto the railing, balancing with his arms outstretched. So this was it, he thought. He raised his face to the heavens. An invisible jet raced across the sky-blue sky trailing a white mist. All he needed to do was lean forward.

That's when he made his mistake. He looked down. The mountain angled below him, covered with rocks and trees. His muscles tightened and his left foot slipped. He felt himself falling. Do it, he thought. Just let go and let it happen.

No! Without thinking, he grabbed the railing as he fell. The bare metal was freezing but he couldn't force his fingers open. It was agony, but he held on anyway.

"What's going on here?" The chirping voice came from the door of the station. Light footsteps approached.

"HELP!" Terror strengthened Dick's grip but he knew he couldn't hold on long.

"I'm here. Take my hand!" The woman's face appeared, her small plump hand outstretched.

"I CAN'T LET GO!"

"There's no one around but me. If you don't let me help you, you'll die." She gripped his left wrist with her right hand. Her glasses dangled from a chain around her neck. She was older than he was. How was she going to save him?

His left toe found a nook in the under carriage of the deck. It gave him enough leverage to pull forward with his right hand. The woman tugged with all her might on his left. He swung his right leg up. The railing was too high and it caused him to fall backwards.

"Help me!"

"I've got you. I won't let go."

"Don't bullshit me. You can't lift shit."

The woman pursed her lips. "Then you are dead, young man. Do you feel dead?"

Who *was* this idiot? He swung his right leg again. This time his heel caught on the top rail. She clung to his forearm. As he came over the railing, she fell backwards onto her butt.

Dangling

He jumped down and helped her to her feet. "You are crazy. You could have been hurt."

"Crazy?" She puffed. "I'm not the one standing on top of the rail pretending to be God." She wasn't wearing a coat and her teeth chattered.

He rotated his arm, wincing. He'd wrenched his shoulder. "I'm sorry. I didn't mean to put you in danger."

"Let's get inside, young man. I'm freezing." She turned her back on him and headed for the station. He hung his head and followed her obediently. He hoped she wasn't going to call the police and get him in trouble. Now that he wasn't going to die, he didn't want the attention.

She went into the ticket booth and poured them each a Styrofoam cup full of black coffee. "I don't have any cream. We drink it black around here."

"Thanks." His fingers were numb. He held the cup in both hands, enjoying the heat on his aching hands.

"You going to tell me what that's all about?"

"You aren't going to call the cops?"

"Do you want me to? She sat down on a wooden bench and motioned for him to join her. Her breasts were large. Her hips and legs tiny. She wore a colorful satin jacket over a black blouse and black pants.

He thought about how it would feel to put his hands around her neck. "I'd rather you didn't."

"I oughta spank you. You scared the bejesus out of me."

"I didn't mean to scare you."

"Life that awful for you?"

"No, it hasn't been awful. Maybe scary sometimes." He stared at the palm of his left hand. There was a splinter in the flesh below his thumb.

"Here, let me fix that for you. I got something that will burn like hell."

"Okay."

She hurried into the office and returned with a piece of gauze, some rubbing alcohol and a needle. "I have to make do. I didn't expect I'd have to doctor up someone who was damn fool enough to do what you did."

Yes, ma'am." He held out his hand like a child, his chin trembling.

"There are people who love you. What would this do to them?"

He tried to think. Did anyone love him?

"Well, there are certainly people that YOU love." She must have read his mind.

He thought of his girls and nodded.

"There you are. You have things you are supposed to do in life. Did you ever see that movie with Jimmy Stewart?"

"Harvey?"

"No, the one about the angel needing wings."

"It's a Wonderful Life."

"Remember what they said? Each person has an impact on the lives of everyone they know or will know. You have a destiny, young man. You can't throw that away." She dug into his hand with the needle. He whimpered. She glanced up into his eyes. "Oh, grow up. That didn't hurt that much." She held the splinter between her fingernails.

"It did too hurt." He opened and closed his fist.

Dangling

"You big baby." She dabbed at the tiny wound with the alcohol soaked gauze. "You are going to be fine."

"Thank you again."

"My name is Winnie Rose. What's yours?" She patted him on the shoulder.

"Willie Wanger."

She rolled her eyes and the corner of her mouth twitched. He thought she was going hassle him for lying to her, but she just sighed. "Nice to meet you, Willie. Now you go on back down the mountain and get on with your life."

She was right. He should do what he was supposed to do until he couldn't anymore or until someone stopped him. Either way, it was out of his hands. He was like that saber-toothed tiger. He would keep on hunting until he died. It was the natural order of things.

The office was empty. She stood up and he stood as well. "You saved my life," he said. He couldn't tell if there was someone in the small room operating the Incline. They walked towards the main lobby. It was empty too.

"You want a souvenir?" She pointed to a stylized line drawing of the Golden Triangle. "Maybe it would help you remember this day."

He maneuvered so that he was behind her. "That sounds good. How much would it cost?"

"Oh, I'll give it to you." She bent over to retrieve the drawing from a low shelf.

He raised his hands, the fingers spread. One more moment and he'd be in position. His raw penis stiffened, his balls tightened.

The front doors crashed open and a group of teenage boys came inside the foyer, stamping their feet and blowing on their hands. "Afternoon, Miz Rose. How ya doing?" One of them called.

Dick jerked his hands down and held them behind his back.

Winnie rolled the drawing and stuck it into a cardboard tube. "I'm okay. What are you characters up to this fine day?"

"Going down to Station Square. My uncle is going to pick us up and drive us over to the University. He used to go there and he's going to give us a tour."

"Well, you have a wonderful time."

"Thanks, we will." The boys each bought a ticket.

"It'll just be a minute." Winnie Rose told them. They trooped around to the entrance and waited. "Get yourself on board too, Willie. This will be between you and me." She put the tube into a paper bag and handed it to him.

"Thank you, Miz Rose."

She climbed a couple of stairs and opened the door to the operations room. "You come back and see me sometime."

"Oh I will. For sure," he said as he went out to the waiting car filled with kids.

Tuesday, February 4

It was three weeks before Dick took the computer down out of the closet. His paranoia never lasted long, but he was glad when it went away. He hadn't seen Buddy or Grady the Janitor or the Biker Twins from Hell in all that time. John Walsh and Larry King focused on terrorist scumbags for the whole hour. That gave him breathing room.

He was prepared if Linda's ghost appeared again. In fact, it was when he realized he could block her username that he started feeling better. He loved computers when they weren't looking at him.

Dangling

He was gratified to see his ladies missed him. It took hours to go through the emails on each of his usernames. He sipped iced tea and switched to BuddyBoy5. Sorting by date, he scrolled through the spam.

"Bingo!" He said when he saw the message from JenniferB29. He pulled up an email form and tapped out an answer.

"Dear Jennifer,

I'm sorry to be so long getting back to you. A friend of mine died and I have been indisposed. I hope that these past few weeks have been good ones for you.

I understand your loneliness. It seems that I have been alone all of my life. I was never close to my parents. Even so, they died when I was in my twenties and that was a long time ago. I spent my adult years focused on my work. No time for a wife or family. Not anything an ordinary woman could understand. That's why my wife left me. She said she couldn't compete. In reality, she couldn't. My work is all-absorbing. That's why I need a relationship that is flexible.

I am a man of some wealth, which means I can travel and I'm not limited. I have a beautiful recreational vehicle that I often take on my trips. Perhaps I can come visit you and we can see some of the country together.

Your friend,

Willie"

He paused for a moment, re-reading it. "Come to me, little pussy," he said as he hit the SEND key.

Chapter 24 – Dialogue
<u>Sunday, March 16</u>

Maureen grabbed the stun gun off the nightstand and sat up in bed. The front door was locked tight. The nightmare hung in her mind like a fuzzy cobweb. She was caught in a sticky net suspended in the air. She panicked, flailing about. It gripped her tighter. Then she froze, listening. Deep in the darkness, something monstrous was crawling toward her.

She turned on the lamp and got out of bed. The digital clock flashed 6:00 AM in large cyan numerals. Her mouth was dry, her lips cracked. Reaching around the corner into the great room, she switched on the lights. "God, I've turned into a wimp." She pressed her back against the wall and eased into the room. The room was empty. "Okay," she sighed. "Okay, okay." She crept forward, the stun gun gripped in her right hand.

The kitchen was a dark cavern. Heart pounding, her fingers found the switch plate. She held her breath. The lights blazed on. She let out a long sigh of relief. She filled a teapot and set it on the stove to heat. The teabags were in a china pig cream pitcher. Chamomile seemed the best choice. She was a bundle of nerves since Linda disappeared.

She sat down at the kitchen table and stirred sugar into her tea as she stared out the window toward Linda's house. She needed to plan this carefully. Peter Good or Willie Wanger or whoever was no amateur. Whatever his game was, he played for keeps.

She stared out the window as streaks of light pierced the gloom. Sipping her tea and stacking sugar cubes into elaborate sculptures, she pondered her options. The cyber romance was progressing much as it had with Linda.

Dialogue

First emails, then instant messaging. Now, he wanted to call her. It wouldn't be long before he'd push to meet her. He might try sniffing around early like he did with Linda, but he thought she lived in Clarksburg. The cell number she gave him was untraceable. She sighed with satisfaction.

Her only chance was if he made more mistakes than she did. She decided to use the Grace Kelly come on—frosty exterior with the promise of simmering passion below the surface. Drag her heels. Feign indifference. Make him work hard for each advance. Make him eager. Impatience led to mistakes.

It was half past seven when a car turned into the drive of Linda's house. Maureen recognized Charlie's Bronco. What was he doing here on a Sunday morning? Had he heard something about Linda? What if he walked over to the A-frame? She was reluctant to put on the official Maureen disguise. It was the weekend.

She went into the bedroom and put in the blue contact lenses turning herself into Jennifer. Slipping on a running suit, she rummaged in the closet for her athletic shoes.

It was after 8 when he knocked on her door. By then, she had touched up her makeup and brushed her hair into Jennifer's casual style.

"Good morning." Charlie's smile was broad and toothy.

"Well, hello." She pretended to be surprised. "Have you heard from Linda?"

"No, I'm sorry to say I haven't. I was going to ask the same thing of you."

"It's been so long, Charlie. I'm scared for her." The words slipped out. She ducked her chin, embarrassed.

"We're all worried, especially her parents."

"The police have been here twice."

"I'm glad to hear that. They are keeping me at arm's length for the moment." He examined his boots.

"Why? I thought you were a cop?"

"Well, for one thing, Hinckley isn't my jurisdiction. I'm the Sheriff of Medina County. Not a detective anymore. Besides that, if it turns out that something has happened to Linda, I'd be one of the people they'll look at."

"I can't believe they suspect you of hurting Linda," Jennifer burst out.

"It's not personal. Husbands and ex-husbands are always checked out first."

"That doesn't seem right." Jennifer couldn't imagine Charlie hurting a soul. He had a sweet-natured way about him.

"Crime statistics show that it's someone in the victim's family more often than not."

"Crime statistics." The words caught in her throat.

"I'm surprised to see you here. Where's your friend?"

Jennifer opened her mouth. "I'm—uh, house sitting. Maureen is in —uh, New York visiting friends."

"So you are here all alone?" Charlie leaned against the doorframe. She had not yet invited him in.

"I'm sorry. Where are my manners? Please come in and have some tea with me." She opened the door wide, her cheeks burning.

He took off his hat and stepped inside the great room. "Just for a minute. I came out for Buzzard Sunday and thought I'd come check the property while I was here."

Dialogue

"What is Buzzard Sunday?" She led him into the kitchen and poured them each a cup of hot water. The sugar cubes were stacked into a ten-inch chimney.

"Hinckley's big party—the first Sunday after March 15 when the buzzards come back each year. Linda and I came back every year too. Been doing it since we were seventeen years old." He selected an Earle Grey teabag from the china pig.

"Come back where?" She handed him a spoon.

"Hinckley. Out in the Metroparks, there's a place called Buzzard's Roost. The birds come back every year on March 15."

"How do they know it's March 15?" She knocked over the sugar chimney and pushed the plate across the table toward him.

"I don't know, they just do. There's a legend about the early settlers of Hinckley. They were farmers. During the winter, all kinds of critters preyed on their food stores—raccoons, deer, turkeys, wolves and bears. To get rid of them, the community staged a big hunt. They took the deer and turkey meat back home with them for food, but they left the rest of the carcasses in the snow for the rest of the winter. When the spring thaw came, the rotting meat drew the buzzards. I guess they had such a great meal that they come back every year looking for more." He picked a couple of sugar cubes out of the pile and dropped them into his tea.

"Does someone leave meat out for them?"

"Linda does. She loves those big old birds because they never kill anything. They don't have enough strength in the beaks or talons."

"Buzzards? I thought they were a kind of vulture." Jennifer shuddered at the thought of them. "They stink."

"They will roll over and regurgitate something smelly if you scare them, but they are clean animals. They eat carrion when they can find it, but they eat vegetables too. There's something in their gut that kills viruses and bacteria. When they eat road kill and the like, they clean up the landscape and prevent diseases."

"Yuk!" Jennifer made a face.

"They are smart and friendly too. There was one that Linda named Yoda after that little puppet in Star Wars because he was such a wise bird. He came to see her all the time."

"She made a pet of him?"

"Oh no, he made a friend of her. He landed in the yard and played with an old sponge ball she used to toss out to him. Sometimes he brought other birds with him and they bounced that thing from head to head. She sat out on the porch and watched them." He gestured toward the window, his face twisted with what Maureen guessed was grief.

"Where did she go, Charlie?"

"I don't know. She's never done this before. Her parents are devastated. Not knowing if she's dead or alive is beginning to get to them."

"Surely she would call them. Surely she'd call you?"

"She always has before. That's why I came out today. She loves those crazy birds. Neither of us ever missed Buzzard Sunday before. I was sure she'd be back if she could."

She patted his hand. "I don't know Linda as well as Maureen does, but she seems like a nice woman."

"We were high school sweethearts, did you know that?"

"Yes, Maureen told me."

"I never loved anyone like I love her." He rubbed the rim of his teacup with his thumb.

"Then why the divorce?" Jennifer lowered her voice to almost a whisper.

Dialogue

"I hurt her and she couldn't forgive me. She tried, I'll give her that much. We lost something important between us and couldn't find it again. I was working on my degree, working the streets at night. Being a Cleveland police detective was my goal since I was a kid. Linda needed more of my time—more of someone's time. I thought she would marry again right away. I figured she already had a beau."

Jennifer searched Charlie's eyes. They drew her in. "I suspect she learned to appreciate you long after you had moved on to someone else."

"I never went on to anyone else." He sipped his tea.

"I thought you had a friend."

His eyes glistened. "I have a friend. That's not the same."

Jennifer lowered her eyes to give him a moment to recover. "You always thought you'd get back with Linda?"

"It crossed my mind."

"I think she still loves you too," she said impulsively.

"What did she say?" He sat up straighter. Warning bells went off in her head. He was trying to find out how well she knew Linda. "I never spoke to her about it. I'm just repeating what Maureen thinks." She back peddled.

He sighed. "I'm sorry. I didn't mean to put you in the middle."

Yes you did, she thought. "That's okay. I wish I knew more."

"Was she dating a lot?"

"Not as much as she wanted. She'd call Maureen and make plans. Maureen would adjust her schedule so they could go somewhere. Then some guy would show up and Linda would always cancel her date with Maureen. She expected Maureen to understand. That's why we weren't so worried in the beginning."

"Did she ever tell you who she was meeting?"

She paused. Should she share information with him? Charlie Knight was a cop no matter what he called himself or where he worked. She was in no position to go blabbing about anything to a cop. "She never did." She folded her hands on the table. "That's all I know."

"Well, I need to get going. Why don't you come with me? There's a pancake breakfast over at the elementary school. Then we can go see the buzzards."

"I have plans. Perhaps another day." Was he looking for a substitute? She wanted no part of that.

"It's a great party. All kinds of characters make an appearance every year. People show up in costume. One woman dresses as a buzzard although I think she looks like a turkey. Don't tell her I said that, okay?" He pointed his index fingers at her and she shook her head. "Then we got the biker twins from Medina. They always bring their mother in a sidecar. Stella's from Hinckley originally. It's a stitch. She's seventy if she's a day. They have her all decked out in leathers with a helmet. There are arts and crafts, nature hikes—awww, come on, Jennifer. It'll be fun."

She pushed back from the table, spilling some of her tea.

He stared into her eyes. "I'm not committed to anyone, Jennifer, if that's what you are worried about."

"It's not that, Charlie. I do have plans. If you want to go somewhere, you need to give me more time than this." There was no way she'd go anywhere with someone who dropped in and assumed she didn't have anything better to do.

He stood up. "I'll call ahead next time."

"That would be better. I have a lot on my plate right now."

"Can I have your number?"

"My number?"

Dialogue

"Your telephone number. I can't very well call ahead without it."

He had her there. He'd worked her full circle and she fell for it. She gave him the number for the cell phone she bought under Morton Minor's name. She'd dropped it in the dumpster behind the Cajun Restaurant on Ontario two months ago. He could call that number until he was blue in the face. No one would ever answer it. She'd be long gone herself before he figured it out.

"I'll be getting in touch soon." He sucked in his gut and tucked his shirt into his pants.

"How is Midnight?"

"Restless. He misses living out here. He misses Linda." He closed the screen door behind him.

She stood on the deck and watched him cross the yard back to Linda's house. His shoulders were broad, his hips narrow. Something about him touched her. It had been a long time since she'd been with a man. She shook herself out of it. She had other things to do.

She went back into the kitchen. DAMN! What an idiot! The stun gun lay on the kitchen table next to the china pig. Had he noticed? Don't be silly, she said to herself. Charlie Knight notices everything.

Thursday, March 27

It was mid-afternoon before Miriam Gorman's cell phone rang.

"Hello." His voice was familiar.

"Is this Willie?"

"Yes, Jennifer. This is Willie."

"You sound like that actor. You know, the one in that movie with Kathleen Turner? Where he wrestles an alligator for her?"

"I'm no actor."

"I'm no Kathleen Turner. Is Willie Wanger really your name?"

"Why wouldn't it be?"

"Sounds phony to me—like you made it up." Like Peter Good was a made up name, she thought.

"I assure you, it's my real name. I'll show you my driver's license."

She thought of the dozen or so driver's licenses in her file. "A DC license?"

"Sure."

"How do I know you are who you say you are?"

"Why are you so suspicious? I thought you liked me."

"It's one thing to like someone online. It's quite another to meet them in real life." She held her breath. Was he going to bite?

"This is hard for me. I'm shy."

Like hell you are, she thought. "Do you want to call this off?"

"Oh no. You sound wonderful. Just as I imagined."

"What did you imagine?"

"Someone kind. I've been hurt in my lifetime, Jennifer. I don't want to be hurt again."

Bullshit. "Everyone's been hurt somewhere along the line," she said. "What if you want to hurt me?"

"Why would I do that?" He sounded exasperated.

"It pays a girl to be careful of strangers."

"If you don't trust me, maybe we ought to call this all off."

She called his bluff. "Perhaps we should."

Dialogue

The line crackled. "I don't want to call it off. I want you to trust me."

"I need to know things about you."

"What do you need to know?" He sounded like he was choking.

"What's your real name? Who do you work for? How old are you really? Do you have a recent picture?"

His sigh was long suffering. "My name IS Willie Wanger. You want my social security number?"

"If you don't mind." She smiled to herself, imagining the shock on Peter/Willie's face.

"Get out! I can't give you my social security number." He'd finally lost his prim tone and a natural cadence came through. She thought she recognized the accent, but wasn't sure. Midwest somewhere to begin with. Maybe Pittsburgh in later life.

"So what's your address?"

"Are you going to send me something?"

"I might."

"Willie Wanger, P.O. Box 4572, Washington, DC."

She smiled to herself. She knew the old post office box routine only too well. "And phone number?"

"All I have is a cell."

"So what's the number in case I need to call you?"

"I feel like we are playing a game here."

"Cat and mouse."

"I don't like it." She sensed threat in his voice.

"Fine. Stay away." She hung up and turned off the phone. Let him deal with phone mail, she thought.

Chapter 25 – Cy Gorman
<u>Monday, March 31</u>

Maureen arrived at *First Life* just after 8 AM. Bill Casey wasn't in yet. A new plaque adorned the wall beside his bookcase. She straightened it. A color photograph of beautiful little girl with round cheeks and a half dozen balloons tied to her wrist was etched into metal mounted on a thick piece of walnut. An engraving below the picture said, "I love you, Grandpa!"

Maureen closed her eyes. Bill was good to her. The thought of him ever realizing what she had done made her feel sick. It was time to leave. She laid the envelope on top of his keyboard. She dropped a second envelope for HR in the interoffice mail beside Linda's desk. Linda's Midnight mug sat on a sandstone coaster and her Cleveland Brown's sweater hung off the back of her chair.

Back at her desk, Maureen logged onto the system and started down the list of desperate employees on her phone mail. Once everyone had new passwords, she turned to her emails.

There was a new list of terminations from HR—folks who were leaving the company for one reason or another. She started at the top, blocking their access to the company network.

According to the procedure that Maureen wrote, someone would block her too once Bill and the folks in HR received her resignation letters. That duty fell to her backup, Bick Taylor. Mousy and obedient, he followed the rules blindly. All rules. He didn't have a clue as to how things worked really. That was the key to her operation. She built the system. She knew the holes. As long as Bick followed the rules, she could get in whenever she wanted and no one would be the wiser.

Cy Gorman

Twelve people on the list for today. She squinted through the thick glasses. There was one additional name at the bottom of the email. "Cy Gorman. Deceased. Remove from system."

Maureen sat back in her chair and put her hand over her mouth. "My God, what happened?" she said out loud as she went out to Plain Dealer Website. "Parma Man Killed in Fiery Accident" stood out at the bottom left hand corner of the front page.

"Cyrus Gorman, long time employee of *First Life Insurance Company* headquartered in downtown Cleveland was killed on Sunday night in Clarksburg, West Virginia when his car veered from a country road and struck a house. The impact knocked the house off of its foundation causing the gas meter to tear loose from the pipeline. Neighbors pulled Mr. Gorman from the car but it was too late. Within minutes, the house and car exploded. Fortunately, there was no one in the house at the time and Mr. Gorman was alone.

Gorman is survived by his mother and two children. Services will be held at the Bartel's Family Chapel in Parma."

It had to happen sooner or later. The man had a major problem with alcohol. She checked the clock on her computer. There was a lot to do before she left town. She needed to get a copy of the death certificate right away. That should be no problem with all her identification materials on Miriam Gorman.

She was delighted with her ability to choose targets. It was simply a matter of good solid risk assessment, a little research and patience. This would be a terrific payday and the timing was perfect.

At lunchtime, she ran out to Parma to visit the funeral home. There was no one there except the attendant.

"Can I help you, ma'am?" The man was tall and husky.

She wrinkled her nose. His suit smelled like mothballs. "I've come to get a copy of Cy Gorman's death certificate for my mother. He was my brother."

"I'm very sorry about your brother, Miss." The man was a tenor but he forced his voice down. Trying to sound melancholy, Maureen supposed.

"Thank you. Should I give you my address?"

The man waved her away. "That won't be necessary. If you can wait a moment, I'll get you the documents. Would you like to see your brother? It's difficult after an accident like that, I'm sorry to say, but I believe we did a wonderful job on him."

That was the last thing Maureen wanted. She still had nightmares about seeing Sean's body. "Oh, that's okay. I can wait for the wake."

"Here, let me show you his presentation." The man guided her into a small room several doors down from the lobby. "You spend time with your loved one while I get you that copy."

"That's okay, I don't want ..."The door swung shut behind him.

Maureen held her bag to her bosom. Floral arrangements surrounded the coffin. Red roses adorned the silver casket. She checked the names on the flowers. A large bouquet of carnations on a stand with a wide ribbon with the words, "In Memoriam", was from *First Life*. A small wreath was from 'Your loving mother, Miriam.' Another wreath bore a ribbon that said, "Dearest Father."

Maureen rummaged in her bag for a notepad. She didn't have to do this anymore, but she was prepared just in case. She recorded the names of everyone in the black leather bound guest book lying open on an elaborate podium beside the door. Perhaps one of them would have a good credit rating. Maybe one of them was sick or dying or lived a risky lifestyle.

Alone in the viewing room, she tiptoed forward. She'd never met Cy Gorman even though she spoke with him on the phone several times. Of course, as Jennifer, she followed him to Clarksburg several times but she never got close enough to see his face.

Shiny gray satin lined the coffin. Cy's head rested on a matching pillow. He was a small man with deep acne scars on his chin and cheeks. Someone had combed his thinning ginger hair across a bald spot on the crown of his head. She fancied she smelled the booze on him.

She avoided funerals since her parents died so many years ago. Of course, she was in no condition to make decisions then. Her aunt made all the arrangements. Maureen glanced around her. The room had fifteen chairs set up in three rows of five, facing the coffin like it was on stage. She hated the idea of showing off the dead like they were dolls. Cy seemed small and alone. She reached out to touch him. "I'm sorry that you weren't happy," she whispered.

What was she saying? She'd made a fortune off unhappy folks. Where would she be if they had been careful? She supposed she ought to feel guilty—or at least bad, but that was beyond her. Hell, she didn't even know them. She just took advantage of situations these people created for themselves. She didn't make them do the stupid things that drew her to them like buzzards to road kill.

"Here you are, Miss. Please give my regards to your mother." The man gave her an envelope and patted her hand with a sorrowful look on his face. He did this all day long every day, she realized. He didn't care about Cy Gorman or any of the other people on display in his establishment. He made his living off the tragedies of others—just like she did.

She nodded and slipped the envelope into her bag.

Outside the big mahogany doors, she ran into Bill Casey coming up the steps.

"What are you doing here?" He looked uncomfortable in his dark suit. His shirt collar was too tight and his face was redder than normal. Little blue veins dotted his cheeks and nose and the whites of his eyes. She wondered if his blood pressure was up.

"I came to see an employee of ours who was killed." She couldn't think fast enough to lie.

"Cy?"

She lowered her eyes and nodded. "I didn't realize that you knew him."

"Cy and I grew up together here in Parma. He's the reason *First Life* hired me. In fact, he dated Morgana while I was in Vietnam. I came home and stole her away from him."

"I'm sorry, Bill."

"Why don't you come back in with me? Morgana couldn't get off this early and I don't want to be alone." He pushed open the door. She couldn't think of a reason to refuse. She went back in, ducking under his arm.

The attendant nodded at Maureen. Praying he wouldn't give her away, she acknowledged him before putting her hand on Bill's arm and guiding him back to the viewing room. She sank into one of the chairs while Bill approached Cy Gorman, putting his hand on the rail of the casket. Maureen crossed her legs and looked away. It was too personal.

After a minute, the floor squeaked and Bill sat down beside her, unbuttoning his jacket so that his belly was unrestricted. "He was a pissy little runt, I'll give him that much. Drank his life away."

"You knew he was in trouble?"

"No, I can't say that I did. He hasn't spoken to me in years—not since I was promoted to General Manager. He tried to be happy for me, but he couldn't do it. His marriage was a catastrophe. I don't think they ever loved each other. Pushed his kids away, too. Maybe it's my own jealousy, but I don't think he ever got over

Morgana so we kept our distance." Bill's voice caught before the tears came.

Maureen sat back in surprise, listening to his ragged breathing. Then she put her hand on his shoulder. "I'm sure he'd be glad to know you were here."

"Even back then, I should have seen what was happening to him. It's too late now. I should have gone to see him when things could be fixed." Bill's freckles stood out on his face and hands in the lurid neon lighting. She'd never noticed them before.

"How could you fix anything? Cy chose his lifestyle."

"I could have tried. I gave up on him a long time ago, just like everyone else."

"You can only take care of yourself. In the long run, that's the only thing you can control. You can't count on anyone else. They leave you or they die or they turn out not to be what you thought they were." She realized that he was looking at her with big sad eyes.

"Has life been like that?"

She blushed. "Everyone has baggage."

"I suppose they do. I have been lucky. When I came back from Nam, I decided to leave my baggage at the airport. I wanted the rest of my life to be happy, so I went about making it happy."

"Happy?" She snorted. "That's a bit much to ask. Security? Now, that's achievable if you work really hard."

He tugged at his collar. "What made you feel that way, Maureen?"

"When my parents died, they had no insurance. There was barely enough money to bury them. I was in the hospital for months after the accident. The medical bills took everything including their house. By the time I was well, I was broke and had to depend on my aunt until I could learn enough to make a living for myself. A bolt out of the blue and everything that you have can be gone."

"How old were you?"

"Nineteen. I was home from college on spring break when it happened. So much for school."

"You didn't give up like my friend Cy. You made something of yourself. You have a nice car, a nice apartment, a good job. You'll make director in a couple of years. I'm sure you have tons of insurance."

Her stomach twisted with anxiety. "I hope it's enough."

The silence in the viewing room was broken by piped in organ music. They both jumped. "I guess they thought this shindig needed something cheerful." He chuckled.

"Sounds like a soap opera to me." She stood up, slipping her bag over her shoulder. "I need to get back to the office."

"You didn't tell me how you got to know Cy." He stood too, sucking in his stomach and buttoning his coat.

"He was a friend of Linda's. She introduced him to me at Danny's Bar."

Bill accepted the lie without question. "Linda got around, didn't she? Everyone liked that crazy girl. Where do you suppose she went?"

They went out into the hallway. The carpet was dark red. "I don't know, Bill. I can't figure it out. Why would she just leave like that?"

In the parking lot, Bill opened the car door for her. "You should know that I have replaced her. The new gal starts next week. I didn't have much choice. It's been months."

"Is she fired?" Maureen slipped in behind the steering wheel and put the key in the ignition.

"We'll cross that bridge if she ever comes back."

"Are you coming back to the office?"

"I think I'll go back and sit with Cy a bit. It's too little too late for him, but maybe it'll make me feel better for abandoning a friend in need." He smiled and tapped the roof of her car before heading back into the funeral home.

Maureen spent the rest of the afternoon thinking about Linda. She knew in her heart that she must be dead. She'd gone over to the Hinckley Reservoir twice, walking the trails looking for any sign of unusual buzzard activity. She had no idea why this particular patch of woods attracted her. Linda could be anywhere, but it soothed her to think that she might be nearby.

It was only reasonable to believe Peter Good dumped Linda where no one could find her. As long as no one knew for sure, there would be no death certificate. No one could scavenge her belongings. No one would put her on display in a silver coffin.

Maureen called up the revenue program she had altered and scrolled through the lines of code. Her focus lasted a few minutes before it wavered. Linda was goofy and selfish. Her headlong pursuit of love made her the object of amused gossip amongst her friends and co-workers. Her naiveté put her in danger time after time, and yet, there was something brave about her—she said out loud what most folks only thought.

Maureen was sure Peter/Willie had been in the cottage with her that night. Of course, he didn't know JenniferB29 was the same woman he attacked before. That was her secret weapon. Nevertheless, she was sure The Lone Wolf was setting her up for the kill.

She gritted her teeth as she logged off the network. He wouldn't succeed. She wouldn't let him. She was going to take him. If he had any money, she was going to walk away with it. It would be a slow, inevitable drain and he'd never be able to stop her.

It was almost dark when Maureen parked up the street from Charlie's house in Medina. The lights were out in the neighbors' houses as well. She should have changed. The bulky disguise made it difficult to run. The damp grass made her feet cold. She took a step and waited, half expecting someone to see her and raise the alarm. The pen was in the backyard. Inside the doghouse, Midnight's eyes glowed.

"Here boy, here boy." She stuck a piece of sirloin steak through the fence.

Midnight licked her hand, whimpering.

"I know, I've missed you too, fellow," she whispered before she went back to her car.

Hinckley wasn't much more than a charming crossroads. The white clapboard administration buildings included the fire and police departments. Across the street, the tiny library was supposed to be haunted. Turning left onto River Road, Maureen found her way back to the cottage. The Saturn sat next to the deck. The young family buying it would pick it up tomorrow. The cash would supplement her war chest.

She got the car detailed so as to eliminate any fingerprints, fibers or hairs. The buyer's ten-month-old daughter would soon cover the seats with drool and cookies. Before a week went by, it would be impossible to track the car back to her.

She examined the surrounding area before opening the garage door. Staying inside the Acura until the garage door closed, she gripped the stun gun and checked out the storage room. Upstairs, she toured the house checking for evidence of an intruder. She turned on the cell phone and collected her messages.

"We got cut off," he said. The hostility was unmistakable. "I'd like to talk with you again. Your voice was so beautiful. I'm dying to meet you. Please, check me out. I'm sure you'll find that I'm what I profess to be. I'll be waiting for your answer."

The next message was darker. "I've been waiting to hear from you. Please don't do me this way. I won't stand for it. I'll be online if you don't feel like calling."

The next two messages were short bursts of angry silence. Maureen shivered. The guy gave her the willies. She stripped off her disguise and wrapped herself in a green velveteen robe.

From the loft, Linda's house was visible in the moonlight, dark and abandoned. BuddyBoy5 IM'd her before her computer finished logging onto the Internet. "Where have you been?"

"Working. Us poor folks have to work you know," she answered.

"If you give me your work number, I'll call you there."

"They don't allow us to take private calls at work."

"I've been on pins and needles, waiting for your answer. Can we begin again?"

"I'm not like your other women, Willie."

"Who said I have other women?"

"You are fifty-three years old."

"I'm fifty-five. I lied to you. I thought you wouldn't like me if you knew how old I am."

"Why would you think that?"

"Younger women are sometimes petty."

"Things will change for you if we meet." She smiled to herself. Would he be able to resist?

"What things?"

"You'll find out."

Chapter 26—The Escape
<u>Monday, March 31—8:10 PM</u>

The new Jennifer ran her fingers over the side door of the Acura. The deep dents and scratched paint irritated her. The bastard! Willie Wanger was Peter Good and she was sure Peter Good took Linda. What if Peter Good WASN'T the one who attacked her here in the garage? She popped the trunk and lifted the boxes into the deep compartment. She didn't care. She'd make him pay anyway.

Leaving the Maureen Tippleton identity behind for good was liberating. Her passport, driver's license, *First Life* badge and other personal papers were ashes in the cottage fireplace. Big garbage bags full of Maureen's prosthetics, wigs and large size clothes sat beside the car. The big glasses and brown contact lenses lay on the front seat inside a pink plastic makeup case. She planned on leaving the clothes at the Church on the corner of Center and Ridge on her way out of Hinckley and tossing everything else into dumpsters all over the west side of Cleveland.

She packed her computer into the backseat along with all of the peripherals. It took a long time to assemble this equipment and she was going to miss it. The hard drive, Linda's laptop and a box full of CDs sat in the front passenger foot well in a red backpack. Her suitcases were soft duffels on wheels. They fit between the front and back seats.

In the kitchen, she filled a pail with soapy water and carried it into the great room. She only lived there a few months, but she didn't want to leave even one fingerprint. Not that her prints were on file anywhere, but she wanted to be sure. She dropped a sponge into the bucket.

The phone rang. She ignored it and wrung out the sponge. After four rings, the machine picked up.

"Maureen, this is Bill Casey. Please call me back."

She gritted her teeth and climbed up on a chair to clean the bookshelves mounted on the rock façade beside the fireplace. Bill's phone mail messages usually droned on and on about this or that idea he had for some project. This one and the four others on the tape were short and to the point. Call back. He must have read her resignation letter and wanted to discuss it.

It was better to leave the conversation outside Bartel's Funeral Home as the last one, she thought. She pushed a heavy book back as she wiped down the edges of the shelf. Was this Linda's Bible? Or Charlie's? A scraping, clattering sound startled her. What was that?

She pulled the book away from the wall. A loose piece of sandstone rocked in its place. Two fingernails broke as she pulled it out. A small manila envelope lay under it, wrinkled and dirty.

She tore it open. "Ah", she said out loud. Photographs of Linda, the doctor's wife and several other older women fell to the floor. All were naked and in compromising positions. A name, date and time was written on the back of each print. She recognized the neat square handwriting. Now she knew what Sean Harper's scam was. He was setting these women up for blackmail.

She tossed the envelope onto the coffee table. Maybe she could use it someday if she needed a little extra money. She finished wiping down the mantel and climbed down from the chair.

The phone rang again.

"Maureen, I hope you get this message. If you don't want to call back, that's okay. I just wanted to tell you a few things. I hate to lose you, but I understand wanting to take advantage of a new opportunity. I don't know why you didn't tell me you were leaving this afternoon, but I wish you well. You've been a great employee. If you ever need a recommendation, give me a call. Good luck."

She stared at the phone. "Dammit, Bill." She picked up the packet of pictures from the coffee table, squatted in front of the hearth and opened the flue. Tossing the envelope onto the grate of the fireplace, she opened the tall tube sitting on the hearth and took out a long match. The paper caught quickly, the smoke drawn up the flue. She wiped her eyes as Sean's blackmail scheme turned to ashes.

Tuesday, April 1

5:32 AM

Dick Longren packed his laptop computer into its knapsack. The RV awaited him in Indianapolis, a little over an hour away by plane. They didn't expect him in Asheville until the end of next week. No one would even start looking for him until then.

Using liquid cleaner in a pump bottle, he sprayed all the surfaces of the kitchen table and wiped them down with a thick cotton sock stuck on his hand. Most of the furniture was upholstered but he focused on anything wood or tile or chrome in the little apartment. No sense making it easy on them after he was gone.

Wearing thin latex gloves, he put the cleaning products under the counter. The refrigerator was empty. He dropped jars of pickles, mayonnaise and Parmesan cheese into garbage bags. He'd get rid of them on his way out of town. Removing the shelves, he soaked them in the sink and scrubbed them down with hot soapy water and a sponge.

It was high time he moved on. He'd worked for the old woman for years, using her cars and living on her property. She gave him plenty of time off to deliver the RVs and paid him a good salary.

He was frugal during the off-season, but when he hunted he spent freely. He had small savings accounts in several banks in several states under several names. Unlike the early years when they came to him with cash, he didn't make much off most of his victims, although once in a while he found a few bucks in their things. One woman in California had a grand in her purse.

He used his girls' Mastercards and Visas to pay for small things, like socks, but it was too dangerous to keep them long. After a couple of days, he cut up their credit cards and tossed the strips out the window as he sped along dark country roads.

The RV gig netted him $40—50 K a year and he stashed all of it in long-term certificates of deposit. He was 56 years old and he had just over a million dollars when you figured in the money he put back when he was Lance the airline steward.

Before cleaning the bathroom, he used his nose scissors to cut his hair very short. He liked Baby Shampoo. It didn't burn if it got into his eyes. Pouring the golden stuff over his head, he scrubbed until his scalp was sudsy. He had a bag full of disposable razors. It took twenty minutes and two razors before his head was clean. He rinsed it with warm water, running his hands over the skin. Squeezing the last of the aloe lotion he used when he masturbated into the palm of his hand, he rubbed it over his smooth, shiny scalp.

Leaning closer to the mirror, he smiled at himself. There was a piece of food stuck between his front incisors. He picked it out with his fingernail and grimaced again. Using a Q-tip and a new tube of sable-colored mascara, he darkened his bushy eyebrows. A close shave would keep the white bristles at bay for a few hours. He packed the remaining razors in his round travel bag in case he needed a touch-up right before meeting Jennifer.

He slipped on low-slung jeans and a white western shirt. The boots were old and a bit run-down on the heels but they would

The Escape

do. The belt was thin, carved leather with a big silver and turquoise buckle. He turned sideways. The outfit emphasized his poochy little belly and tiny ass.

A small case sat on the back of the commode. Peeling it loose from the backing, he held the moustache up. It was dark and flowing. He placed it under his nose and held it with one finger. It was even grander than the ones sported by the biker twins, drooping down below the corners of his mouth. With new gold-framed glasses and the Stetson, not even his mother would recognize him.

7:12 AM

Jennifer stopped at the end of the driveway and looked back. The cottage rose above the mist, the glass sparkling in the early morning sunshine. She imagined Linda and Charlie as lovers wrestling on the deck, giggling together. Midnight raced around the pond below them chasing ducks and geese. Before the accident, she'd wanted a life like that—someone to play with, travel with and love with.

The car crash not only killed her parents but also her ability to ever have a new family. The long piece of steel that pierced her abdomen and perforated her uterus and the infection that followed ended those dreams before she left girlhood. She learned the importance of insurance that year—and money.

She never wanted to be that vulnerable again. Perhaps now that she was rich, she'd find someone like Charlie—someone who cared whether she lived or died.

She tucked the long tendrils of nylon hair behind her ears. The fashionable rectangular-lensed glasses were light on her face compared to Maureen's big round ones. She was a new woman and she felt light as a feather. She pulled out in front of a pickup truck. It honked and swerved. She hit the accelerator and sped off.

USERNAME

7:42 AM

At long last, it was time. The copied key slipped into the lock. His footsteps echoed in the cavernous foyer of the mansion. The cleaning staff wouldn't be here until the day after tomorrow. The cook came in once a week and left Oona Barrett fourteen meals in Tupperware containers stashed in the freezer. That was yesterday. No one would come into the house for a while. Now was his chance.

The stairs creaked as he went up them, but it didn't matter. The old woman was practically deaf. She sat in a rocker in front of a big screen TV in her sitting room, a bag of Cheetos in her lap. She was watching *Rebecca*, an old movie about a woman with no name.

He picked out her scarf years ago, bright red and extra-long. He crept up behind her and slipped it around her neck. She heaved and rocked forward. He wrapped another loop around her throat and jerked, his biceps tensing. The moment life left her body was thrilling. He pulled her out of the chair and spent a few minutes enjoying her vulnerability. All these years, he'd been her possession now she was his. It was fair.

The safe was behind a huge painting of a pride of lions plunging their claws into the flesh of a dying buffalo. The latex gloves were sticky. He preferred working the combination lock with his bare fingers, but after a few tries, he felt the tumblers fall into place.

There wasn't as much inside as he had hoped. He filled his briefcase with the cash, a few dollars short of five thousand. There was a debit card to her brokerage account. It was only good until the day after they found her, but if he went to a Mac Machine and took the maximum every day for the next week, his take would be significant. He rummaged through the papers until he found the envelope with her pin number in it. He laughed out loud. Her birth date. She was so predictable!

He stepped over her body, pausing to leave a kiss on her forehead. He loved all of his girls.

8:15 AM

Over the past few weeks, Jennifer deposited cash advances from several credit card companies into her various accounts. Now, in downtown Cleveland, she parked the Acura in an indoor lot off of East Ninth, and made the rounds using different cards to check balances and collect money from ATMs.

Using Iliana Johnson's debit cards, Jennifer had access to just over $50,000. She cleaned out Cy Gorman's accounts, filling her wallet with cash. Miriam Gorman had credit amounting to $50,000. With all the different identities available to her, Jennifer could live for a long time without even touching her Swiss accounts.

Slinging her bag over one shoulder, she turned up Superior and headed toward the Terminal Tower. She checked her watch. She was supposed to meet Willie Wanger at the Ohio Valley Mall in Belmont several hours south of Cleveland.

He thought she was coming from Clarksburg and timed the meeting based on his drive time from DC. She let him choose the place and time but she planned on beating him there. It never hurt to check things out in advance. Even so, she didn't need to leave right away.

She bought traveler's checks from American Express. A few doors down, she found a travel agent and purchased plane tickets using Morton Minor's Amex card. On impulse, she collected several brochures on world cruises. After all, working was a thing of the past.

Down the way, she pressed her nose to the glass of a shop decorated in shades of pink. Women sat around in fluffy pink robes and slippers, sipping something from champagne glasses. A tall slim woman in Elvira black beckoned to her. She ran a finger over her freshly broken nails. This was the first day of her new life. A full-body Swedish Massage was $75 per hour. Manicure/Pedicure was $50. She checked her watch. Why not?

9:00 AM

Dick Longren swaggered down Concourse B. He saw Grady the Janitor pushing a cart. Stopping at a newsstand, Dick pulled the Stetson down over his eyes and picked up a magazine, not breathing until Grady disappeared into a bathroom. It was unlikely the chubby man would recognize him anyway, but why take chances?

The flight to Indianapolis was on time. He saw John Walsh sitting in first class as he side-stepped down the narrow aisle to his seat. Dick clutched his computer bag to his chest and examined the ceiling of the aircraft. Walsh must have been preoccupied with scumbag terrorists because he didn't notice Dick Longren.

Dick relaxed. It must be a sign that this was going to be a successful trip. After his rendezvous with Jennifer, he would head south and catch a boat for Costa Rica—his final escape.

10:24 AM

Jennifer paid for her manicure and left a large tip for the nail technician. She went down the steps, enjoying the bustle of Tower City. Outside, the sky was pale blue. She twirled around, smiling. The last time she would see Cleveland. The buildings rose around her. She held up her hands. The nails were blood red and shiny. A passing man turned to look at her with approving eyes. She wasn't invisible anymore.

She retrieved the Acura and headed out St. Clair to the rental garages. Using the small key she kept on the key fob, she unlocked the garage door and pushed it up. The Trooper sat inside. She opened the back hatch and transferred her duffels and the backpack into the truck. Even though covered with a layer of dust and spider webs on the outside, it smelled new on the inside.

Clinging to the steering wheel, she put one foot on the skinny running board and pulled herself up into the driver's seat. The engine started right up and she backed it out into the alley behind the garage. Leaving it running, she got out and pulled the Acura in. Disconnecting the storage key from the key chain, she pulled down the garage door and locked it.

The Trooper needed a bath and fuel. A filling station was two blocks down the street. Sliding Miriam Gorman's credit card through the reader, she lifted the handle and inserted the nozzle into the tank. The digital display showed 20 gallons when the pump clicked off. Her money would go quick with this damn thing.

The car wash was just around the corner. She sat inside while the machines squirted soap, wax and hot air over the truck. She turned on the stereo. Music filled the Trooper. She guessed Peter Good left Linda with an appreciation of Italian tenors. As she pulled out into traffic, she dropped the garage key out the window.

🦁

11:03 AM

Well, look at you! Going to a rodeo?"

"You think the cowgirls will like me?" Dick held out his hands palm up and cocked his head.

The man shook his head and laughed. "You wrestle a bull for them and they'll be all over you."

The recreation vehicle was thirty feet long, a diesel push. It smelled of plastic and fabric when he pulled open the door.

"This one goes to a picky customer." The factory dealer explained. Dick climbed the steps and crashed his head into the corner of the TV monitor mounted over the passenger's seat.

"Is everything as he ordered it?" He rubbed his forehead. A large bump formed over his right eye.

The man polished the corner of the TV with his handkerchief and checked for any damage to the wood. "And then some. But I tell you right now, he's a stinker. We had to reorder three times until we got the right stereo system. It had to be the exact brand and model that he wanted. We custom built a closet for the stacked washer/dryer. He didn't like it and we had to redo it."

"Nothing wrong with that, Hoyt. If you pay a quarter million for something like this, you want what you want." Dick squeezed into the driver's seat of *The Grand Escape* and checked out the options.

It was pretty standard. Upholstered in taupe leather, the seats looked like expensive recliners. A small screen showed the driver what was directly behind him using closed circuit TV cameras. Another one displayed the map of the GPS navigation program.

"He's never driven one of these before, not even a small one. People like him think they that just because they have a driver's license they can drive anything. I can imagine the phone calls I'm going to get when he gives it a try and it doesn't respond like he expects. You better plan on giving him a lesson or two when you deliver it." Hoyt did a final inspection of the interior, a checklist in his hand.

"No problem. These babies are awkward—maybe a little top heavy, but they aren't that bad once you get used to them. I'll leave some time to put him through his paces though." Dick gripped the steering wheel and leaned back. The large mirrors on each side of the bus-like vehicle gave a good view of the sides. He fumbled along the wrap around dash with his left hand until he found the button to adjust them electronically.

"That's what you say now." The man tapped the documentation, which had been taped to the kitchen counter. "Make sure he sees these papers. He called me three times this week to remind me."

"Relax, will ya? How many of these things have I delivered with no problem? He'll be fine. I'll be fine."

"That's why I'm having you do this one. I don't want any trouble."

"No trouble. I'll call you when I make the delivery, okay?"

"Don't forget your stuff setting out here."

"You get going. I need to get familiar with this old girl. I'll load her up in a minute."

"Have a safe trip, buddy. Nail one of those rodeo sweethearts for me." They shook hands.

Chapter 27 – Closing In

11:20 AM

Jennifer parked the Trooper in Charlie's driveway. It was risky, but she was sure she could pull it off. Besides, it was the middle of the day so the chances of Charlie being home were remote.

She got out and opened the wide hatch. Rummaging through a plastic bag from DAWG BONZ filled with snacks and toys, she picked out a small rubber duckie. Holding the toy by her thigh, she walked around to the backyard where the big lab sat in his pen. He yelped when he saw her and stood on his hind legs, putting his paws on the fence.

"Here ya go, sweetheart." Midnight recognized her no matter who she was. She pushed a dog yummy through the fence and he snapped it up.

"You wanna come with me, baby? Wanna go for a ride?"

Midnight recognized the word 'ride' and barked, his tail wagging back and forth. She opened the gate. He dashed out of the pen and galloped around the small yard, his ears flopping.

"What's the matter with that guy keeping you locked up this way?" She scratched his ears and gave him the rubber duckie. He bit into it and it squawked. Dropping it, he bounded around until Jennifer got a hand inside his chain collar and hooked his leash into a link. "You aren't going to lose this, are you?" She picked up the duck.

A face appeared in the kitchen window of the house next door. A dark-haired woman scowled at her. Jennifer waved and smiled. The woman nodded and went back to her dishes.

"Come on, boy. Let's get you in the truck." Midnight ran toward the front yard pulling her along behind him. Seeing the Trooper in the driveway, he circled it, trying to find a way in. The big blue carrier was inside the back storage area.

Midnight was so eager to get into the truck that he jumped into the carrier before he realized what it was.

"I'm sorry about this, boy." Jennifer closed the carrier door and locked it. Midnight sat back on his haunches and howled.

"Ssssh." She handed him his squeak toy. The dog howled again, his head back. She found another yummy and pushed it into the cage. Midnight gobbled it up. "Okay, okay." She dumped several into the carrier with him. "I'll get you some water first stop, okay?"

Midnight lay down on his stomach, his chin on his paws, chewing on the squeak toy. Jennifer closed the back hatch. She was sweating as she backed out of Charlie's driveway.

"We are going to have a wonderful time, Midnight. You'll see things ordinary dogs never see, go exciting places, eat wonderful food. We'll fly on a big plane tomorrow and maybe ride on a big boat one of these days. It'll be great fun. I'll take care of you, you'll see. I just have to take care of one thing first." She over steered the SUV and nearly went into the ditch. "And we'll never have to ride in this damn thing again after tomorrow."

11:43 AM

Jennifer drove past the old courthouse on the square in downtown Medina. "This is trouble," she told Midnight, craning her neck as she followed the street signs, looking for Route 42. "Let's pray Charlie isn't around."

She checked her watch as she turned south toward I-71. "Timing's about right." A neon sign on her left caught her attention. SOUTH PAW. A one story log building that looked like a bar with a parking lot filled with motorcycles and pickup trucks. "Damn!" Her eyes focused on two figures leaning against the bumper of a white Bronco. It was Charlie and Bill Casey! She tried not to look at them as she passed.

She glanced in the rear view mirror, chewing her bottom lip. Did they see her? She doubted either of them would recognize her and the truck wasn't that unique except for Linda's damned vanity plates.

Don't panic, she told herself. They weren't expecting to see her and people only see what they expect to see. She thought of Bill's obscene plaque and chuckled. Even when Linda pointed it out to him, he missed it. Charlie was another matter though.

Midnight whimpered. "I know, boy. As soon as we find a rest stop." She pulled onto the highway and accelerated toward Belmont.

"You never told me Charlie knew Bill Casey." She turned to look at Midnight. "Does everyone in Ohio know each other?"

2:13 PM

The Grand Escape was a wonderful vehicle. If Dick was a buying man, he would have chosen one like this — but his RV days were over after this run. Time to start checking out sailboats. He thought about the beaches of Costa Rica. No more snow. He puffed up his chest. It felt good to be on the road again.

As he crested a hill, he saw that an Ohio State Police officer had stopped a small red car with yellow flames painted on the front fenders. Buddy leaned forward, his hands on the roof of the Camero, his legs spread—a tall trooper patting him down.

"Ha!" Dick hit the steering wheel with the heel of his hand. You dope! He checked his speed. Fifty-three miles an hour. Take no chances when hunting was his number one rule. After all, that's how they caught the Son of Sam killer. The dumb ass parked illegally near the scene of one of his crimes. Not Dick. No sirree!

His thoughts went back to the surly woman he was to meet in a few hours. He flipped open the cell phone and tapped in a number.

"Hello?" Her voice was chilly.

"Jennifer, this is Willie."

"Yes?" He could hear the road noise through her phone.

"I wanted to tell you where I'll be parked."

"I can't imagine there will be many RV's there."

The woman was maddening. Dick paused a moment. "I'll be on the south end by Sears."

"Fine." Either he lost the signal or she hung up on him. Women had changed over the years, but once he got her inside *The Grand Escape*, she would be his — just like the others.

2:17 PM

The bastard was eager. Good! She'd make him sorry he ever messed with her—and maybe even make a few bucks off of him in the process. She wondered what he'd done to Linda. Ugly possibilities flashed through her mind. She shivered. No, she couldn't think about it. She picked up the stun gun laying on the seat beside her. It had a built-in flashlight. She flicked it on and off, wondering how it felt to get stunned. She hoped it hurt like hell.

Midnight snored in his dog carrier. She felt better with him in the truck with her. Charlie would miss him, but she didn't care. Charlie had other friends. Hell, he and Bill Casey were bosom buddies. Seeing them like that spoiled her day. She liked keeping the various parts of her life compartmentalized. It was too confusing to mix Maureen's people with Jennifer's.

What if Charlie was following her? She squinted in the mirror. Was that a white truck in the distance? She twisted her head. A woman in a PT Cruiser full of potted plants passed in the right lane. A Ryder truck coasted along a quarter mile back. No white Broncos.

She dialed Charlie's number. The phone rang and rang. Now what? Was he following her or not? If he were still at the bar, she could relax. She dialed information. "South Paw—it's a bar on Route 42 outside of Medina."

"South Paw." A familiar voice answered.

She froze. What was Bill Casey doing answering the phone there? She closed the phone and tossed it down on the seat beside her. She'd take her chances. If Charlie hadn't found her by now, maybe he never would.

7:03 PM

The Ohio Valley Mall was just off of I-70 in St. Clairsville. Dick Longren pulled onto Mall Road and circled the big group of buildings. All the usual stores—Sears, Penney's, K-mart were clustered together along with smaller shops selling dresses, sports gear, books, sunglasses and other goods. The north end of the parking lot was too near the highway. Although he realized that the area would clear out when the mall closed, the south end was a less conspicuous place for his meeting with Jennifer.

It would be a few hours before she arrived. There were dozens of cars parked in the south lot. He turned off the engine. Locking the vehicle, he walked around the corner and across the Mall Road to a restaurant.

"Smoking or non-smoking?" The hostess asked. He eyed her thick soled shoes with disappointment. He preferred open-toed pumps with ankle straps.

Noticing a booth full of pretty young women having dinner in non-smoking he said, "Non-smoking." Each girl had a tall glass of something alcoholic. Stacks of presents wrapped in white paper with silver ribbons sat next to the table. A foil balloon floated above them, anchored with little cardboard feet, "Here Comes the Bride" printed on both sides.

The hostess put him at a small table a few paces from the party. Inspecting a menu printed on a breadboard, he ordered a large schooner of beer and a thick, blackened steak. The women chattered, their voices carrying across the room. The bride was a small dark-eyed girl with terrific breasts. The waiter brought his salad and he dug in, glancing at those perky breasts from time to time.

7:31 PM

It was dark when Jennifer pulled into the mall. She cruised down to the south end. There were quite a few cars in the lot. Then she saw it.

"Look, boy. There's an RV. You think that belongs to Willie?"

Midnight bumped against the walls of his carrier and whimpered.

She slowed as she passed *The Grand Escape* and parked a few yards away. "It looks empty. I better check it out while I can." She slipped the stun gun's strap over her wrist and got out of the Trooper, locking it with the key fob as she walked away. Midnight's whine followed her across the parking lot.

The RV's dark windows spooked her. Taking a deep breath, she tried the door. Locked. She squatted. There was plenty of room for a person to crawl under it. She ran her hand across the storage bins. No way to open them without a key. She circled the vehicle.

Most of the windows were high over her head. However, the roof was accessible by built-in steps molded into the back of the bus.

She grabbed the aluminum hand rail and climbed up onto the first step. She could reach the small back window by standing on her toes. It was half open. Pressing her nose against the screen, she could make out the interior of the RV. No way would she allow him to get her in there. A long narrow aisle edged with cabinets and built-in furniture, it would be impossible to get away from him. There was not enough room to fight and no place to hide.

The bed was below the window. It would soften the landing of anyone squeezing in through the casement. If she could get in now while he was gone, maybe she could steal his IDs and never have to meet up with the mysterious Mr. Wanger at all. She pulled a small penknife out of her back pocket and inserted the blade at the top corner of the screen. Cutting around the edges, she created a large flap and pulled it toward her.

The RV rocked and a light went on near the front door. There was a loud crash. "DAMN!" Someone growled. She ducked, clinging to the hand rail and cringing against the back panel. "I'm going to rip that damned TV set out and leave it by the side of the road." Footsteps came toward the bedroom. She prayed that the blinds hid where she'd cut the screen.

"Where are my girls?" The voice seemed deeper than on the phone. Her heart pounded. She had no doubts anymore. This was the man who attacked her in the garage of the cottage.

The bed squeaked.

She waited a minute and peeked in again. He lay on his side, holding a thick book against his chest, rubbing what looked like a faded blue rag against his cheek.

She looked around, not daring to breathe. She was lighter than him, but the vehicle was bound to move when she jumped down.

Closing In

She closed her eyes, remembering his incredible strength. This was stupid. She didn't have a chance in a direct confrontation. Why put herself in the hands of an insane man? What's more, here she was hanging off the back of an expensive RV in a mall parking lot. What if someone called the police?

She peeked again. He was asleep. She felt for the pavement with her toe. As soon as she landed, she whirled and ran for the Trooper.

🦁

9:55 PM

Dick Longren switched on the sconce over the bed and checked his watch. Jennifer wasn't due for another thirty minutes. He sat up and rubbed his forehead. Other than bashing in his head every time he came into the RV, he'd had a wonderful evening. The steak was a bit tough but the beer was first rate. Then, when he came out of the restaurant, he found a beat-up Toyota decorated with balloons and ribbons. A sign attached to the back bumper said, "Congratulations Sandy and Bill."

He opened his hand and examined the license plate number that he'd written on his palm. "I'll come back for you, Sandy girl, right after I stash Jennifer." A double! He was back on track again, as good as ever.

A breeze rattled the blinds and a flash of light from a lamp post hit Dick in the eye. "Ach!" He winced. Something flickered. "What the hell?"

He clambered across the bed and pulled open the blinds. He touched the cut screen with his finger and it moved outward. Standing on the bed, he scanned the lot behind the RV. No one was around.

He ran down the aisle to the front door. Using a flashlight, he trained the beam on every inch of *The Grand Escape*. Other than the slit screen, it seemed fine. "Goddamned kids!" He shook the flashlight in the air at vandals he couldn't see.

10:10 PM

Jennifer sobbed as she sped down the highway. There was no one but Midnight in the truck with her, but she had to sneak a peek into the back seat anyway. As the miles passed and her terror subsided, her breathing returned to normal. Spying a rest area, she slowed the Trooper and pulled into a parking slot in front of a cement block restroom.

"What did I think I was going to do? Ask him not to sneak up on me? Ask him what he did to Linda?" She bumped her forehead lightly against the steering wheel. "WHO THE HELL IS THIS GUY ANYWAY?" She yelled. Midnight startled and barked.

She'd spent hours trying to find data on Willie Wanger. What a silly name! There was no trace of such a person. No Peter Good, for that matter.

She started this venture thinking she would find out who he was and empty his bank account—her own revenge for the attack in the garage. Then she'd turn him in to the police. Maybe send Charlie an anonymous letter. It might not be Charlie's jurisdiction, but Charlie cared about Linda. He'd make sure they did something about Willie Wanger.

When her research turned up nothing, she realized that she'd have to meet Willie to get what she needed.

Who was she kidding? This bastard killed Linda. He was a murderer! This was the big time. She was a petty thief. What chance did she have?

Closing In

"He doesn't know my name. He hasn't a clue where I am or where I'm going." She turned in her seat to look at Midnight. "But what if he DOES find me?"

Midnight had no answer.

"I don't owe anyone anything."

The dog rattled the cage.

"Let's get out of here, boy." She put the Trooper in gear and headed toward Pennsylvania. She could spend the night at the airport hotel. It was new and luxurious. She and Midnight had tickets out of Pittsburgh International at 9 AM the next morning. Why spoil her first evening of freedom dealing with Willie Wanger?

She drove twenty miles, happy with her decision. Then she had a sudden thought. "No one else knows about this guy!" A chill went through her. "What if he's done this before? Of course, he's done this before. He'll do it again too. After all, who's going to stop him?"

Midnight gnawed on his squeak toy.

She pulled over to the berm and sat thinking. An eighteen-wheeler rushed past, shaking the Trooper. She could STILL send Charlie a letter with her suspicions.

"The police could subpoena the Internet service and find out who Buddyboy5 and The Lone Wolf are. Of course, that doesn't mean the name of the person who paid the bill was Willie Wanger." The passing traffic muffled her voice.

Should she continue the con? Her mouth was dry. Could she handle him? She pulled back into the highway. A big Caddy beeped its horn at her when she swerved into his lane.

"Damn truck," she muttered as she got the SUV back under control. She pulled off at the next exit and turned around.

10:26 PM

The Grand Escape was alone under the lamppost. The mall was closing for the evening. Dick went through the RV turning on lights. His girls were a bit nervous at first. He wanted to make everything seemed warm and inviting—well-lit, safe.

Jennifer's scarf was still in the box. He took it out and laid it across the fur bedspread. She was a classy broad, an independent businesswoman. He'd selected an expensive silk with a small print, very tasteful.

He took a bottle of wine out of a Styrofoam ice chest. Wine was a good way to get his girls to relax although individuals had different tastes. One boozer in Florida wanted scotch straight up. She passed out in the john before they went ten miles. It was disappointing. He had to clean her vomit from the bathroom before delivering the RV.

He stood at the doorway. Everything was set. He never missed with the RV scam. They all thought it was exciting to be with a wealthy man.

He hitched up his pants and tightened his belt. His wallet made an unattractive lump over his right buttock. He took it out and tossed it into a small bin in the console between the seats.

Ten more minutes before Jennifer's arrival. The chaise lounge was stored in the luggage compartments under the floor. He unfolded it and set it in the circle of light thrown by the street lamp.

Chapter 28—Confrontation

10:40 PM

Jennifer circled the perimeter of the mall. The parking lots were empty. At the south end, all the lights were on in the RV and someone was sitting outside on lawn furniture. She slowed as she passed. A tall, well-built man turned to watch her.

The door to *The Grand Escape* was wide open. "I will NOT go in," she told Midnight. "No matter what he says, I have to stay out in the open."

It would be idiotic to approach him empty-handed. The pepper spray was in her purse setting on the passenger seat, the stun gun in her pocket. It would incapacitate him long enough for her to get away. The Trooper was her best weapon. It was big and heavy and all the doors locked remotely. And darkness. She should stay in the dark.

She was approaching the south end again. Should she stay or leave? She glanced over her shoulder. Midnight stood in the carrier, his eyes glowing.

10:47 PM

The big black and silver SUV had been around once. Dick sat upright in the lounge, smoking a Pall Mall. The boots pinched his toes. The belt was too tight around his abdomen. Maybe Jennifer decided not to come after all. He'd give her a few more minutes and if she didn't show, he'd go after Sandy when she came out of the restaurant.

He heard an engine. The truck was coming back. It cleared the corner and pulled into the parking lot. He watched as it approached, slowing. It stopped outside the circle of light projected by the lamp, a shadowy shape behind the bright headlights. He tossed the cigarette butt aside and stood up, shading his eyes with his forearm.

The headlights went off. The engine shut down. Blue and pink circles loomed in front of his eyes for a moment, then his vision cleared. What was she doing? Sitting out there in the dark?

10:49 PM

Jennifer tightened and loosened her grip on the steering wheel. What was she going to say to him? What did she want to hear back? She caressed the can of pepper spray. "It's now or never, Midnight!" She took off her glasses and put them in her purse. They would only be in the way. She slipped the keys out of the ignition and got out. The truck chirped when she locked the doors. Midnight growled.

He heard the door slam and lock, but he couldn't see her. Somewhere in the blackness, a dog whimpered. He squinted into the night. Her footsteps were light. A small woman. Good. He liked the big ones but it was easier to stow little girls. They fit better into the plastic bags.

She stepped into the light. Slim. With bright red hair. He'd not had a red-head in a long time. His cock twitched. She wasn't at all what he expected. She was seductive online, almost rude on the phone. This woman looked delicate. He wondered if the triangle between her legs was red too. He licked his lips in anticipation.

He beckoned for her to come closer, but she stood at the edge of the light. Shy? You had to coax some of them. He wanted her near the RV when he pounced. It wasn't smart to carry on too much of this business out in the open even though the mall closed over an hour ago. Every moment they were exposed was a risk.

293

The dog's whimpers turned to yelps. What was wrong with that damned beast? It was unnerving. Was there someone out there that he couldn't see?

He glanced around. There was no one in sight.

He moved forward, keeping his back to the RV. Ah. The woman was lovely. He was within four yards when she spoke.

"So you are The Lone Wolf. It's about time we meet."

He stopped, the smile draining from his face. How did SHE know about The Lone Wolf? He was Willie Wanger, Buddyboy5. He hadn't been The Lone Wolf since that girl in Hinckley.

Or had he?

His mind raced. What had he told Jennifer? There were so many divorcees and he had told them so many different things.

Her eyes were green. Definitely, green. Devil eyes. The night crackled. Desire and fear melded in the pit of his stomach. He tensed his muscles. Omnipotence rushed up from his groin.

The dog's yelping grew louder. Frantic. It distracted him. Interfered with the moment. His rising cock deflated.

Was this a trap? Had she lured him out here on false pretenses? He looked for the SWAT team in the gloom beyond the ring of lamplight. Was John Walsh out there? Buddy? The Biker Twins? No, there was nothing but that damned howling dog.

He reached for her—an affectionate opening gesture, but she stepped back and raised her right hand. What was she holding? A gun? Something hissed. A wet spray hit the side of his face and his left ear. His eyes watered and his nasal passages filled.

She was trying to hurt him! The BITCH!

He grabbed her wrist. She jerked upwards, stripping his fingers off her arm. His fist hit what felt like a can. It clanked to the ground and went rolling across the pavement into the darkness.

USERNAME

Rage replaced caution. He lowered his head and charged.

The woman turned sideways and kicked the side of his left knee with her right heel. He screamed and bent to rub his leg. She twirled around and faced him, her fists clenched—bouncing on her toes. Who did she think she was? Jackie Chan?

Enough of this business, whether she liked it or not, she was coming into *The Grand Escape* where they could talk. He unbuckled his belt and stripped it out of his jeans as he got to his feet. Wrapping the leather end of it around his hand, he swung the buckle in a wide under-handed arch. She threw up her left arm to fend off the blow. The buckle caught her below the elbow. He felt the impact of metal into flesh, heard her moan under her breath. That'll take her down, he thought—and loosened his grip.

She staggered backwards and grabbed the belt, jerking it out of his hands and over her head. Dick watched it fly through the air and land several yards away.

He clenched his fists. The bitch wasn't human. He'd show her what pain felt like. He would tear her apart.

He lunged at her. She hit him in the chest with both hands but his momentum carried him forward. Gripping the front of his cowboy shirt, she fell backwards onto the asphalt and pulled him with her.

He was falling. The pavement came up to meet him. He ducked his head and landed on his back, a complete somersault. The air went out of his lungs. The back of his head hurt where it slammed against the ground.

Opening his mouth wide, he tried to suck in air. He lifted his head, opening and closing his fists, gasping. The dog's hysterical barking raised the hair on his arms like chalk squeaking on a blackboard.

Jennifer sprang to her feet. The man lay on his back just behind her, arms and legs flailing as he tried to breathe. She wiggled her fingers. The maneuver had snapped the partially healed bone in her pinkie. SHIT!

She drew back her foot to kick him in the ribs. He looked up at her, his eyes moist and pleading. An old man, he seemed scared. Concerned, she lowered her foot and bent over him.

The soft, human glow in his eyes changed to a reptilian glitter. His lips twisted into a snarl. Horrified, she jerked her hand away—her heart thudding in her chest, her palms sweating.

He was between her and the Trooper. She sidestepped around him as he rolled onto his stomach. He grabbed at her ankle, but she danced clear. She kicked at him again, her foot slicing the air near his head. He pushed up to his knees and growled like a wounded animal. No match for this kind of insanity, she whirled and ran toward the truck.

It was several yards back in the darkness. She stuck her hand in her pants pocket as she ran. Where was it? Where? Her fingers curled around the key fob. Holding her arm straight out in front of her, she pressed a button.

She was no fun. She fought too hard. Clutching his knee, he struggled to stand. There was easier prey at the restaurant across the street. He didn't need this hassle. He turned to go, rubbing his elbow. Who ever heard of a woman who could toss a man over her head like a rag doll? He'd only run into one other woman who fought like this.

He stopped and looked over his shoulder. He didn't know how, but she'd found him. Why? What did she know? What did she want? He searched for her in the night, disoriented.

Her footsteps receded. She was getting away.

He couldn't let that happen. He limped after her.

The lights blinked when the engine started. He startled. What was going on? She was still running. Had she abandoned the truck for some reason? He lumbered toward the sound of her footsteps. His leg was stiff but he couldn't worry about aches and pains now.

What was that? She'd opened the car door. He had to get to her before she locked them again.

The dog's incessant howling grew louder. Less than five yards in front of him, she climbed into the truck. The lights came on. He stopped and threw his arms up to protect his face. The beams focused right on him. The bitch was going to run over him! The door was still open when she gunned the engine and the Trooper leapt forward.

At the last moment, he jumped to the right and the front fender caught his left hip sending him sprawling. The swinging door missed slicing open his head by millimeters.

Her breath came in shallow gasps. She felt the thud of the truck hitting his body through the steering wheel. Her scalp under the wig prickled. Was he still after her? She peered into the rear view mirror—then the right and left side mirrors. She braked, reached out and closed the door. Punching a tiny button on the key fob, she locked all four doors. Twisting around, she narrowed her eyes. He'd been swallowed up by the darkness.

The key was still in her hand. She didn't quite know what to do since the engine was running. Her knit shirt was wet with sweat—under the arms, on her back, on her chest. She fumbled trying to stick the key into the ignition.

OH GOD! The RV was coming up. She slammed on the brakes and turned the wheel to the right, sliding sideways. Midnight's barking turned to high-pitched shrieks.

The truck skidded to a stop a few feet from *The Grand Escape*. She sat for a moment, staring out the passenger window toward where she last saw him. Was he still there?

She pressed the accelerator again and made a tight right turn. He had to be somewhere outside the circle of light. The squealing in her ears was either the tires or Midnight.

The Trooper rose up on two wheels. The damned thing was going to tip over. She slowed and spun the wheel to the left. The SUV bounced back on four wheels, slamming her knee against the bottom of the steering column.

She scanned the parking lot, twisting her head first one way and then the other. Midnight quieted. The sudden silence terrified her. She turned around. The dog stiffened, staring into the darkness beyond the windshield. She followed his gaze.

The man was sprawled on the pavement, arms and legs akimbo. She eased forward so that the area where he lay was lit by her headlights. "He's dead! OH GOD! OH GOD! OH GOD!" She covered her mouth with her hands to smother her shrieks.

Breathing deeply, she fought off her own hysteria. She had to be calm. There were things she had to do. Should she get out and see if she could help him?

She gripped the door handle. Okay, okay, okay. It was a chant that turned into a bad case of the hiccups. What she'd seen in his eyes chilled her soul. NO! Let the bastard be. Besides, if he was dead, he was dead.

Her mind cleared. What should she do? She couldn't afford to get caught with Linda's car. What if there were dents? What if there was blood or God knows what else on the undercarriage? Hiccup. She drove past the body and parked close to *The Grand Escape*.

"Not much longer, Midnight." She hiccupped again, holding her hand over her mouth.

Grabbing her purse and backpack, she jumped out of the Trooper. The RV was luxurious. She stepped inside. Tossing her purse on the passenger seat, she turned to inspect *The Grand Escape*.

The cockpit was lower than the living area. Overstuffed sofas lined an aisle that led to a well equipped kitchen. A bathroom with a tiny shower opened off to the right, a sliding door closet to the left. Then a large bedroom filled the rear of the vehicle.

"Wow!" Her mouth dropped open when she realized the dark stuff on the bed beneath the protecting plastic was fur. There was no one there. Relieved, she opened the closet door in the hallway. Willie Wanger's knapsack sat in the corner.

She hung her backpack on a hook. The hook came off the wall and the bag crashed to the bottom of the closet, causing a large scrapbook to fall off the top shelf. It hit her on the head and fell open on the thick carpet. She squatted. She turned a page, then another.

Near the back of the book was a picture of Linda and a pair of size 8 panties. Jennifer's scream was shrill and went on for several seconds. She leaned her head against the wall, hitting the paneling with her fist. She staggered out of *The Grand Escape* and took deep breaths of the cool night air.

Willie Wanger lay stretched out on the pavement several yards beyond the lamp post. She wanted to kill him again. To kick and pummel his body until the anger and grief went away. She took several steps in his direction, her fists clenched.

Midnight cried when he saw her headed away from the Trooper. She stopped and opened her hands. The murderous rage drained away. She choked back a sob. "You're right, boy. I can go crazy later. Let's get out of here."

Pulling open both doors of the back hatch, she hooked Midnight's leash into his collar before unlatching the dog carrier. He rushed toward her, eager to get out of the cage. She grunted as the full weight of the animal bounced against her chest and she nearly fell. She eased him to the pavement and he hurried over to lift his leg and pee on the front tire of *The Grand Escape*. She tugged at his leash to get him into the RV.

Once inside, the dog bounded around, jumping on furniture and sniffing the plastic covered carpet. She wrapped the leash around the door knob to keep him from getting out.

Back at the Trooper, Jennifer slid the duffels out of the luggage compartment. She rolled them across the cement and stowed them under the RV. Using both hands to close the bins, she sat on the ground trying to catch her breath. Her left arm ached where he'd hit her with the belt buckle, her broken finger throbbed.

The image of Linda's lifeless body popped into her mind, unbidden. "NO!" She squeezed her eyes closed. "I can't think about her now." Her back was to the blackness. A cool breeze raised goose bumps between her shoulder blades. Was someone watching her? Jumping to her feet, she spun around. Something still out there? She looked again. Had to be him.

It took several minutes to wrestle Midnight's cage into the RV. The door was narrow and the step was high. Her strength was waning and her arm hurt. Squeezing past Midnight who tried to lick her sore hand, she pulled the door shut behind her and stepped down into the driver's seat. It was like folding herself into a small drawer.

She stared at the console. She'd never seen anything like it. She turned on a light and squinted at the bank of buttons and switches, trying to read the labels. Picking the most likely one, she hit it with her thumb. The RV started—or maybe it started. The sound of the engine was so far away. Several monitors flashed as computers booted up.

Midnight whimpered, straining at his leash.

"Okay, okay." She got up and freed him.

"There you go, boy." She crawled into the cockpit and examined the dash. Midnight jumped over the console between the seats and knocked a briefcase to the floor where it popped open. He squeezed into the foot well, sniffing.

"What is it, boy? What's in there?" She leaned over. Neat packets of bills lay on the carpet. She picked up the case. It was filled with money and socks. "Looney tunes!" She told Midnight as she held up an unopened package of Thorlos. "The bastard."

Fumbling for a Kleenex, she found a wallet in the console. No time for this, she thought. No time. She opened it anyway. It was thick with money.

"Good." She returned to the problem at hand. "How does this thing work, Midnight?"

The dog lifted his head and looked at her with huge brown eyes, his tail wagging.

The outside mirrors showed her the sides of *The Grand Escape* but not the road beside and behind her. The thought of taking this monster onto the freeway was intimidating—especially since she didn't know which button controlled the mirrors and she couldn't find the headlights.

"Stay here, boy." She shook a finger at him as she got up. Panting, she closed the door behind her and ran around the front of the RV to the left side. Pushing with the heels of her hands, she got the mirror to move.

Now that her eyes had re-adjusted to the dark again, she saw the Trooper sitting near the circle of light. Funny. She couldn't see Willie anymore. She took the stun gun out of her pocket and flicked on the flashlight. Nothing.

Midnight began barking again.

"God!" She ran to the door. She could hear Midnight running around inside the RV. She glanced over her shoulder. Nothing.

She crawled inside, slamming the door behind. The lock clicked into place. Okay. Okay. Okay. She slipped into the driver's seat again, leaning forward to study the dash. There. She turned on the headlights.

Willie stood in front of *The Grand Escape*.

Jennifer jumped and screamed.

"My girls!" He shook his fist. "I want my girls!"

She waved him away. "Get out of my way. I'll run you down, I swear."

He started toward her, dragging one leg behind him.

She hit the start button again. The starter growled. The engine was already running. She put the RV in gear.

"GIVE ME MY GIRLS!" Willie pounded on the door.

Midnight ran to the door—showing his teeth, his upper lip quivering.

Willie threw himself against the side of the RV again and again.

Jennifer pressed the accelerator to the floor. Nothing. The RV wouldn't budge. What is it? What's wrong?

"I'll cut your heart out and eat it!" Willie bellowed, kicking the door with the sharp toes of his cowboy boots. "Don't think you can get away from me."

There! Air Brakes! She hit the button. A loud whoosh. She floored it again. Nothing.

Willie's assault on the RV stopped. Jennifer turned to stare at the door knob. Could he get in another way? Through the roof? From underneath? Midnight nosed closer to the entry way.

"What happened, boy? Where did he go?" She whispered.

Midnight backed away from the door, turning to face the bedroom down the hall, his tail stiff behind him—listening.

The bus shuddered.

The window!

Midnight ran toward the back of the RV, barking.

Jennifer clambered out of the cockpit. A quick glance reassured her that the bathroom was empty. The lights blazed, blinding her to what was beyond the bedroom window. Tripping over Midnight who yelped and jumped out of her way, she jumped on the bed and reached to pull down the sash.

A thick hand reached through the ripped away screen and grabbed her right arm. She screamed, fighting as Willie yanked the top part of her body out of the window. The glass was half way down and her head hit the side of the frame, stunning her.

Chapter 29—Consummation

He couldn't let the bitch drive off with his girls. He clung to the railing with one hand, praying that the worn heels of the cowboy boots wouldn't slip off the tread of the molded step.

He pulled hard and her head cleared the bottom of the sash. One more yank and she'd be out of the window. Suddenly, she was fighting back, flailing at him with her left hand and screaming.

"I just want my girls." He winced as her fist found his eye. "Give me my girls."

Midnight jumped on the bed behind Jennifer, barking. He spun in a circle, leapt down to the floor and ran into the living area. A moment later he was back again.

Jennifer writhed but couldn't break Willie's grasp. Her feet dangled an inch above the bed. She kicked, trying to get some leverage, knocking the sconce off the wall with her knee. Despite her broken finger, she punched him again and again.

He was slightly below her and gravity was on his side. Her shoulders slid through the opening. No. NO! She felt herself tipping forward, head down. She beat against the side of his body with the hand of her pinned arm. "Wait, wait!" She begged. "Let go of me and I'll come out to you."

"You hurt me!" Anger contorted Willie's face.

She jerked her arm sideways and then down, breaking his grip. She kicked and dropped backwards so that her feet touched the bed.

"Oh no, you don't." He leapt and grabbed her left elbow before she could withdraw inside the window. She flipped the stun gun dangling from her right wrist so that it landed in the palm of her hand.

"Let me go!" She held up the Taser so he could see it.

He couldn't or wouldn't understand her warning. "Give me my girls," he insisted.

She placed the stun gun between Willie's eyes.

He waited a moment. When she didn't press the button, he let go of the hand rail and clung to her left arm with both hands, trying to jerk it out of the socket.

Her scream turned into a shriek. He wasn't going to let this bitch get away with *The Grand Escape*. He wasn't going to let her steal his girls. He yanked again and twisted, enjoying her pain.

Jennifer squared her shoulders. "LET GO!" Her voice was commanding.

His grin was slow and malicious. It pissed her off.

He'd been in her house. He'd tried to kill her. Twice! He'd broken her finger. Twice! He was trying to break her arm. He'd taken Linda.

Poor lonely Linda who was struggling to make a life for herself. BASTARD! She pushed the button just as he jumped off the step, pulling on her arm with all his weight.

Dick had her now. A loud crackle filled his ears. Was that her arm breaking? He smelled the bright light that arced a few inches from his face. Stunned, he let go and fell backwards.

Consummation

Jennifer dropped onto the bed, wincing and cradling her arm. "Damn!"

Midnight jumped up against the wall, his front paws on the sill, barking out the open window. She struggled to her feet, balancing on the springy mattress. Gritting her teeth, she slid the sash down and locked it. "There." She leaned her back against the paneling and hiccupped. "There."

Midnight stopped barking. He turned to look at her, his tongue dangling out of his mouth.

"What is it, boy?" Jennifer peered through the window with him. They could barely see him, just visible below the back bumper. "Stay down," she muttered. "Stay down."

Something broke her concentration. Sirens. Someone must have heard her screaming or Midnight barking. She hiccupped. The RV was full of evidence. Linda's truck was a few feet away.

She jumped off the bed and ran to the cockpit. The engine was still running. Midnight crawled into the seat beside her. Holding her breath, she pressed the accelerator to the floor. The RV lurched forward.

The sirens grew closer. The RV swerved across the parking lot toward the outside railing along Mall Road. She hit the brakes. They skidded to a stop with the front bumper less than a foot from the fence.

Midnight whimpered.

"I know. I know. This is worse than the damned Trooper," she told him. Unused to the mirrors and forgetting to check the rear video monitor, she backed up too far to the left, then too far to the right. A crunch.

"What the hell?" She stood up and bashed her head against the TV mounted above the cockpit. Her vision blurred. She'd lost one of the green contact lenses. No time to look for it now.

Holding one hand over her eye, she peeked through the blinds over the kitchen sink. She'd backed over the chaise lounge and into the lamp post, missing the Trooper by inches.

She squinted. "How the hell am I going to get this thing out of here without hitting the Trooper?" She unlocked the outside door.

Midnight growled.

"It's okay, boy. The stun gun will keep him down for ten minutes. I'm just going to see how close I am to the truck."

She opened the door.

Dick Longren grabbed the front of her shirt and pulled her out of the RV.

"NO!" She flailed at him.

"You didn't think I'd let you get away twice, did you?" He threw her up against *The Grand Escape*, his hands finding her neck. "Give up," he hissed through his broken top plate. "Give up. I have you now."

His thumbs dug into her throat. Her eyes bulged. He lifted her by her neck and shook her. She gasped, her tongue protruding. Her punches weakened and he took the opportunity to squeeze tighter. He felt death coming and his cock hardened. He closed his eyes, enjoying the moment.

A black demon with red eyes roared and leapt through the darkness, burying its fangs in Dick's bicep.

"What the f...?" Dick released his hold on Jennifer. She fell to the pavement and crumpled.

Consummation

Jennifer rolled onto her back and sucked in air. As she came around, the first thing she heard was the siren. Yes! Maybe they were coming to save her. She couldn't fight anymore. Her body hurt. Her head hurt. Her arm throbbed. Her finger was broken—again. She didn't care if she got caught anymore. She just wanted to sleep.

Lights flashed in the distance as the fire truck rushed by on the highway. "Not for us," she sobbed. "Not for us."

As air filled her lungs, she became aware of Midnight's ferocious growling and Willie Wanger's curses and screams. She sat up, holding her neck.

Midnight wouldn't let go of Willie's arm. Willie rolled on the pavement, punching the big dog in the nose again and again. "Get him off of me."

"Stop hitting him." She got to her feet.

"Call him off or I'll kill him."

"And then you'll kill me?" She backed along the side of the RV.

Willie yelled as Midnight bit deeper into his arm. "Let's call a truce. Okay? I'll go my way and you go yours."

"Like I would believe you."

"I give up. You win. Get him off of me."

"I don't know how." Jennifer climbed into *The Grand Escape* and hurried to the cockpit, the sounds of the battle between Willie and Midnight continuing.

It was bad enough when she could see clearly. The world beyond the windscreen was fuzzy. She put the RV in gear and pressed the accelerator, praying she'd miss Linda's truck. Two bumps and she was back over the chaise lounge.

She swung the steering wheel hard to the right and circled the Trooper and lamp post. Midnight let go of Willie's arm and took off after her, barking.

Jennifer hurdled around the parking lot. As she came back around, she braked. The door swung open and Midnight scurried into the RV.

She hit the gas pedal and the RV shot forward.

Dick Longren rolled to his feet. The dog had torn the muscle in his right arm. He couldn't move it. His shirt was slimy with blood. He planted his feet, ready to grab hold of the swinging door. If a damned dog could do it, he certainly could. *The Grand Escape* came straight at him. At the last moment, he stepped to the side, focused on the door.

She jerked the wheel to the left to avoid the Trooper and then back to the right, heading for Mall Road. From the darkness, Willie jumped out at her. The side mirror caught him dead center and lifted him off his feet. The crunch was sickening.

He clung to the huge mirror with his left hand, squirming and kicking. She couldn't take her eyes off of him as the RV continued to circle. In the darkness ahead, the Trooper reappeared as a fuzzy black blob. She slammed on the brakes.

The wheels locked and *The Grand Escape* slid forward, throwing Willie onto the pavement. Jennifer closed her eyes. Willie's screams were cut short as the RV rolled over his body.

Epilogue – Key West
<u>September 30</u>

Sails taut with wind, *The Danger* skimmed across the water, heading back toward Key West. Near the stern of the boat, a small woman rubbed cocoa butter on her thighs and leaned back on her elbows, lifting her face to the sun. The black dog at her feet sniffed her toes, then laid down and put his snout on his front paws. After a long day of snorkeling, they were both tired.

A slim boy in flowered swim trunks stood over her with a tray of cut up fruit. "Miriam?"

Her eyes were closed behind her dark glasses.

"Miss Gorman?"

The dog jumped up on the cushion beside her, placing his body between her and the boy.

She pushed the Oakleys up over her forehead.

"Do you want some fruit? We have two kinds of melon, fresh pineapple and papaya." The boy lowered the plate and she picked up a chunk of pineapple and bit into it. "You should take another bottle of Evian, ma'am. It's easy to get dehydrated out on the water like this." He pointed to a cooler near the middle of the boat.

"Thanks, Max. I'll get some in a minute." She repositioned her sunglasses and waited until he moved on to the honeymoon couple from Atlanta sitting in the bow.

Midnight whimpered.

"Oh you big baby." Her voice was like a caress. She opened her hand and the dog gobbled up the remaining pineapple.

"He's a beauty." The captain sat behind the big wheel, one bare foot propped on the side of the boat. He wore thin white shorts, a T-shirt and a shiny gold wedding ring on his finger. "My brother had a chocolate lab. A real sweetheart."

She stroked the dog's head. "Midnight's a thief. I'm surprised he waited for the fruit to be passed around."

The dog licked the pineapple juice off her fingers.

The captain took a sip of Evian and smacked his lips. "He was in the water for hours. Probably just wants to be lazy for a while."

"I know I do." She yawned and stretched, conscious of his eyes on her. It was a relief to be able to relax at last. Oh, she might still be using another name, but there was no longer a need for disguises. She got away clean.

"Are you on vacation?" The man interrupted her thoughts.

"Sort of."

"Where are you staying?"

She bit her lip, thinking. He didn't seem like the type who'd come visiting without an invitation. Still, you never knew. "I rented a house."

He waved at a family in a passing speedboat, before turning back to her. "How long are you staying?"

"Until I'm tired of the Keys, I guess."

"In that case, you may be here awhile." His eyes sparkled when he smiled. "By the way, my name's Jack Frazier."

"You said. When we came aboard?" She couldn't help but smile back. Midnight nosed under her crooked finger, forcing her to pet him. He got nervous when other people showed too much interest these days.

"When did you get here?"

Key West

She narrowed her eyes, flirting. "Are we playing twenty questions?"

"Why not? That leaves me at least eighteen more." He guided the sleek white boat past a sandy key filled with handsome cottages.

"Do I get one of the remaining eighteen?"

"Shoot." Jack laughed. "My life is an open book."

"What about that ring?" She pointed.

He covered it with his thumb. "I've worn it so long that I feel naked without it, I guess." He sighed before meeting her eyes. "I'm a widower. My wife died three years ago."

She didn't know what to think. Another liar? She didn't hold it against him, of course. She'd been fooling people for years. It was easy. Folks pretty much believed whatever you told them unless they had reason to doubt you.

"Am I being shut down?"

Something in his voice touched her. "I'm sorry. I didn't mean to be rude."

"Would you like to see a picture of her?"

"Who?"

"My wife." He fished his wallet out of his pocket and tossed it in her lap. Midnight yelped and drew back.

She stared at it. How many wallets had she stolen over the years? Held together with Velcro, this one was made of blue nylon. Her fingers trembled as she pulled it open. Trying not to look at the credit cards in the side pockets, she flipped through the pictures. The woman was good-looking. Long blonde hair, dangling earrings. A wide smile.

"Her name was Sherry."

"What happened to her?" She looked up to find him staring at her intently.

"Cancer."

"Oh." She searched for something to say. "Did you have any children?"

He pointed to the boy sitting in the bow with the honeymoon couple. "Max is our son."

"I see." Her eyes returned to the photograph. Midnight put his paws on her thighs and sniffed the plastic coated pictures. She closed the wallet and handed it back without memorizing Jack's driver's license information.

The sails rattled and he corrected their course. "So, Miriam, have you seen all the sights of Key West?"

"We've been here two days. This is our first tour."

"I figured."

She raised her eyebrows. "How did you figure that?"

"You're a little pink around the edges. The tan will come later."

She glanced down at bare shoulders, which were reddening alongside the straps of her swimsuit. "We spent the summer in Alaska. I thought maybe Key West would be fun for the winter. I've never been here before."

"It's a wild and crazy place." Jack shook his head as though describing the exploits of a beloved, naughty nephew. "Max and I sailed down from Boston a year ago. To get away from things, you know. We liked it so much that we decided to stay. We live in my boat."

"This one?" She looked around. *The Danger* was great for an afternoon but it hardly seemed big enough for two people to live on.

"Oh no. Mine's smaller than this." He rushed on, stumbling over his words. "We spend our days doing charters. There's an Internet

313

Café in the middle of town for Max to keep in touch with his buddies. I spend my spare time in the library or at Sloppy Joes. We go fishing with friends. A lot of the local bars have TVs now so we can watch football." His voice dropped off. "Mostly we just sleep in the boat."

If he was lying, he was bad at it. She decided to believe him. It was a big step for her. "It sounds like a pleasant life."

"We'll be back at the marina in about ten minutes, so I better work fast here. Would you like to have dinner?" He cleared his throat. "With me, I mean."

She thought about it. It had been years since she had a date. Back in the early 90s in Vineland, New Jersey. No, that one didn't count as a date. She'd stolen his electric bill off the kitchen table when he went to the bathroom. The one before that didn't count either since she ran out on him before dessert.

"I keep telling Max that I'm going to get back into the swing of things again, but the truth is, I was never very good at it in the first place." Jack hung his head in mock humility. "Sherry ended up asking me out."

"Does that mean the offer's no good?" She heard herself saying.

"Really?" His smile was tentative. "You want to go?"

"When?" The marina was in sight. She wanted to seal the deal before they docked.

"Tonight?" Apparently, Jack did too.

"Great." No time to think about it. Just do it. Pleased with herself, she pulled on white shorts over her swimsuit and slipped her feet into a pair of Teva sandals.

"I'll pick you up at nine, okay?"

"Sure." She stuffed her damp towel into a tote. "No. I'll meet you somewhere." She clipped the leash to Midnight's collar.

"Do you know Lola's? On Duval across from the food court?"

"I can find it."

"Let's meet there in the bar. Around 8:30? I'll see if I can get us into the Café Marquesa for dinner."

She gathered her belongings and stood up. "I'll be there."

"Watch the boom." Jack waved her back down as *The Danger* skirted a couple of giant cruise ships that sat near the harbor. He motioned to Max and the two of them set about lowering the sails so that they could motor into port.

At the dock, she slipped a twenty-dollar bill into Max's hand before stepping off the boat. Midnight barked at a seagull and took off up the walkway, his ears flopping.

"Tonight!" She called over her shoulder as the big dog dragged her away.

"Tonight." Jack waved and turned to hug Max who pretended to punch his father's arm.

"It was the dinner hour at Lola's and the patio restaurant was busy. A few drinkers lounged around the upstairs bar—mostly fishermen and tourists. Two large windows were thrown open and the street sounds from Duval added to the cacophony of voices filling the room.

"Hot stuff!" A blue and gold parrot perched on top of his cage greeted her as she came through the door.

She crawled up on a stool at the end of the mahogany bar. Looking down on Duval Street through an open window, she saw a man with a twenty-foot yellow snake wrapped around his torso. He strolled back and forth on the sidewalk, pausing to allow passersby to photograph him and the serpent.

Key West

"Can I help you?" A pretty Asian girl with a British accent laid a cocktail napkin on the bar in front of her.

"Rum and Coke?" Miriam fished a ten-dollar bill out of her purse.

"Coming right up." The bartender took a glass from a rack over her head and filled it with ice.

Miriam gazed out the window, enjoying the endless stream of artists, tourists and fishermen trudging up and down Duval. She planned on retiring as Iliana Johnson, but Willie Wanger's book of horrors changed all that. She congratulated herself on having the foresight to keep at least one back-up identity on hand.

A very tall woman avoided the man with the yellow snake out front and hurried up the steps to the bar. The parrot whistled at her as she came in.

"Oh pu-lease." The woman tugged on her striped tube top and rolled her eyes. "Suni? Suni, darling. Get me a frozen daiquiri and some conch fritters." Her voice reminded Miriam of Darth Vader — a breathy bass.

"Be with you in a minute, Scarlett." The Asian girl poured a shot of Bacardi into Miriam's glass and filled it with Coke.

"Take your time." Scarlett pulled up her tight skirt and sat on the stool next to Miriam, crossing her long legs. "You mind if I switch channels? A friend of mine is supposed to be in the audience of the Jerry Springer show."

"I don't mind if no one else does. The remote is at the end of the bar." Suni served Miriam her drink.

Scarlett looked around the room. A couple sat in the corner staring into each other's eyes. A group of middle-aged partiers elbowed each other and reminisced about a girl they knew in college. ESPN played to an inattentive audience. "Say, sweetheart." She touched Miriam's arm, pointing to the remote. "Do you mind?"

"Oh, no. Go ahead." Miriam handed Scarlett the remote.

Scarlett switched channels. "Commercials. Always commercials." She hit the mute button.

"Here you go, dearie." Suni brought Scarlett her daiquiri. "The fritters will be out in a moment."

Scarlett took a sip of her drink, leaving a dark lipstick mark on her straw. "Whew, it's hot in here. Don't you think it's hot?"

Miriam smiled and shook her head.

"Oh well, then. It must be me. Another hot flash." Scarlett fanned herself with her bejeweled hand. "I love your blouse. I've been looking for something like that but I'm so busty."

Despite her efforts to avoid it, Miriam's eyes dropped to the cantaloupe-sized mounds under Scarlett's tube top. Prosthetics, she thought. Good ones. "I ordered it off the Internet," she said thinking about her days as Maureen in Cleveland. "Here, give me your email address and I'll send you the URL."

"Aren't you a doll? My name's Scarlett O'Haira. With an I." She drew an 'I' in the air, making a 'Pttt' sound as she dotted it with her finger. "Oh, pu-lease. Don't give me that look. This is Key West. You can be anyone you want down here."

"Good. Then, I'm Miriam Gorman." Miriam eyed Scarlett's elaborate Dolly Parton poof, wondering if O'Haira was a stage name.

Scarlett scribbled her email address in Miriam's book. A blue anchor was tattooed on her forearm just above her shell bracelet. "You're new in town, aren't you?"

"Brand new, but I like it here already." Miriam wondered what kind of scam Scarlett was working. Hiding from the law? An ex-wife? Hustling the gay community? Of course, it was possible Scarlett was just another drag queen, but Miriam doubted it. It takes a crook to recognize one, she thought as she tucked her address book into her purse.

"Welcome, Miriam. I hope I see you around." Scarlett turned back to the television.

The sound blared on. "This is a picture of Linda Knight, thought to have killed a man in Belmont, Ohio last spring. If —."

"Oh pooh!" Scarlett switched stations. "Where's Jerry Springer?"

"What was that?" Miriam's heart pounded.

"What was what?"

"That TV show. What was it?"

"That show with John Walsh?"

"Do you mind?"

Scarlett lowered her eyes and surrendered the remote. "No sugar, I don't mind. I must have got my wires crossed about Jerry."

Miriam switched channels. How the hell did the cops mess things up so bad? She thought of Willie's pictures of Linda and tears stung her eyes. She'd torn them out of the photo album and ripped them to shreds. The bastard.

"An anonymous tip to *America's Most Wanted* in April led police to a motor home parked behind a Mexican food restaurant near the Pittsburgh International Airport." A raspy voice reported. "Investigators traced the recreational vehicle to an Indiana dealer who hired a man by the name of Dick Longren to deliver it to a customer. He claimed Longren stiffed him and disappeared with the merchandise.

"Inside the RV, Pittsburgh cops found evidence that this was more than just theft. Computer equipment, a journal and a photo album led officers to conclude that Longren was a serial killer who'd been operating in the mid-west for some time. Insiders say that there may be a connection between this lowlife and the murder of Susanna Hancock whose body was found last spring in a pond near Indianapolis."

Miriam glanced at Scarlett. Should she turn off the show? If she was suspicious of Scarlett, might not Scarlett think she was hinky? It was unlikely anyone would connect either Maureen or Jennifer to that body in Belmont. Even more unlikely anyone could connect them to Miriam Gorman of Key West, but she'd been living on edge for months. Contacting the show might have been stupid, but the faces of those women—all those dead women—haunted her. She had to do something and calling the police was not an option.

Miriam turned her attention back to the show.

"After reviewing files on Longren's computer, cops linked this thug to a seemingly unrelated incident in Belmont County Ohio. One that we covered here on *America's Most Wanted* in June.

"On April 1st of this year, Linda Louise Knight ran over an unidentified man in the Sears parking lot at the Ohio Valley Mall sometime after 10 PM. Her Isuzu Trooper was abandoned at the scene and she fled on foot or was picked up by an accomplice.

"The victim carried no identification. A wallet found in a storage room on Mrs. Knight's property bore the man's fingerprints. Identification found in wallet bore the name of Peter Good. However, the ID was a fake.

"Linda Knight had gone missing several months earlier, but appeared at her ex-husband's residence in Medina, Ohio on the day of the incident. Finding no one at home, she took the couples' large black dog, known as Midnight and hasn't been seen since."

The stupid neighbor. Linda was six inches taller and fifty pounds heavier. Was the woman blind? Sure, the cops were bound to think there was a link to Linda because Willie was lying dead near her truck. It never occurred to her that they'd find his wallet. All she could think of at the time was getting the hell out of there.

"Information found in Longren's effects led investigators to conclude that Longren and Peter Good were the same person. The

Indiana dealer confirmed this when he identified the body in Belmont as the man who picked up the RV in April.

"Ohio cops think that this scumbag kidnapped Linda and kept her with him for weeks. Whatever occurred in Belmont, Linda's parents are very worried."

The video showed an older couple. Charlie Knight stood behind them, his handsome face dark with anxiety. Linda's father was tall and lean, her mother short and plump. "We're so worried, Linda. No matter what's happened, we love you and want you to come home."

"Dorotheee! Come home, Dorothee! And bring your little dog too." Scarlett cupped her hands around her mouth sounding like Auntie Em and the wicked witch all rolled into one.

"Now, Scarlett, that's a bit insensitive, don't you think?" Jack Frazier came up behind them. He looked cool and comfortable in a light tropical shirt and white slacks.

Miriam quickly muted the sound and turned to smile at Jack.

Scarlett rolled her eyes. "Oh pu-lease! It's a television show. They probably make up half of it."

Jack laid his hand on the back of Miriam's bar stool. "Did you meet Miriam?"

"I met her, but she didn't tell me that she was your new squeeze." Scarlett moved over to allow Jack to sit down.

Jack blushed. "It's our first date, Scarlett. Give a man a chance."

Suni set Scarlett's fritters on the bar in front of her and turned to Jack. "What can I do for you, love?"

"The usual."

"So, what were you two up to?" Jack rubbed his palms together. Miriam noticed that he'd removed his ring.

"We were watching that hunky John Walsh talk about some loony tune in Ohio." Scarlett put her bag on the counter and sorted through it, laying a tiny cell phone on the counter. She took out a silver compact mirror and examined herself. "He's always looking for someone on that show."

"He makes me feel bad." Jack turned to Miriam. "And tonight I want to feel good."

"Why bad?" It was the first thing she'd said to him.

"He's been through what every parent fears and dreads." Jack's eyes changed.

"What is that?"

"The loss of a child."

Miriam glanced over her shoulder to see that AMW had moved on to a different story before she relaxed. "It's awful to lose anyone, don't you think?"

"I've lost my parents, a teacher, friends — my wife." Jack accepted his Bass Ale from Suni. "All horrible things, but the thought of losing Max terrifies me. If something happened to him like it did Walsh's kid, I don't think I could stand it."

"Oh, Jack." Miriam reached for his hand. It was something that Linda used to do when someone she cared about felt bad.

"The worst part would be not knowing. Is he in pain? Is he scared?" His voice dropped. "Is he dead?" Jack took a quick drink of his beer and wiped his mouth on the back of his sleeve. "I'm sorry. Let's not talk about it, anymore."

"Fine with me, gloomy Gus." Scarlett straightened her wig and put on fresh lipstick. "I could sit around my apartment and mope all by myself if I wanted to think about things like that. Lola's is for partying."

Key West

"That's right. I want to get to know this lovely lady here." Jack patted Miriam's hand now that he had it. "Tell me about yourself, Miriam."

Was this just a rest stop? Did she dare start a life for herself here? Jack was a very handsome man—kind of sweet and vulnerable. He even smelled good. She opened her mouth, and then closed it. "I have one more thing I have to do, Jack. Can you give me a few minutes? I'll be right back."

Disappointment flashed over his face. "Sure."

He thought she was dumping him, she realized. "I promise." She stood on tiptoe to kiss his cheek, her hand sliding across the bar.

She felt his eyes on her as she crossed the room.

"Don't you know better than to leave a good looking man like Jack alone?" Scarlett called after her.

"There's a pretty bitch." The parrot chimed in as she went down the stairs looking for the bathroom.

She locked herself in the back stall and tapped a number onto Scarlett's tiny cell, extending the antenna. This will do it, she thought as the phone rang. Once I do this, it'll be over and I can move on.

"Hello."

The sound of Charlie's voice shattered her illusions. What if he recognized her voice? What if they traced the call?

"Hello?"

She swallowed. What was she going to say? Linda's dead and laying in a shallow grave somewhere but I don't know where?

"Is that you, Linda?"

She took a ragged breath.

"It doesn't matter, baby. Just come home. I love you. I always have. I kick myself every day for what I did to you—but that doesn't matter now. Your parents ... "

She closed the phone, tears streaming down her cheeks. Maybe it was better not to know after all. That way Charlie could keep on pretending that Linda might come home someday.

She wiped her eyes with toilet paper and blew her nose.

"Show us your tits, baby!" The parrot welcomed her back to the bar.

Scarlett and Jack were discussing sailboats.

"There she is." Jack seemed thrilled to see her. No one had ever been thrilled to see her. It felt wonderful. "Is everything okay?" He pulled out a stool for her.

"As okay as I can make it." She dropped the phone into Scarlett's purse as she passed. "You know, Scarlett, I wonder if you could tell me where I could get my nails done like yours?"

"Oh girlfriend, it's called Georgine's and it's the cutest little place over on Simonton." Scarlett stood and picked up her purse. "Maybe I can take you over one day and introduce you to the girls."

"I'd like that."

"Email me. We can have lunch at Kelly's first." She headed for the door.

"Pretty boy!" The parrot screamed.

"Oh pooh. Suni, can't you do something about this bird?" Scarlett wiggled her fingers over her shoulder as she went down the stairs. "Have fun, you two."

"I thought she'd never leave." Jack whispered behind his hand. "Scarlett's a bit irascible, but you seemed to hit it off."

Key West

"We have a lot in common," Miriam said.

"Are you ready for dinner?"

She smiled. "I'm ready."

Other Books by Joyce Faulkner

Chance … and other horrors (Pyschological Thriller)
In the Shadow of Suribachi, 2006 Military Writers Society of America Gold Medal for Historical Fiction
Losing Patience, 2006 Honorable Mention, Writers' Notes Magazine
For Shrieking Out Loud (Humor)

Coauthored with Pat McGrath Avery

Role Call: Women's Voices (History/Biography)
Sunchon Tunnel Massacre Survivors, 2010 Gold Medal Branson Stars and Flags Book Award (History)

Contact Joyce Faulkner at <u>JoyceKFaulkner@gmail.com</u>

Books by Pat McGrath Avery

Murder is for the Birds (Mystery)
Murder Takes a Ride (Mystery)
The Sharon Rogers Band: Laughed Together, Cried Together, Crashed & Almost Died Together (History)
They Came Home: Korean War POWs Tell Their Stories (History)
Letters from Korea: A Story of the Korean War (Children/History)
Tommy's War (Children/History)

Contact Pat at <u>patmcgrathavery@gmail.com</u>
Website: <u>www.patmcgrathavery.com</u>
Blog: <u>www.iwritemyworld.com</u>
Facebook: patmcgrathavery

www.ingramcontent.com/pod-product-compliance
Lightning Source LLC
Chambersburg PA
CBHW072055020726
47501CB00003B/597